KU-490-555

Praise for The Martingale Cycle

'A fascinating and hair-raising examination of just how much
we are in thrall to computers, and how willingly we give up our
privacy'
Guardian

'An amazing book'
Trisha Goddard, BBC Radio London

'Impossible to put down once you've picked it up, it cements
Matthew Blakstad's place as a writer of
considerable talent, a writer who knows exactly how to grab
his audience, and keep them involved – and highly entertained
– until his story is done'
Reader Dad

'Embedded with techy jargon and shards of wit,
Sockpuppet takes a snapshot of our age of online shaming and
oversharing and runs it through a skewed, feverish filter. The
result is compelling'
Financial Times

'A woven web of tech and trauma, human foibles and group
shenanigans, all mixed up into a beautiful hotpot of a story
where nothing is ever quite as it seems'
Liz Loves Books

'Thrives on the tension between private, public and corporate
interests… the author touches a raw nerve
when he confronts the anxiety around information
used to harass'
SciFi Now

12837939

About the Author

Matthew's first career was as a professional child actor. From the age of ten, he had roles in TV dramas, in films and on stage at theatres including the Royal Court. After graduating from Oxford with a degree in Mathematics and Philosophy, he began a career in online communications, consulting for a wide range of clients from the BBC to major banks. Since 2008, he has been in public service, using his communication skills to help the British population understand and manage their money. In 2012 Matthew took the Writing a Novel course at Faber Academy. *Lucky Ghost* is his second full-length novel.

Also by Matthew Blakstad

Fallen Angel
Sockpuppet

Matthew Blakstad

Lucky Ghost

HODDER

First published in Great Britain in 2017 by Hodder & Stoughton
An Hachette UK company

First published in paperback in 2018

1

Copyright © Matthew Blakstad 2017

The right of Matthew Blakstad to be identified as the
Author of the Work has been asserted by him in accordance
with the Copyright, Designs and Patents Act 1988.

All rights reserved. No part of this publication may be
reproduced, stored in a retrieval system, or transmitted, in any
form or by any means without the prior written permission of
the publisher, nor be otherwise circulated in any form of binding
or cover other than that in which it is published and without a
similar condition being imposed on the subsequent purchaser.

All characters in this publication are fictitious and any
resemblance to real persons, living or dead is purely coincidental.

A CIP catalogue record for this title is
available from the British Library

Paperback ISBN 978 1 473 62477 1

Typeset in Sabon MT by Hewer Text UK Ltd, Edinburgh
Printed and bound by Clays Ltd, St Ives plc

Hodder & Stoughton policy is to use papers that are
natural, renewable and recyclable products and made
from wood grown in sustainable forests. The logging and
manufacturing processes are expected to conform to the
environmental regulations of the country of origin.

Hodder & Stoughton Ltd
Carmelite House
50 Victoria Embankment
London EC4Y 0DZ

www.hodder.co.uk

For Sally,
who would have been my first reader

PART ONE:

'It's cold out there.'

—*Tom Waits, 'Emotional Weather Report'*

A LONG, LONG WAY AWAY

One moment Alex is dry heaving into the West End gutter; the next it's 1952. Grey light ripples round her face with a fizz of static. She wipes bile from her mouth, makes to stand straight, like a 1950s lady should. Too fast: the panic-monster starts hammering again inside her forehead. Sickness wells up in a dizzy fuzz and she leans forward, pressing hands against knees. She makes a couple more empty heaves but nothing comes.

She dares a look around.

She's on a vintage railway platform. A stopping-point on some country branch line. From the steamed windows of the cafeteria, amber light seeps out into the evening gloom – though back in the real world it's barely five a.m. The brick walls are freshly whitewashed and pastel posters promote the temptations of Buxton, the Cornish Riviera and, anachronistically, *Grazia* magazine. Over the surging orchestral bed a whistle shrills. Across the platform tweedy ghosts check watches, pick up leather cases and turn to face the steam train as it clanks to a halt.

Alex's glowheart hovers by her elbow. FEAR and ANTICIPATION brim inside it in apple red and watermelon pink. She breathes with its beats until the FEAR subsides; then she stands up slowly. She doesn't vomit or pass out, which is progress. Cheery magenta letters swoop in and jostle together.

‹slap him›

they say. OK, but slap who? Alex searches face after well-rendered male face. None pay her any mind. They stub cigarettes, remove hats and open slam-doors for their pinch-waisted wives, speaking in that clipped pronunciation that only exists in black and white. So distant, so familiar.

Alex always knew she'd be at home in the 1950s. Never mind she'd have ended up a housewife, or a maiden aunt who was *not the marrying kind*. This is her era. Which is why, when she was on the brink of exploding with panic, the Strange has landed her here. It knows her so well now, after weeks of gnawing through her data.

⟨slap him⟩

The words edge closer. Alex scrubs at them with an unsteady hand but they're reluctant to budge. She strokes the dragon tattooed along her scapula, silencing the fizzing embeds, but she can't stop her heart from pounding like it's trying to tunnel out of her ribcage. The prompt edges closer, cajoling.

⟨right now⟩

⟨slap him⟩

A stocky man in a dark green overcoat and sweet homburg steps forward from the crowd. An amber pulse traces his outline and for a second he seems to expand and contract. This is the other player.

⟨in the face⟩

He's thirty-ish, austerity-starved but muscular, and handsome. A low-rent Cary Grant, smoking a tobacco cigarette. There's something close and familiar about him. Something Alex wishes she could place. His glowheart bulges with PRIDE and SATISFACTION. He must have been Strange for quite some time to have a heart so fat and present. Alex still wears her own heart out of view.

The whistle shrills again and the train puffs up, preparing to depart. Steam envelops Alex and the man.

‹slap him hard›

It's a weird-ass opening cue – but the motto here is, *try everything new*. Before she can change her mind, she walks up and slaps the man's cheek, hard. He shies back, cockeyed smile replaced by fury – then he gets it. Alex shakes her stinging palm.

'Whatever you believe you saw this afternoon—' he says.

The Strange feeds Alex her cue.

‹no›

‹we shall not speak of it Charles›

'No,' she says, surprised at the wealth of feeling ejected through that word. 'We shall not speak of it, Charles.'

Her voice emerges in that same cut-glass vintage accent.

'If you cared one fraction of how I care, Elyse, perhaps this might not have happened.'

Elyse? Her character's name is Elyse? That's interesting.

'Of course!' she tumbles onto the next line. 'When a man transgresses there is always a woman to blame!'

'I have the Morris outside. Let me take you home. Do not take an irrevocable step in anger.'

He's actually pretty good. His ease with the scene is confidence-building.

'And that is it? You believe you can have this both ways? Keep me with you and keep with – whoever else? *What*ever else?'

'I have truly cared for you – after my fashion. Can you not see that?'

People on the platform are starting to take notice.

'If you expect me to speak of this here—' she hisses.

As she turns to grasp the handle of the compartment door, real tears prickle at the corners of her eyes. A sticker on the window says SMOKING in Gill Sans capitals. Charles grabs her arm.

'But where will you go, my darling?' he says. 'You cannot simply step into the unknown.'

OK, game. Very subtle. *Step into the unknown?* That's exactly what Alex is supposed to do this morning, out in the real world. They want her to speak to five million people; but she can't. That's why she ran away. That's why, with this challenge, the Encounter's asking her, *do you dare or don't you?* She doesn't know the answer. Inside the Encounter, Alex is a character – and the nature of characters is, they face conflict. They get to make choices. The lady or the tiger? Fight or flight? Just like real people, characters travel down narrow forking corridors of possibility. Free will boiled down to multi-choice. Still, choices are empowering. Time to decide.

Elyse pulls her arm from Charles's grip. and steps up into the carriage. She nods politely at a brace of elderly ladies nestled on the tartan bench seat, in identical floral flocks. Each has a basket clutched to her stomach. Elyse turns back to Charles.

'Yet how can I stay?' she says. 'When it's you, my darling, who have made that impossible?'

The whistle sounds again, more insistent. Charles turns his head away, visibly fighting tears.

'And what of our son?' he says.

Her view shimmers. For a moment she sees the real man, in the present day. The clothes he's wearing – green overcoat, homburg hat – are pretty much the same as his character's, but his profile is less honed, more vicious. His fingers tickle a spider's web tattooed on his throat. Odd detail on such a dapper dresser. Familiar detail.

The scene reasserts. Alex wishes her cheap-arse mesh didn't keep fritzing out like that.

'You are strong, Elyse,' says Charles, not looking her way. 'Remember, it is you who are strong and I who am weak. One day you will forgive me.'

He steps back and closes the train door. Their eyes lock through smoky glass. Elyse screws up her eyes, seeking out the unaugmented man. Why does she know him?

'Alex Kubelick!' booms a voice.

Alex starts. That isn't her name in here. She turns. A bulldoggy, dishevelled man has appeared on the bench seat between the two ladies, to their evident disgust. He's dressed in a synthetic windcheater and woollen beanie, from which a low-cost Chubba mesh dangles before his eyes like chain mail. He's eating something sticky with a great amount of finger-licking. Even so, he might fit into the scene, if he wasn't so blue. His face, clothes, hair – all cyan. A colour that screams against the mossy fifties' palette.

Mickey Gallant has gate-crashed Alex's story as a ghost. He gazes around with vague interest, munching.

'Nifty Encounter,' he says. 'Do you always play Martingale era?'

With two short jolts the train begins to pull away. Alex steadies herself, though the motion isn't real. She hurries to the window and peers out through soot and condensation. Her co-star has vanished. The platform heads sideways with increasing speed. A magenta prompt rolls past.

<what is Charles's secret?>

Whoever Charles was, he's gone. The Encounter won't reassert itself until Alex and he next meet in the real world. Which is probably never. Shame, but most casual Encounters end that way, unresolved. She plonks herself on the bench seat opposite Mickey. Her backside strikes something hard. Whatever she's sitting on in the real isn't cushioned. She glares at Mickey.

'You can't load anything on me,' she says. 'Not today.'

Mickey is transparently crestfallen.

'You don't know what I've got,' he says in his foghorn voice.

She screws her eyes at his hazy outline.

'Where actually are you?'

'You're anchoring the show this morning. Don't you want to make a splash?'

With that simple reminder, PANIC beats against the walls of Alex's glowheart. She stares it down until it softens to a pulse.

'I don't care what you have. I'm not— hold up, wait. How did you know I'm supposed to be presenting?'

'Sources!' says Mickey, loving whatever joke he thinks he's made.

His booming voice draws prim glances from the ladies.

'God, *indoor voice*,' hisses Alex, though the ladies are sprites and Mickey isn't really there. 'Please?'

Mickey screws up his face, delighting at the attention. His cheeks are patchy with four-day stubble. He's in as much of a mess as Alex has ever seen him; but that's part of his schtick. This belligerent scruff gets under the skin of his targets, Columbo-style, makes them let their guards down. He has a knack for finding dirt beneath the nails of the squeakiest-clean politician, the most polished CEO. He used to toss Alex regular scoops, back when she worked outside the network. Before she broke down and vanished. She owes him, but the guy's a walking IED.

'Lovely as it obviously is to see you,' she says, standing, 'I have to get back.'

It seems she's made a decision. She is going back. Going on air. The rattling of the train beneath her feet is astonishingly real. That's the haptic tattoos on the soles of her feet.

'Smint?' says Mickey, offering a dispenser.

Alex sighs and sits back down. Be kind to an abandoned dog, it'll only start following you around. Yet Mickey's never let her down.

'I'm good, Mickey. Thank you. Look, I know I'll regret this, but tell me what you have and then, I don't know, dematerialise. OK?'

Mickey fumbles in his satchel. Alex checks the count on her glowheart. A clump of pink-and-magenta nuggets have landed in it. Her reward from the Encounter. Forty Coin, denominated in CONTEMPT – her character's primary emotion. Not bad.

CONTEMPT is up in value this week. Is it the Coin that's lending her this sudden bump of pride, or slapping that man? It was a fleeting cutscene but it's wiped her away her fright. She wishes she could place the man, though.

A wheel of retro handbags carousels into Alex's field of vision. Each bag was being carried by one of the walk-on characters in the station. Each is rated in SERENITY and ADMIRATION. She flicks the ad away and finds the train compartment gone. In its place is a deserted London street. It's dark in the real world, where it's five a.m. on a February morning. Alex is sitting on the bonnet of a self-driving Toyota that's hibernating at a charging point – the real-life version of the train's bench seat. No wonder it felt so hard. Her mesh still covers her eyes and ears – she's still in the Strange – but the scene's returned to the present day. Even here, though, there's augmentation. The sodium glare of the street is dampened by a soft mist. Lamp posts twist into spiny birch trees. The shush of Oxford Street traffic comes through as a woodland rustle, cut by the chirrups of unseen birds. This wallpaper's called Autumn Woodland. It cost Alex twenty Emoticoin and she over-lays it on everything. It makes her life mellower. These days, her whole world is curated. Her colours, her soundtrack.

She slides off the bonnet of the car. The Strange's main navigation glides in:

<REMEMBRANCE>

<ENCOUNTER>

<FAVOUR>

<GHOST>

She makes a crumpling motion with her hand, collapsing the menu, then throws it away. Mickey's ghost is still with her, sitting in mid-air, clutching a wodge of dog-eared papers.

'I just happen to have come across a certain item,' he says. 'Top-notch leak.'

Alex shakes her head. Barely ten minutes have passed since she fled from her workplace out here onto the street, and most of that time she's spent in the 1950s. This was meant to be a training day. Like every other morning for the past three weeks, she arrived at the production office at four a.m., did her best to blend into the pre-dawn hubbub. She's been loving her month as a trainee radio host. She wasn't due to go on air for at least a fortnight. This morning was her chance to shadow the amazing Sally Robsart – to find out how Sally, with those doe eyes and that hot-chocolate voice, still manages to knock ten shades of shit out of every politician she interviews. Yet Sally was nowhere to be seen.

Alex found herself some busy-work to do, hacking out notes for a discussion link, until her boss, Siobhán, came over to tell her Sally was down with the vomiting alpaca flu that's doing the rounds. Alex would need to go on air instead. Anchor this morning's show. Speak to millions, in less than an hour and a half.

'Amazing,' she said, when what she meant was, *No! I'm not ready.*

No sooner did Siobhán swoop off than a full-blown panic roared over Alex. She barely managed to mutter '*Cigarette*' before stumbling down to the building's forecourt. Her only thought was escape. She'd hop into the first driverless that trundled by, make it drive until its batteries died. Before she even made it to the kerb her knees buckled and blotches of black light blinded her. She grabbed at a lamp post as her guts ejected three espressos and a slice of toasted white. She gazed into the sorry gutter-puddle. Here she was, fucking up in full view of the building. Everyone who'd ever dissed her would know they'd been dead right. She was still the gibbering fuck-up who six months before had stumbled away from journalism, vanished into a sink-pit of misery. She should never have returned.

Six months ago this would have triggered a spiralling descent, a glut of pills and an obstinate refusal to consider a talking cure.

Not today. Today she has a safe place that she carries around with her. It's called the Strange. Standing over the tidy patch of puke she put on her thrift shop tea-hat and let its mesh veil descend around her face. It shimmered into life – and dropped her onto the gamestage of the railway platform. The game has moderated her panic – until Mickey came along to remind her she's about to go on air.

Here he is now, shaking his papers at her like a box of Kit-e-Kat.

'I guarantee you do *not* want to pass on this hot little number,' he says. 'Guaranteed.'

'Hot as in stolen or hot as in dangerous?'

'That's Siobhán talking. Did she pick you because you have a voice like a sex-chat girl or because you're a dynamite reporter?'

'*Sex chat?*' says Alex.

'They need you more that you need them. They're all about fake objectivity. You're first person.'

'If you say so.'

Alex's gaze dwells on the white stone frontage of the Corporation. They'll be wondering where she is.

'Their Rajars are through the floor,' says Mickey. 'Your interviews on *Doorstep* were super-hot.'

'Look, Mickey, I love you to bits but they need me up there. I have a show to prepare.'

For a second or two her glowheart fizzes with fern-green FEAR; then it subsides. She starts walking.

In the movies – the flat black-and-white ones where they dress in the styles that everyone's started wearing again today – in those movies, when a woman got 'hysterical', some hardboiled beefcake would slap her. Maybe shake her by the shoulders for good measure. In the Encounter, it was Alex who got to slap the beefcake. Weird, but she does feel better for it. All round the surface of her glowheart, green and orange peak in time with her beatbox heart, but since the slap they're steadier. Another prompt appears.

‹these eleven tips will make you›

‹stronger and sexier at work›

She claps the blinkbait away. Ghost Mickey has followed her to the revolving doors.

'You have Susan Harridan up,' he says. 'At seven fifty.'

Alex frowns at his delighted face.

'She's called *Hardiman*, you sexist twat. And how is it you know my running order better than I do?'

'I guess someone forgot to change the passwords on the scheduler. You're doing Hardiman.'

Alex gives him a level look.

'All right. And?'

'And fucking this.'

His blue hand holds up a piece of blue paper. Alex can't stop her eyes skipping down the printed-out email. After a moment she snatches it off him. It travels with her fingers as though it were an actual piece of paper. She reads it properly. Mickey's grin says he knows he has her.

'How did you get ahold of this?' she says.

He taps the soft flesh of his blue and often-broken nose.

WATERING HOLE

A pig's face appears at the driver's-side window.

— You coming with? it says.

The rubber crumples the voice of the lady behind the pig mask. She sounds like the tannoy in a supermarket. Thimblerig nods in reply but he doesn't stop typing or shift from the passenger seat of the burned-out Prius. His feet are up on the dashboard and his crablet's legs are clamped to his thighs. This leaves his hands free to type. He'd be sitting in the driver's seat — which has a better view of the office building — except that this is the kind of old-style car with a steering wheel and that wouldn't leave him room to type.

The woman waits. She's expecting more. She peers around the charred interior of the car. At least she's actually wearing her mask — unlike some of the demonstrators knocking round the tarmac of this light-industrial plot. Half of them have taken their masks off to sip from smart-cups of coffee.

Thimblerig types in the chat window.

Thimblerig: These people think anonymity is something you can turn on and off.

After a second Eponymous replies from wherever he is.

eponymous: *8=(:

At least none of these fair-weather hacktivists were stupid enough to wear their mesh. Also they've powered down their tattoos. That's something.

The lady adjusts her mask and tries again.

— So, she says, the thread said six thirty a.m.? It was super-specific. But there's nothing so to speak happening?

Thimblerig keeps typing. He doesn't look at the pig-face lady. He's already noticed how her bra is showing through the gauzy T-shirt. Now she's leaning in through the window he could easily turn around and see the pale headlands of her breasts. These activist ladies don't seem to care who stares at them but Thimblerig cares. Through the eye sockets of his mask his eyes bear down on the screen of his crablet. His cheeks are hot against the rubber.

— Because, says the lady, we read that Thimblerig was going to be here this morning doing some tech shit and we were wondering – since you're – you know. Typing and so on. Are you maybe—?

Ten metres behind her the other sixteen Cockaigne activists jostle and shout in the half-light of the abandoned lot. Each has the same pink rubber mask pulled down over their heads. People always stand a few centimetres taller when they're in the pig mask. Maybe it's the anonymity. Maybe it's because they know what it stands for: Cockaigne. The movement. In the masks they're no longer a rabble of back-bedroom conspirators. they're part of an infamous hacker network that brings down corporations. Aids rebels. Shames governments.

Though for all the noise this lot are making you'd think they were on a night out rather than prepping for a Cockaigne opera-tion. Maybe some of them have come here from mesh clubs or whatever. Thimblerig has never been to a place like that so he has no idea what time one shuts. He can't understand why anyone would want to wrap their head in mesh and fill it with so much sound and noise they can't even tell what an idiot they look like as they prance around a silent dance floor. Why would anyone go to a public place just to stay wrapped in a private place? Strangers are strange.

The pig-people blow into cupped hands and lean on placards. It's night-time chilly on the outskirts of this Swindon business park. A funny sight when you think about it. No one remembers why Cockaigne protestors wear the pig mask. The reason's lost in the ancient history of the movement, back when it had another name.

— So are you, says the lady with a muffled sniff, actually an *adult* or whatever?

Thimblerig hunches further into the seat. This is the problem with IRL. People judge you because you're seventeen. He's been keeping his distance from the civilians by hiding in this burned-out wreck of a car but they've sniffed out that he knows what he's doing. This pierced and grubby lady is their ambassador. She wants him to tell them what to do. People like this are incapable of self-organising. None of them are hackers. They're the kind of hangers-on who want to feel part of a movement but don't even know how to jailbreak their own mesh. That's fine though. All they have to do is try to break into a building that's impossible to break into. They're here to cause as much disruption as possible before police arrive to chase them away.

Thimblerig's the last person who would tell anybody what to do. He's only here because he needs to get his cat within ten metres of the east wall of the Occidental Data Partnerships office building. The demo is to give him cover to get the cat close enough to connect.

The lady tuts and walks away. That's the other thing about amateurs. No patience.

Thimblerig never runs with a crowd. He barely ever wears the pig mask. It's not that he's afraid exactly but at demos everyone gets shoved together, shouting and sweating, and that makes him scratchy and uncomfortable. He works best looking into a situation from outside. That way he can see how things are constructed before he takes them apart and reassembles them the way they're meant to be.

eponymous: we good?
Thimblerig: Any second.

Eponymous is right. He needs to get up off his bottom. The sun's already starting to rise – though shadows still lie thick across the patch of waste ground where the pig masks are mustering. He'll move in a minute. He just needs to review the router script once more. To be certain.

The inside of his mask smells of wee or something. Also, it's too big for his head which makes it hard to see clearly through the eye sockets – but that's OK. He could type blindfold. Literally he sometimes does that.

OK. Nothing left to test. No more excuses. He looks up at the target. The UK headquarters of Occidental Data Partnerships is just the other side of a chain-link fence at the end of the lot. It's a floodlit building whose fake marble cladding looks like Lego. The brown-tinted mirror glass windows make it impossible to see inside. Unless of course you hack your way in.

Cockaigne has been wanting to land a blow on Occidental for months. Thimblerig's been working all hours to persuade them this 'Internet security firm' is anything but. The way Occidental makes money is by buying and selling system vulnerabilities. They buy these malicious hacks from the nastiest crackers on the planet then flip them to rogue corporations. Or to the security services of governments. They know full well these clients will use the tools to attack business rivals or oppress opposition activists. Even worse – no sooner have Occidental sold the warez to the bad guys than they contact the victims of these attacks to sell them system defences.

This is like what was happening in Thimblerig's home country just before he was forced to leave. Out of the blue one day the extremists would move into a town.

— We're going to protect you, they'd say to the people of the town.

— Against what? the people would reply.

— Against the infidel, du'h. And BTW to help us protect you you're going to need to give us all your money and resources and unmarried women over the age of thirteen.

Except unlike the extremists Occidental don't even have the courage to get their own hands dirty. They're the worst kind of people. And their UK Chief Executive Doug Raynor is the worst of the worst.

How does Thimblerig know this? Because he has intelligence on Doug Raynor. A few months ago he came across this information and it changed his life. It gave him mission and purpose at long last. He doesn't have proof but this morning for the very first time he's on the point of getting it. To the rest of the Cockaigne crew this is just another corporate takedown. It's a great deal more to Thimblerig.

He goes onto the thread where they're organising the demo and types a single word.

Thimblerig: GO

It isn't original but it's clear. A ripple of movement wavers through the crowd. They pull on their masks and power down their cigarettes. Four of them jog over to the wall to gather equipment. Under cover of the pig faces they harden up and walk with straighter spines. They're good people when they drop their pointless banter and start to act. With just two letters Thimblerig has activated a crew of men and ladies who are all at least five years older than him. It's like remote-controlling a squad of soldiers. A shiver rattles down his spine. It's like he's had some kind of premonition. It's probably just the morning cold.

Through the grime of the windscreen he watches the crew move in on the chain-link fence. At the lead two pigs have bolt cutters slung over their shoulders. Behind them three more lug an extendible ladder. At the front is the lady from the window. The one with the see-through top. The pack enters a splodge of yellow arc light by the fence. The two with the cutters start to snip a vertical slice of chain-link. Thimblerig watches as the pigs peel back a section of fence then pile inside like rice through a hole in the packet. They surge around the building towards the floodlit forecourt at its west side. Some of them raise placards while others extend the ladder. Four or five are livestreaming. Thimblerig stacks their feeds along the side of his screen. The protestors start a call-and-response.

— *STOP US IF YOU'VE GOT THE SKILLS,*
— *RAYNOR! RAYNOR!*
— *WE'VE SHOPPED YOU TO THE O-OLD BILL,*
— *DOUG RAYNOR, HEY!*

Even leaving aside what Raynor did to Thimblerig's family nobody could claim he's a good citizen. A pumped-up tech bro with a buzz cut and connections to the alt-right. His 'private security' work involved an awful lot of travel to the mid-east in the early 2000s. He wears narrow expensive suits and leaves too many shirt buttons open at the neck. Gym muscles bulge through the fabric.

Taking Raynor down is the goal of the present operation. As far as the chanting pigs are concerned the mission is to get something incriminating on Raynor before the demo is broken up. Behind this Thimblerig is seeking something far more specific. Something on Raynor's activities during the civil war back home. Years ago.

As planned the chanting has drawn the attention of Occidental's wage-slave security men. Two black uniforms emerge onto the forecourt to confront the chanting crew. This is Thimblerig's cue. He twists around and shouts into the car's dark footwell.

— اتحركي

A streak of gunmetal launches from the footwell and streaks out through the staved-in rear window. Thimblerig tracks the grey bolt as it pelts across the tarmac. It moves in and out of pools of sodium then through the gap in the fence where it vanishes into the shadows at the east side of the building. To the west the demonstrators run mocking circles round the guards. Thimblerig leans back into the seat and waits.

It's better to stay on the fringes. As a child living in the camps – before the authorities broke them up – his charity caseworker used to say that he'd become an outsider as a direct result of making his own way north at such an early age. She said this was why he refused to participate in group activities. That story was rubbish. It's true he's an outsider. Just as it's true he has a wavery relationship with this country and its language and its soft green gardens. But he'd have been this way however his story ran. His father was just the same. He lived his whole life on the outskirts of life. Never held down a state job for very long despite his skill at electronics. When the uprising came he rose without a thought. It was like he'd been waiting his whole life for the chance to rebel.

But that's a whole other part of the story.

Thimblerig checks his feed. The cat is returning null pings. It'll keep working its way through the shadows to the west of the building until it finds a signal from one specific wireless router. Once it's logged into the router it'll hunker down and set itself up as a bridge.

Thimblerig got the login details and location for this router from the dumbest watering-hole attack he's ever run. A week ago Lucky Ghost tipped him off to the fact that Doug Raynor and his senior staff are addicted to a restaurant in the centre of Swindon called the Taj Garden. Somehow Lucky Ghost found out that every few nights – when Raynor and his colleagues are working late – they go online and order a delivery of macho triple-chilli dishes. Based on this information Thimblerig hacked the Taj Garden's noddy e-commerce and planted malware. Next time one of Raynor's team opened an SSL to pay by credit card Thimblerig punched straight onto the man's crablet. Unfortunately the crablet was a personal device that wasn't networked to anything in Occidental's building but after a bit of rooting around Thimblerig uncovered a synched and unencrypted copy of the man's email folders. It turned out he was a senior sysadmin. Thimblerig mined the mails. He found a lot of random but damaging information that he passed on to various contacts. With any luck some of those stories will have made it to the blogs. The mainstream media will take longer. So some of this stuff might land a blow on Occidental but none of this was helping Thimblerig get to Raynor. Then he found in the Sent Items folder an email containing the location and settings of a wireless router on the same subdomain as Occidental's in-house servers. This is the router that Thimblerig's cat is currently –

```
resolving . . .
host found ID F0AA139B
connecting . . .
enter username: odptmpuser03
enter password: ●●●●●●●●●●●●●
welcome
```

The cat's connected and Thimblerig's script is running. He cracks his knuckles and opens a terminal window. It takes seven minutes to seize root under the ID of the curry-loving sysadmin. Occidental makes its money selling system vulnerabilities. It should know better than to leave its back door open like this. Thimblerig's a decent cracker but any twelve-year old with a Raspberry Pi could've pulled off this exploit.

Another port opens. Eponymous – who's been following the action remotely – has entered on Thimblerig's coat-tails. His job is to look for evidence of the freelance contractors Occidental use to scout for bad hacks. That'll keep the rest of Cockaigne happy while Thimblerig pursues his own goals. He starts by poking the Exchange server. He pulls up two windows. In the left-hand window he loads the past month's worth of Doug Raynor's email. The right-hand one he fills with a year's worth of mails dated a decade past.

Eponymous pops up in chat.

eponymous: nicely done
Thimblerig: You on yet?

eponymous: (^ ^)b
   smooth as
   give me an hour ill have doxed the living shit out of every
   blackhat on their payroll
   any smoking guns on email?

Naturally Eponymous isn't interested in deep cuts from the decade-old mails. Thimblerig will need to give him something from the recent cache. He scans the left-hand window. He's only gone down three scrolls when he sees something. Well – isn't Raynor the early bird?

Thimblerig: Here's one from Raynor to his top brass.
   Sent half an hour ago.
   They have a zero-day hack called Kaa.
eponymous: (-_-;
   like the snake?
Thimblerig: Snake?
eponymous: idiot
Thimblerig: Best I can make out Kaa exploits a flaw in Transax
eponymous: transax?
   ¯_(ツ)_/¯
   you going to make me google everything?
Thimblerig: Moron.
eponymous: *im* the moron but *youve* never seen jungle
   book?
Thimblerig: Raynor sent this email to all his senior managers
   telling them
   hold on

Thimblerig rereads one particular passage. Which makes no sense.

eponymous: what?
   telling them what?

(C_C)
wtf is transax anyway?

In this mail Raynor contradicts himself every two lines. First he tells his managers Kaa is a vital part of '*Monday's big exploit*'. Next he says '*This is my hack and if those head office cucks don't pay for it they aint getting their hands on it, simple as*'. It's like reading the email of a teen with no impulse control.

The video feeds at the side of Thimblerig's screen are getting jolty. There are shouts. Thimblerig peers through the windscreen. Something's kicking off at the building's entrance. He squints against the sunlight scissoring low across the tarmac. Two ladies are climbing the ladder up the side of the building. The uniformed guards are shouting up at them. The pig-faced Cockaigners chant and buffet the guards. All as it should be. But a new variable has entered the fray. Four or five figures in what look like Spider-Man suits have materialised among the protestors. Eight or nine now. Planting their feet wide apart in hero poses they form a cordon around the guards. One of them points at the pig crew and declaims something Thimblerig can't hear. More Spider-Men appear.

No harm some other crew joining the demo. The more chaos the better. But Thimblerig's never heard of superhero hacktivists. Maybe Swindon locals. He goes back to the chat where Eponymous is still asking about Transax.

Thimblerig: It's the system that manages bank-to-bank
transfers.
I did some freelance pen testing on it last year
It's tight
Nobody's ever got close
But apparently Kaa can take it down
eponymous: (@ @)
raynor has a hack that can take over BANKS?
srs???

must have made $$ much
any clue who he sold it to?

Thimblerig: That's the thing
He didn't

eponymous: oo-
makes no sense

Thimblerig: But it's big
Maybe bigger than anything we've found.

More shouting. A fight has broken out by the Occidental building. The Spider-Men are striking exaggerated combat poses and throwing wild punches at the pigs. The pigs are shoving back. One has grabbed a Spider-Man and is trying to kick him. A knot of red-and-blue Lycra has got hold of the bottom of the ladder and is shaking it about. The lady in black gauze is clinging on at the top and screaming something at the people below.

The buzzing of the crablet draws Thimblerig's attention to the screen. Eponymous has been shooting off more messages.

eponymous: shit man

then

eponymous: this isnt a smoking gun

then

eponymous: it's a smoking bazooka
(p^-^)p

then

eponymous: we need to put this out there NOW

He's right of course: but. Thimblerig thinks a moment before he types. How would Lucky Ghost handle this?

Thimblerig: No
eponymous: :-O
   wts man we have to
Thimblerig: No, this is bigger.
   If we waste it shaming them we'll never find out what
   Raynor's planning to do with it.
eponymous: so?
Thimblerig: So you put out a dump of the dox on the blackhat
   hackers.
   The police'll follow that up.
   Meanwhile I'll talk to Lucky Ghost.
eponymous: (¬_¬)
   aw cmon really tho
Thimblerig: The Ghost'll know what to do.
eponymous: sure because shes working for the feds
Thimblerig: Can we not have this conversation now?
eponymous: you do know she isnt really elyse martingale
   don't you bro?
   you do know saint elyse died last century?

Of course Thimblerig knows. It's hard to overstate the importance of the late Professor Elyse Martingale to a Cockaigne hacker, especially Thimblerig. Even his handle is lifted from a passage by Elyse:

Each of us must become fully versed in the use and function of the computing machine. Else we shall be as callow bumpkins, falling victim to the three-cup thimblerig of any streetside mountebank.

He's still deciding how to come back at Eponymous when he hears the scream and looks up. Beyond the fence the ladder is teetering away from the building. The woman in the see-through top clings to it like a sailor on the crow's nest of a sinking ship.

She makes a desperate grab at the guttering on the side of the building. Misses. The ladder sways away. At its base a tide of Spider-Men shoves against a counter-tide of pigs. The ladder wavers then twists and topples towards the fence. It lands across the top of the chain-link and bounces. The lady's thrown up then onto the tarmac in the shadow of a giant yellow skip.

Thimblerig wrestles with the rusted catch of the car door. The lady's body is very still. Pig-masked protestors surge through the gap in the fence and peel off hither and thither across the lot pursued by Spider-Men. Thimblerig swivels in his seat and kicks at the jammed car door. Two protestors run to the crumpled woman and kneel by her. One pulls off his mask and leans in to listen to her breath or heart. The security guards walk up and hover anxiously beside the skip.

Thimblerig kicks again and with a *crack!* the car door swings open and bounces back at him. He shoves it open and tumbles out of the car. The kneeling man stops listening to the woman's heart. He sits back on his ankles and shakes his head towards the guards. Thimblerig looks around for someone to help but the lot is suddenly empty of pigs and superheroes both.

For the longest time nobody moves. Then the cat comes streaking out through the gap in the fence. It runs between the legs of one of the guards. He lifts his foot and hops around in a half-circle to watch the grey flash tear towards Thimblerig. The cat skids to a stop at his feet then coils and springs into his arms. He catches it and pulls its sturdy lightness to his chest. He and the security guard stare at one another across the abandoned lot. There's movement at the top of the skip. A Spider-Man clambers out of it and onto the rim. He balances there and scans the gloom. His eyes fix on Thimblerig. He points at him with a big sweep of his arm.

— *Hold it right there, citizen!* he shouts.

Thimblerig clutches the cat to his chest and flees.

CRASH THE PIPS

'Thank fuck!' says Siobhán Tooley. 'Our young digital renegade returns.'

Alex's boss is the Corporation's Deputy Head of Actuality. She has a face and figure that suit the post-war style that's so achingly hip right now. In her chevron-striped skirt-suit and matching fedora she looks like a cross between Rosalind Russell in *His Girl Friday*, and a Vegas magician. A couple of years ago this outfit would have looked clownish. Now it's standard office wear, Martingale style being pretty much mainstream these days.

'Oh,' says Alex, attempting a smile. 'Is that what I am?'

The production office is really just two banks of desks in the centre of a massive open-plan space outside the radio studios. All that demarcates it from HR or IT is a sign hanging from the ceiling, with the show's logo on it. Plus the chaos of newspapers and script sheets that coat every surface, and the commotion of production staff churning round the desks.

Alex has taken off her hat and mesh, putting her back at the mercy of the blue-white strip lights. No way to overlay her gentle forest wallpaper on the office – the Strange is blocked inside the building. Allegedly it interferes with transmission, though Alex suspects it's the Corporation's distaste for new disruptive channels. So as soon as she entered the security gates downstairs, the ad-crawls vanished and her woodland overlay fritzed out, leaving undecorated whiteness. Anxiety descended like a bolt.

And, of course, the second she emerged onto the fifth floor, Siobhán was on her.

'I'm hearing you've been – dancing around on the forecourt?' Siobhán says now. 'Collecting pocket monsters?'

Her voice is so loaded with vocal fry you could cook your breakfast on it, but her usual ironic tone is tinged with concern. Bless her, too, for the out-of-date pop culture reference.

'Yeah, sorry about that,' says Alex, gesturing vaguely towards the entrance. 'I had a bit of a . . .'

She tails off. Siobhán smiles dimly, studying her face.

'So,' she says, 'Ready to speak to the nation?'

Alex nods.

'Or at least,' says Siobhán conspiratorially, 'to a few million middle-class white people who *think* they're the nation?'

'Absolutely,' says Alex, who isn't ready for anything.

Siobhán takes her by the arm, as though to prevent her bolting.

'Great,' she says. 'Let's get you set up.'

Siobhán must never know how bad things got for Alex six months ago. There's no way she'd have given her this anchor job if she knew the vlog wasn't just on 'temporary hiatus'; if she realised Alex had had to jack it in at risk of serious collapse.

Alex only applied for this job as a crazy gambit in the hope it might offer some kind of out from her cracked and broken world. Yet against the odds, journalistic outsider as she surely was, she got the job. For a month it was a parting of the clouds. The darkness of the past half year were swept away by a fresh wind. Then reality turned about and hit her full force. This was when she started losing sleep again. *National. Live. Broadcast. Radio.* What the hell was she thinking? This wasn't her. How could even *greater* exposure be the solution to anything? At least ten times she'd started a letter of resignation, saying how sorry she was, explaining how the whole thing was an insane mistake. Then, ten times, at Harmony's insistence, she'd deleted the letters.

In the end it was the Strange that saved her. The immersive game that overlays your world – minding your worst feelings, fostering your best – became the answer to her rising panic. A few weeks back, her tattoos arrived by drone. She laid the dragon across her chest and the climbing roses down her forearms, letting the stalks twine round her fingers. A kvetching Harmony laid the leafless tree down the length of her back, letting its roots spread over her buttocks. The tattoos stung as they eased their tiny cilia into Alex's skin, but only for a second.

Her mesh arrived just after. She fitted it as a veil to the brim of her favourite tea hat. When she first put on the hat, and the mesh fell around her face and ears, she tumbled forward into the Strange like Alice down the hole. At once her experience was kinder, her vision recoloured to a palette that'd been tested before on hundreds of thousands of users, to hone in on the precise shades that would foster positive emotions. Her empty glowheart appeared beside her, ready to track her feelings. The whole awful stew of her emotions lifted outside her body, where she could monitor and moderate it.

A glowheart is a glimpse into her quantified soul. Little wonder nobody ever gives up the Strange once they taste it.

Since then the mesh has been Alex's armour against the worst her wracked emotions can throw at her. Every time the fears of the radio job have sent her to the edge, the algaerhythm has heard her silent screams and crafted an Encounter to coax her back. The most recent took place outside on the forecourt, just minutes ago. A slap, a man, a parting train. A story crafted just for Alex. She can't figure out why it was so effective at staunching her latest panic attack, but that's the genius of the Strange. It second-guesses the very thing you'd have asked for if you'd only thought to want it, and it finds another Stranger who's ready to give it to you. In this case a guy she could slap. A weirdly familiar guy. Which felt good. Hear-me-roar good.

Siobhán takes Alex by the upper arm and leads her past the humming production desks towards the studio. Her heart thuds like a trashy dance track. She looks for her glowheart but of course it isn't there.

This building is the capital city of the dying media world, yet somehow it remains the voice of the nation. In an hour, when Alex's microphone lights up green, she'll speak live to 5.4 million people. More than twice the visitor count of her old vlog. Her stomach turns again.

'First stop, the green room,' says Siobhán. 'Coffee's on.'

In the absence of the Strange, a coffee might just be Alex's salvation.

Alex manages not to spit out the stewy muck. Only now does she see the clods of white gathering on its surface. But still: caffeine. She dares another sip and looks through the glass wall into the studio. A runner (Emmy? she doesn't have all the names down yet) is setting out jugs of water and adjusting the mics on their anglepoise arms. Alex will be safe in that air- and sound-conditioned space. Back when she produced her vlog, she'd regularly put herself in the path of physical danger. It was a compulsion. Door-stepping corporate trolls, sidestepping their goons, gave her the energy to keep on fighting. Until that one last time when she finally took an actual beating. That threw her life clean off its tracks. Here, though, she's safe and subsidised – and salaried.

Beyond the studio, through another glass wall, is the control room where Siobhán will sit to steer the broadcast. In its low light, Alex can see the engineer setting levels on the gleaming mixer desk. The Captain America mesh-mask rolled up on his forehead is the only contemporary item in the whole room.

Radio news. A dinosaur that only keeps lumbering on because its nervous system's so slow, its brain doesn't yet know it died five years ago. What *is* Alex doing here?

'Ready for the airwaves?'

Talk about nothing changing: here's Thomas Causey, offering a bony hand. *Tom*, as he is to Alex now. Her unexpected co-host this morning.

'I guess,' she says.

She tries to map these drawn features into the Thomas Causey she knew from the TV news when she was a kid. All the things she's been wanting to tell this man: how he used to transfix her with his take-downs of politicians, his unstinting questions and merciless silence; how he inspired her to set out on her own journalistic course. Seeing him in the flesh reduces him – and something else is odd. Ah: no hat. Seeing anyone these days without a hat or mask is weirdly old-fashioned.

Tom's small fierce pupils bore into her.

'I see you've sampled our witch's brew?' he says, patting the urn.

Alex laughs.

'It has caffeine. It's fine.'

Thomas puts a cup under the spigot. Finding she has nothing else to say, Alex smiles and watches the tarry flow fill his cup.

'I understand,' he says, 'I'm to be teamed up with our very own blogger-in-residence?'

Alex is puzzled for a moment by the third-person construction – then realised he means her.

'Oh – we tend to call it live vlogging.'

Thomas drops two sugars into the murk.

'I rather thought we'd been *live* here for some time?'

'Yes, yes, of course. Live audio is so hot right now.'

'I'm pleased to hear it. Though I must admit, I hadn't previously noticed the temperature drop.'

He takes a slow sip and replaces the cup on its saucer.

'Siobhán tells me you're ready,' he says. 'It's good to hear she has such confidence.'

Alex raises her brows.

'Because?' she says, knowing she's rising to bait.

Thomas affects a moment of careful thought.

'Online, you can do things that are frankly beyond us. While we paint in the details you ignore in search of – ah, "clickbait".'

There is a particular kind of hell for people who put quote marks around ten-year old Internet terms as though they're somehow exotic. Tom takes a custard cream and swallows it whole, like an anaconda taking a yearling lamb.

'Siobhán thinks you have something,' he says, 'that will appeal to a younger demographic who have not yet acquired the habit of morning radio news.'

Younger demographic. Exactly what Mickey said.

'It's all very well,' says Tom, 'to ambush someone on their doorstep for a thirty-second "viral" video. Here, we favour a more forensic style of journalism. I'm sure you'll pick it up if you follow my lead.'

He brushes crumbs from his hands. Alex has a flash of the guy in the railway scene. The man she slapped. Why is his face still nagging at her? Where has she seen those spider tattoos?

Thank the goddess for a slow-news day. The stories in the first hour read like a bullet list of the lazy boom-time the nation's living through. Record results from Old Street tech firms; preparations for the launch of the RedShot Mars lander. The only hard-edged news a report of a fatal accident at a hacktivist demo in Swindon. Alex settles into the show's beats: how links, tape packages and discussions bounce between her and Tom. She makes it to the first news bulletin without a glitch. When she slips off her cans and rests them around her neck, Tom gives her a thumbs up and 30 per cent of a smile. More flattered than she expects, she looks down at the stick of dynamite splaying from under her pile of script pages. The printout of Mickey's emails.

The second hour drags. She's itching to take her shot at Susan Hardiman. With twenty-one minutes to go, Tom intros a package about the teetering fortunes of a British retail institution – the DIY chain Handy Frank's. They need the government to agree a bail-out package by Monday, or they go under. The mood music is that Frank's is too big – too iconic – to fail.

Alex shudders. Why did Handy Frank's have to bully its way into her radio debut? She knows all about that double-dealing business. Six months ago, she door-stepped its CEO for her vlog and it ended badly for both sides. She was left stumbling, shaking and bruised, from the scene; put out of action for the long haul. The tear-down interview she briefly shared played a part in the firm's current troubles. Rightly so. She barely scraped the surface of Handy Frank's dodgy dealings.

The next few items are wrenchingly slow. Tom leads into an item about the revival of big-band swing in East London clubs. He can't decide whether to be chipper about the comeback of a classic art form, or sneering about the thought of lindy-hopping hipsters. As the tape package rolls, the engineer patches into Alex's cans a press officer from the Department for Business, who hands off in turn to the minister, Susan Hardiman. Everyone says hello. To get a level, the engineer asks the minister what she had for breakfast. Home-made granola and blueberries, apparently. Alex silently calls bullshit. Even when there's nobody listening, politicians lie.

Seven fifty on the nail, her mic lights up. She intros Hardiman, twirling a pencil and staring into the spit-guard. In response to Alex's soft-ball opening question, Hardiman rolls off a bland statement about the morning's growth stats. She'll be sitting in some bunkered radio room at the ministry, with soundproof foam peeling from its walls. Opposite her will be sitting the press officer, scribbling notes to hold up should the minister stray from her lines: *GROWTH; HARD-WORKING FAMILIES; PROSPERITY.*

Alex needles Hardiman gently on the numbers but doesn't put up a fight. Let her think she's getting an easy ride from the newbie.

Then, apropos of nothing, Alex says, 'Perhaps now we can turn the discussion towards carpets?'

The line falls silent. Alex pictures Susan and her advisers exchanging looks; but what can you do when you're live on national radio?

'Excuse me,' says Hardiman, 'I don't—'

'Alex?' says Siobhán from the booth. 'What are you—'

'Most specifically,' says Alex, 'handwoven pure Dalesford wool carpets. Do you have a view on them, Minister?'

Siobhán gestures frantically through the glass.

'Fucking muppet has the wrong script!' she says, knowing Alex can hear.

'The, um,' says Hardiman. 'The handmade carpet sector is a great example of how our resurgent manufacturing – ah—'

'Am I right in thinking you sit on the standards committee, Minister?'

Pause.

'Ye-es?'

'So you'll be able to tell me: is it normal for a professional lobbyist to pay for the refurbishment of an MP's constituency office?'

Longer pause. Put a note in front of that, bitches.

Deep inside Alex's cans the small voice of Siobhán says, 'What's happening?'

'Last month's necessary refurbishment,' says Hardiman at length, 'was funded through a donation from a generous private source. Which has been declared. The Standards office is satisfied I acted with complete probity. Now if we can return to the topic at hand—'

'In which case you'll have disclosed the email that I have in front of me now – sent by your constituency manager to the lobbying professional Sam Corrigan – saying, quote, *I'm sure that won't present a barrier to your making the payment. Susan is very comfortable taking a hard line on that package. She's known as a hawk on government intervention so this will be a consistent position for her to take.*'

Pause.

'That—' says Hardiman.

Over the crystal fidelity of her headphones Alex hears a scuffle of papers.

'I am unaware of any such email,' Hardiman says at last.

'Surprising, given how carefully you looked into this matter. So you're unaware of the *package of government intervention* Mr Corrigan refers to in his mail?'

There was silence.

'Ho-ly fu-ck-king . . .' says Siobhán into Alex's cans.

'You could, I'm sure,' she says, 'satisfy the Parliamentary Standards Office of the *probity* of your dealing with this lobbyist, Sam Corrigan?'

'I am unaware of any such email. This is a matter for my constituency staff. Now if we could turn to the policy announcement I'm making today—'

'Did you accept a bribe, Minister?'

'Alex! *SHIT!*'

'That is an outrageous—'

'If you'd be so good as to answer the question, Minister. What was the *position* you were so ready to take in exchange for this money?'

'The New Compact For Jobs is a win–win policy. It's good for business and good for the hard-working—'

'Did you accept a bribe, Minister?'

'—for the hard-working families of—'

'Well, unfortunately we're out of time. Susan Hardiman, Minister for Competitiveness, thank you. Tom.'

Thomas, who's been staring blankly at Alex, fumbles for his script and cues in the weather. Dan, the weatherman, who entered the studio during the interview, has been sitting hypnotised but now he stumbles through his forty seconds of spits and spots of rain, while Alex kicks back her chair and lets out a breath, exhausted by the bout. By the time Dan hands back to Tom they're twenty seconds behind. Tom gabbles out his cue and ends by crashing into the time pips as they sound the hour.

Slowly he removes his cans, staring flatly at Alex. He probably hasn't crashed the pips once in his whole twenty years on the show. Alex returns his stare as they go to news.

Alex gathers her papers and pushes out of the silence of the studio hallway into the open-plan cacophony. Raging with the triumph of her coup, she can barely remember the show's final hour.

Her phone buzzes in her pocket. The sensation surprises her. These days she only uses the thing to text her mother. It's a message from her former economics professor, Lukaš Caron.

> **Lukas**
>
> Alex. I just heard your piece. A splendid interview.
> As it happens I have a story you might be inter-
> ested in. My new book, STRANGERS IN PARADISE,
> is out on Monday. It explores the new emotional
> economy of the Strange. My publicist has been
> speaking to your editor about a spot but I don't

The message goes below the fold but Alex doesn't scroll. This is a taste of how things will be now. She's an influencer. Her heart putters as she navigates a gauntlet of pats on the back and heads for the post-show huddle, which is held on the ring of uncomfortable pouffes by Siobhán's desk. Most of the team are gathered there already. The backchat stops the second they catch sight of Alex. Siobhán is standing by her desk, jaw set, arms folded. Alex stops dead a few metres from the huddle. Siobhán calls over.

'Do you have a minute, Alex?'

The tone is jaunty but the fury on her face is a new thing. Alex has been naive. She wasn't seeing beyond the blow she landed on Hardiman. All the warnings she's had – about process, about referring all decisions up to management – she just ignored, on her first morning at the mic. While she was doing her *Doorstop* vlog, the only point was to land a blow. She always did, at whatever cost. She had nobody to answer to but the baying appetites of her followers. At this vast and fragile institution, things are different. She knew that, but this morning she decided to forget.

'Oh – two minutes?' she says to Siobhán, pointing towards the ladies'.

Siobhán nods slowly and tracks Alex's progress to the loos. Once there, Alex slams the cubicle door. Her mesh being inactive, she pulls out her phone to message Mickey.

> Your source. It is corroborated?

The message is quickly flagged as read but it takes the better part of a minute before Mickey starts typing his reply.

> **Mickey Gallant**
> Will be soon. Working on it now.

> But – the email?
> I just read it out on air.
> Like YOU SAID.

> **Mickey Gallant**
> Yes, sure, the email is almost
> certainly a real thing

> ALMOST???

> **Mickey Gallant**
> Look, it's just a piece of paper OK? I could
> have typed it up myself this morning.

Alex whitens.

> Please please tell me that isn't
> what you did. Tell me that at least.

> **Mickey Gallant**
> It's a good source I just haven't jumped
> through all the hoops yet.

Alex smashes her fist three times into the cubicle wall. After a pause, there's a voice from just the other side of the door.

'Everything all right, Alex?' says Siobhán.

ZERO DAY

Thimblerig runs over tarmac towards the green giant. The cat's claws dig into his belly where he's clutching it to him. The giant's a glowing beacon. In the half light of early morning it hovers above the empty car park. Summoning Thimblerig to its protection.

The cat hisses. Thimblerig hears running feet to his five o'clock. Some distance away but closing in. Without turning to look he dives behind a driverless car that's idling at a charging station. He puts his hands out to break his fall as he hits the pavement. The cat leaps free and lands in a tight crouch. The footsteps pass on the other side of the car.

He waits a while then levers himself up to his knees. The heel of his left hand stings where he landed. Probably grazed but it's too dark to tell. The cat steps up and licks his palm with its moist tongue. The antiseptic stings a little. He pats the cat on the head and uses the wheel arch of the car to lever himself up.

‹Kindly do not touch the paintwork›

says the car's windscreen.

— Sorry, says Thimblerig, stepping back.

He scans the car park in all directions. No more Spider-Men for the moment. He can't work out whether they're some daft stunt by a rival hacker crew. Or something else. Either way he doesn't care to let one catch him.

His chest burns from all the running. His sweaty T-shirt's cold against his back – though the inside of his pig mask's hot and damp from his frantic breath. He wiggles it back into place and trots towards the giant. The cat follows at his side. Inside her is the data he pulled from Occidental. The emails about the Kaa hack. And maybe in the older mails there's evidence on how Occidental's CEO Doug Raynor sealed the fate of Thimblerig's father.

This giant is winking down from the forecourt of a warehouse store two hundred metres ahead. It's the last in a row of seven superstores linked by an access road. The fibreglass giant is dressed in bright green dungarees and a matching cap. Emblazoned on the chest flap of his dungarees is a vast red 'F' for 'Frank'. Green neon outlines his cartoon features. That winking eye and outsize thumbs-up are the trademarks of the Happy Handyman – the mascot of the Handy Frank's DIY store. *The nation's favourite home helper* it says on the ads.

By this point Thimblerig's completely lost. The Spider-Men have chased him over what felt like a hundred office parks and ring roads. Now the green light of the Handyman is calling him in to the superstore like a lighthouse in a storm.

Thimblerig loves Handy Frank's. He's done so ever since he came to England with nothing to his name but a ziplock bag containing a bundle of forged papers and a battered copy of a book about the future. The twinkle in that unwinking eye stands for everything good in the people of his adopted nation. Their reliable mischief. Their anti-authority pragmatism. Maybe also the racist stuff, but he prefers not to think about that.

Thimblerig trips as he hops across a low concrete divide but he rights himself and jogs towards the sign. The store's hours are displayed on a board beneath it. It won't open till ten a.m. There's at least an hour before the first shift arrives. He's spent so long in Frank's stores that he knows their schedules better than most employees. The first British money he ever earned was by fixing the radios and phones of his compatriots who lived with him in Mr Wassouf's row of houses. Every pound he earned was spent at

Handy Frank's on tools and components for the repair work. And for his own home-brew computers. He was nine. Frank's has been his refuge ever since. It's the one place he can be sure to find someone to speak to about the things that really matter: i.e. solder and transistors and microcircuitry.

He passes under the buzzing illumination of the Happy Handyman and the shuttered displays at the front of the building. The staff entrance should be at the rear of the building. As he rounds the corner he almost runs into a row of recycling bins. Standing on top of the SMALL ELECTRONICS bin – picked out in yellow floodlight – is a Spider-Man.

Thimblerig freezes. The Spider-Man is three metres away. His bootied feet are level with Thimblerig's face. Legs apart and fists on hips he scans the car park with his back to Thimblerig. The smart rubber of the blue-and-red suit can't hide the tyre of fat around the man's waist.

Thimblerig bends to pick up the cat and steps back silently the way he came. He's almost made it around the breeze-block corner of the store when the Spider-Man's head darts round and fixes its blank pointed eyes on Thimblerig. Blue flickers over the eyepieces. It wasn't Spider-Sense that made him look. There's mesh inside those sockets. This Spider-Man is a Stranger.

Thimblerig breaks away and runs to the opposite side of the store. From behind him comes a metallic crash and a cry of pain. Seems this Spider-Man doesn't share the arachnid agility of the original. Thimblerig vaults and scrabbles over a green plastic hopper filled with sacks of smokeless coal and rounds the corner. He tears down the alley between a wooden fence and the featureless wall of the superstore. Halfway along is a staff entrance. From the front of the building comes the *tap-slip tap-slip tap-slip* of a superhero with a twisted ankle. Thimblerig fumbles in his backpack for the plastic wallet where he keeps his cloned entry cards. He finds the card with *HF* written on it in Sharpie and swipes his way in. There's a security camera above the door. What will the face recognition make of a grinning pig arriving early for work? He yanks the door shut behind him. Through the narrowing crack he sees the Spider-Man limping into the alley.

Thimblerig puts the cat down as the lights flick on. He's in a narrow staffroom lined with aluminium lockers and three large vending machines. With any luck, the Spider-Man's mesh didn't pick him up before the door shut. He's got no devices or implants that a mesh could detect electronically – so it's down to whether one of its thousands of links had line of sight on him. He switches on the entry system beside the door. The screen lights up with a grainy monochrome image of the alley and the staff car park beyond. The Spider-Man is hobbling across the car park and towards the chevroned entry barrier.

Thimblerig blows out a breath of air to clear his head. He hangs up the entryphone and heads between the rows of lockers towards a door that – if this Frank's is laid out the same way as all the others he's been in – will lead to the storeroom. The cat lopes dutifully beside him.

These lockers are where the Handy Johns and Handy Janes stow their green dungarees. Thimblerig has always liked the Handy Frank's staff. They're so famously cheerful they've recently generated their own meme. It always takes the same form. On the left is a photo of something ghastly – e.g., last week's fire-bombing of a school in Oklahoma. On the right a Handy John or Jane gives the trademark thumbs-up and winks at the camera. Above his or her head is a speech bubble saying e.g. *Phew! That'll save stripping out all that asbestos!*

Thimblerig doesn't like people mocking the Handy lads and lasses. They were the first grown-ups on this island to ever make him welcome. Always ready with practical tips to fill the gaps in what his father taught him. Never seeming to mind him loitering in the aisles for hours without buying anything. Eponymous likes to tease him about his love for a hokey old store. He says high street DIY is a busted business model. Nobody owns a toolkit any more – they just go onto the Strange and ask a fellow-Stranger to lend them the exact-sized spanner or drill bit they need. Which might explain why the company is faring so badly. The chatter on the boards says the government's planning to rescue them. That's good. Thimblerig's not the only one who'd go into a major gloom if this national treasure shut up shop.

He swipes into the storeroom with the key card that he cloned months ago from a Handy Frank's regional manager as she bawled out a staff member at the till of Thimblerig's local store. He pretended to check out a display of battery packs while quietly running his portable skimmer over the key card that was hanging from the manager's belt. The card he wrote from that impression has got him through every door in every store he's tried it on since. Along the way, it's helped him pick up one or two items he couldn't afford to buy.

In the chilly storeroom he makes his way between high-stacked shelves of boxes containing a multitude of tools and fixtures and garden furniture. Lights hiccup on as he walks the aisles. He reaches the locked cage that protects the racks of more expensive electronics and slips his lockpicks from his backpack. The cage door's secured with a mid-range five cylinder Yale. He holds up the first two barrels with a straight pick and wiggles the angled pick until its curve sets the last three tumblers into line. He flicks the lock open and shuts himself in the cage. He drops into a ball in the corner and tears off his pig mask. The cameras will have seen a pig-man break into the cage. None are pointing down into this corner. He can be himself.

He rubs his hands through his mess of hair then looks around the aluminium racks. There must be a thousand different chipsets and components in this tight space. He shudders but he's out of danger. Locked in a cage with all this digital gear is as close to a safe place as Thimblerig can get.

Now the mask is off he can smell the soot and scorched rubber he's been carrying with him. The front of his favourite Martingale T-shirt is smeared with grime from the burned-out car. He shudders again. Dirt bugs him. Also he just saw a lady possibly die on his account.

Throughout his escape his crablet has been latched to his left forearm. He gives it a gentle tug. It unclenches its six articulated legs and he moves it to his thighs where latches hold and fires up its display. He pulls up a terminal window and posts a Martingale quotation – *Naked and unadorned we stand* – to a nondescript chat thread on the hacker forum known as Brine. This is the signal that will call Lucky Ghost to his side. Only he knows this formula and he guards it with his life.

Leaving the display live he picks up the cat and pulls it to his chest. He nestles his cheek on its hard head and feels the purring vibration of its motor. The ceiling lights tick off one by one until he's in the dark. Now all he needs to do is wait for Ghost to come online.

Lucky Ghost first appeared a year ago. It was two in the morning and Thimblerig was on a Brine channel called #martingale_ops where he's one of the moderators. A bunch of Cockaigne hackers were flaming each other about where and how to share a massive data dump they'd recently snared containing the home addresses of every single cyber protection officer in the Greater Manchester Police. Everyone agreed they should share it – information is meant to be free. The disagreement was over how to make the maximum noise. Things were getting somewhat out of hand when an unapproved user appeared out of nowhere and posted to this ultra-private thread.

Lucky Ghost: I suppose one should be flattered to find one's name being used for a den of such notorious brigands.

The user's name was Lucky Ghost. Her multicoloured avatar leapt at Thimblerig from the chat window. Everyone else on this thread was lurking as usual behind the default system avatar – a grey head-and-shoulder weeble. Not Lucky Ghost. Her custom avi was based on the classic posterised image of Professor Elyse Martingale: the twentieth-century's prophetess of tech and the anti-state. Which was quite a calling card in those circles.

Even the noisiest of the hackers was stunned into silence for a moment. This person had strolled onto a permission-only channel and simply joined in the chat. It was like when a lone gunman strides into a saloon and all the townsfolk fall silent and stare. As channel moderator, Thimblerig was the first to respond.

Thimblerig: How did you get on here?
Lucky Ghost: As the name suggests, my dear, I am a ghost.
eponymous: tits or youre bounced

That was the standard greeting for anyone presenting as female on that channel. Girls are supposed to prove they're game. Usually this means a topless selfie.

Lucky Ghost: Try it, dear boy, and I'll share this little tidbit on the home page of The Huffington Post.

And just like that up popped a screen-cap of a chubby white male with his top off. The man's face and man-breasts were sprayed with light thrown up from his laptop. The wall behind him was unfinished concrete. He was staring at his screen and reaching down to create some action in the region of his crotch. His face was contorted in what looked like bowel pain but was presumably ecstasy. Eponymous vanished from the board and it took him two days to show his face again. At his bedroom desk Thimblerig barked with involuntary laughter. He'd never seen a picture of any of his other cohorts but that *must* have been Eponymous.

This was the way to make an entrance. Top-flight crackers don't tell – they do. From that first night the Cockaigne team has listened to Ghost. Except for Eponymous who refuses to even chat with her. Everything the Ghost provides is gold. It's her who gave Thimblerig the information that turned him onto Occidental Data Partnerships and Raynor. That exploit went so smoothly – until the Spider-Men arrived.

* * *

The cat's eyes light up in the dark of the cage.

— *My dear boy*, she says. *What a dreadful outcome.*

Lucky Ghost is here. When Thimblerig's alone she always speaks through the cat. This voice is constructed from samples of Elyse Martingale that he's digitised and cleansed from vintage recordings. The result is distant and maternal – and comforting. It's as close as Thimblerig can get to speaking to Elyse.

— It went so wrong, says Thimblerig.

— *You could not have known.*

Tiny servos fire to tilt the cat's head sideways as it studies Thimblerig's face. He realises he's crying. Sloppy tears are burning traces through the grime on his cheeks. He wipes his face. There's nobody here to judge. Nobody but Ghost.

— I grabbed the cat and ran, he says. But I think she died. The lady.

— *Her name was Winter Green,* says Ghost.

For some reason that's the saddest thing Thimblerig has ever heard. He sobs once then slaps a hand to his mouth. Is it strange he should turn to this anonymous presence at a time like this? He'd never open up to his Cockaigne friends the way he does to Ghost. He's trusted her since that first night when she doxxed Eponymous.

Trust is weird on anonymous channels. Ghost could have shopped Eponymous at any time. The fact that she didn't means she's either on the level or playing the mole. Someone with her skills can just as easily be spy or ally. Everyone's only trustworthy as their past behaviour makes them out to be. Thimblerig lives in the narrow space between trust and betrayal. It's the best he can hope for.

The cat eyes him as he wipes his face. As matter of factly as he can muster he tells Ghost about the data he pulled from Occidental. And about the hack called Kaa.

— It's a zero day, he says.

A zero-day hack is a pearl you only find after prising open a thousand shells. It's the hack that nobody else has discovered yet.

That nobody has been able to spend a single day defending against. His gut tells him this zero day called Kaa is a key that can decrypt this apparently chaotic morning and create some sense from it. This morning he learned that a live bomb is primed and hidden inside the banking system. Kaa is the fuse. So why has nobody lit it?

— From what I read in those mails, he says, Doug Raynor could have sold this thing for millions but he didn't. Why?

If he can figure this out then maybe he'll understand why this morning's stunt was taken down by cavorting superguys. Why the lady called Winter Green had to die. The urge to know is an ache in his belly.

— *Perhaps,* says Lucky Ghost, *he did not want it used.*

— But why?

— *Raynor represents autocracy and power. Using this Kaa would land a blow for liberty. Perhaps his corporate masters are stopping him.*

That chimes.

— I can't even work out, says Thimblerig, what would happen if the banks stopped working. If money went blue-screen-of-death.

Money is strange and Thimblerig doesn't understand how it works. He was a child when he left his home city. Soon after that the siege began to truly bite and the stores all emptied. People who survived through that time say that money soon lost its purpose. After a while they stopped carrying it. They found other ways to remember what they owed one another. As Elyse Martingale says: *A bank is the instrument by which Capital extracts obligations from working people. Money is a false promise. Is it not time we replaced it with a true one?*

— *The only way to find out,* says Ghost, *is to use Kaa. No spanner thrown into the gears of institutional control is ever wasted.*

It's sometimes hard to tell whether Lucky Ghost is quoting the great Elyse or speaking for herself. This is part of a bigger puzzle: is she a human person at all? Or just a very sophisticated bot?

— *Have you understood*, she says, *why they call it Kaa?*

He hasn't. Ghost sends him a short loop of some old-time cartoon snake wrapped around a branch. He plays it on the crablet.

— *Trust in me . . .* the snake sings.

Its voice is tinny and slight in the cavernous storeroom.

— *Trust in me . . .*

— *Trust in me . . .*

After the third loop he kills the clip.

— *You, my lad, have unearthed a snake in the capitalist Eden of trust.*

Thimblerig's tears dry as he puzzles this out. He gets nowhere.

— Do you understand what Kaa does? There's so little information here.

— *The question is, do you? Start with what you do know and work backwards.*

— The mails say it attacks Transax. That's the system banks use for moving money between them.

— *And what does Transax do?*

Thimblerig thinks a moment before replying.

— Transax lives inside the money system. When one bank lends money to another it's Transax that tells both systems who to trust with the transaction. And who to not.

Thimblerig reads every blog he can find about this stuff. Know your enemy.

— *So then. If Kaa disrupted this clearing system?*

— . . . the payments would be rejected?

— *And yet this concerns far more than money.*

— No one would know who to trust anymore. Kaa hacks trust.

— *Now you have it.*

What would happen to our money if one day trust was erased from the system? There have been so many financial crises. Money – like Thimblerig's father's money – can disappear completely in a flash. Which proves there was never really anything there in the first place. Nothing real happens without money but money is an *ifrit*. A vanishing spirit. Thimblerig's temples hurt from thinking about it. One thing's clear though: Kaa's a powerful hack.

Deep in Thimblerig's gut is an urge to make the system crash and leave people free to do what they want. This is why he hooked up with Cockaigne in the first place. For years now they've been wanting to hurt the banks. Maybe this moment is what it's all been for. All the loss and hopelessness. Even Winter Green's death.

— We need to get hold of Kaa, he says.

— *Good lad. But how?*

Except none of this is what he set out to do this morning.

— You said if I hacked Occidental, I'd be able to prove it was Raynor.

He doesn't need to say what he wants to prove. Lucky Ghost knows. Two months ago she pointed him to a cache of CIA documents lurking deep in the bowels of WikiLeaks. Dox dating back to the Syrian war. They'd been lifted from a laptop seized by US special forces from an extremist group. Among billions of uncatalogued bytes Ghost had extracted a single snatch of logfile from a decade-old chat session. Thimblerig has read and reread this chat a hundred times. It's a terse conversation that by rights should not exist. An extremist exchanging intelligence with an American operative. They're making a trade. That in itself would be explosive if any journalist had bothered to root it out but the conversation has a far more specific meaning to Thimblerig.

The American is a so-called 'private security contractor'. He's identified only by the handle *drainer*. During the chat this *drainer* gives the extremist detailed technical information on the communication systems of a rebel platoon based in the city. This information seems to be the price for the release of a US serviceman held by the group and *drainer* is some kind of full-deniability middleman between the US authorities and the jihadis. Two weeks later all nine leaders of this rebel outfit were dead or kidnapped. One day after that the serviceman was dumped blindfold at a Kurdish outpost near the Turkish border.

This narrative fits with certain information Thimblerig's already assembled. It fits as neatly as a plug in a socket. The identity of *drainer* is a cryptographic key that could unscramble everything that's been hidden for so long. Ghost says *drainer* is none other than Doug Raynor. Beyond the obvious wordplay she's been unable to produce any proof. Yet when has Lucky Ghost been wrong? Since then Thimblerig's dug and scraped for anything he can find on Raynor and his organisation. Evidence of past online handles and activities during that disastrous war. What he's turned up so far is suggestive but it's not enough. Now the information he's hacked from Occidental Data Partnerships could be the thing that makes the difference.

Why go to such lengths to implicate Raynor? Because one of those nine rebel leaders was Thimblerig's father.

— *You captured Raynor's email archive?* says Lucky Ghost. *From ten years past? The evidence may be in your hands.*

Or in his cat. Thimblerig strokes the silky plastic on the back of its head.

— A whole year's worth, he says.

– *So, then.*

— But Ghost, it'll take days to mine them. Do I go after Kaa? Or finish the job and get to Raynor?

— *Are those mails going anywhere?*

Thimblerig looks at the sturdy cat-shaped robot curled in his lap. He nods in the dark of the warehouse. Ghost can't see this. She only ever links with the cat on audio.

— All right, he says. I'll steal Kaa. I'll take it out of Raynor's hands. I'll go back to the building and log back on. With time I should be able to locate the Kaa code.

— *That could be a challenge. Our friends in the Wiltshire constabulary are out in force after your little stunt.*

Thimblerig tugs at the clump of hair hanging over his forehead. A small noise escapes his mouth like something breaking. The cat watches with lidless eyes. He's been so stupid. If the police are at the site already that means Eponymous has put out the info on Raynor's dodgy contractors. Just like Thimblerig told him to do.

— They'll have wiped everything by now.

— *That would be the unfortunate conclusion.*

Thimblerig's amateur stunt has stopped him getting to the prize.

— I've ruined everything.

— *Perhaps not.*

There's one of those pauses you sometimes get with Ghost. People who claim she's just a machine often point to these blank-outs as evidence. But what if she is? A few years back the Cockaigne movement was kicked off by the actions of a chat-bot. An artificial construct programmed to speak like a person. But it wasn't a person. If someone speaks truth it doesn't matter if they're person or machine.

Ghost still hasn't returned to the cat. Thimblerig thinks briefly about the little delivery he sent by drone to a certain address in north-west London. He wishes he had time to follow up on that but there isn't the time.

His buttocks are getting numb on the cold concrete. The cat stirs in his lap as he shifts. From the dark a blue light ripples at the edge of his vision. He turns to catch it.

On the far side of the cage is some kind of display stand decked with strips of fabric. One of the strips flickers blue. It isn't fabric: it's mesh. Thimblerig picks up the cat and points it at the display.

— ضوّي he says.

The cat's eyes light up. Flattened in the halogen beam is a point-of-sale display for five varieties of mesh – low-grade RuggedMesh to the near-invisible top-line models. These are the veils the Strangers use to swaddle their heads from the world. They twist and twirl their hands to follow its cartoon illusions. They dance like helpless lunatics. At least that's how they look to anyone watching from the real world.

Each mesh is a swatch of translucent net made up of tiny micro-filament links. Strangers place these audio-visual veils across their eyes and ears – usually hanging them from the brim of a hat. Which is why everyone seems to wear a hat and dress like a character from the black-and-white movies that Thimblerig's neena used to watch.

Each link in a mesh is intelligent in its own right. Each has a tiny laser. Hundreds of these lasers working together can paint a hyper-realistic 3D image onto the retinas of the mesh-head. The links also have tiny speakers that are tagged together to form an audio surround. Plus tiny cameras to interpret the world outside the mesh.

That tinge of blue means one of the strips is powered up. Which means hundreds of nano cameras are capturing Thimblerig's face right now and sharing it with thousands of nearby nodes in the algaerhythm.

He puts a hand on the cat's back.

— طفي he says.

The torch in the cat's eyes powers down but they're still gently aglow. Ghost has returned.

— *It seems*, she says, *that early this morning Mr Raynor left a case of hard drives in the care of a secure storage firm called Gordion. Just outside Swindon. A few miles from the site of your ill-starred demonstration.*

— Early this morning? Before he sent the Kaa emails to his senior team?

— *Indeed.*

Obviously. Raynor wouldn't junk a hack of this magnitude.

— So what do we do?

— *What do YOU want to do, dear?*

Recently Thimblerig has been thinking a lot about the time after his father was killed and he made his slow way north. How his family's assets were seized by the authorities back home. How the international banks abetted this. The very same banks that sit cosy on the high street and commercial Internet of the UK. Thimblerig's still young but he sees through their branded gloss. Even today those banks continue to shore up that despicable regime and conceal its pillaged assets. The true evils of the world are lodged behind the cool numerics of the banks.

— We need to steal Kaa, he says. We need to *use* it.

— *Very well, dear. Give me a few minutes.*

She's gone again. Thimblerig stands and stretches. The strip lights over the cage tick on. He must have passed under a sensor. He returns the passive gaze of the mesh strip on the display stand then looks around the cage. He didn't come equipped for a break-in but that's OK. Everything he needs is here. Now the mesh has seen him he needs to move fast. The Strange knows he's here. Maybe more Spider-Men will come – or others. He doesn't have time to figure out where these Strangers are coming from or why.

The cat's eyes follow as Thimblerig picks up his backpack. Time to go 'shopping'.

HUGE IF TRUE

Mickey Gallant lives life on caps lock. He clatters up the Old Kent Road, through the simmering heart of London's densest community of Strange, phasing in and out of other people's stories. This part of town is close to home as means a damn to Mickey. A stocky bustle of interference and curiosity, he slaps palms and garbles one-liners, leaving behind a trail of small-denomination Coin: today, it's mostly *DISTRACTION, INTEREST* and *JOY*.

He stops outside an artisanal Judean street-food outlet called *Judus S. Carry-Out*. A gaggle of Strangers in suits from assorted nineties kids' shows is gathered on a grimy concrete patch – Power Rangers, and a Ninja Turtle. Alongside each floats a fat glow-heart, busy with colour. Their hands move rapidly, patterning the details of the story they're playing. Micky checks: it's season 4 of *The Martingale Saga*. Mickey orders a leavened wrap and steps into their playspace.

Maybe half of all Encounters reanimate that great twentieth-century prophet of tech, Elyse Martingale. Many overlay her story with superpowers or spy plots, but this Encounter's more realistic. Mickey's in parkland, walking downhill from a red-brick manor house towards a well-rendered lake. If he recalls right, Elyse led some kind of groovy sixties research facility. The cluster of Strangers stand by the lake, their lurex suits and helmets transposed to duffle coats, chunky black gasses and long tousled hair. All are smoking: vapes in the real, Woodbines in the Strange. The Pink Ranger is Elyse, complete with trademark tweed twinset and bird's-nest hair. Everyone clams up as Mickey approaches. The Encounter has accommodated him into the guise of some paunchy official. It feeds him a line.

<may I remind you I remain director of this facility?>

Mickey's free to extemporise but he hasn't viewed the *Previously On*, so he plays it safe and reels off the cue verbatim. His voice is transposed to a colonial bray. The lorded Elyse fires back with both barrels.

'I am hardly likely to forget, Mr Cadby.'

'And yet,' says officious Mickey, 'you continue to install undesirables and radicals on my campus without my permission. This is not some Notting Hill "commune", may I remind you?'

The guy he's playing is some kind of a dick.

'Judging by the quality of people on *your* staff,' says La Martingale, 'I should think it a relief to all concerned that you've had no hand in recruiting *mine*.'

Cue barely suppressed guffaws from the long-hair crew. Steam spurts from fake Mickey's veiny nose and he storms back up the rise to the big house: though in the real all he does is turn to the food counter, where his wrap is waiting. It's the spicy option so he pays the man 60 RAGE.

'Mr Cadby?' says the Pink Ranger/Elyse – which is weird because Mickey's left the Encounter.

He skirts the gamers. The Pink Ranger's helmet tracks his progress.

He's seen this group before. They hang out here much of the day, immersed in Elyse's story. From the full-body costumes they're fully Strange, meaning they worship Martingale. She represents the liberation that comes when you give yourself up to the electronic commune. Not everyone has the chops to do that. The deeper you travel into the Strange, the more distant you grow from friends or families; the more you rely on random strangers for momentary solace and support. Hence the brand name.

Mickey, too, has cut the cords connecting him to other people, but he's too jaded to go full coslife, like these dudes. In their eyes, the fact that he wears his mesh as a simple veil brands him a dabbler. Maybe that's fair, but he can't imagine waking up to see C-3PO in the mirror, or whatever. That's how you got to live if you want to go fully Strange.

He pulls away from the blank gaze of the Ranger and trundles north, gnawing on the wrap. Which he's too queasy to enjoy. It's not like him to lose his appetite, but all he can think about is the specific creek where he's dropped Alex Kubelick, paddleless. He completely failed to do the usual dotting and crossing of 'i's and 't's before sharing intelligence like that. He was so excited to discover that she was interviewing the Hardiman harridan that very morning. So he went for it. Which was monumentally fucking stupid. After Alex hammered Hardiman, he finally followed up his source; but all he got was an undelivered bounceback. As in, not good. Mickey, for all his shambolic detachment, is not a man to leave a colleague sinking in the mire on his account. If his source has gone to ground, he needs to send a terrier down the nearest rabbit hole. The particular terrier he has in mind goes by the name of Hairy Jacko.

Mickey polishes off the wrap. He's been watching his mesh all morning for traces of Jacko. Now he's picked up the trail. He dials down alerts to focus on Jacko's whispered conversations. Like most command-line types, Jacko's a Strange refusenik, so his trail's constructed out of footage from the mesh of Strangers. It's like tracking down an enormous bearded Pokémon. *Hairyama*, maybe? *Beardadon*? Mickey grins as he follows the 3D flickbook of Jacko's progress down the street. His mesh pays a tiny tick of Coin for every image he acquires. Spies are so cheap these days and this part of south-east London is fat with Strangers. Among these all-night supermarkets and jerk chicken outlets you're as likely to see a Stranger as a civilian. It's a way of life here.

The trail crosses the street and enters – big surprise – Hass's Pie Plaice. The exact spot where Mickey's search would have started anyway. Mickey crosses, barging through the ghosts of Jacko's progress. They puff to nothing in his wake. Halfway across the road a slow-moving car stops with a tiny jolt, just short of Mickey. He hadn't seen it glide up. The empty car throws a boldface message onto Mickey's field of vision.

‹please cross thank you›

‹please cross thank you›

Mickey gives it the Vs and crosses slowly as he pleases. Pass-agg autonomous vehicles shouldn't show their windscreens in this part of town. This is a Stranger zone.

Outside Hass's, a battered drone the size of a blackbird hovers, dragonfly blades shuttering silently. This must be Jacko's sentinel. As Mickey pushes inside the caff, he catches a reflection in the misted glass of the door. He doesn't turn to check what he's seen but he's sure. The pink Power Ranger from before – the one who played Elyse – is trailing ten metres behind, eyes locked on Mickey's back. Something about the Ranger's stride jolts a thought in Mickey's mind: he's still in the Strange. Still playing Elyse.

Mickey opens the door and enters a welcoming fug of grease and steam. Hassan himself is behind the counter, sporting a Millwall shirt and a glum expression. As the door swings shut the condensation on its glass conceals him from the street. Hairy Jacko is the only person in the caff, seated in his usual spot at the corner table, just in front of the orange Formica counter. His long face hangs in swags from his skull. His hair and beard, which are the colour of dirty tarmac, reach below the table, giving the impression that he's hair all the way on down, like Cousin It. On the table in front of him is a preindustrial laptop whose screen is thicker than Mickey's hand. It's an odd sight. These days, you walk into a Starbucks, there are no laptops on tables: just Strangers typing on air, watching info riot about them. Jacko favours the old ways.

As Mickey peels up his mesh, Jacko looks up and goes through a tiny symphony of facial expressions. He clocks Mickey; recognises him; checks out the open flap of the counter behind him; smiles broadly back at Mickey – all in the space of half a second.

'Geezer,' he says, in a voice like rush-hour traffic. 'What you got for me?'

Which is his standard greeting. Mickey levers himself into the vinyl of Jacko's booth. He's just able to squeeze between the tight arrangement of bench seat and table.

'Coin,' says Mickey. 'Assuming you've something for *me*.'

A low growl starts behind Jacko's beard: this is laughter.

'Thing about you Bizarros,' he says, 'is, there's never any give without take.'

'*Strangers*,' says Mickey, placing his fingers on his chest. 'You wound me, Jack.'

'I might just do that, Mickey. I might just.'

They stare this one out a while. Mickey's the first to drop his gaze. There's something eerie in the sewagey whites of Jacko's eyes.

'You don't exactly hide yourself,' says Mickey. 'I just followed your trail right through the Strange. Hardcore fellow like you could make yourself invisible with a wave of your hand.'

'Maybe I want to be found. Finding me isn't the same as seeing what's in here.'

Jacko spreads out the fingers of both hands above his clunky grey laptop, as though blessing it, still eyeballing Mickey.

'I'm looking for a cracker,' says Mickey. 'Understand you might know a guy.'

More of the growling. Jacko's laughing because the idea he knows 'a guy' – as in just one – is tearaway nonsense. He may look like a homeless man nursing a stagnant cup of tea for the whole afternoon, but Jacko's proof that judging by looks is a chronic error. He has this rebel army behind him – a bunch of anarchist tech fringies who call themselves Cockaigne. They use their considerable skills to wage war on the big data moguls, liberating their imprisoned information. Not lads you'd want to be the wrong side of.

Jacko stops laughing when Mickey places a hard copy of the Hardiman email on the tacky surface of the table. The version of the mail he passed to Alex was printed out using default settings: just the tos, ccs and subject line. Here, he's printed off full header information, showing how the mail was routed. The kind of server-speak that Mickey doesn't understand but Jacko reads like a native.

Mickey uses hard copy wherever he can. In a world where everything you write is remembered for ever, paper is helpfully amnesiac.

'There was a hack,' Mickey says. 'This snippet found its way to me. Source gave me just enough to show the material was on the up and up, but nowhere near enough to figure out who he was. From which I conclude he's done this more than once, and he's careful. But I'm thinking this mail might be part of a bigger hack I only saw a tiny scrape of. I'm thinking you might be able to direct me to who did the hack. On the QT.'

The door jangles open. Both men turn. Mickey fears it'll be the curious Pink Ranger – but it's only Hass's wife, Fatima, with a hefty bag of groceries. Mickey and Jacko watch her lug the bag behind the counter. Nobody, including the impassive Hass, moves to help her.

Jacko starts to slide the paper back towards Mickey but it sticks in a splot of ketchup.

'How would I even know?' he says.

'You're the grand vizier, Jacko. You know everything about everything.'

Jacko regards Mickey's poker face and shuts his laptop. That black slab of metal looks like a hunk of landfall but it's the nexus of all the invisible shit going down in London.

'Let me get this straight,' he says. 'A man whose only source of income is passing intel to the cockroaches—'

Meaning the media.

'—wants me to give up the identity of a guy – or girl – whose motive is clearly anti-state? Why would I even?'

'First, because I'll make it worth your while, *and*—' Mickey presses on before Jacko can interrupt '—because I've no intention of exposing him. Or her. All I need is enough corroboration that a friend of mine doesn't get the boot for—'

Saying more would be a tell. Jacko grins, with teeth like a row of cracked bollards.

'This *friend* of yours wouldn't be of the young female persuasion? Is this the famous Gallant gallantry? Which is, I have to say, nominative determinism at its finest.'

'She happens to be a dyke.'

'So? I know the way your fantasy life works, Mickey. I know a-a-l-l-l about that.'

More macho action with the eyes. Once again, Mickey's the first to look away. Jacko's not bluffing. It'd be a miracle if he doesn't already know every sad detail of Mickey's private transactions.

'She's a friend and a client,' he says, 'who I don't want to end up in the shit so early in—'

He stops short again.

'Yeah,' says Jacko, 'but she's hot, though? Little Miss Kubelick.'

He chuckle-growls at Mickey's discomfort, then flips open his laptop and types for a silent while.

'OK,' he says at last, leaning back and folding his arms across an untamed bush of beard. 'So here's what I suggest.'

Mickey clears his throat expectantly and does his best to hold Jacko's stare.

'I suggest,' says Jacko, 'you get up and walk out of here. I suggest you go through the kitchen and use the back door. And I suggest you do that before the group of seven coslifers gathered outside with baseball bats comes in through that door.'

He nods at the front entrance. Mickey follows his gaze but the front windows are still opaque with condensation.

'You what?' he says, standing awkwardly in the gap between bench and table.

Jacko nods at Hass, who raises the flap on the counter without altering his blank expression. Mickey slips out of the booth and hovers, one eye on the street door.

'My little bird tells me they're making a move,' says Jacko, eyes fixed on the laptop.

As Mickey breaks for the gap in the counter, Jacko places the stub of an index finger on the email.

'But,' he says. 'But. Let's say I was to talk to this person or persons. What do I see in return?'

'I can do you ten thousand REMORSE,' says Mickey from the kitchen door.

'Ten thou?'

'I've been hoarding REMORSE.'

Jacko gives him more of the gimlet eye.

'Yeah, mate,' he says, 'I reckon you probably have.'

He turns back to the screen. Mickey slips past Hass into the dingy kitchen.

SO MANY FEELINGS ABOUT THIS

This Encounter is called *The Curious Case of the Money That Never Was*.

Alex's day so far has been an endless rigmarole of meetings with Corporation high-ups. Her interview with Susan Hardiman has stirred a nest of corporate hornets, each of which wanted to sting her in turn. It's after three p.m. when she finally leaves the building. The second she passes the turnstiles, she reinstates her mesh. The Strange is ready with an encounter, casting her as the grizzled gumshoe.

<where next Marnie?>

It asks her.

'Sam Corrigan,' she tells it. 'Political huckster. Office in Soho.'
It takes three seconds for the game to respond.

<got him>

it says.

<lemme send you the deets>

A ball of honey light forms at waist height, then weaves off down the crowded pavement, leaving a flaming thread. A game route leading Alex to her real-life target. She straightens her hat and sets out after it. Every few turns a thug in a tan mac appears on her trail. She makes sudden reverses to throw them off. One time she hops on a bus for a single stop. Later, with two goons on her heels, she dodges into Top Shop and loses herself in the scrum. A glowing woman is present for a while, hawking underwear, until Alex dismisses her with a puff of air. A kiss-off that still seems rude to Alex, though the woman's just an ad-bot.

When she exits the store, she's thrown off the goons. Her heart is pounding with the chase. Each hood she shakes earns her another hundred VIGILANCE. Only the Strange can take a short walk to the office of a political lobbyist, and make it a heroic quest. All kinds of things she thinks about her character, Marnie. Marnie is good and clear-headed and bold. She doesn't quiver and turn to jelly as soon as she gets a stern look from her boss. Marnie doesn't have a boss.

Fifteen minutes later, Alex is walking south along the terraced gully of Wardour Street. It's extra dank and seamy in her noir reality. She weaves through the low-life bustle the game has manufactured from Soho's human traffic. The golden destination marker glows around the corner on D'Arblay Street. An electric bell starts clanging on repeat.

Alex cocks her head and traces the sound to an old-style red phone box that's standing outside a sex-bot shop. There's no such thing as this phone box. She walks over and waves her hand through it, just to confirm. The tattoos on her palm create force feedback as her flesh passes through glass and metal. The mesh-head crowd is making a wide berth around this box. They can see it, too. Alex pretends to heave open the non-existent door and steps inside. The ringing is louder here. As she lifts the Bakelite handset the haptics in her palm lend it realistic heft.

'Hello?' she says into the phone.

'Weird question, Ally?' says Harmony's voice.

'Oh, hello, Pie.'

Instant guilt: Alex hasn't called Harm all day. She didn't even warn her own wife she was going on air. She certainly hasn't let on about all this compliance business at work.

'Don't take this the wrong way,' says Harm, 'but did you order a little green man?'

Her voice is cracked and distant.

'A what?' says Alex. 'Are you OK?'

'He arrived by drone. The little green man.'

There's something in Harm's voice. It's hard to tell exactly what, over this crappy line. She's using her ancient Android smartphone. She flat-out refuses to wear a mesh, which doesn't just mean appalling audio, it means Alex can't *see* her. How are you supposed to gauge your loved one's feelings when you can't even see her face?

As if reading Alex's mind, the Strange fills the absence. A burst of yellow light replaces one whole face of the phone box. In splices a life-size animated loop of Harmony. It's like a split-screen effect from an old detective flick.

The image is lifted from Alex's library of ghosts. In it, Harm's wearing a blue-stripe Breton top. She turns to give Alex an uninflected grin. Her dark fizz of hair is pulled back in a scrunchie, Jackie O shades resting on top. The image flickers, then she turns again. And again. And again. Each loop brings with it a pang for that time, two years back.

This is Alex's favourite recording of Harm. It brings out that perfect mash-up of a face. Those almond eyes, full lips and skintone like the perfect flat white. Like Harm has cherry-picked the best components of the global gene pool. Her Veronica Lake curves are such an on-trend body shape. Such a contrast to Alex's string-beam frame that shouts *anxiety hag* to every passer-by. Although of course the image does have a couple of filters applied.

'Sorry,' says Alex to the recorded Harm. 'We're talking about an *alien*?'

Harm makes that sucking sound in her teeth, like a Jamaican grandma.

'A man, dim-bulb. A little green plastic man in overalls. The delivery drone was hovering outside the door of the apartment when I got home from class.'

On Thursday mornings, Harmony teaches her FE college students, on a course called *Introduction to selfistics: the cult of the ego in digital society.*

'It was a timed delivery,' she goes on, 'for eleven this morning. Did you order him?'

Harm's schedule keeps her at the college till after lunchtime. On any other Thursday, Alex would have been home from training at eleven. So this plastic man was meant for her. This green man.

Oh, shit. Alex bites the joint of her forefinger.

'Does he have a letter written on him?' she says urgently. 'The man?'

She knows the answer. A bright green letter—

'F,' says Harm. 'He has an F on his dungarees. So wait – he *is* yours?'

The little green man is a Happy Handyman. One of the figurines they give away in branches of Handy Frank's. If Alex had got home first, as she was meant to do, she'd have received it and got the message right away. She'd have known precisely who sent it. To add to her current fun, the Handyman is stepping up his game.

'That's kind of a relief,' says Harm. 'It was freaky coming back to him. What on earth's he for?'

Alex stares out through the windows of the phone box. The Handyman has left her alone for weeks. She hoped maybe for good. Pathetic, naive. He'll never quit.

It's all surging back on her. Six months of this shit and still he isn't done.

The people jostling around the box interrogate her with their stares. Like they know.

'How does he always know exactly when to do these things?' she says out loud.

'*He*, who?' says Harm.

Alex lets go the non-existent handset and steps out through the phone-box wall. It dissolves and casts her into the real. Passers-by revert to their own selves. Mostly tweedy hipsters, plus two Star Wars Universe Stormtroopers and a claque of furries. Alex scans the unmasked faces until she remembers she's no idea what the Handyman looks like in real life.

'The complaint this morning,' she says, 'now this green man. Fuck! He's right back at it.'

'Ally? Are you OK?'

Harm's voice is still with her, though the phone box has gone.

'He'll never let this go,' says Alex.

She takes cover in the scuzzy doorway leading to the flats above the sex-bot shop. The kind of door that'll stand open later in the day, a handwritten MODEL sign on the wall. Alex lets out her breath and sinks into a squat, her back against the door. The video loop follows.

'Ally?' says Harm. 'You're not –?'

Alex's breath is coming in stupid heaves. Oh, Jesus, not the panic. Not when she needs to figure this out.

'Take your time,' says Harm. 'Focus on my voice, OK? And breathe.'

She draws out the last word. Alex takes in a breath, and chokes. The air in the doorway reeks of piss. Of men on the hunt.

'Ally? Stay with me, darling.'

All these men streaming by, treading so close with their hulking feet. Alex fumbles at the Strange's navigation and pulls up a Remembrance to blot them away. A sunlit stone wall slides in, decked with fishing nets. The urban rumble submerges under the surge of ocean breakers and the din of gulls, binge-drunk on stolen pasties. The salty zest of the sea is metallic, as though it's come from a can, but realistic enough to send Alex shooting back. She recorded this scene two years back, in the Cornish village where she and Harm spent a blissful fortnight.

And there's Harm now, waiting at the harbour steps in her Breton top, sunlight around her blindingly pure. Same image as in the video loop. Alex is breathing more easily now.

'*There* you go,' murmurs Harm. 'OK now?'

Alex fumbles out a tissue and slides it under her mesh to blot her eyes.

'I think so. Yes. Thank you, Pie.'

She balls up the tissue and takes a deep breath.

'OK,' she says. 'So I need to tell you something.'

There's a long pause before Harm says, 'Go on,' in a level voice. Alex swallows.

'So,' she says. 'There's this – man.'

'*Man.*'

'I call him the Happy Handyman. That's his avatar.'

Alex can't remember a point in her life when she hasn't been the target of some faceless goon who can only get a power-up by lancing a successful women with his spite. She used to pretend she could ignore the blows – but the Handyman was always her special case. Six months ago, he drove her mania to such a peak she had to shut down her vlog. Even then he didn't let up his campaign. His favourite meme was a wraparound video he'd modified from some porno, where a giant demonic version of the Happy Handyman repeatedly thrust his hose of a cock into a gagged, bound and pneumatically enhanced woman with Alex's face. He'd push this at her over and over, make it appear in the most private and the most public areas of her life.

Now, for the past month, since she landed a serious job with a serious profile, he's been moving his sallies to the physical world.

'He used to message me a lot online. A *lot*. But recently he's been leaving these . . . notes.'

'*Notes*? As in pieces of paper notes?'

The first was tucked into the glass on the street door of Alex and Harm's apartment building.

DEAR COLD-BLOOD DYKE WHORE

it said

I'M BAK AGAIN THE HAPPY HANDYMAN. THIS TIME IM
COMIN FOR YOUR HALF-CASTE BITCH OF A GIRLFRIEND.
SHES SOME PIECE ISN'T SHE? BET SHE COULD TAKE MA
HOT FAT HANDY COCK TWELVE INCHES INSIDE.

The next was dropped in their numbered letter box, inside the lobby; the third pushed under the door of the flat. Always making out to be from the Happy Handyman. Somehow Alex managed to get to all of these before Harm saw them.

She leans her head back against the door's thick paint.

'Just . . . messages,' she says. 'This is only the past few weeks, a month tops.'

'A month without you *telling* me? Why wouldn't you tell me?'

'Oh, I don't know, because maybe I wanted to avoid this exact conversation?'

'You know what these pigs did to you last time. We need to call the police.'

'He's just some dickless goon who needs his balls chopping off. But today he's . . .'

She waves her hands about, uselessly since Harm can't see her.

'He's what?' says Harm. 'Today what?'

Alex's head is going hammer and tongs. How to explain this?

'This isn't just about a plastic man, is it?' says Harm. 'There's something else.'

Zing. Straight to the nub as always. Alex gazes up at the artificial blue of the Cornish sky.

'Thing is,' she says, 'the Corporation received a complaint this morning.'

'Complaint? From?'

'Oh, come on. A complaint. Obviously it was anonymous.'

'I'm just asking.'

'No, sorry. But it was absolutely definitely from the Handyman.'

Harmony whistles through her teeth.

'He's trolling you at work, too?'

'It was kind of clever.'

'You're calling this clever?'

'Because when it landed I'd already had three hours of Siobhán plus yay many other management types hauling me over live coals.'

'Your boss, Siobhán? Oh shit. This was about the interview? The one with the politician? Ally, what have—?'

'It's *fine*. It's fine. It's just this, quote, *compliance* process, you know? I need to dot some i's and – whatever.'

She doesn't mention her refusal to name Mickey as her source. Nor the formal written warning Siobhán slapped on the table. Nor the ultimatum: corroborate the bribery accusation by Monday or Alex's radio career is over before it's begun. She'll broach all that later, when things are calmer.

'It's just Siobhán,' she says. 'I told you what a ball-breaker she is.'

'A what-the-Hell?'

'Jesus, a *hardass*. But look, the point is, by late morning I thought the whole thing was over. Then Siobhán marches in and slaps down this *complaint*.'

In the frozen air of that meeting room, Siobhán's face was set and blank, like some cheaply rendered character from an Encounter. All the motherly cosseting she's given Alex these past weeks? All her *darling this* and *darling* that? Completely gone.

The Strange, text-mining the conversation, has offered up an ad.

‹unfair treatment at work?›

‹no win no fee›

Alex snaps it away.

'And,' says Harm, 'it was left by this troll?'

'This Handyman.'

The complaint was just so *targeted*. How does he always know what buttons to press?

'I got the sense,' says Alex, 'that without it, things would've been sticky but OK. I could feel Siobhán *willing* me to toe the line and get through the whole kangaroo-court thing.'

'What the hell did it say?'

Alex can't help hearing this as, *What the hell have you done?* Always this assumption that Alex has fucked up, blundered into things like some amateur.

'He made allegations,' she says, 'about one of my old interviews.'

'On the vlog.'

'Yeah, on *Doorstop*. Specifically the one I did with a certain Francis Gunnell.'

'That superannuated thug?'

The second Siobhán mentioned Gunnell's name, Alex's heart kicked into an agitated bossa nova. Gunnell is CEO of high-street DIY chain Handy Frank's. No friend to Alex. Not after she nailed him last August on her vlog over bribery allegations. Back then, Handy Frank's was riding high, officially, at least. These days, its back's against the ropes. Store closures, layoffs, banks calling in debts; and it's Susan Hardiman's government department that's considering whether to bail them out.

'I don't know,' she says. 'Falsified evidence, theft of confidential documents—'

'Oh, *what* ?' says Harm.

'Don't,' says Alex. 'I'm telling you what he *wrote*. It's bullshit. But it's clever bullshit. Because of the legals. You know, the stuff I can't talk about and not be sued.'

At this stage, Siobhán said at the end of the grilling, *these are only allegations. But they warrant serious investigation. We believe in corroboration, Alex. As you seemed to forget this morning.*

'So,' says Harm, 'even Siobhán knows about this Happy Handyman, but you weren't planning on telling *me*?'

'Just *stop* it. You've *never* understood how much I need this job to work out for me.'

'And now it turns out he's been targeting us for *weeks*?'

'I honestly think it's me he's targeting.'

'He knows where we live!'

'But he's not going to *do* anything. He just wants a reaction.'

'Well, I'm reacting, right now. I'm calling a locksmith.'

'OK, OK, but don't do that. I can get a Stranger to do the locks much cheaper, for Coin.'

'Sure, because you only ever want to deal with Strangers these days.'

'What does that mean?'

'Just . . . look, just come home, Ally. You know you're not in a great place. I only want to—'

Alex beats the stub of her hand on the stone step.

'Why do you always assume I can't handle myself?'

Harm's voice is brutally calm.

'Well, my love, I was actually in the building with you six months ago?'

Alex lurches to her feet and makes to move. To do what, she doesn't know. The Cornish wall dissolves. Pedestrians stride through from reality, accompanied by the barking of the congested traffic. From within the crowd, a Stranger with a red-striped jumper glances at Alex in alarm from behind a pair of big round spectacles, worn over a mesh that dangles from his red-and-white bobble hat. A small-ish drone is hovering just above his head. It, too, seems to be looking straight at Alex: except of course it isn't. Sparkles fill her field of vision until she crouches back down. Drone and pedestrians vanish. The harbour wall re-forms, a shush of ocean beyond it.

'Do you think it's possible I'm being watched?' she says.

'Ally . . .'

'Why is that so crazy? There's always *someone* watching me. Judging.'

'This from the woman who used to check her vlog's follower count every three minutes.'

'Until the watching got to be too much. I can hide in the Strange. That's why I'm in here. It keeps me safe.'

'Ally. Darling. You think I can't hear the anxiety in your voice? All this time in Wonderland, yet still so anxious?'

'I just need to find this one guy. I was on his trail when you rang. I'm losing points right now.'

Harm sighs long and deep.

'This is the way we live now,' she says. 'We mustn't lose our *points*. Everything's permanently on the brink of some disaster. Our country's about to drop off the edge of history. We need some kind of validation. So, *points*. Whatever keeps us drinking from the corporate tap.'

'It's only gameplay.'

'It's *life*, Ally. Or it should be. You swaddle yourself. Wallow in phoney pasts. Play superheroes, or what is it this time – superspies?'

'I know you don't get it but I need it.'

'Oh, I get it,' says Harm. 'Whoever controls your anxiety controls you. That's all I'm trying to tell you. Just because they help you nullify bad feelings, doesn't make them your friend.'

Alex curls her legs under herself, sitting on a piss-soaked Soho doorstep like a wino. The Strange's Cornwall bleeds away.

'I know you want to help,' she says.

The golden thread returns, pulsing insistently, calling Alex to her mission. She nods at it.

'It's just so important you're OK,' says Harm. 'I'm not trying to be a bitch.'

'I know. And you do help. Always.'

And it's true. Pulses of TRUST and SERENITY alternate through Alex's glowheart.

There's a long pause. Alex and Harm used to be mad chatter-boxes. So much silence now.

'You were brilliant this morning,' says Harm. 'Though it was, you know, a surprise to wake up to your voice coming out of the radio.'

The golden thread flashes more urgently.

'Sorry, yes. Sorry. I should have told you. I was just—'

'We can talk about it later, OK? Right now I'm going to do my marking. And you're coming *straight home*. All right?'

'Oh no, I just – I do need to finish this task.'

'Your game?'

'No, but honestly, it's a real thing, too – to do with this compliance rap. I'm almost done with it.'

More pausing.

'OK – but just this one "task"?' says Harm at last. 'Then you come home to me?'

'Just one.'

With an analogue click, Harm's gone. Alex stands. The golden pathway weaves off through the crowd, rippling between reality and Encounter. A coslife Stranger in a Predator costume pelts down the centre of the road, dodging and vaulting invisible obstacles, pausing to fire off rounds from a non-existent pistol. He races off and is swallowed by the crowd. Prick.

As Alex follows the thread onto D'Arblay Street there's a dull toot. Incongruous, yet close at hand. It sounds again: the whistle of a steam train. Smoke billows through the Soho bustle. The whitewashed wall of a station platform asserts itself along the shopfronts, then fades. That was the station Encounter from this morning. The game should only present itself when the guy is close – the vaguely familiar guy from this morning.

The station wipes. Alex looks around but can't see the guy. Four hundred VIGILANCE land in her glowheart.

‹congrats›

‹you made it Marnie›

Her task is done. In the terrace opposite, one narrow house is painted in shining gold. Quite a contrast to the crust of pollution coating its neighbours. The gold isn't real, though. It's the Strange's destination marker. That's the building where Sam Corrigan has his office.

Corrigan's the man who sent the incriminating email Alex read on air this morning. He's this notorious Westminster hanger-on-cum-lobbyist. Alex searches the entry buzzers and finds a crisp little card with *INFLUENCE* printed on it. Corrigan's company name. She lets her finger hover over the button.

Assuming Mickey Gallant keeps on not returning her messages, Alex's best hope of getting corroboration is to get Corrigan to admit the mail is genuine. It rankles that she'd need the help of a jerk like that. What's she planning to say to him, anyway? She withdraws her finger from the buzzer. She's not ready to march into a political bear pit. Her glowheart starts to simmer puce with ANGER. How could she not be angry? She fucked up this morning, but how does that give Siobhán licence to treat her like a rookie? Why can't anybody trust her?

Today is – oh Christ, how is all of this happening now, when everything was starting to get back to an even keel? Alex wants to find a random fantastic Encounter where she can truly lose herself. Vanish from Harm, from work, but she can't. She has to fix the Hardiman thing by Monday. Four days to clean up her own mess. So: she needs to be smart with Corrigan, subtle.

I know this hasn't been your way in the past, Siobhán told her this morning. *You're used to pulling a rug from under your targets. Surprise generates drama, but rarely cogent answers.*

So you prefer, said Alex, *to give your targets time to work out how to lie?*

Siobhán winced.

You do understand, Alex, that Hardiman's after your blood?

The minister doesn't just want an apology; she wants Alex fired. Given the choice between pissing off the government and dumping a fractious new recruit, there's no doubt which way Siobhán will swing. But the thing every fucker is ignoring is: *a government minister took a bribe*. What's needed here is an actual investigation. Instead of which, everyone wants to shit on Alex.

Well, you know what, Ms Minister of State Susan Hardiman? thinks Alex. *Investigation is precisely what I do. You're not after my blood now, Susan. I'm after yours.*

Her glowheart swells with EMPOWERMENT. Alex may not be able to go after the anonymous Handyman but she can land a blow on Hardiman, and slimy lobbyist Sam Corrigan is her way in. She reaches again for the entry buzzer. Before her finger touches it, a male voice fizzes from the speaker.

'*Are you planning to come in, or just stand there glaring at my door knocker?*'

The deadlock clunks open.

FOLLOWER COUNT

Connor watches Alex Kubelick step into the dingy hall. The hair cascading from under the brim of her hat is deep red, spiced with some kind of optical sizzle. She's attractive – or would be with a bit more flesh on her. The door shuts under its own weight.

Like most Strangers, Connor's a nut for Martingale-era black and whites. So as soon as he started tailing Kubelick at four this morning, he recognised her tan skirt suit and the broad-brimmed hat as the outfit Ingrid Bergman wears to give Bogart the kiss-off in the final scene of *Casablanca*.

He touches his cheek where she slapped him in the railway station Encounter. There was some kind of electricity between them as she stepped up onto that departing train. Connor's been a Stranger long enough to know that Encounters don't come about by accident. The algaerhythm must have nosed out some compatibility between them, in the corners of their data. If he had a chance to speak to her in the real, what might she tell him? He's been watching her long enough. She has to know so many things that Connor wishes he knew, too.

If you'd asked his opinion five minutes ago, he'd've said she was on the level. That changed the second she entered that black front door. She's visiting that PR cunt. Dad's right, as the old man always is. She's mixed up in this business. So, no. Talking is not the thing he needs to do to her.

Tailing her's not an option, either, any more. Now that the railway Encounter's begun, it's going to keep looking for any opportunity to complete the story. If he strays too close to Kubelick, they'll get dragged in again. It almost happened on the corner just now, until Connor backed away. Eventually, she's bound to clock him. That won't help Dad's cause. He needs to stop sneaking after her. His next stop has to be her home address. He'll have a clear run while she's in with Corrigan.

He flips the Strange to Memory and winds back the last few minutes until Kubelick reverses out of the door. He strokes at her with a finger. Her name appears. He peels back her name and tugs out the mess of crisp little cards with all the data he's assembled on her. He riffles through and pinches out her home address, throws it into the air. It whips up and speeds off, leaving a flaming trail down Wardour Street. A driverless cab hums to a stop. With a final look up at Corrigan's office window, Connor slips inside.

SPECIAL PROMOTIONAL
CONSIDERATION PROVIDED BY

'Clearly I've got no idea why you're here. And I have precisely—' Corrigan makes a flourish of checking his chunky analogue wristwatch '—eight minutes before my next meeting. So?'

He splays his arms across the violet plush of the armchair. Alex stands with a hand unsteady on the door handle. She had to let herself in – Corrigan didn't budge from his chair. His office is the size of a walk-in wardrobe. Crammed into it is the kind of dayglo furniture that was hip three years ago, before everyone's taste shifted to the tempered palettes of post-war austerity. The fat pile of the carpet is trodden bare.

She holds out a hand to shake but Corrigan simply fixes her with crisp grey eyes. If it weren't for the odd electric sparkle, Alex would think he's meshless. That and the glowheart slouching by his elbow, fat with SATISFACTION.

Alex's mesh throws her some motivation.

‹your best you is your boldest you›

She swallows, drops her hand and perches on a puce sofa, facing Corrigan. The furniture's so close together their knees almost touch.

'Fine,' she says. 'Let's skip the chit-chat. I'm assuming you heard me with Hardiman this morning?'

Corrigan gives nothing back. This is psy-ops bullshit and damn him but it's working. The air's laced with peppermint vape and behind it, something sewery. The walls keep closing in whenever Alex isn't looking. *What's the time, Mr Wolf?*

She clears her throat.

'Of course you did,' she says. 'So you'll have noticed I didn't mention the most screwy thing about that payment to her office. That bribe.'

Still nothing. Back in the day – i.e., six months ago – Alex lived on the adrenal surge of confrontation, loving that her risks were consumed by millions of followers. Why now is her glowheart spiking with peak FEAR?

She calls up the second email – the one she didn't use on air, that confirms the payment to the minister's office. She makes a magician's pass, sharing it onto Corrigan's mesh, unpinches to zoom on the second para and twists it his way. He studies it with polite interest, as though he didn't write the words himself.

> You should see 200,000 REMORSE on your office
> heart. Do let me know if there's any problem with
> the transfer or if you have any other queries.

REMORSE. A flavour of Emoticoin, striped half pale pink for BOREDOM, half lilac for PENSIVENESS. Two hundred thousand toy tokens from the world's most immersive game. The aggregate sum of thousands of tiny feels, exchanged and rewarded in the Strange.

Corrigan nods to acknowledge he's read it. Doesn't waste his breath denying or admitting that he sent it.

'Why bribe a minister in Monopoly money?' she says. 'Pounds sterling too old-fashioned?'

The more Alex thinks about this, the less sense it makes. Emoticoin are for carshares and Encounters, not political corruption.

A slender busty girl with a black bob and translucent skin drifts in from a door at the back of the office. Corrigan keeps his eyes on Alex as the girl glides through the confined space and stands beside him. Her eyes are clogged with make-up. Again, yesterday's look. She gazes at Alex with baby-doll eyes. She's not real. Corrigan is a modder, and this a fake squeeze he's built himself in the Strange.

He strokes the small of his imaginary girlfriend's back.

'What's your balance, Alex?' he says.

His steel eyes intrude into her space. The girl shifts, realistically.

'Let's say low thousands,' says Alex.

'OK, so – a newbie. Nothing to be ashamed of. Though I guess this is why I don't see your heart?'

He grins sleekly. His own heart brims by the arm of his chair. Has he turned the heating up? Sweat is forming under Alex's mesh. The girl sits on the arm of Corrigan's chair and furls herself against him.

'I've nothing to hide,' says Alex.

'I've been Strange since before there was a Strange. You've been here five minutes.'

Most Strangers fall into one of two tribes. Mostly it's hipsters in faux-1940s gear – like Alex, if she's honest. They hang their mesh from thrift-store hats. Then there's the hard core of fully Strange who go coslife, with mesh built into the eyeholes of their character masks. Corrigan doesn't fit in either tribe. His slim and shiny suit is pure 2010s. It's like his life was frozen a decade back.

'So help me out here,' she says. 'What kind of lobbyist uses game currency to bribe a government official?'

Corrigan takes a slow sip from a glass that's frosted with condensation from the close air. He places it down with exquisite care on a lime-green occasional table. Alex wets her lips.

'Suppose,' he says, 'you had evidence this mail is real – though we both know if you did, you wouldn't be here. You claim Susan failed to register this alleged payment with the Standards committee? Well, why should she? Emoticoin aren't money.'

Oh, what's this now?

'No, but they're—'

Alex stops. What exactly are Coin? They only exist inside the Strange. Strangers trade in them. Use them in the real world, even – though mostly to pay for craft beers. But Hardiman's office used them for carpets and paint. Doesn't get much more real-world than that.

'They have value,' she tries.

A disappointed expression dances over Corrigan's face, though no emotion dwells there long. Alex's glowheart is veiled but he has to hear the unsteadiness in her voice.

'How can I best explain this to someone like you, Alex?'

He pats the girl's thigh. She stands and saunters out of the door. Corrigan leans forward, elbows on knees; manspreading.

'Why *are* you in the Strange?' he says. 'This was a recent decision?'

'It takes me places I need to go.'

She doesn't say, sometimes it knows her better than she does herself.

Corrigan nods.

'What you didn't say is, you don't pay a penny for the privilege.'

Alex shrugs.

'I get ads. But they're better ads than I get outside.'

Corrigan leans back and stretches his arms across the chair's back. He shimmers slightly in the grimy February light inching in through the sash windows.

'Let me tell you a story,' he says.

The grinding sound of D'Arblay Street drops away. Alex's mesh brings up a bed of ambient music.

'Once,' says Corrigan, 'a powerful witch lived in a tall, tall tower at the head of the valley.'

Alex cocks her head.

'Oh, really? A witch now?'

Corrigan's eyes are fixed on hers. She moves her bag from by her side to her lap. Folds her hands over it.

'One day she stumbled on a spell that let her scrape in people's private realities by reading the flicker of their pulse and the sound of their breath. She used this spell to build an artificial world where she cocooned the people of the valley. And the people paid a tithe for their captivity.'

'You're talking about Dani Farr,' says Alex. 'Calling her a witch – a tiny bit gendered?'

Dani Farr is the genius who created the Strange. She was the very first person to go fully Strange herself, observed by millions on an open feed. She's some kind of cult hero in the community, in spite of – or because of – the fact she's never seen these days, in the real or otherwise.

'People loved the story world,' says Corrigan, 'because it *knew* them. Knew who they lusted for, what thrilled and terrified them. It transported them back into their true memories, and forward into fantasies of the witch's concoction. The story world became their counsellor and truest friend. But soon the witch realised she'd created a rod for her back. The more the people gave of themselves, the harder it was to read their myriad tales, retell them in her story world.'

Alex notices her left leg is jiggling like crazy. She places a hand on it.

'We're getting to a point around now?' she says.

'The witch was wise. She realised she couldn't continue reading every story on her own. So she magicked up a legion of tiny imps to swarm across the valley, embedding themselves in people's possessions – in the clothes upon their backs. Reading their stories.'

'Look, fuck this, sorry,' says Alex. 'What are you hoping to get from telling me what I already know?'

She heard all this, in a less prissy format, back when she covered Farr on her vlog. He's talking about the algaerhythm.

It happened a couple of years back. The Strange had become a victim of its own popularity. Mondan, the company that runs it, was running out of server power to handle the firehose of data splurging in from Strangers' cameras, mics and haptic tattoos. So Farr adapted some existing viral code into a multitude of tiny autonomous software creatures she called *algae*. Now the algae live inside every connected device, signalling one another like the neurones in a titanic global brain, reading and encoding their human hosts; devising Favours and Encounters to sate people's needs. The algaerhythm is the drumbeat every Stranger's life is danced to.

'You're no Stranger are you, Alex? You're too grounded in the real to properly enter a story.'

'And you're too far up your own arse to realise there's anybody else in the room.'

He smiles.

'OK,' he says, sipping a tiny dose of water. 'Let me précis. Emoticoin took Dani by surprise.'

There's something in his eyes when he mentions Farr's name. A twist of the lips. Like Dani's the mistress he's cheating on his wife with, and he's afraid that Alex suspects.

'Coin were only ever meant as soft rewards,' he says. 'Tiny endorphin hits to repay us every time we lend our feelings to the game. To keep us playing. But over time we started using them for so much more. To reward one another when we traded favours. So Dani made these Favours an official part of the game.'

In the Strange you can exchange whatever you desire. A high five, a hug, a kiss, a touch. A compliment, an errand, a meal, a lift. A couple of hours together on the sofa, a massage, a dinner date. Sex. Not just stories any more.

'And,' says Corrigan, 'it became something wonderful. You know this, Alex, even though you don't dare let yourself embrace it.'

'You don't know a thing about me.'

'It's become a society of the known, where everything is shared and transparent. Where each gives according to their talents, rewarded for the thoughts and favours we share with one another. For the first time, wealth isn't flowing up to a coterie of tech wizards in gleaming towers. Do you know what the Strange has become?'

'I know millions of people manage to use it without bribing politicians.'

'It's become Elyse Martingale's vision for a free society of information.'

He's not showing any signs of taking the piss. There's a dreary male earnestness about everything he says.

'Not sure,' she says, 'what Red Elyse would make of some corporation getting wealthy on the back of her digital utopia. Of it being full of ads. Being part of—' she does scare quotes with her fingers '—"the Spectacle".'

Alex believes in the Strange but she also hears a lot of this sort of smoke-blowing from the mouthier Strangers.

'Bravo,' says the condescending shit-bag. 'You know your Martingale. But it doesn't matter who runs it. How it's funded. It's become an alternative place to live a human life. See, these days? We're way past the question, *how do I make this work?* We can make anything *work*. The challenge is, how do we make the thing *pleasurable*? Who cares about the things we buy because of what they do? Our greatest share of wallet goes to things that make us *feel*. Instead of simply telling stories, the witch's magic world gave the people of the valley everything their hearts desired.'

He takes another long sip of water, ice-drill eyes boring into Alex.

'Maybe,' she says, 'we can stay out of Happy Valley, and stick to politics?'

Corrigan shrugs.

'Somewhere under your layers of bullshit,' says Alex, 'you're saying that no real money exchanges hands in the Strange. Which, OK.'

She wishes she was recording this. It would make an interesting feature. Then she remembers she doesn't have a vlog any more; and she's suspended from her day job.

'Anything your heart desires,' says Corrigan with a dashing smile.

'But so this is my point. Coin *do* have real value.'

Corrigan sits forward, shaking his head.

'Now you're playing with the meaning of "value". The value of Emoticoin is based on what we *feel*. There's no monetary value in here.' He taps his forehead – meaning his mesh. 'No central bank, no gold reserves. No issuing government.'

What game is Corrigan playing? Whatever it is, Alex feels more like a piece than a participant. This triple-shot arsehole is getting high on his own private TED Talk.

'People are so attached to the notion of cash,' he says, 'they haven't noticed how the banks have snatched money out of government hands. The *banks* make the money now. Let me ask you a question, Alex.'

'I'm doing my best to ask you one.'

'How much have you paid to banks in fees – let's say in the last year?'

'I hardly see—'

'A few per cent of your income. Just to hold on to your money, advance you some when you need it. Now tell me another thing. Do you *trust* banks?'

'Why is that—?'

'I didn't think so. So what picture do we have here? An institution that insists you go through it to be an actor in the modern world, yet that you do not trust, and that takes money from you for the privilege of blowing your nose.'

'You're dodging the—'

'The Strange frees you from the tyranny of institutional trust. Trust that charges rent. Bloody liberty. Let's just trust each other and not charge each other for the privilege. Let's get rid of money.'

He gives her another ten seconds of those gimlet eyes.

'OK, look,' she says. 'I get it. I do. Maybe the Strange is this – this paradise of sharing. But the world outside isn't. Politics isn't.

A payment of Coin can influence what a person does in the real world, and sorry, but that's wrong.'

Corrigan leans back, sighing like Caligula, weary at the mundanity of his subjects.

'Everything *influences* us, Alex. I'm a scare-quotes "spin-doctor". *Influence* is my stock in trade. The right words, framed the right way, in the right tone of voice: they can persuade you to do something, with never any money changing hands. Do I need to register my *words* with Parliament, before I speak to a politician? No. So why should I have to account for, as you say, *Monopoly money*?'

This is nuts. This guy's corrupt as hell but he's talking like a freedom fighter.

'Now *you're* playing with words,' she says.

'Me? I am?'

All at once he's standing. Alex's eyes are level with the well-packed crotch of his fitted suit.

'Maybe,' he says, letting his height bear down on her, 'you should read what it says on my fucking business card?'

She stands, too. Her 1.8 metres makes up the better part of his lanky frame.

'Hey,' she says, 'ease off. You and I both know you sent that email. I don't care how much *Electronic Radical* bullshit you spin me.'

As Corrigan leans back on his heels, his image ripples.

'Screw this,' he says. 'You don't even begin to get it. You know when I called down to you before? When you were fannying around not pressing the buzzer? Did you think that was because I saw you on the entryphone? Nope.' He steps forward sharply, forcing Alex to jerk away. '*I could see you walking up the street.* Crying in that fucking doorway. Do you even know how much of what you do is being watched? Sorry, Alex, but you're entry level.'

This is what Harm is always saying: how the Strange exposes Alex to every random nutter. She draws herself up to her full height.

'Being Strange is all about being seen,' she says, in a more pompous tone than she was batting for.

'But do you actually know what *you're* seeing? For instance—'

Corrigan clicks his fingers and he's gone. Alex looks around baffled. She lifts her mesh like a curtain to see the uninflected room. It's identical to the image on her mesh. There's no Corrigan in either version. His glass has vanished from the table.

He was never here.

SEEMS LEGIT

Minutes of Occidental Data Partnerships
Senior Executive Group meeting #327

Attending: Mr Ox: CEO
  Ms Okapi: Chief Financial Officer
  Mr Lemur: Executive Director of Operations
  Mr Antelope: Executive Director of Technology
  Ms Mongoose: Executive Director of Corporate Services
  Item 3 only: Mr Honey Badger: UK Implementation Lead

Location: None

Minutes taken by Ms Pangolin

Agenda item 1: CEO update

Mr Ox gave update on January accounts. He commented that
  additional performance management measures utilised on
  regional managers have proved highly effective in driving up
  receipts. He regretted the unexpected and swift departure of
  Mr Pine Martin but it was agreed that the consequent positive impact on cross-divisional performance was to be
  welcomed.

Mr Ox went on to provide overview of his Vision Statement. He
  drew meeting's attention to further increases to levels of
  outsourcing, in order that ODP can ruthlessly focus on its

core competencies of Market Insight, Aggressive Pricing and Enforcement. **Mr Ox** ended by recommending all Executive Directors read book, *The Nimble Corporation: Managing for Market Uncertainty* by Prof. Rogers F Peattie, from which he drew extensively in drafting the Vision Statement. The Nimble Corporation, he explained, comes together in hive style, aggregating optimal skill sets to solve problems, then rapidly moving to the next challenge. The Old Corporation is hampered by labour laws and local regulations. Truly nimble organisations, like ODP, can route around such problems.

Action: All Executive Directors to return comments on Vision Statement.

Agenda item 2: Investment portfolio

Ms Okapi provided update on adoption of Emoticoin ('Coin') as key liquid asset class for payments and inter-territorial transfers. She reminded meeting of Key Benefits provided by Coin: lack of traceability; robust year-on-year exchange rate growth against Dollar, Euro, Karuna and Hryvnia; arbitrage potential through use of 32 separately priced emotional denominations. **Ms Okapi** requested approval to transfer remaining Bitcoin, Dogecoin and Litecoin holdings (USD value $353,947,033) into initial balanced portfolio of DISTRACTION, SUBMISSION, LOATHING and ECSTASY.

Decision: Transfers approved.

Action: Ms Okapi to report to next meeting confirming transfers and outlining active trading strategy for Coin.

Agenda item 3: Performance of UK contracts

Mr Ox requested update from **Mr Honey Badger** on implementation contracts in the UK. He explained that ongoing Project Domino contract in that territory will require significant implementation and execution resource, often with very limited lead times. **Mr Honey Badger** expressed full confidence in delivery against plan. He went on to question **Mr Ox's** decision to agree to providing services below usual rates as the opportunity cost on Project Domino is extremely high. He pointed out that no compensation had been provided him in consideration of Kaa software and that as a consequence he would continue to seek other commercial partnerships in this regard.

Mr Ox expressed dissatisfaction with this report and instructed a representative in the UK office to carry out disciplinary procedures on **Mr Honey Badger**. While procedures were under way, he emphasised to **Mr Honey Badger** that the specific benefits of Project Domino were known only to himself. Further to this, information was conveyed to **Mr Honey Badger** concerning the whereabouts of certain family members.

Action: Mr Honey Badger to review readiness of UK implementation network and report to Friday management team meeting.

Any other business

There being no other business the meeting adjourned.

GR-R-REAT!

After thirty seconds searching the tiny office, Alex confirms that Corrigan isn't hiding under the sofa or in the tiny toilet. Well, he did say he had an appointment. Guess he was already at it. Alex was talking to his ghost.

Her first thought is, effing liberty; then it occurs to her she's alone in his office. Was always alone there, it seems. It would be a poor investigative journalist who didn't seize the situation. She scans the outmoded furnishings crammed in the narrow room but there's nothing resembling a computer — let alone physical files to poke about in. The desk is a minimalist slab of orange enamel — no drawers or compartments. The only kind of paper is a set of four children's picture books sitting catty-corner on a shelf. Alex flicks through one but can't see anything special about the poorly rendered illustrations of pigs that fill it.

She shuts the book with a puff of dust. The office has an air of neglect. Which makes her think: maybe it's not just that Corrigan isn't here *now*. Maybe he's *never* here. This is a guy with a lot of haters. A lot of people calling with accusations. Maybe it's convenient to have a business address he can advertise, where he can remotely buzz visitors in from the street and meet them while being somewhere else.

The door at the back of the room drifts open. The black-haired ghost-girl wonders in. She folds her arms and looks around the room disgustedly. Her ink-dot eyes land on Alex. This is to let her know she's being watched. OK, fine. She sits in Corrigan's ergonomic swivel chair and lets her weight carry it around a full 360, rotating herself into his mind-set. The girl watches from under heavy lids.

Even if Corrigan wasn't here, they did at least have a conversation. Albeit a weird one. Why did he tell her that story-version of the Strange's genesis? On the surface, he was defending his bribe, without admitting he'd made it. Telling her it's fine to bribe a politician, provided you do it inside a game. Yet there was something more. Why go off on that rant about the new economy of feels? Dani Farr may be a corporate sell-out but from everything Alex knows of her she'd hate to see Emoticoin used for petty corruption.

But all that is only what Corrigan wanted Alex to hear. It has to have been a diversion. She was right before: she should never have come here half-cocked, without an ounce of leverage. She still needs something a lot more solid than an uncorroborated email.

So: she's back to *corroboration*. It's still possible Mickey will come up with the goods on his source but the longer he stays silent, the more Alex doubts. Her best shot is still to prove that Corrigan actually paid the bribe. But how?

She bangs her head against the contoured headrest, which gently nudges her back. Her job's on the line and she's still nowhere. If this was a briefcase-full-of-cash situation, that'd be something, but how do you prove someone used a game to corrupt a politician? She's so ignorant about the workings of the Strange, though she uses it every day.

Although. Maybe Corrigan's fable was illuminating, after all. He said there's a new kind of money moving around the Strange. And it's true: Alex saw this herself last year, when she interviewed Edina Mathers.

A year back, Alex did a story on her vlog about how the Strange was cutting a swathe through low-paid service jobs. A growing mass of Strangers was offering labour in exchange for the glister of Emoticoin. Alex wanted to show how this was screwing with people's livelihoods and she'd tracked down the perfect interviewee. A trained chef, Edina Mathers had the kind of sob-story that would stir up the feels among Alex's followers. Wembley Park, where Edina lived, had recently gone fully Strange. Since then she'd been unable to find restaurant work. Everyone was eating food prepared by other Strangers, trading it for Coin. The restaurants were boarded up, their kitchens stripped for scrap metal. Over the course of three months, Edina had lost 100 per cent of her income and was receiving only Emoticoin. Alex had nosed out the first big scandal of the sharing age.

Except the story fell flat. It turned out Edina didn't care. She hadn't lost income, she said, she'd gained freedom. She could cook when she wanted and for whom she chose, The community of Strange gave her things money never could have bought.

Alex puts her feet up on the desk and crosses her ankles. The chair creaks grudgingly as it reclines. Think about Edina. If you can buy a meal with Coin, why not a politician? If an honest worker like Edina can make a living from it, why not a corrupt one? Alex has always seen the Strange as a place of escape, a community where people share and barter in good faith. To Corrigan, it's all about money. What he was describing is an alternative economy. As an economics graduate, Alex should have picked up on this. She recalls a catchphrase of her old professor, Lukaš Caron: *Money is power, yes – this is obvious. But then you must ask: what is money?* Why should there have to be a pound or dollar or renminbi sign in front of every number?

She pulls her legs to her chest and spins round twice; then grabs the desk to brake herself. What would Lukaš say, if he turned his impassive eyes on this problem?

She knows exactly: *In this scenario, who stands to gain?*

Which is of course the point. She needs to prove a bribe was paid inside the Strange. She's been obsessing about carpets and Emoticoin, but all of that is incidental. What matters is *why* the bribe was paid in the first place. So: who stands to gain from bribing Susan Hardiman?

A flicker of movement, just to Alex's left. She goes into a defensive crouch but it's only the familiar avatar of Harmony, smiling at Alex, announcing a call. There's an analogue click, then Harmony's voice kicks in.

'This is a pre-emptive strike apology,' she says.

Alex's smile is for herself. Harm can't see her.

'I get it,' she says teasingly, 'you reckon that gives you moral high ground?'

'Wife-points at least.'

'Like two hundred thousand REMORSE?' says Alex before she has a chance to censor herself.

'I don't understand that so I'm going to ignore it.'

'Probably wise,' says Alex.

She takes a last look around the room. The dark-haired girl is glaring daggers still. Alex sticks her tongue out at her and makes for the door. She's no idea where she's going but she needs to get out of the pomade-scented air of Corrigan's tiny office.

'Did you finish your marking?' she says as she pulls the door shut behind her.

'I was too distracted,' says Harm. 'I wasn't kind to you just now. Are you coming home?'

Alex descends the narrow stairwell. There's a rank smell, like spunk or rotting flesh. Place must be alive with roaches. She needs to find Hardiman, get to her right away. Confront her in the street, perhaps, on her way to her ministerial car.

And ask her what?

'I'm not sure,' she says. 'There's stuff I need to find out.'

'So he helped you?' says Harm. 'Your lead?'

'Ha. So not. Though in a way, yes.'

Alex finds the door release. It clunks open, letting in the Soho wild track.

'Well that's good and clear,' says Harm. 'You know, I thought for tonight I might make you a – *what are you doing*?'

'Huh? Well, I'm—'

'*Get off me!*'

There's a thud, then the squawk of Harmony's phone hitting something hard.

'Pie! What's—?'

The voice comes back muffled and distant.

'What the hell are you—? Stop!'

The line goes dead. Alex runs into the street, searching for an empty driverless – but it's chock a block with honking gridlock.

'Bike!' she shouts into her mesh.

‹your nearest Beth Bike is ten seconds away›

A strobing blot appears on the corner of St Anne's Court. Alex jogs to it. In the dusk of the street, the blue dot resolves to a bike, quivering at the kerb. Media types love these driverless hire bikes, so Soho's full of them.

'Home!' says Alex as she shifts onto the saddle.

The bike lurches into motion, taking a narrow channel between the line of unmoving traffic and the cars parked up along the kerb.

There's someone in the flat. Harm spoke to someone, there was a scuffle, and then—

A sickening taste of guilt rises in Alex's throat. The Handyman. Harm said they should call the police but pig-headed Alex had to play it down. Now he's *in the flat*.

The bike escapes the traffic jam and trundles up to speed on an empty stretch of Wardour Street, heading for Oxford Street.

'999 Police!' says Alex into her mesh.

‹thank you Alex›

‹police emergency treble-nine›

‹how may I assist you›

Before she can speak a great beast rears out from behind a parked white van.

'Jesus!' she says, throwing up a hand.

The creature is striped in orange and black. It's seven foot tall. The bike does its best to swerve around it, but it can only tilt so far before gravity takes hold. Alex lands hard on tarmac. The saddle smashes her pelvis as the bike skids and flips over her.

'*Gah*!' she shouts as the bike clatters to the kerb.

She extracts her leg, shouting at the pain that shoots down her left side. The costumed figure lumbers at her. It's a Tony the Tiger. She scrambles up but he's on her before she can find her feet.

'Not so fast, Katya!' screams the Tony.

His great striped club of a foot swings at Alex. She twists away but it catches her in the ribs. Its soft weight shoves her back on her arse with a painful jolt. The fallen bike is making circles on the pavement, spinning its gyro back to vertical. The Tony swings another massive foot. Alex grabs it and shoves. The Tony tumbles back and lands on its bulky backside. Which probably didn't hurt at all, through the plushy mass of costume.

The bike has righted itself. It rolls up to hover by where Alex is lying. She puts a hand on its swaying saddle to pull herself up, ignoring the shout of pain from the base of her spine. A circle of pedestrians has formed to watch the performance – some meshed, some not. Alex wonders what version of this comedy the Strangers are seeing.

'Those were good men you killed!' cries the muffled voice of the Tony as it struggles to its feet.

Alex hops onto the saddle. The bike jolts her as it lurches off the pavement, motor whining. As it gets up to speed, the Tony lunges at Alex with both arms. She ducks over the handlebars. As the bike speeds off she turns to watch the tiger trotting after, waving a bundled orange fist.

'You'll never escape!' he cries. 'We are legion!'

The bike banks sharply left onto Oxford Street and she loses sight of the tiger. She gives her head a rapid shake. Did that just happen?

At the bottom right of her field of vision she catches a flash of blue light. The police bot is waiting. Never mind the tiger. Harmony. She needs to get to Harm.

AN EXPLOIT

Thimblerig keeps low behind the scraggy bushes fringing the car park. He watches the drones begin their tour of the building's sides. When they finish this run it's time to move.

The drones have been on the same routine for hours. First all four make a zig-zag sweep down the glass front of the Gordion Offsite Storage building – two at ground level and two along the upper storey. Then the pairs loop off down the sides of the building to take in every door and window. They meet at the rear and park in a charging station on the roof. Five minutes later the whole routine kicks off again. This is how it runs 24/7.

Thimblerig glances behind him at the service road. It's only just gone six p.m. but this out-of-town business park is quieter than the zombie apocalypse. He's spent all day in concrete hinterlands. Barely seeing anyone since he shed the last of the Spider-Men. The only person here right now is Gordion's night-shift security man. Who has already settled in for the night. His peaked cap's upturned on the desk as he unpacks a Thermos and a parade of foil-wrapped snacks. Given all the drones there's no reason to have human security. It must make Gordion's clients feel better.

The nearest drone swoops past the fire door at the side of the building – Thimblerig's entry point. Three minutes five seconds.

Lucky Ghost found out from wherever she finds things out that Doug Raynor has stowed his case of hard drives in a secure cage here at Gordion. The cage is in a fireproof chamber accessible only by thumbprint and a keypad code that changes daily. So basically impregnable. Especially with only a few hours to prepare. But that's where the Kaa hack is and Thimblerig needs to get to Kaa.

At some point when he has time he'll delve into Raynor's ancient emails and prove his connection to the fate of Thimblerig's father. Until then he needs to keep his cat close beside him. For now it holds the only copy of the mails.

He checks his keys and pass card. All present. Enough double-checking. He hooks on the earpiece he liberated from Handy Frank's. As he does so he has a flash-frame image – his father hooking on a similar Bluetooth earpiece as he patrols a bombed-out street. Clad all in black. This isn't a true memory – it's an image from a YouTube video Thimblerig discovered several years after he came to England.

He pulls on his pig mask – which smells even ranker than before – and peeks over the hedge to watch the drones complete their rounds. Twenty seconds. Hot spirit bubbles through him. Something of his father's still inside him. The drones swoop up to their resting place on the roof.

'*Go!*' whispers Thimblerig.

'*Check,*' comes back Eponymous's whisper from the earpiece.

'*You don't need to whisper, too.*'

'*Oh, yeah, sorry,*' whispers Eponymous.

Thimblerig stands and vaults the tatty hedge. A branch cracks and he belly flops onto it. Brambles scrape his face.

'*Ow,*' he whispers.

'*What mate what what?*' says Eponymous. '*What?*'

'*Nothing. Radio silence.*'

'*You started it with your "ow" shit.*'

Thimblerig rolls off the hedge.

'*Ow. Never mind.*'

He scrabbles to his feet and starts a rolling jog across the tarmac to the fire-exit door. His breath is hot and wet inside the mask. His left ankle screams each time it lands but he keeps up the loping pace – wincing at every second footfall.

'*Three minutes fifty-five,*' whispers Eponymous.

'*Shut up.*'

Thimblerig makes it to the door without dying of asphyxiation. He falls to his knees panting and fumbles for the key ring. He printed these keys an hour ago. The day guard finished his shift at five thirty. Thimbelrig followed him to a café on the ring road and watched him order up a glistening plateload of pork by-products. When the guard went to have a loud pee at the back Thimblerig photographed every key on his key ring and cloned his pass card. Then he went to a Kinkos up the road and used the photos to 3D print a set of keys.

Kneeling at the door he tries each key in turn. His hand shakes but he does his best to be methodical. Eponymous's breathing on the earpiece is like holding a seashell to his ear. He tries the fourth key. It sticks. He's on the point of pulling it out when some cue from his fingers tells him to try again. This time the key turns. Holding it in place with his left hand he takes out the cloned swipe card with his right and runs it through the slot. Nothing happens. Maybe fifteen seconds left. He swipes again more slowly. Nothing. His fingers ache from holding the key against the spring of the lock.

He mutters something like a prayer – Arabic borrowed from his mother. The swipe flashes green. He's through the door and into the building.

'*In,*' he whispers with his back glued to the inside of the door. '*Over to you.*'

'*Check,*' says Eponymous and disconnects.

Thimblerig's standing in a well-lit anonymous corridor running along the outer wall of the building. It takes a sharp right when it hits the wall of the secure storage area at the rear. Raynor's disks and the Kaa hack are in a locked cage on the far side of that wall. Between Thimblerig and those disks are a dozen security measures. Plus at least as many human beings. Humans are easier to fool than tech but it's still a tall order to get past so many. Just as well Thimblerig doesn't need to do that.

While he waits for Eponymous to make the first call he works his way along the wall checking doors. This spur of the corridor contains only toilets and a cleaning cupboard. He heads for the corner and peers around. There's a security camera fixed to the ceiling above his head. It's pointed along a stretch of corridor where two more doors face each other from opposite walls. Then the corridor bends away towards the front reception and the guard. The door to Thimblerig's left leads into the secure storage area. That door is solid metal with no handle. Arranged beside it are any number of swipes and fingerprint pads. Those look hard enough to get through but this is only an outer door. Beyond it there'll be a holding area then an even more secure door that can only be opened while the first is closed.

Thimblerig isn't planning to get through any of those doors. What interests him is the humble office door opposite. That has just a single card swipe. Above the swipe is a little sign. By leaning forward and squinting he makes out the words *CLIENT MEETING ROOM*. That's where he's headed but he can't make a move with the night guard out front watching the CCTV. He needs to wait for Eponymous.

Right on cue the earpiece gives out a low intermittent tone.

— Yessir, says the slurred voice of the guard, picking up.

He sounds half asleep though he's only an hour into his shift.

— Oh hello, yes, says an accented voice that Thimblerig would never recognise as Eponymous. Please, is this the front desk at Gordion Offsites – um – Storings?

Thimblerig's hearing this call over a femtocell – a brick-sized cellphone repeater he assembled this morning from components lifted from the Handy Frank's storeroom. When he got to the Gordian storage building he gaffer-taped the femtocell to the trunk of a tree on the forecourt. Since then he's been using his earpiece to monitor it. Femtocells are super handy in areas like this where cell coverage is poor. Any mobile telephone hunting for a tower will find the femtocell first. At which point the call will go through Thimblerig on its way to the mobile network.

— That's right, says the night guard. Gordion Storage. Who can I connect you with?

— Oh good, good. Listen, my friend, I'm calling from the Kitchen and Bathroom Depot opposite your building.

— Oh, is this Emmanuel?

— Ah, no, Mr Emmanuel is unwell. I am – Samuel.

That's apparently the best Eponymous can do but it seems to go down OK. Even though his accent's veering all over North Africa and into the Middle East.

— Listen my friend, he goes on. I have seen three bad lads this evening hanging about at the front entrance to your car park. Up to no good. One I have seen with a can of spray paint. I am thinking you will wish to investigate this.

— Ah, thanks, mate. Are they there now?

— Let me check for you sir.

There's a dull *bip*. Not from the call but from the corridor where Thimblerig is standing. The card reader beside the secure metal door is flashing orange. Someone's about to emerge from the storage area. Eponymous returns to the call.

— I cannot see them from here but I think you will want to be checking this as soon as possible.

— You're a pal, said the guard. I'll do that.

There's a clunk from the other side of the door. The inner security door has shut. After perhaps five seconds the outer door will open onto the corridor. If the person coming out of the secure zone heads for reception, they won't see Thimblerig. If they're heading for the toilets, they will. Not a chance worth taking. Thimblerig has to get into the client room before the door opens.

Inside the rubber mask his breath is stifling. Come *on*, Eponymous. That guard needs not to be at the CCTV screens *right now*.

— It is the least I can do, says Eponymous, for a fellow guardian of security.

— All right, mate, catch you later.

— Goodbye my friend.

The call ends. The outer security door beeps and clunks. Thimblerig moves into range of the camera. No time to wait and be sure. He has to hope the guard's already left his desk to check on the fictional kids.

The security door swings open as he reaches the door to the client room. He swipes his card. The sensor tips to green. He slips inside.

Blood pounds in his sweaty ears. No alarm. Nobody asking why a pig-faced man just walked into the client meeting room. He flips on the light.

This internal room has no windows and is sparsely kitted out. Everything looks as though it comes from a Handy Frank's Home Warehouse. At the centre of the room is a veneer table with a small plastic stand at its centre – a static-free surface where Gordion places sensitive electronics for client inspection. Around the table are four upright chairs. A standard lamp stands unplugged in the corner. Opposite the door is a low cabinet on which is a microwave. A kettle. Jars with teabags and instant coffee. The only sign the room is ever used is the sugar spilled around the stack of styrofoam cups. On the wall are faded prints of pre-electronic safes and locks.

That's all. No other doors. No obvious place to hide – but the hack depends on a hiding space.

Thimblerig heads for the cabinet and slides open the door to the right-hand section. The beeping of his headset alerts him to the start of Eponymous's second and most important call. The duty manager answers after two rings.

— This is Andy Battesby, says a new voice, at Gordion Offsite Storage. How may I help you?

Thimblerig bends down to look inside the low wooden cabinet. It's empty except for a few stray pens and elastic bands.

— Good to speak to you, Andy, says Eponymous. This is Martin Kazan of Occidental Data Partnerships LLP.

This new voice is functional. A little posh.

— Yes, hello, Martin, says the manager, may I take your pass-code please?

Thimblerig wiggles the cabinet's middle shelf. It's loose. He edges it out and tucks it behind the cabinet. Eponymous rattles off the ID code they intercepted earlier. Thimblerig slides the cupboard doors across and removes the shelf from the left-hand side. Stows that away. There still isn't room to crawl into either side. He needs to remove the central divider but it's fixed more solidly into place.

— Thank you, Martin, says the duty manager after a pause. How can I help you?

The code checked out.

— Seriously, I hope you can. You know my boss, Doug Raynor?

— Sure.

Thimblerig wiggles off his backpack. He reaches under the hibernating cat for the wrap of tools he acquired from Handy Frank's. The cat doesn't mind. Being a robot.

— Well then, you'll know what a ballbreaker he is.

The duty manager laughs but doesn't say anything. He's too clever to be disrespectful to a client. Thimblerig extracts a flat-head screwdriver and lies on the ground to duck his shoulders inside the cabinet. He flips off the rubber snap-caps at all four corners of the central divider.

—Yeah, well, says Eponymous, I'm the lucky guy who needs to arrange for Doug to access a case of hard drives he left with you this morning at – let's see, oh-three forty-six.

— Sure, I know the one. Doug can come in any time and we'll extract that case from your cage.

Thimblerig checks the screw heads and swaps his flathead for a 4mm hex.

— That's exactly what I told Doug but he isn't in the mood for waiting. To be honest it was – you know like in *Stop the Pigeon*? When the colonel shouts down the phone?

— Dick Dastardly? Hah. Yeah.

Good, good. Andy made three cartoon character references during earlier conversations. Eponymous is using that.

— Totally blew out my eardrum.

Thimblerig is starting on the first screw when there's a thud from the corridor. He freezes.

— You all right, mate? says Eponymous on the line.

The thud came from Thimblerig's earpiece and simultaneously from the hallway. The duty manager is just outside the door. Thimblerig removes the second screw and starts on the third.

— Yeah, sorry, I'm trundling a bloody great filing cabinet to the client room. An *empty* filing cabinet. Boss says it needs to look more professional in there. If you can believe it.

— Oh, into the *CLIENT ROOM*? says Eponymous in too loud a voice.

Yes, yes. Thimblerig got that the first time. He starts on the final screw.

— Totally pointless, says the duty manager. Just one second while I get my swipe card.

He's right outside the door.

— Err – sure! says Eponymous.

The final screw is out. Thimblerig pushes on the interior divider. It doesn't budge. He wiggles out of the cabinet, turns around and braces his feet against it. There's a beep from outside the door. He pushes his feet against the divider. The door to the room swings open. The divider starts to move.

From where Thimblerig is lying with his feet inside the cupboard he has a good view under the table to the duty manager's feet. Luckily the man's view of Thimblerig is blocked by the table. He presses a foot against the base of a filing cabinet just outside the door and tips it onto a two-wheel trolley. A drawer of the cabinet rattles open. Andy curses and pushes it back into place. Under cover of this sound Thimblerig gives the divider a final shove. It slides halfway down the opposite side of the cabinet. That'll have to do. Thimblerig crawls into the tight space and folds his legs against his chest. He pulls his backpack in and slides the door shut. Then he breathes.

Through the cabinet door come the sounds of the duty manager manoeuvring the filing cabinet into the room. It lands with a thud then rattles a couple of times as Andy manoeuvres it into place.

— Phew. Done. Sorry about that, mate.

His voice comes in stereo from the earpiece and through the cupboard door.

— No worries. Looks like we both have the shit end this evening.

— So don't tell me. When Doug arrives he's going to expect his case to magically appear out of the cage in seconds flat?

— That's pretty much it. I think if he has to wait for you to go through the process he might actually combust. So I was wondering—

— Can I go through the extraction process now and have the case ready and waiting when he gets here?

— I know he'll need to ID himself and everything but at least he won't have to wait. I'll tell you, Andy, you'll be saving my job. My life when it comes to it. And believe you me. It'll mean a lot less grief for you, too.

This is good social-engineering practice. Appeal to the target's altruistic desire to help a fellow wage slave – rather than try to browbeat them.

— How long do we reckon before he gets here? says the manager.

— Twenty-five minutes, tops. He's driving over now.

There's a pause while the manager weighs his options. Eponymous knows better than to push. He stays silent and lets the meat-hack work.

— You're actually in luck, says the manager at last. Now I've finished being a removal man I have a few minutes spare. I'll call up that case and stow it here in the client room. The desk will alert me when Doug arrives.

Nobody tries to hack a physical security system from scratch. They certainly don't do this with a four-hour turnaround. But Thimblerig doesn't need to do anything of the kind. Most systems are smart but people are stupid and unreliable. Social engineering is more effective than any software hack.

— Thanks, mate, says Eponymous as the manager leaves the room.

— Nah, you're good, says the manager as the door clicks shut.

In the dark of the cabinet Thimblerig lets out a breath into the confines of his mask. Now all he has to do is wait.

There's a low beep in his earpiece – probably Eponymous returning to the line. But the voice that says *Hello* is not Eponymous. It's the same duty manager – the man named Andy. This is a new intercepted mobile call. A call that's not in the plan.

A second voice comes on the line.

— Who am I speaking to please?

A new voice. Male. American. Familiar.

— This is Andy Battesby at Gordion Offsite Storage. How may I help you?

— Hi Andy, says the other voice. My name is Doug Raynor and I'm calling from Occidental Data Partnerships. I need to access some of our material. I apologise for not having made a booking through your site but I'm heading to you right now.

— Oh yes, sure, Doug. I was just speaking to your colleague Martin about that. I'm about to call up the case you wanted.

— My colleague who? says Raynor.

In the dark of the cupboard Thimblerig lets out a whimper.

SHIT GOT REAL

The street door is swinging open onto the dark forecourt, security glass staved in. FEAR flares puce on Alex's glowheart. She flicks away a mindfulness exercise. As she steps inside, her patent leather shoes crunch a snowfall of broken glass.

It took twenty-five minutes to get here by bike, the whole way repeat-dialling Harmony's phone and landing on voicemail, trying to persuade herself it was fine. A dropped phone. Harmony flaking out in some adorable fashion. Now she's here the smashed glass tells her otherwise. The lock engages as she shuts the door. Someone smashed the glass and reached through to flip the catch, then – what?

She jogs up the stairs. The Handyman. It has to be the Handyman. She bursts out onto the fourth-floor landing, black dots spattering her vision.

⟨deep breaths Alex⟩

⟨from the diaphragm⟩

The door to the flat is down the end of the corridor, closed and normal. Everything normal. She walks a gauntlet of tailored ads. The Strange charges advertisers more for spots outside the user's home.

⟨Yeo Valley salted butter 2 for 1⟩

Yes, thinks Alex: they do need butter.

When she gets to the door, she knocks. Why? She has keys, there's a bell. Why knock? Her head riots with violent scenarios. Blood on the walls, the door in splinters. But the door is fine. There's no blood. Pressure-balls pop inside her forehead. The door opens.

Harmony.

Alex falls tearfully onto her. Harm is fine. She's fine.

'Ow! Shit!' says Harm.

Alex pulls back.

'What did I do? Did I hurt you?'

'Oh, *you're* crying?' says Harm.

Alex realises, yes: she's crying.

'Great,' says Harm. 'When I'm the one with size twelve boot marks down my side.'

'Oh, Christ, darling is it true? I tried so hard to get here – but I didn't know—'

She's losing her breath. Her glowheart peaks. Red waves crash against her eyes. Harmony examines her, then puts up her hands, palms facing Alex.

'No,' she says. 'Sorry, I can't have this right now.'

She turns away. Alex pulls her back, trying to take her, comfort her, ask her, but her words are a babble of mocking crows. Harmony pulls away, wincing from a pain in her left side. Alex forgot that she's hurt.

'ImsorryImsorry,' she says.

'*Shh*!' Harm hisses, pointing to the sitting room. '*We. Have. Company.*'

Two women get up awkwardly from their seats as Harm leads Alex into the sitting room: a uniformed policewoman, younger than Alex, a smart eyepiece over her left eye and her wavy black hair scraped back into a ponytail; plus an older woman whose walnut skin is darkened by the cheap mesh hanging from her vintage pillbox hat. Three half-drunk mugs of tea on the table.

There's that cluttered silence you get when strangers meet at a wake, then Harm does the introductions.

'Sarah here,' she says, putting a hand on the policewoman's sleeve, 'broke in to help me but the guy was already gone.'

'The glass—' Alex manages through thick breaths. 'The front door—'

The policewoman nods.

'Yes, sorry for that. We're waiting for someone to come and board it up.'

'And Artemis here,' says Harm, pointing out the older lady, 'heard me cry out and called the police. She's in flat 46, below. Luckily Sarah was on the estate already, and took the call.'

Alex shakes her head. She can't get the timeline straight.

'No,' she says, '*I* called the police.'

Harmony glares at this, but the old woman smiles benignly.

'I hear Harmony scream and I call for police,' she says, laying fingers on the fringe of her mesh. 'Then I shout up the stairs. I do not hear Sarah knock. I don't want to leave my apartment. Which is why she must break the glass.'

'Either Mrs Metaxas's shouts,' says the policewoman, 'or myself banging on the front door, seem to have panicked Ms Adcock's assailant. He took off down the fire escape. Before Ms Adcock could identify him, unfortunately.'

There's a silence. Alex reaches out to take Harm's hand but she quickly folds her arms.

'He was in our flat,' she says, not looking at Alex. 'This huge guy. I thought for a second he was the locksmith, then I was on the ground and he was *kicking* me. And do you want to know what I saw while I was down there with his boot in my ribs?'

Now she does look at Alex, and there's something hurtful in her eyes. Alex takes her upper arm but she wriggles it away and taps the back of her fingers against Alex's mesh.

'More of *this* shit! All blacked out over his face while he kicked and kicked.'

'Oh. Listen, Pie—'

Harm's attacker was a Stranger. That won't help Alex's cause.

'It's *him*,' says Harm, 'isn't it?'

Alex takes a step back.

'I'm still trying to piece this together myself,' she says, 'I'm just so glad you're OK.'

Harm snorts and rears her head back.

'I'm *OK*, am I?' She fumbles at the side of her blue silk shirt. 'Would you like to see the rissole he turned my side into?'

'Rissole?' says Alex, laughing in spite of it all.

'As I was saying,' says the policewoman, 'I do think I should accompany Ms Adcock to A&E at the Royal Free.'

'How can you laugh?' says Harm. 'He's one of your lot, Ally. Got up like Spencer Tracey, with those creepy tattoos on his neck.'

That's when it finally clicks.

'Tattoos?' says Alex. 'What kind?'

'You *know* what kind. Stranger tattoos.'

'No, no – I mean, what pattern?'

'How does that matter? He was *kicking* me!'

'The pattern.'

'God! Spider's web.'

So now Alex knows who attacked Harm. Knows why someone wanted to bribe Hardiman. Knows who it was she slapped this morning, on that station platform. Knows the whole deal.

The Strange rewards this moment with a dose of VIGILANCE. She didn't even realise she was still playing the detective Encounter.

'It's not the Handyman,' she says.

'This is a dangerous stalker, Ally. He's a threat to me as well as you.'

'This was not! The Handyman! Can you *LISTEN*?'

Harmony steps back, raising her palms.

'Jesus. Have you actually taken your meds?'

No, Alex hasn't. Not since she first entered the Strange. She hasn't needed to.

'None of this would have happened,' says Harm, 'if you hadn't put on that obnoxious *thing*.'

'By which you mean the mesh?'

'Whatever you want to call it. It's taking you into bad places. Feeding on your anxiety.'

'It's feeding *me*.'

'It's *controlling* you.'

'This, this awful thing happens,' says Alex. 'Why do you have to turn it into—'

'*Yes,* this *awful thing*!' shouts Harm. 'This thing that happened to *ME*! Do you even get that?'

The policewoman manoeuvres herself between them.

'I suggest everybody counts to ten,' she says in the voice of someone who's witnessed a million domestics.

'Tell her, Ally!' says Harm from over the policewoman's shoulder. 'Tell Sarah about that sicko.'

'It's. Not. The Handyman,' says Alex. 'I'm trying to tell you.' She lowers her voice to speak to the policewoman. 'It's tied up with this payment, you see, well, no, it was a bribe really, that's the whole point, but it was paid in Coin, Emoticoin I mean, and I know who paid it. Who bribed the minister.'

The policewoman steps towards Alex with a hand raised. The look on her face tells Alex she's babbling. She stares down at her glowheart until she's synched her breathing with its steady beats. Then she turns to the policewoman and tries again.

'The man who did this—'

'Listen,' says the policewoman. 'Ms Kubelick. Your partner—'

'Wife.'

'—has been the victim of a serious attack that would have turned nastier if Mrs Metaxas hadn't intervened.'

'I called the police. Me. I know who did this. These are powerful men. Francis Gunnell – and, and – Connor! That's his name. That's the man who attacked you, Harm. They run a business called Handy Frank's. But they're into some—'

The policewoman laughs openly – a single *Ha*! that bursts from her. She clamps her hand over her mouth, aware she's broken etiquette.

'I apologise, but – excuse me? *Handy Frank* attacked Ms Adcock?'

'No, fuck it, his son! Why won't you listen?'

'And you have evidence for this accusation? Given that you weren't actually here?'

'What are you trying to say?'

Harm places a hand on her forearm.

'Ally—'

Alex shakes it off.

'Shit, no! The spider's web, the blacked-out mesh. It was him.'

'My God, Ally! Because of a tattoo?'

'No! Because of—'

But she can't find the words to say why she's so certain. The other three women are standing in a ring, a cautious distance from her. The policewoman steps forward, taking hold of the situation. The situation apparently being Alex.

'Do you know,' says the policewoman in a professionally level voice, 'how many attacks like this there are in London every single day? Committed by some random man who decides it would be fun to harm a woman?'

'Don't teach *me* how to be a feminist.'

'Your wife is the victim of an assault. Right now she's in need of medical attention. Would you please allow me to deal with the matter at hand?'

How old is this girl? Twenty-four, twenty-five?

'Since when are you her wife? *I'll* take her to the fucking hospital – right, Pie?

Harmony folds her arms and glares at the kilim pattern of the rug. Artemis's eyes dart between the three women as though this is the most fabulous daytime show that ever aired.

MEGAFLOP

Lucky Ghost: My dear boy. You have landed yourself in a pickle.

Thimblerig's legs have started to tremor at being folded against his chest so long. He's hugging them with his arm to stop them hammering on the cabinet door. This leaves his other hand free to type on the crablet clamped to his right thigh. He taps the words slowly so the duty manager won't hear.

Thimblerig: I'm in a cupboard. I have less than half an hour. I don't know what to do.

The manager's standing just outside the cabinet talking to his boss on the telephone. They're speaking about how persons unknown just tried to spoof Raynor's backup disks out of the storage area. Thimblerig has his earpiece turned down so he can't hear the boss talk – but the manager's side of the conversation is clear enough.

Lucky Ghost: Update me. Be quick.

He does and he is. He fills her in on how the hack ran super-smooth until Raynor called and blew it open. How he's driving over here to rescue his drives while Gordion goes on lockdown.

Lucky Ghost: One moment. I should like to confer with a source. I shall return shortly.

Thimblerig: Hurry.

Lucky Ghost: Courage, lad.

Strange how this anonymous voice can sooth his fear. It's because of the trace it carries of Elyse Martingale.

Elyse has been a presence in Thimblerig's life since before he came to England. If there are two people who made him – if anyone can ever 'make' somebody – then they are his father and Elyse. Both wizards with machines. Both fighters against regimes. Both dead. He might call Elyse a mother except he once had a mother of his own. All of Elyse he had to suckle on as a child was a yellowed copy of her 1969 book *This is Tomorrow.* Her imagined future that never came to be. When he was eight he had to carry that thin book north by train and truck and on foot.

He only got round to reading *The Electronic Radical* much later. Then he saw Elyse's picture on the cover – those stern, assuring eyes – and realised his 'Professor Martingale' was a woman. How was he to know? There was no photo in his copy of *This is Tomorrow.* The biography only said *Professor Martingale did this. Professor Martingale did that.* When the only Western names he knew were Tony Stark, Steve Rogers and Bruce Banner, why wouldn't he think Elyse was a man? Would he have worshipped her so if he'd known she was a woman? He doesn't know and counterfactuals have no meaning.

Outside the cupboard the manager's still talking on his phone.

— What I can't work out, he says, is what they planned to do with the disks once we called them up. They'd never've made it further than the client room.

From inside the cupboard Thimblerig wills the manager not to think through the consequence of what he just said – i.e. that the hackers he's talking about must have penetrated the client room before calling up the disks. And therefore the manager should look in the one place a desperate kid might be huddled. i.e. inside the cabinet.

He consoles himself with the thought that nobody ever sees the holes in their own security. They wrap themselves in so many protections they think they're invulnerable.

The duty manager laughs at something his boss has said.

— Right, he says. I'd love to see some hacker turning up in a bald wig, pretending to be Doug Raynor.

Having seen pictures of Raynor – his black button eyes in a shaved and bullet-shaped head – Thimblerig smiles into the dark.

Ghost is back.

Lucky Ghost: As best I can make out, Raynor has found a buyer for Kaa.
Thimblerig: With the police all over him?
Lucky Ghost: Clearly he is unafraid of the bold agents of the law - will wonders never cease? It seems he is running a, shall we say, fire sale.

Outside the cabinet the duty manager ends the call.

Thimblerig: It's a big risk though.
Lucky Ghost: He is a reckless man. Which is why I importuned you to obtain Kaa as soon as possible. Lest this be the last remaining copy.
Thimblerig: t's the only copy.
Lucky Ghost: But my dear boy, how could you know that?
Thimblerig: Doug Raynor's coming to Gordion in person. Even though the law might be following. This must be his only copy.
Lucky Ghost: Ah. Clever lad.
Thimblerig: And I can't stop him.

The door beeps and clicks as the duty manager leaves the room.

Lucky Ghost: There is one course of action. Destroy it.
Thimblerig: Wipe Kaa?

Lucky Ghost: I'd hoped to be the one who decided how and when this thing was be used, but that can no longer be. Nobody must have that opportunity.

So painful to think of destroying that sweet hack.

Thimblerig: Why not let someone else use Kaa? If they harm the bankers is that bad?

Lucky Ghost: It must be deployed in the right place at the right time, not as a weapon of corporate or national aggression.

Not for the first time Ghost speaks like an agent of some wider system. Thimblerig longs to quiz her but this isn't the time. There's no way for he can wound the bankers as he'd hoped. But still he can hurt the bully Raynor.

Thimblerig: I'll do it.
Lucky Ghost: Good lad. Hurry.

Thimblerig closes the chat and slides the door open a chink. The coast is clear. He pushes the cupboard door fully open and rolls gratefully out of the tight enclosure. He gets to his hands and knees and stands like a newborn foal. He looks at the plastic display stand atop the table. This is an insulated plastic cuboid where the Gordion team places the electronics they bring out for handling by clients. Especially anything that shouldn't be hit by a static charge. Like a hard drive for instance.

There'll only be a narrow window of opportunity. Thimblerig needs to improvise.

He shakes his legs to work blood into them then crouches down to extract his tools. Working quickly but quietly he tips the microwave onto its back and removes the bottom panel with a Phillips #2. He disconnects the wires to free the base from the body of the oven and stows this behind the cupboard with the shelves. The transformer – a heavy metal cube – is just behind the microwave's control panel. Avoiding the capacitor – which most likely holds charge – he unscrews and lifts out the transformer block. It's held together by screws instead of bolts. Good. He won't have to drill them out. He snips off the thick protruding wires and opens up the block.

It takes seven minutes of frantic levering and occasional whacks from a hammer to slide out every one of the layered metal plates that alternate through the centre of the coil. By the time he gets the core free his hands are covered with tiny scratches from the sharp edges of the plates. He holds up the coil. It's a square spool with rounded corners – like a roll of fishing wire with straight edges.

He blows sweaty hair from his eyes and cocks his head to listen for movement outside the door. He rips the plastic tape from the tight-wound coil of coated magnet wire. This coil would do the job but it's too small – less than half as big as the anti-static display stand. So he sits on one of the chairs and starts to uncoil the wire. He looks around for something the right size to work as a template for his larger coil. His eyes land on the kettle. Perfect.

Before too long a messy cloud of copper wire is looped around his ankles. He picks up the kettle and sits at the table to coil the wire around its base. As he forms a neat copper stripe he pictures what's about to happen in this room. Doug Raynor will arrive in a matter of minutes. The man who betrayed Thimblerig's father will walk through that door and stand two metres from where Thimblerig is hiding in his cupboard. From where – assuming none of a hundred things goes wrong – he'll wipe the Kaa hack from the backup disks and deny his enemy the chance to profit from it.

He'll have struck a blow. But shouldn't revenge mean more than fiddling with wires? But what instead? Leap out of the cupboard and attack a trained killer with a flathead screwdriver? Perhaps he should. This is the closest he'll ever get to the man responsible for his father's death.

Unless that's not true. This decision would be far easier if Thimblerig knew for certain Raynor's the man he's looking for.

What proof he has took years to compile but it's not enough. He used to think he could prove anything if he could only penetrate far enough into the flow of secrets that passes constantly underfoot in hidden ducts and passages. He thought the truth was one more layer of encryption away. Now he understands that everything is always to some degree uncertain. At some point you simply have to decide for yourself. Maybe this is that time?

The coppery wire is getting twisted up. Thimblerig whips it in the air to shed the mess of loops then continues winding.

What he does know comes mostly from a man he met three years ago on a subreddit used by Syrians resettled in Europe. This man – now housed in a day-workers' camp in Bavaria – had once been the owner of a phone shop in Salah al-Din. When the store was bombed out he found his way into a rebel platoon headed by Thimblerig's father. As the only member of the squad with tech skills he was soon running their systems. Though not competent enough to notice their comms being hacked. Only after all nine of his commanders were taken by extremists did he think to check the logs. It took some time but he managed to pinpoint the SSL injection that had let the extremists monitor the rebels' voice and text traffic.

That was one part of the puzzle. Now – thanks to Lucky Ghost – Thimblerig has another. A chat transcript from WikiLeaks. Where an American security contractor called *drainer* does a trade with an extremist cell based on the outskirts of Aleppo. This *drainer* sends the cell the code and instructions for an SSL hack. Plus the IP address of a rebel unit's communication server. Ten days later the rebels' comms are hacked. Three days after that the extremists take out nine rebel leaders in a single afternoon. Including Thimblerig's father.

Put the pieces together and a picture forms. Yet the centre remains dark. Who is *drainer*? Ghost says she knows him to be Raynor but she's shown no proof. So Thimblerig's spent the past few weeks rooting through Raynor's complex online footprint. He's established that Raynor was in the right region at the right time – this was mentioned at the Aleppo hearings in evidence given by an unnamed US intelligence officer. He's referred to as an officer of a private security firm used by the CIA to broker relationships on the ground at a time when the US was not officially present in Syria.

So: here's a character called *drainer* who knew the right things and was in the right place to be Doug Raynor. That's much more than a coincidence of names but it's not definitive. Yet what is definitive? In Thimblerig's dim-lit world there's no such thing as certainty. All he can trust in is his sense of the right. But in this case he doesn't know what's right.

The coil is fully wound. Thimblerig lifts it gently off the kettle and fishes out the wireless mains switch that caught his eye at Handy Frank's. This is a nifty device he can turn on remotely from his crablet. He binds his newly wound coil with electric tape then gaffer-tapes it to the bottom of the display stand on the table. Then he fetches the standard lamp from the corner of the room and turns it upside down. The mains flex runs all the way inside its hollow stalk. Good: he needs as much length as possible. He yanks the cord until the full length of cable decouples from the terminals at the top. He tips out the flex. With his battery-powered drill he makes a 5mm hole in the tabletop under the display stand. He runs the bare end of the mains flex up through the hole and solders the flex in a circuit with the wireless switch and coil. With a few more strips of gaffer he runs the flex along the bottom of the table and down one leg. Then he plugs the whole assembly into a mains socket under a hinged plate in the floor.

The whole job has taken eighteen minutes. Thimblerig uses one of the pictures from the wall to waft away the smell of solder. Then he stands back to check his handiwork. He hasn't been able to conceal the flex where it runs into the floor panel. But in every other way the table looks exactly as it did before. With luck his improvised degausser won't hum so loudly that Raynor hears it. With even more luck it won't get so hot that it melts the plastic display stand. Luck's a major component of an improvised hack.

He does his best to return the room to the state it was in before. He's halfway through fitting the casing back onto the now-disabled microwave when he hears the voices in the hall. Stupid. He'd been waiting to hear another call come in over his earpiece but he has the volume turned down to zero. The beep of a card swipe sounds outside the door. He ducks and crawls back into the cupboard. Ignoring the shout of pain from his leg he pulls the backpack inside and slides the door shut as Raynor's voice enters the room.

— You're telling me what? That you were just going to hand my disks over to these pricks?

— Oh, definitely not, sir. We'd never have given them access to the building.

Thimblerig winnows his crablet from underneath him and calls up the app that will trigger the wireless switch. He hasn't had time to test it. He has to hope.

— My colleague will be here with the disks in just a few seconds.

— He better be.

The pause that follows is very very awkward.

— So, says the manager, what happened to your, er . . .

— To my what?

— I mean – the bruises on your face?

There's a silence. Thimblerig isn't in the easiest of predicaments but at this point he's extremely glad he's not the duty manager.

— I got them, says Raynor, headbutting the last guy who asked me too many questions.

This situation is interrupted by a knocking. Thimblerig startles. Is someone banging on the cupboard? No – it came from the door to the room. Which opens with a beep of the release. There's a muttered conversation then it shuts again.

— All right, Mr Raynor, sir! Your disks, all secure.

— I can see that, doofus.

— Let me just set these out here for you where they'll be insulated.

— Jesus shit, hurry it up.

— There. All set. Now if I could just get you to sign this—

— Yes, yes, whatever. There. Done. Now scoot. I have a call to make.

Thimblerig can't help thinking the duty manager is more than happy to comply. The door beeps open and shuts. There's a series of shuffles. Thimblerig's thumb hovers over the icon that will activate the wireless switch and — he hopes — set off the degausser. He's pretty sure the manager put the disks on the display stand. In which case a minute or so of mains AC pumping through the coil should be more than sufficient to demagnetise them. It'll probably brick them completely.

But what if the disks aren't on the display stand? What if Raynor chased off the manager before he had a chance to set them out? What if Thimblerig kicks off his kludged degausser while the disks are outside its probably pathetic range?

He twists his thumb away from the icon.

— It's me, says Raynor.

He's talking on his phone. Thimblerig turns up his earpiece to hear both ends of the conversation. He catches a male voice on the far end of the line.

— . . . had an arrangement, it's saying.

— Any *arrangement* we had became null and void, says Raynor, the second you tried to steal my shit from under me.

— That is a paranoid response. Your employer told me you were a man one could do business with.

The voice is flat and posh. As though Raynor's speaking to a telephone response bot.

— I don't have an employer, says Raynor. I'm a contractor. But I rang to tell you your stunt got you nowhere. I'm at Gordion now and I have my disks. How do you fucking like that?

— Mr Ox promised me Kaa. I suggest you discuss your course of action with him.

— Yeah, well I *suggest* you quit getting up in my business. I'm looking at the disks right now. Here. Lemme show you a picture.

There's the shutter of a phone taking a photo. The whoosh of a file sending. Thimblerig scrambles for his phone and checks the screen. A picture of three neat stacks of uncased hard drives lined up on a plastic display stand.

He activates the wireless switch.

— See that there? says Raynor. Would you like those drives? Tough shit. The second I'm done talking to your ass I'm taking them direct to a guy who's prepared to pay the proper price.

Thimblerig's sure he can hear the degausser buzz. He prays this is imagination. And/or that Raynor's too caught up in bragging to hear it.

— Do as you must, says the voice. Kaa is but a single domino. Let us see how your employer takes this.

Thimblerig finishes counting to sixty and turns off the switch.

— Like I say, I'm a contractor. I do what I'm paid to do. And nobody's paid for me not to fuck with your ass.

— You should hear yourself, Mr Raynor. Subconscious word choices are so revealing. You would appear to have a powerful anal fixation.

— Fixate this, you pussy.

The line goes dead with a low *boop*. There's a clatter as Raynor packs away his disks. He bangs on the door and whistles loudly.

— Hey! he shouts. Service here!

The door clicks open and shuts. The room is silent. Thimblerig wriggles around to get to his crablet.

Thimblerig: Done. The disks should be wiped clean.
Lucky Ghost: Well done, lad.

Yes. Very well done. Except that it's late in the evening and Thimblerig's stuck inside a cupboard in a room that's guarded by video cameras in a building on lockdown. And he's just realised he's desperate for a pee.

VALUE AT RISK

Not for the first time, Mr Ox finds himself exercised about the balance sheet. Unable to concentrate on his correspondence, he takes a handful of walnuts and raises his shape from his reinforced chair. He strides to the corner window and looks out over his city's half-constructed future. The Minsk dusk is gassy and sliced with arc light from sites where cranes and crews are already winding to a stop. No discipline, these workers. Mr Ox sighs and picks a walnut from his handful. If he had the time or inclination, he would offer his services to these shoddy Serbian construction firms, deliver them a hockey-curve uptick in productivity. He cracks the nut between thumb and forefinger, tosses the meat in the air and snatches it in his mouth. He crunches thoughtfully.

As the city dips into darkness Mr Ox's mind comes alive. None but he can see the present dangers. To an external observer, Occidental Data Partnerships is riding high. It has ventures in an expanding portfolio of markets. Bulk Identity Vending and Alternative Narrative Creation remain core propositions; Enhanced Influencing a growth area. They are market leaders, too, in Personnel Removal. Right across its service lines, the firm continues to draw significant investment. Business is after all risk management – and investors know that if they place their money with Mr Ox, they can rest assured he will manage away all barriers to profit.

On the surface, therefore, the balance sheet is in excellent trim. Yet, as Mr Ox is well aware, this robust health depends on Ms

Okapi and her liberal approach to mark-to-market valuation. A third of their assets are lifted from a projected future and translated into present wealth through accounting techniques Mr Ox must confess – though only ever to himself – he does not comprehend.

This fosters heightened sensitivities to fortune. The slightest disruption to their growth curves would unnerve investors and set their numbers crumbling like a housing development into a sinkhole. Furthermore, economic times are tougher than is yet apparent. In a marketplace where certain product lines – the direct distribution of specialist pharmaceuticals, for instance – continue to be aggressively disintermediated by nimbler start-ups, Project Domino is a vital source of revenue. However, one cannot be blind to the risks of resting so much on a single contract. This breeds dependency, systemic risks. Risks Mr Ox fears may materialise all too soon.

Through the floor of the office comes a succession of dull crashes and a squeal of pain. Mr Ox tuts: he must have Facilities better soundproof the ceilings of the data extraction rooms on the floor below.

He gazes across the darkening concrete towers of the part-completed Minsk Planet district, in which Occidental's building stands. Barely a dozen blocks illuminated in this cluster. This pattern repeats as far as he can see. The footprint of this eternally re-starting and re-ceasing construction programme spreads across a hundred soccer pitches. It has been under construction for nearly two decades, yet still is not complete. The grandeur and frustration of this endeavour capture well the character of Mr Ox's home city. He would not wish any other base of operations.

He pivots his bulk around and propels it to his desk.

His first focus is to winnow out all threats to Project Domino. It is a source of deep frustration that the cluster of hopping fleas who style themselves Cockaigne should have chosen to step up their campaign of interference. Their bites are tiny but they itch;

and their volume is on the rise. At a time when Domino activities are ramping up, such a threat to core operations is not only corrosive to cash flows; it drives reputational risks that threaten a solid order book.

Mr Ox's Senior Executive Group colleagues see Cockaigne as a mere distraction; but as Vintner says in his seminal *Embracing Unknowables: A Scenario-Based Approach to Corporate Risk Management*, one must not only control the hazards one faces today; one must also foresee outlying risks that, though merely probabilities, will have the most severe of impacts should they materialise. Cockaigne has become such a risk, and, thanks to a communication from the Project Domino client, Occidental has solid information Mr Honey Badger may act upon.

If only Mr Honey Badger did not himself present a risk. His freelance activities, his unwillingness to buy into corporate values, are disquieting. A business is only as robust as each link of its chain of command.

Mr Honey Badger has managed yet again to irritate the client – this time badly. Mr Ox was able to patch up the relationship, on the basis that his errant Director of UK Operations is essential to short-term success. To switch personnel at a critical stage of roll-out would be sub-optimal. Happily, the client relented, on the condition that Mr Honey Badger is suitably disciplined following full delivery of the services. It's a mark of how Honey Badger has fallen in Mr Ox's estimation that he agreed so willingly to these terms.

Mr Honey Badger has never understood the primacy of relationship management. Mr Ox shall make him read *Satisfaction is not enough! Nine Surefire Tips That Will Generate Love From Your Client Base,* by the excellent Mr Harry Taborin.

So: the time is ripe for a decisive test of Mr Honey Badger's mettle. The new information from the client provides an opportunity to stem these vexatious incursions; but only if it is acted upon swiftly and without remorse. A dose of insecticide, one might say, applied to the nagging insects of Cockaigne.

Mr Ox presses the loudspeaker button on his prized Soviet-era desk tannoy.

'Yes, sir?' comes the crackling voice of Ms Pangolin.

'You wound me, Ms Pangolin,' says Mr Ox. 'Please: "Sergei".'

'Yes, Sergei,' says Ms Pangolin.

Her voice remains brisk but Mr Ox can tell that she is pleased. As Ryan Salzburg writes in his excellent *Stop Your Excuses NOW! Eight Invaluable Ways To Be Bolder In The Workplace*, such small intangible tokens can generate the appearance of equality with one's subordinates, without eroding authority.

'Have Raynor come to me at once,' he says.

On the screen of the vintage Juku ES101 that it pleases Mr Ox to use, he calls up the records the client sent through. Very detailed files on the Cockaigne hacker known as Thimblerig – including, crucially, a home address, and comprehensive details of the hacker's recent activities. This *agent provocateur* has been placing thorns in Occidental's side for no little time. What a pleasure it will be to see this problem staunched.

A tentative rap sounds. This is the ringtone Mr Ox – an inveterate traditionalist – insists on using to announce a ghostly visitor.

'*Enter*!' he bellows.

A hazy reproduction of Raynor slides into the room. The bruises on the side of his shaved head are already fading.

'You're a careless man, Mr Honey Badger,' says Mr Ox.

Honey Badger has his feet planted wide apart and his head back. As a brave man might face down a firing squad.

'Careful enough to fox your dickweed client.'

'I don't think so. But that's not what I'm referring to. Mr Lemur has had your premises, and those of your pet lobbyist, under scrutiny. Using the technology provided by our client.'

'Lemur's army of morons has been watching my building? Without my say-so?'

'You say morons. Yet this army has proved remarkably effective in detecting breaches. You had visitors today of whom you were not even aware.'

Mr Ox flicks up the images of the Ayyash boy, recovered from the mesh of their work-for-hire ground agents. Honey Badger's image glances at them without acknowledgement.

'And Lemur's creepazoids,' he says. 'Did they stop or even catch this *visitor*?'

All the walnuts in Mr Ox's hand are suddenly squeezed to powder. Distractedly he drops the remnants into his standard-issue KGB waste bin.

'That is beside the point. You and I both have skin in this particular ball game. This individual stands to hinder us both. Both of us lose if Project Domino does not deploy effectively on Monday.'

The image of Mr Honey Badger flickers like some cine film recovered from the previous century. He folds his arms and relaxes his stance. The man is too easy to read, even over remote link.

'You're asking for my *help*?' he says. 'I assumed this was the last rites.'

'What I am asking is that you complete your contractual commitment.'

'Shit me. You must be desperate. Guess it's not enough to have an army of dipshit gamers on the ground here, huh? You realise I'm not giving you Kaa?'

'I realise you have nothing left to give in that department. Thanks once again to the efforts of our ingenious client.'

The man takes a braggadocious pose; pointing a furious finger, of all things, at Mr Ox's face.

'That brainiac's gonna get a piece of my mind.'

'Assuming you find out who he is, Mr Honey Badger. You think even *I* know?'

The two men regard each other for the better part of a minute. Staring matches are rendered abstract over the Strange; more a video game than a test of mettle. At length, Mr Honey Badger seems to reach some conclusion.

'OK,' he says, 'so what kind of cover do you have for the space rocket?

All at once the man is nothing but business. Here is why, in spite of his rogue behaviour, Mr Ox cannot but like him.

'The technology,' he says, 'is covered. We need tactical support on the ground.'

Honey Badger nods.

'And the artist? His little "accident"?'

'We have a squad ready. But they require leadership.'

Mr Honey Badger's eyes defocus as he studies the full list of tactical deployments that Mr Ox has transmitted.

'That's some coordination job in such a short window.'

'The client is most insistent about timing.'

Honey Badger strides to the suspended portraits of Ayyash, places hands on hips as he studies them. One sees his training in the limber set of his haunches: ready to spring into action at a second's notice. He turns to Mr Ox and indicates the target with a thumb.

'And,' he says, 'you want me to remove interference from the ay-rab dweeb?'

By not replying, Mr Ox signals that his patience for discussing implementation is exhausted. He composes himself behind his monolithic desk. A sphinx with the face of Rameses.

'Suppose,' he says, 'I were to offer a completion bonus of, let us say, three million DESPAIR. You would honour our contract?'

Honey Badger blinks but says nothing.

'Or,' says Mr Ox, cantilevering his upper body forward across the desk, 'is this to be our final discussion on the subject?'

Honey Badger shrugs.

'Guess my diary's pretty clear, next couple days.'

Mr Ox's lips crease into some form of a smile.

BAD PENNY

The figure stands in the Edwardian porch, silhouetted by light from the frosted window of the door. It could be man or woman. From a hundred metres away and across the road, Mickey can see light moving vaguely behind its eye-slits. It twists its head his way. He about-turns and starts a brisk walk down the dark pavement.

This clinches it: he's being tailed. Everywhere he's been, it's taken less than half an hour for some Stranger to appear and start checking him out. None of them made any kind of move. They've all just . . . *been there*. Mickey was hoping he could sneak back home to grab his things, head out of town and hole up while he waits for Hairy Jacko to get back to him, but the phantom Strangers are here ahead of him.

He dares a look over his shoulder. The black-clad figure is matching his pace some distance behind, on the opposite side of the heavily parked street. A cape flows behind it. As it moves into a pool of sticky yellow street light, Mickey sees that it's dressed in full-body Martian Manhunter. Mickey picks up his pace. As he reaches the junction of Ackroyd Road, he makes a steering-wheel motion with his hands. Thirty seconds later, up pulls a steel-grey Prius, driven by a Stranger in a pinstripe suit and silver Mexican wrestler mask. The almond-shaped eyespots are filled with glinting mesh.

'El Hijo del Santo?' says Mickey as he hops in the passenger seat.

The guy nods once. Mickey thought he recognised the mask. As they pull away he twists to see out through the rear window.

Under a pollarded plane tree, the Martian stands arms folded, cape hanging limply. It stares after the departing car but doesn't follow.

Mickey faces forward and gets a map up in the air, taps on the general vicinity of Camberwell. The Stranger takes a slow left onto Brockley Rise, car on silent electric running, then left again towards Honor Oak. Mickey'll have to wave goodbye to the hold-all sitting back in his locker. He'll replace his possessions easily: from Strangers, as always.

Mickey has no home, no ties. Man of means by no means, he's king of the digital road. He gave up his mum's little terrace on Canvey months ago. The Brockley house was just a crashpod – a communal space where each inhabitant has their own three-by-two-metre area of floor, demarcated in rectangles of vinyl tape, paid in SERENITY. No need for privacy when everyone turns on their own reality whenever they're in the crashpod. A medieval castle, a *Firefly*-grade cargo ship, a bar in 1950s' Casablanca – wherever each chooses to live. They wander freely through their imaginary spaces without ever bumping into one another. The algaerhythm running the Strange is their silent choreographer, showing them where to walk without colliding.

The car glides past the dark expanse of Peckham Rye. This stretch of road is mercifully quiet but Mickey still jumps at every Stranger they pass. He needs to get off these streets, find someone open to a spot of house-surfing. Maybe also provide him with a dose of comfort. He puts out the ask. A ripple of voices returns but they're blatant catfish. So many users these days are rogue Personas, dry ghosts programmed to act like people. Mickey slides these bots away and waits for an authentic Stranger, made of fellow flesh. His glowheart rides sidecar, stress emotions running haywire through it.

A true response comes in while the car's idling at traffic lights in Denmark Hill. Mickey hops out without saying a word. Twelve thousand SATISFACTION passes to the masked driver as the car hums off. Mickey's eyes follow a trail of dotted green across the

street and up to the first-floor flat above a food outlet named
TASTY JERK CENTRE. A woman's outline shows full-figured
through the wall above the shop. She moves to the window and
parts the curtain, looks down on Mickey.

⟨names penny⟩

Mickey accepts.

Five minutes later his head's resting on the warm folds of
Penny's lap. The fabric of her bathrobe is scratchy acrylic the
colour of old ladies' hair-rinse; but the flesh below is soft. He
breathes her powdery scent and the lavender of her vape. She
strokes his hair in a distracted rhythm as they watch a gameshow
host strut on the corner kitchenette. The host tells a joke and
wraps his arm so far around the contestant's shoulders his fingers
brush her breast. Mickey can't hear the joke or the canned laughter. His mesh is on mute.

He pulls his legs into a foetal curl. This is better. The Strange
erases the bitter dark, with affection on tap on every corner. Yet
Mickey can't shake the sense of everything coming to an end, of
silent furies on his heels. Unless this pursuit is just some dark
Encounter, offered him as symbol of all he's retreating from. His
whole dark world of loss.

Unawares, Mickey's started to cry. He looks up at Penny's full
chin, the blue acrylic undersides of her tits.

'Can I just tell you—?' he says.

Penny shifts on the sofa, pushing his neck to a painful angle.
She gives a low snort and keeps on watching the silent show.

'I've lost everyone,' he says.

She glances down.

'You didn't order EMPATHY, darling,' she says.

Mickey stiffens. He clambers off her lap and gets to his feet,
head thumping and mouth dry.

'All I—' he starts, then stops and stumbles off to the dark and
oily bathroom.

He throws the catch and raises his mesh to throw water in his eyes. He stares at his sodden features in the murky mirror. His face looks like it's covered in razor burn. What does he even want right now? Any minute, Jacko will be in touch with news of his source. He'll put things right for Alex. Then what? Is there any story left to run for Mickey Gallant?

He drops his mesh. The Strange answers, as it always will. The words appear in perspective, angled towards the half-tiled partition wall. On the other side, Penny will be seeing them, too.

‹a happy ending›

The Strange has chosen to play him a porno and it's right. That's exactly what he needs to shake the jags from his mind. Penny accepts the Favour and an R&B soundtrack winds up to full volume. In the mirror stands a burley beefcake Mickey. His cock twitches in anticipation of how Penny's been transformed. There's a thump from outside, like she's punched the wall. Mickey hopes not. She can't completely hate him, or she wouldn't have accepted the Favour.

He opens the bathroom door to a flood of amber light and a woman's groans of pleasure. Penny's pneumatic self gazes coolly from the velour chaise longue her DFS sofa's become. Her silken dressing gown is undone and a section of tan lace bra shows round each breast. Mickey's hard. His return is showing as 25 ECSTASY. Penny will get a lot more, as the provider of the Favour. ACCEPTANCE, or SERENITY. Giver emotions.

'*Thank you* for cleaning out my pipes,' coos Penny in the voice of Ava Gardner. 'Really, I didn't know *what* I was going to do. I was wet all over when you got here. How can I possibly thank you?'

She plumps the cushions, revealing more bra. Mickey plonks himself on the sofa, ignoring his cues. There's zero character drama anyway. She unbuckles him and yanks down the tony slacks that have replaced his stained chinos. She squirts baby lotion and rubs her palms. The squelching goes straight to Mickey's dick. As she works him, he leans back into the musty cushions and lets out a moan. It'll be a miracle if this little vignette lasts a minute. Her movements send shivers through her right breast. He reaches his hand to it.

'Tits is extra,' she says in the voice of an angel, moving his wrist away with her slimy hand.

Mickey shifts focus to the peripheral options. Tits is a hundred JOY. He accepts. Penny reaches inside her gown to flip the catch. Her breasts fall heavy. Mickey grabs hold as she starts a firmer motion. They gaze impassively into each other's eyes. Mickey's on the point of exploding. His grip tightens. She flinches and works him faster. Just as he's about to come her eyes flick to a space behind the sofa. As he ejaculates, Mickey's earnings flash before him, a slot-machine jackpot. Two hundred and fifty REMORSE.

Something about this Favour was worth a bonus. Before he can take in the unexpected reward, Mickey's head jack-knifes forwards. The head of a plumber's wrench has smashed into the back of his neck, striking at the fold where spine meets skull. The head of the wrench lands with such force that the atlas and axis vertebrae are torn away and forced up into the cranial base, where they lodge in spinal matter at the entrance to the foramen magnum. An area of occipital bone six centimetres in diameter crumples into the soft matter of the medulla.

Penny leaps deftly aside. The second blow lands on Mickey's right temple, throwing his body sideways. The Stranger in the sky-blue bunny suit clambers over the back of the sofa and sits astride Mickey, lodging a furry thigh on either side of his body. Penny slips into the hall. The bunny lands the wrench five times onto Mickey's face then sits back breathless, inspecting the wreck of blood and cartilage where the nose was.

The blue rabbit drops the wrench on Mickey's lap and uses both hands to wiggle his head back into place. Penny appears at the door where she freezes and takes an intake of breath.

'Do you want me to pop that in the machine?' she says.

The rabbit gets up off Mickey's body and looks down its front. Spatters of Mickey's face and brain decorate the plush bib of the costume. There are red streaks down the side of its tall right ear, where it used its bloody paw to adjust its headpiece.

'When I'm done,' it says thickly.

The rabbit kneels in front of Mickey, tugs the mesh from his head and tosses it aside, then rolls up his right sleeve and leans in, inspecting Mickey's forearm through the domes of blue crystal set over its eyes. Lights dart about inside its eyes like fireflies at midnight.

'Embeds,' it says. 'I need to take them out.'

'I'll get something for the floor.'

She fetches a candlewick bedspread and lays it out. Three minutes have passed since Mickey's embeds logged the cessation of his heartbeat. That's the grace period allowed for temporary loss of service before confirmation of mortis, which is why, as the blood-streaked rabbit lifts Mickey's body by the armpits and side-steps to the bedspread, his death is confirmed by the host. This is the cue for each of his 1,325,722 Coin to empty from his wallet and return to the issuer, leaving a balance of zero.

Emoticoin are locked to their owner: they die with him.

PART TWO:

RAGE

No one likes to believe that his or her personal economic interest is in conflict with the greater public need. To invent a plausible ideology in defence of self-interest is thus a natural course. A corps of willing and talented craftsmen is available for the task.'

—JK Galbraith, *The Good Society*

'VR has the potential for apocalyptic creepiness, too.'

—Jaron Lanier, in the *New Yorker*

ONLY HOPE

The flat is silent, if you don't count the tapping of the central heating. Alex is splayed on her back on the sitting-room carpet, knees up and a tumbler of Petit Chablis by her hand. Between her and the plain white ceiling, she's racked up a three-dimensional mish-mash of documents. She's shuffling them into groups, layers, associations.

Her breathing is clockwork. Harm was right. She hasn't been taking her meds, not since she put on her mesh. The Strange is a better regulator than any antidepressant they've ever dosed her with. Until yesterday, when it all went haywire. Now, with her back extended on the rough weave of the Afghan rug, she has it under control. The fear's still there, peaking in pulses on her glowheart, but it's contained. She knows now that it's *real*. Someone is after her. Connor Gunnell, and his father Francis. Hence why her rounders bat is lying an arm's length to her right.

She flicks a series of photos of the Gunnell boys, working to stop her heart from skipping at every image. These men have lurked under bridges every way she's turned, ever since the interview that wrecked her vlog and, for a time, herself. It landed her in a low, dark place it took months of meds and behavioural therapy to clamber out of. It wasn't just the Gunnells – there was also her troll, the Handyman. But the interview was the trigger. She's been dodging its memory ever since.

She has her mesh on mute to focus only on the visuals, so she almost missed Harmony calling from the hospital earlier. Harm sounded cooler-headed but wasn't saying much. The nurses had triaged her and given the contradictory messages that she was OK enough to go to the bottom of the queue for a doctor, but in enough danger they wouldn't let her home. Alex asked if she wanted company. She didn't much like the way Harm said no.

Still, it's given her time and permission to riffle through these documents on Francis Gunnell. Everything she dug up six months ago is even truer today. The tax evasion through offshore shells. The associations with the Dayell crime family from the West Midlands. The allegations of graft and muscle. Alex's exposé didn't do a thing to clean up Gunnell's act. If anything, he's got worse. His old-world business – whoever it is that actually buys tools any more – is waning under the remorseless winds of the new economy. Hence his recent plea to government – specifically, Susan Hardiman's department – for a bail-out. Thirty million to tide the firm along. Amazingly, the government didn't tell him to fuck off, and they're in the process of assessing the bid. The announcement's due at the start of next week. From all the signals, it seems foregone. Gunnell will get his money, provided Hardiman can extract an OK from the button-pushers in the Treasury. She's been crowing about the importance of Handy Frank's to *the nation's homes, gardens and hearts.*

So: here's a version of events. Gunnell bribes Hardiman to secure his bail-out and shore up his crumbling empire. The bribe, delivered through Corrigan, is one of the sweeteners. No wonder the minister's desperate to see Alex slapped down for confronting her publicly.

Yet some facts don't snap so neatly into that narrative. Why, for instance, was Connor on Alex's tail *before* she exposed the bribe on-air? Then there's the nature of that bribe. Gunnell's old-school as a wind-up fob watch. His stock-in-trade is knuckledusters and suitcases stuffed with cash. Paying off a politician in digital currency isn't his style.

Still, the Gunnells are surely after her. More than ever, what she needs is solid proof of how that bribe was paid. Some way into

Emoticoin. Something that links together Francis Gunnell, Sam Corrigan and—

There's someone in the room.

By the window.

Alex's right hand lands on the rounders bat. She tucks her feet against her butt and rolls her weight forward, comes up in a crouch and launches herself, using her momentum to swing the bat at the chest of the man standing by the window. Her documents flap in a virtual wave of paper, clearing a path for her bat as it passes through the man and smashes into the blue glass stand of Harmony's favourite Indian lamp. The bulb explodes and coloured shards hail against the wall. The documents cower in a holding pattern to her right.

Alex drops the bat and stands panting.

'Shit,' she says, surveying the wreckage.

Last November, after the scuffle with Connor Gunnell, Alex took a martial arts course. The kind that's a hodgepodge of different disciplines, teaching women self-defence with a thin layer of spiritual practice dusted on top. The sensei would tell her, 'Your reflexes are excellent. But your aim is terrible.' Guy knew what he was talking about.

The man by the window is a ghost. Yet another visit from a man who isn't there. Is this why she joined the Strange? For endless men to materialise and give her their opinions?

'Oh, who are you now?' she says. 'The ghost of Internet yet to come?'

He's slightly less than Alex's 1.8 metres. His hair's the better part of him. It starts in a thicket above his head, then twines and tumbles in knots around his face and down in a fat bib to his crotch. The face that glares out through a gap in this hedgerow is sharp, dewlapped and furious. He could be a haggard sixty-year-old, or a guy in his thirties who's lost four stone in weight, leaving his face a hollowed-out fold.

'Why didn't I need to ask you in?' says Alex.

Like vampires, Strangers can only come indoors when invited. The man points to Alex's right. She turns to see.

She doesn't remember installing a two-metre-tall 1990s cathode-ray computer monitor in her sitting room. Funny the things you forget when life gets busy. The screen is fat and rounded. Its tube bulges outwards, catching the light in a curved band. A trick of rendering, since the thing isn't there. The back of the CRT's deep casing projects back through the wall.

> Name's Jacko.

says the screen.
Alex looks at the rendered man, but he points again at the screen. She turns back to it.

> I prefer text.

it says.
'I do not,' says Alex, 'understand the smallest part of what is going on here.'
As she speaks, words appear on the screen.

> I do not understand the smallest part of what is going on
here.

The curser blinks waiting. The programming heft it must be taking to render this giant photorealistic screen, just so this guy can backtrack on thirty years of user interface improvements. Whoever this 'Jacko' is, he's some kind of wizard.

> So start using your grey cells.

She glances at the man. He's still – but not frozen. No obvious sign he's typing these words.

> Name's Jacko. It's about Mickey Gallant.

Alex takes a step towards the screen. She speaks, and again her words appear on the command line.

> OK Jacko, you have my attention.
> I've seen you digging. You're on to something with Francis Gunnell.
> How the hell do you –
> If you will leave your papers lying around.

On cue, the ranked array of documents shears up from their huddle and cascades into the outstretched hand of the man called Jacko. He grins as he tucks them under the fold of his beard. Nobody but Alex should be able to even see those documents, let alone manipulate them. She turns back to the giant screen and speaks at it.

> OK, you like your theatrics and you've hacked the Strange, even though nobody's ever hacked it.
> Nobody's TALKED about hacking it.
> You have my attention. What about Mickey?
> He came to me yesterday. He wanted to find the source of those leaked emails. The ones that got him killed.

Alex snaps to attention, as though slapped. She glances at her glowheart, which is strobing red, then turns to Jacko.
'What the fuck are you talking about?'
Jacko looks at his watch. Points at the screen. Alex turns again, wishing she could ignore this silent ghost's imperious directions.

> Should be any minute now.
> What are you talking – look, would you please stop doing that to everything I say?
> Three, two – there we go.

Another figure manifests right next to Alex. It's standing with its back to her, legs vanishing into the coffee table, where three mugs of tea still stand uncleared. This new ghost is green and near-transparent. It's wearing a jade-green cagoule and a green woolly hat.

'Mickey?' she says.

A sketch of Mickey made from strokes of tarnished green, in the dark air of her sitting room.

'Alex?' says the sketch to the Mondrian print above the sofa.

It can't see her. This is playback, not a conversation. Help me, Ally-Wan Kenobi, you're my only hope. Alex shakes the weird from her head. Mickey's ghost ripples.

'Yes, Mickey,' she says, though she knows he won't answer.

'I've got nothing,' he says to the black, red and yellow blocks of the Mondrian. 'And you know, sorry for that and everything. I tried but. At this point all I can tell you is what I sniffed straight away, and that's the green: or no. It's not green any more, is it? Just that glow we keep receiving in return, keep needing more of. Sorry, I'm off on one. I need to —'

The sketch wipes its nose on its sleeve. It looks around and shivers, as though a wind is blowing through it.

'I need to go. They're on me, somehow. Keep coming forward from the Strange, no matter how I shift. Following me. I need to give you this thing that's been stuck in my head since they started. And it's this.'

The outline sets its heavy shoulders. There's something of the living man's persistent sorrow in this outline. Alex has always seen his vulnerability, his desperation to be liked. In spite of that she's treated him like shit. Maybe because of that.

'Follow the money, Alex. You've always had the knack. Follow the Coin.'

Blink: gone.

This is how Strangers do legacy. When they go Strange they can select a loved one to receive their pre-record when they die. Usually, they just say, *Sorry – I know you never understood why I stepped off the tracks.* And so forth. They try to explain why they entered the glowing shadows of the Strange and went dark on everyone they'd known. Usually, they fail. Usually, these black-box recordings simply horrify their survivors. Mothers, brothers and former lovers have come to dread the moment when their missing one will manifest from nowhere, speak haltingly, apologise for not having found the words, then vanish into the dark, a ghost descending.

'He's dead?' says Alex.

Silence. She turns to the screen where her question and Mickey's answer are waiting for her.

> He's dead?
> Somewhere between midnight and two a.m. Body found in a dumpster in Peckham. Every inch of him scoured with Cillit Bang.
> When the hell were you going to tell me this?
> You don't have a monopoly on sorrow.

'How fucking dar—'

> How fucking dar#

Alex's words are silenced. Not just on the screen but from her throat. How is that possible? Can this wizard Jacko hack her body, too? Is it the tattooed embeds on her throat?

> Mickey came to me yesterday to ask who hacked those mails. I held back on him. The only reason he was asking was to save your job and that wasn't worth betraying a confidence.

Alex stares at the screen. Mickey did that for her and got himself killed.

> I regret this now. I would talk to the source myself but he's no friend of mine. Ideally I'd give this intel to someone I trust. You'll have to do.

Alex wants to tell him to fuck himself but she doesn't dare test her vocal cords. Oh God: Mickey. Is it true, what she just saw?

> Mickey spoke up for you, in spite of the trouble you caused him. So. Those emails were lifted by a script-kiddie named Abul Ala Ayyash. Address in Crawley. I've put his details in your book. You want to know who did for Mickey? Go to Ayyash.

Alex reaches into the contacts on her mesh and flicks to *Ayyash, Abul Ala*. She'd gladly kick in the monstrous black glass of the screen, if there was the slightest chance it would have an effect.

'I have literally no idea,' she says, 'who you are.'

> I have literally no idea who you are.

Seems she's now permitted to speak. She continues.

> And if it's true that Mickey's dead –
> You saw for yourself.
> Oh, sure. Because everything I'm seeing at this point is completely, definitely real.

She turns to fake Jacko, who's assumed the most dickishly smug expression Alex has ever seen. Her every instinct is to punch this wanker in his doubtless hairy balls. She wants this to be the kind of clever bullshit she's a demon for cutting through. Then she could put this scary bastard back in his hole. But it isn't and she can't.

'*If* Mickey's dead,' she says to his avatar, 'it must have been the Gunnells who did it – or more probably their gangster mates. This wouldn't be the first time someone who got in their way has vanished. This is exactly what I was trying to prove when – oh shit—'

She takes two breaths. Prods a finger at Jacko's intangible chest. Tries again.

'I don't care about your hacker pal,' she says. 'It doesn't matter who passed those mails to Mickey. This is about Francis Gunnell and the thirty million pounds he wants from the government.'

She turns back to the screen. Jacko has already typed his reply.

> Take this to Gunnell, you think you'll get any different? Any case he's a fragment. You need to see the big picture. Ayyash.

She shudders at the thought of confronting Gunnell. She's no intention of going anywhere near that thug, either.

> You're saying I'm in danger?
> You put yourself in danger the second you read that email on air. Mickey, too. Now put it right. What I'm telling you is the only smart way to proceed. Go to Abul. Go to him now.

Alex reels. This cold, objectionable man has invaded her space with dreadful news. Now he's trying to use her shock to order her about. If she's going to get through this awfulness she needs to get out from under Gunnell, Corrigan, the Handyman and this self-satisfied bully Jacko. She looks from man to screen, then back again. Then she rips off her mesh and tosses it onto the sofa. Jacko and screen vanish. The room is dim and grey outside the Strange, but at least she's not under his boot. She takes three level breaths and mutters a mantra. Stepping outside the Strange is like leaving an airlock and step-ping into airless cold, but better this than have Jacko trying to rule her shit.

She checks the clock. It's nearly eight. Good. She can head out right away. She knows exactly where to go. She knows Lukaš' routines. It's Friday morning. Ever since Alex was his student, that's been the day for his open-door surgery. By now he'll have kissed goodbye to his slender Finnish wife as she serves organic granola to their three immaculate kids in their vast white kitchen. He'll be driving to work in some sleek German car, a baroque sonata on the sound system. By the time Alex gets into town he'll have been in his office for half an hour.

Alex goes to the kitchen for her bag. The little plastic Handy Frank is standing on the kitchen table, where it's stood since Harm took delivery of it yesterday. Alex picks it up. This cheery homunculus in its bright green dungarees is based on the real likeness of Frances Gunnell himself, though it's a hell of a lot more friendly than its model. It grins and winks at Alex, prompting a pang of guilt. If Harm hadn't found this thing, she'd never have known about the Handyman's campaign. Best she doesn't find it here when she returns from hospital. Alex stuffs the mannequin in her bag and composes a brief note for her wife.

Like she told Mickey, she's no intention of confronting Gunnell. The idea of it makes her skin crawl. For once in her life she's going to do the smart thing. The thing she should have done before she went to Corrigan. Rather than shoot off half-cocked again, and stumble into some even bigger mess, she's going to ask someone who'll know more about the situation than she does.

She returns to the sitting room and takes up her mesh. Hesitates before putting it back on. Mickey said it himself in his parting words: *Follow the Coin.* Alex needs to prove that Gunnell paid off Hardiman. It's the key to the whole thing – to the attack on Harm, to the thing she still can't quite believe has happened to Mickey. And the thing is, Alex happens to know the leading expert on the emotional economy and the Strange. Happens to know him very well. She'll go to him and find out how to end this thing before anyone else gets hurt.

She allows the mesh to slip itself into place along the brim of her hat. The room recolours and her glowheart surfaces, registering new-found certitude. The navigation slides in. No giant computer screen. No arrogant hippy by the window.

OK, good. Time for Alex to go back to uni.

GRAFT

Francis Gunnell heaves the duffel from the back of his van. He shoulders it, feeling its weight, and starts to trudge the two hundred yards from the dark railway arch to the London home of Susan Hardiman MP. He checks the dial of his father's mechanical wristwatch. Eight thirty, Friday morning. Seventy-two hours from the decision on the bail-out package. Three days left to save his business; his life. He's had it with the lad's route. The time for subtle is way past. This ends now.

It's always so. Each day he fights the same damn battle over again, scraping and scratching. Who knows where he finds the energy to carry on, at his age, when this greedy sinkhole of a world keeps sucking down every last damn thing he builds? Since his Jules passed, the business is all he's had. He's created something the country loves, embedded it on every high street. Sure, he's cut corners, broken legs. So what? He gives the people what they want. Yet always someone's trying to pull him down.

He stops where the street bends and gently slopes down an avenue of detached villas. This part of north London, you might as well be in some village on the South Downs. From here he can see Hardiman's house. A climbing rose twines around some iron railings that Francis can see, even from this distance, are modern repro. The originals would've been stripped out in the war, under cover of the government lie they'd be melted down for Spitfires.

He extracts his baccie pouch from the pocket of his all-weather jacket and rolls up, watching a pink-faced man jog painstakingly past Hardiman's front gate. Flabby on soft money, like every fucker on this street. Politicians, ad execs, bankers. Francis lights up, shakes the match and chucks it over the fence of the nearest house. These cunts don't know work. They think a spreadsheet is work. They think Emoticoin are a badge of worth. They never drove a four-ton through the night on their tod, slow and dumb from more sleepless nights than they can even count, to Folkestone, propping up eyelids with cigarettes, for two dozen pallets of roofing felt. Never loaded it solo at three a.m. with sweat pouring off them in the freezing air of the depot. All so they can have it set out on the forecourt by opening time, on a two-for-one special, bank holiday Friday.

Francis pulls the smoke until it scratches his lungs. He won't let them judge him. They can compete with him, they can undercut him. Maybe they'll break him. But they can't judge him. For all his success, the most important lesson Francis ever learned came during those years, driving through the pelting rain in the dead of night. It's this: don't get some other cunt to do it for you – get off your arse and fix it yourself.

He keeps watching the unchanging house front until his ciggie burns his finger. Then he flicks the butt and grinds it with the heel of his work boot. He spits in the gutter and checks his watch. Eight forty. Hardiman hasn't emerged but he's tired of waiting. He shoulders the duffel and heads for her house.

'Dad!'

Connor's voice comes from the direction of the van. Francis doesn't turn. Feet slap tarmac then a hand grabs his shoulder. He punches it away.

'Whoa, whoa, whoa!' Connor backs off, hands up. 'Easy, Dad.'

They face off between the bonnet of a driverless Merc and the rear hatch of a Volvo people carrier.

'This isn't your job, son,' Francis says at last.

'No? What's this "job", exactly?'

He reaches for the duffel. Francis heaves it further up his shoulder, out of reach. The contents clank.

'Jesus, Dad. You can't fix this the old way. This isn't some county council planning chair. Hardiman's a player.'

Francis tuts and heads off across the road towards Hardiman's pad. Connor chases after, pulling him back.

'Yeah?' says Francis.

He pulls his arm free. The butt of his hand strikes his son's face, scraping mesh against cheek.

'Ow, fuck!' shouts Connor.

'Lay hands on your dad, is it?'

Francis grabs the felt lapels of Connor's coat and heaves him up a notch. He has the edge on his lad, in height at least, though the boy could floor him if he had a mind to, with those muscles made on a gym bench, instead of by graft. They stare at each other, then catch the twinkle in each other's eyes.

'Fucksake,' says Francis, letting go.

They laugh and lean their backsides on the side panel of the Merc. Francis pulls out his pouch and starts to roll another ciggie. He offers it to the boy.

'Nah,' says Connor, 'you're good.'

Match scrapes matchbox. Both men look across the road at the dead exterior of Hardiman's mock-Tudor.

'Any luck at the Kubelick bitch's flat?' says Francis, shaking the match.

He sucks on his roll-up. Connor shakes his head.

'I was barely inside when her other half got home.'

'The brown girl? Did you see to her?'

'She walked right in on me.' Connor stands abruptly and walks off a couple of paces. Spins back round.

'She has nothing to do with this. You know that?'

Francis turns from the sight of his son turning soft. Or if he's honest, this is far from new.

'You didn't let her see you?' he says.

'I was careful. I think I really hurt her, Dad.'

'D'you find anything?'

'I keep telling you. This is the Sharing Twenties. People don't use paper any more, much less leave it lying about.'

'Well, what the fuck do you suggest?' says Francis, standing. 'We need *something* on that sarky cunt.'

'If it's her.'

'You kidding me?' says Francis, stepping towards the boy. 'You saw her go into Corrigan's office. You heard her on the radio.'

'She didn't even mention Frank's. It's Hardiman she was after. I think she's – decent. You had me tailing her for days – before any of that. This is your grudge, not mine.'

'Because she's fucking with my business.' He gets up in Connor's face. 'Why can't you just—'

Connor breaks away, takes a few steps up the hill. Frances raised the lad to be hard, but he can be such a lady's blouse he wants to shake him sometimes.

'Just my opinion,' mutters Connor.

Like a teenage child. Like this thing wasn't threatening everything. Never a shred of responsibility.

'Yeah?' says Francis to his back, 'well, let me tell you *my* opinion.'

But he doesn't have the words. His breath is getting the better of him like it does so often these days. Connor turns, ready for a fight; then clocks the expression on his father's face.

'You OK?' he says.

'It's just that—' Francis gathers himself, starts over. 'Listen, son. If this thing goes south, I want you to know—'

'Don't talk as if we've lost.'

'I want you to know Jules would have been proud of you.'

'Oh come on. What is this?'

Avoiding the concern on Connor's face, Francis scans the villa fronts.

'Look at these,' he says. 'Nice homes. You know? This is what it's all for. What we help people do.'

He looks hard into Connor's eyes. It's his son's turn to look away.

'That's what I want for you, son,' says Francis. 'What your ma would've wanted.'

'We live in a mansion.'

'But your *own* home. You don't want to stop with your old dad until you're feeding him through a tube. Your own home and – that someone special.'

There's some difficult silence as they avoid touching on the thing Connor knows Francis means, but never finds a way to say out loud – or tell Connor he's learned to be OK with it – or not OK, but still he'd prefer a son who's chosen one way or another, than no son at all.

Connor nods at the duffle.

'You got a shooter in there or what?'

Francis lets out a lungful of air, relieved and disappointed the moment's passed.

'Me? Nah. Just some tools and what have you.'

'Fucksake, Dad.'

'I'm only putting the scares on.'

'Here?' Connor gestures around, over-dramatic as ever.

'I need to hear it from her.'

'This isn't how we do things any more.'

'Oh, because we *outsource* our muscle? Because you're too squeamish to do it yourself?'

'I'm just saying, there are other ways.'

'I need to know who's putting the squeeze on Hardiman. Who's paying the Kubelick cunt to spoil us.'

'Are you listening to a thing I say?'

'Don't you—'

A door slams. They turn to see a glossy family emerge from the house opposite Hardiman's. Slender Mum, Dad with a clipped beard, two poppets. The lad is Spider-Man. Francis doesn't know who the girl is. Saturday breakfast chit-chat spills onto the street as they pile into the family Volvo. As the father opens the driver-side door, his eyes land on Francis and Connor standing in the road. On instinct Francis gives the trademark wink and thumbs-up. The man's face flickers with recognition as he climbs into the people-mover.

'Shit,' says Francis as the Volvo revs and starts zigzagging from its space.

'Told you,' says Connor. 'Broad daylight.'

As the Volvo passes, Spider-Boy waves through the rear window. Connor waves back. Francis glares. The car turns a bend. Father and son lean back onto the Merc. Francis rolls his third cigarette.

'You see that story yesterday?' says Francis, gesturing with his unlit ciggie.

Connor shrugs.

'About?'

'You know the one,' says Francis, lighting up. 'This kid. Fourteen, fifteen, something. Left home with no warning and started living on the street, dressed as Superman.'

'Daredevil.'

'So you do know.'

'Superman doesn't wear a facemask. Wouldn't work for coslife.' Connor points at his eyes, one at a time. 'Nowhere to fit the mesh.'

Francis looks his son in the eyes, which are rendered chalky by the veil of mesh.

'Did you see,' he says, picking tobacco from his teeth, 'what this lad did when his mother tracked him down? Spat in her face. Told her he didn't know her. Is that the cult you're into?'

Connor folds his arms and sighs.

'There are always people who take a thing too far. You can't judge the Strange by one story.'

'I can judge it's tearing families apart.'

'You're always telling me business is about relationships.'

'And?'

Connor shrugs again. The petulance all wrong on a big lad like him.

'And the Strange is where I make relationships.'

'With some beanpole dyke who wants to drag us under?'

'I'm just saying,' says Connor, 'we—'

He spots short. Francis follows his eyeline. Hardiman's at her porch with a gym bag. She nudges the front door shut with her hip. She's in weekend dress-down – plaid shirt and mum jeans – but her crash helmet of politician's hair still hovers over her head. Francis and Connor launch themselves from the side of the car and stride towards her. Hardiman's halfway out of her gate before she spots them.

'Mornin', Susan,' says Francis with a grin.

She stares wild for a moment then her chin goes up.

'For heaven's sake,' she says.

She shuts the gate, shooting a wary look up and down the road, and trots towards a carriage-green Range Rover at the kerb.

'Don't worry, Susan,' says Francis, tagging her as she bleeps the car open. 'No press here today. No Alex Kubelick to yank your chain.'

Hardiman stops sharply.

'This is completely inappropriate,' she hisses, waving her key. 'Do you want to scupper your bail-out?'

'Oh, *me* scupper it?'

Francis reaches for his duffel. Connor puts a hand on his arm.

'Dad—'

Francis glares.

'So,' says Hardiman, 'this is Mr Gunnell, junior. What a pleasure to meet you and how utterly amateurish of you both.'

Francis starts to unlace his duffel, fixing Hardiman with a stare.

'Get in the car,' he says to her flatly.

'Excuse me?' she says.

'Dad—' says Connor. 'The feller just now. The Volvo?'

Francis makes to speak again, but falters.

'How you could possibly imagine this kind of stunt would help your—' says Hardiman.

'I honestly suggest,' says Connor, studying his father's face, 'you shut it, Mrs Hardiman.'

'Ex*cuse* me?' she says.

Francis breathes through his nose like a bull in the arena.

'Both of you can it!' he shouts, dropping the duffel and shoving past his son, getting up close to the politician. 'I knew something had happened, last week, when your office stopped taking calls.'

'It really is easier to manage an impartial process without the beneficiary badgering my officials.'

'Then Kubelick did that stunt on air. That bullshit about a bribe.'

'Well,' says Hardiman, 'I'm glad we agree on that.'

'Shut the fuck up, you trumped-up bitch.'

'*What* did you say to me?'

'Dad—'

'Say that again, Mr Gunnell.'

'You think I don't know a stunt?' says Francis. 'You think I don't know when something's been cooked up to fuck with me?'

Connor grips his upper arm, hard. Even with her elevated hairdo, Hardiman barely comes up to Francis's top button, but she faces him down, fury spilling off her. Then her face softens.

'Mr Gunnell,' she says.

'What.'

'Let me tell you something.'

'All ears.'

'When I took the ministerial brief I was expecting opposition. Press gibes. Insults. Eggs, even. The thing I never prepared for was how much time and energy people put into constructing conspiracies to account for my every action. Conspiracies that always place themselves at the centre of the narrative.'

'Don't make me laugh.'

'In particular,' she says, 'it seems to be men who do this. Seriously, Francis. If you think at this point I have any more control over my destiny than you do, good luck. There is no conspiracy but there is also nothing you or I can do. Our fates were sealed the moment Ms Kubelick decided to read out that mail on air.'

'What in the name of shit does that mean?'

Hardiman steps to her Range Rover and opens the oversize door, eyeing Francis for further signs of threat. He doesn't make a move to stop her.

'I suggest,' she says as she steps up into the car, 'that you put your house in order. We all have a busy week ahead.'

'Hold it, hold it,' says Connor, limply. 'What *exactly* are you saying here?'

'Have you really not caught on?' she says. 'This isn't just me, or just you. The bail-out. This is about to become, as you would doubtless say, an utter shit storm.'

The profanity sounds especially filthy in her cut-glass vowels. In spite of himself, Francis smirks. Hardiman heaves the car door shut. The engine starts up, then the window eases open.

'Now,' she says through it. 'If you'll excuse me, I'm off to kick the living crap out of a punching bag. Good day. *Gym*.'

That last word was for the car.

The two men watch the four-by-four glide silently down the hill.

I PROMISE

'Should you not be at home with your – ah – partner? At such a time?'

'Wife,' says Alex. 'I'm fine.'

'And yet,' says Professor Lukaš Caron, leaning forward on his glass-top desk, 'that is what you would always say while heading into one of your—' He clears his throat. One of her meltdowns, he means. '—episodes.'

It's true. Three times Alex crashed while studying here, spectacularly and publicly. Three times Lukaš eased her to her feet, wary of her fragile state yet somehow fascinated by it. Probably she was just another cold case for his analytical intelligence – but there was a kind of affection there. Or perhaps that's wishful thinking. Child of a broken home, father substitute, blah, blah, blah.

Standing at his desk, Alex takes a couple of tempered breaths.

'I'm fine. I need to figure something out in a hurry and I thought you could help.'

Lukaš removes his half-moon glasses and leans back. His Danish chair accommodates the movement through silent articulations of its lumbar mechanism. The calm landscape of his brow bunches slightly. He's – what? forty-five? forty-six? – but already his smooth crease of hair is completely colourless.

'Yet that look in your eye,' he says. 'I know that look, I think.'

The piano partita that's been filling the air winds to a resolution.

'Glenn Gould,' says Alex to the silence.

Lukaš twitches one black eyebrow.

'Good,' he says.

That's as much approbation as he ever gives; all Alex ever used to seek.

'So you taught me something,' she says, taking a walk around the wide crescent of his office. 'Congratulations on the promotion, by the way.'

As newly anointed Director of the London School of Economics' Future Economy Unit, Lukaš has been upgraded from his former dingy hutch to this magnificent space overlooking Aldwych. Outside his sweep of windows, a grid of drones hovers the statutory eight metres above the ground, dangling ads at passers-by. Except one, that's flying way too low. It's not showing any ads, just hovering, level with Alex, bug eyes directed right at her.

Something in the room distracting her from the drone. Some kind of silent Encounter has begun beside her. The trace of a large man – a *huge* man – grabs a smaller figure and pushes him into a chair. Traces of suit jacket ripple as the giant straightens his bulk and reaches under his armpit. The man in the chair holds fleeting arms to shield his face. Both men vanish.

'Jesus!' she says, 'did you see that?'

Lukaš studies her from behind his desk.

'Perhaps you should sit down,' he says.

His head is uncovered – no mesh.

'Oh, no, of course you didn't see. Sorry, you must think I'm crazy. It was an Encounter. Trailer for some cop drama.'

'Ah.' Lukaš caps his fat chrome pen, places it on the paper. 'Perhaps you might care to—?' He mimes the lifting of a veil from his face. 'This might help reduce the volume of stimuli you're experiencing.'

Alex doesn't touch her mesh. RAGE and GRIEF pump in her glowheart but their levels are stable.

'You don't approve of the Strange,' she says.

'I disapprove of human desire being commoditised.'

'That's not what it is.'

She turns to the window and watches the drones shimmer in their silver ranks. The small drone is no longer there.

'If desire is the space between the wish and its fulfilment,' says Lukaš, 'then what space for desire, in this utopia? Your Strange is the soul's pornography. Instant, valueless gratification.'

Alex sighs and folds her arms. A rattle of blinkbait ads courses past the window.

'If I taught you anything,' says Lukaš, 'you should be suspicious of a structure where the benefits reside with a few, while the costs are societal.'

'Costs?' says Alex, turning to him – knowing she'll regret it. 'There are no costs to use the Strange.'

Lukaš dismisses that with a wave of his hand. He lifts a remote control from the glass surface of his desk.

'This new office,' he says, 'has a better acoustic, I think.'

More Gould starts up from speakers mounted around the walls in some optimal configuration.

'Goldbergs,' says Alex, after a few notes. 'The '55 recording. Quit trying to distract me.'

Her negatives are dipping again. Lukaš has managed to calm her with these abstractions, as he always can. He gestures at the cluster of chairs across from his desk.

'What *can* I do for you, Alex?'

Reluctant to show he's won, she keeps prowling the curve of windows, running a finger along the sill.

'Something's happened,' she says. 'I've made a mistake.'

'Go on.'

'You sound like a shrink.'

From a low table, Alex picks up a wooden carving of a bearded saint or king. Presumably Czech, like Lukaš. He stiffens to see her handle it but doesn't stop her. Weighing the statuette she tells the story of her on-air stunt. The email.

'As I said in my text message,' Lukaš interrupts, 'congratulations are due in return.'

'You might want to hold the praise,' she says.

She tells him about the complaint from the minister, the Monday deadline to pull up corroborating evidence. How Tom Causey 'kindly volunteered' to take her shifts while she's suspended. The quality of Lukaš' listening is all it ever was: non-judgemental, ruthlessly silent. At some point she sits down after all.

'Alex, this sounds genuinely serious. I'm sorry. I thought your interview a terrific piece of journalism. Tell me how I can help.'

A great shudder rattles through her. Where did *that* come from? GRIEF tips up again.

'It doesn't matter,' she says. 'What I'm trying to tell you is, the man who gave me that email died last night. He was—'

She can't speak it out loud. For a moment she can't decide whether to be sick or black out. It keeps hitting her fresh: Mickey is *dead*. No – shit, understatement of the millennium. He was beaten to a pulp and dumped naked in a Peckham skip, flesh seared with cleaning products. That's what the police confirmed when she finally got through to someone on the way here.

Uh oh – looks like the puking option is on the table again. She puts her head between her knees and swallows porridgy sick. Lukaš stands, pauses a moment, then pads across the cream carpet; stoops to place long fingers on her shoulder.

'How can I help?' he says again.

Alex gives him a long look before speaking. She hasn't earned this sympathy. What did she care for Mickey? Last time she saw him she shoved him away, then blithely used his material on air, like the callous cunt she evidently is. Truth be told she barely knew the guy. They had this transactional relationship is all; and not to speak ill of, but he was a creep. No way she'd be taking this on so hard if he hadn't come to visit her, after he died.

That's another thing: why did he choose *Alex* for his parting words?

'This man,' she says. 'Mickey. He left me a message. "Follow the money", he said.'

Lukaš perches on the edge of his desk.

'As a trained economist,' he says, 'that is hardly advice you need to hear.'

She smiles weakly, though that was a teacherly prompt, not a joke.

'But this bribe? It was paid in Coin. In Emoticoin.'

Lukaš stiffens, stands, and walks back around the desk.

'I went to talk to the man who paid it,' she says, 'but he ran rings around me. I can't prove a thing. This must be the first time in history someone's bribed a senior official inside a game. I need to prove it but I don't understand enough about how Emoticoin works.'

Lukaš is back in his chair. He stays silent a while, hands steepled against his nose. Alex knows to wait. At last he takes a deep breath and leans back.

'What is the most oft repeated lie,' he says, 'in the English language?'

'The most repeated? "I'll call you", probably?'

Lukaš reaches into his pocket and takes out a slim buckskin wallet, from which he draws a crisp twenty-pound note.

'Wow,' says Alex. 'Old skool.'

Lukaš tugs the note taut, making a snapping sound, and places it on the desktop, Queen-side up. He points to a spot at its bottom left.

'*I promise to pay the bearer,*' he reads, '*on demand.*'

With a lurch in her stomach, Alex realises her plea for help has resulted in a tutorial.

'Where does money come from?' says her teacher.

'Banks make it,' she says.

Lukaš nods, says nothing; waiting for more. And Alex is so damn ready to snap back into her student self. All it takes is Lukaš' calm authority. It's a simpler place; comforting, even. Is this the real reason she came here?

'Once upon a time,' she says, hearing the echo of Corrigan's weird tale from yesterday. 'Way back, people didn't need money.

We're talking tribes – tiny communities where everyone knew everyone. They all just kept track of whenever anybody owed a thing to anybody.'

'A mental ledger.'

'Held in the memory of the community. Like mental block-chain. The problem was, when they traded with other communities. They couldn't keep track. So when goods left the immediate tribe, they needed to get back something else of equal value in exchange.'

'A challenge we call——?'

Alex studies Lukaš' inquisitive face, its theatrically raised eyebrows.

Really? We're in seminar mode? Alex racks her memory banks.

'The – double coincidence of . . . wants?' she says.

Lukaš nods and she continues.

'Fast forward to, oh, three thousand BC or thereabouts, and you're getting to more centralised, proto states. Which means if my community shares out more goods than it takes in, that's OK. Now there's a central ledger manager or priest or whatever, who can keep track of what goes on between communities. And that means we don't need to barter all the time. We can keep on trading in the things we need, then settle up every now and then. And to do that we can start using standard units, like, like——'

'Bushels of wheat?' says Lukaš.

'Sure. And at some point people stopped bothering to keep the ledger of transactions and debts. They shifted to the tokens of exchange. The first currencies. Actual gold, for the longest time. Then, in the last few hundred years, we took a step away from the real. We replaced gold with paper dockets you could exchange for gold at a later stage, by taking it to the sovereign; except nobody did. They traded the dockets instead. Soon there was more money than gold; so we uncoupled its value from the metal stuff. The paper *became* the money. Then with computers and so on – we stopped needing paper.'

She slides the twenty back to Lukaš, who ignores it. He's waiting for her to complete a satisfactory answer. She sighs.

'Now, when you ask a bank for an advance of money – this thing we call *credit* – they basically invent some more money for you. Provided you're an OK risk and they haven't exceeded the capital restrictions of the central bank, they create some new money by making an electronic record. Everyone agrees this notional money exists because the financial system's set up to let the banks do this, and we all know they have deposits to draw on if they need to. Everything balances out. Except when it doesn't, at which point the system goes boom. Or rather, bust. So: currency 101. How is this relevant to Susan Hardiman and my friend being murdered?'

'And this process of making money is called?'

She sighs.

'Seignorage. As in *seignor* or lord, denoting the fact that creating money was once the preserve of the king.'

Lukaš nods.

'The lord. First the high priests, then the kings. Now, who? Who issues Emoticoin? Who is your lord, in this brave new artificial world you inhabit?'

He points at her mesh then pockets the twenty. She touches the mesh's fringe.

'Where is its value?' he says. 'Think. You just gave me an excellent tutorial on currency. Where, in your toy world, is the sovereign who promises to pay you on demand?'

'You're going to say, Sean Perce.'

Perce is CEO of Mondan, plc. Widely touted as the king of Britain's newest new economy. Boss of Dani Farr, who invented the Strange.

'A man who, I assure you,' says Lukaš, 'will give nothing in exchange for your Emoticoins. You rightly said: the only person with the power to make money was once the king. Now our king is whichever man has the power to make money.'

'Fancy aphorism.'

'Do you know the total pound value of all the Emoticoin currently being traded and spent in our economy?'

'I – no.'

'No. And neither does anyone else. Excepting Mr Perce.'

Perce is one of the corporate big-wigs Lukaš does lucrative consulting work for. This is why Alex has come to him. He's been telling Perce how to win at the new economy. So isn't it a little ironic for him to come on all Elyse Martingale over Emoticoin?

'Coin is pretend money,' she says. 'A way for Strangers to thank each other.'

'Your time and attention are scarce resources. Yet you give up this vast share of both to Mr Perce, who draws an increasing share of advertising revenue as a consequence. To the point where newspapers, broadcasters – important institutions – suffer. In return, he provides you with an electronic comfort blanket to muffle you from the world. He issues tiny electronic boons, this pretend money, yes, as you accurately called it. So why might people trade this stuff outside the game-world? Why would someone value Emoticoin?'

Alex shrugs. A tickle of unease is moving up her spine. DISTRACTION ticks up on her glowheart. Was it a mistake, with all this horror weighing in on her, to come back to school? Brilliant as he is, can Lukaš help her deal with Mickey's murder? Yet this is where her younger self would run whenever crisis struck. She sits back and lets his words wash over.

'The financial markets,' he says, 'have always traded in sentiment. Money equals mood. When the mood of the market is buoyant, values rise; when the mood is pessimistic, they fall. Investors care only what people *feel*. *Sentiment* is where value lies. So why,' Lukaš gives a short sharp cough, 'should they bother any more with all the complexity involved in tracking the actual supply of oil or gold or, or—'

'Pork bellies,' says Alex.

'Indeed. Why pork bellies? Instead, why not invest directly in the sentiment of a population?'

Lukaš stands and walks to his flipchart. Alex fidgets like an undergrad as he shapes overlapping circles and labels them *GOODS; COMMODITIES;* and *VALUE.* She checks the time on her mesh. However theoretically illuminating this lecture is, Mickey's still lying in a morgue.

'We're past the notion,' he says, 'that a healthy economy must be productive. Making things is a way to generate value, yes, for an immature economy. That is the way we did it for most of our history. But that was only the ladder we climbed to reach the point where value can be isolated from its physical substrate. The precious resources we expended creating goods were never required – just as the gold we used for coinage was only a temporary understudy for the *true* money lying invisible behind it. Now—'

Lukaš slices an 'X' through the circle marked GOODS, then caps the pen and replaces it in the little trough at the base of the flipchart.

'—now we do not trade in goods, but in sentiment alone.'

He walks over to stand behind Alex, uses his hands to make a crown around her head. She holds still and watches his fingers from the corners of her eyes. There's a fleck of green marker pen on his right thumb.

'The emotional centres of your brain,' he says, touching her skull on each side, just behind the temples. 'The limbic system, here. So productive. Amygdala. Gyrus.' His fingers trace the areas. 'They output such a wealth of signal, such rich source code. They generate the wealth of sentiment on which the market has always been founded – yet up to now it has been ineffable, lacking regular structure. Before we can trade a thing we must *commoditise* it. The unique qualities of your anger are of no concern of the market. They are a barrier to trade. Before it can have value, your rage needs to look precisely the same as my rage, as everyone else's rage.'

He removes his fingertips from the sides of her head and returns to his desk.

'It took Ms Farr,' he says, pinching his trousers at the knees to sit, 'to quantify emotions; measure their flow in real time and translate them into tradable commodities. That is why Mr Perce is seizing ownership of large sections of our economy; though as yet nobody has woken up to this.'

Nobody apart from Professor Lukaš Caron, it seems.

'You asked me,' he says, 'is Emoticoin real money? I say in return, people spend it on real goods. And of course – what is money? In part, an accepted medium of exchange. Also a thing that can retain its value. In which case, yes – why should Emoticoin not be money? Why not abandon bank accounts and cards, when fraud and identity theft are so endemic? Why not use a secure token that knows its owner from her biometric fingerprint? Money that will accept no other owner until she tells it to?'

Alex hunches forward. Lukaš is giving her exactly what she asked for but it's leaving her nauseous and exhausted. Because Mickey's dead? Because she fears she's to blame? Yes, sure, but there's something else. Something in the way Lukaš stepped up to his imaginary lectern like it's his god-given right to orate, and hers to listen. Like Corrigan did yesterday.

These men are maybe not so different. Lukaš is so cosied up with his claque of cold-eyed white male entrepreneurs, he uses the word *disruption* seven times before breakfast. He gets paid ten grand a pop to deliver just this kind of spiel in the upstairs rooms of Hoxton restaurants.

Lukaš has paused, usually a sign he's about to pivot to a Key Message.

'Most importantly,' he says, 'if Ms Hardiman received a sum in Coin, neither you nor I nor anyone else will ever know where it came from. Not *ever*.'

Ah. The delayed punchline. Alex's focus comes zooming back to focus square on Lukaš. This is how his lectures work – first the long winding arc, where he casts a sweep over the macroeconomic landscape, then a pause, and in the final sentence, one clean, clear point placed in the listener's hand. He could have said that ten minutes back, if he wasn't Lukaš.

'You want incontrovertible evidence,' says Lukaš, 'that this illicit payment has been made. You cannot. This is not the banking system. There is no central register to track exchange of Emoticoin. Each payment is a private thing, between software algae living in your mesh, my watch. Even Ms Farr could not tell you who paid what to whom, or when. All she sees are the broad tides of exchange.'

It makes sense. Coin's the perfect medium for bribing a politician. Secret, invisible. This might actually be smart.

Lukaš looks ostentatiously at his watch.

'Now,' he says, 'I don't wish to be rude, but . . .'

Alex nods. Her time's up. *It is no longer for me to teach you*, Lukaš used to say as he dismissed his students from a seminar. *It is for you to look at this problem and ask: Where do these incentives lie? When you have answered that question, you will be an economist. Until then there is little more I can do for you.*

Alex stands. Question answered, yes – but no solutions.

'Before you go——?' says Lukaš, looking up from his desk with the shy smile he affects when asking for something.

'Yes,' says Alex, rubbing her face to bring herself back to the world. 'Yes, I spoke to Siobhán before she sent me home. We—'

She stops mid-flow. Directly over Lukaš' shoulder, standing beneath an abstract canvas of white and cream swooshes, stands the ghost-man named Jacko. He's giving her this ultra-significant look and wiggling his eyebrows in a way that would make her laugh in any other situation.

'Yes?' prompts Lukaš.

Alex snaps back to the world.

'Sorry, yes. She may have a spot for you Monday, between seven and eight. It won't be me though, because – obviously. She'll be in touch with your publicist or whatever.'

Lukaš nods and creases his face sympathetically.

'That's kind of you, Alex,' he says. 'I do hesitate to ask at a difficult time for you, but – well.'

Behind him, the ghost of Jacko mouths a word, then another. Alex frowns to tell him she doesn't understand. He mouths the words again.

'And I fear,' says Lukaš, 'I have not been a great deal of assistance?'

Jacko mouths the words a third time.

ABUL. That's the first one. Abul Ala Ayyash. The hacker Jacko told her to follow. The one who gave Mickey the emails. And the second word – oh. It's *DANGER*.

Alex gives Jacko the slightest of nods. He nods back and vanishes. Lukaš is peering at Alex with concern.

'No,' says Alex, staring at the space where Jacko was. 'No. I actually think you have.'

A THOMASSON

Standing on the rusted gantry, ocean seething 100 metres below his feet, Jon Mangan pauses to check his numbers. He's been doing this once an hour since the numbers started mysteriously ramping up three weeks ago. Sure enough, his status shows up fat with the LOVE of another ten thousand Strangers.

Where are they coming from? Jon's under no illusions about his position on the cosmic ladder of celebrity. He's spent his life anatomising the cult of fame, gained a modest following for his quirky output. A year ago, he was running a steady 800,000 follows. Middling-good for a fifty-something artist-cum-cultural-commentator but nowhere near big league. Then his numbers started to rocket overnight. The mood of his followers shifted from a mish-mash of INTEREST, TRUST and ANTICIPATION to all-out LOVE. He keeps wondering if they're mistaking him for some hot new vlogger with a similar name.

No time to puzzle this now: he has a shoot to finish. He wipes his mesh dry and strides to the centre of the giant 'H' painted on the rickety platform that serves as Seatopia's helipad. He sends up Trudy, his trusty panorama drone, to record the piece-to-camera. She unlatches herself from the charging station and whips into the air, taking a flattering angle above Jon's eyeline. He puts on his game face – the amused frown that's become his trademark – and starts his PTC.

'A *Thomasson*,' he says in his mic voice, 'is a structure that no longer serves a purpose, but has somehow been preserved as part of the built environment. You see Thomassons everywhere—'

Here he'll run photos of stairways to nowhere, mid-air doors on the sides of buildings, the pillars of unfinished flyovers.

'—and this evocative category of architectural remnant has become accepted as a form of accidental urban art. They picked up the name "Thomassons" a couple of decades back, in honour of Gary Thomasson, a big-hitting US baseball player who in 1980 was traded to Tokyo's Yomiuri Giants for a record fee.'

Here Jon'll fly in archive footage from Thomasson's career, plus some zany Japanicana of the era. He loves stitching together these cascading tapestries. Post-production's one of the few places these days he gets to create actual visual artworks. True, his show is populist trash, but nothing and no one will stop him treating it as art.

He takes a walk around the helipad, using hand gestures to punctuate his narration. Trudy keeps a bead. The pressure of the chilly east wind keeps trying to slide him across the plate-metal floor.

'Sadly for Thomasson, it was at this point he started hitting wide – or not at all. He was coming close to the Nippon League strike-out record when a knee injury took him out of play for good. He was benched. Functionless. An expensive, useless relic.'

Jon stops and wrinkles his expression to maximum snark.

'Just like . . .'

He throws his arms wide. On cue, Trudy shoots up and back until she takes in the whole concrete platform – its massive tubular legs and the limitless expanse of turbulent sea surrounding it. Jon will be a tiny speck, barely visible at the centre of the helipad.

'. . . this beautiful, ugly, pointless concrete monster!'

This wraparound shot will look awesome on a mesh – especially once Jon has tarted up the grey-greens of the sea and the wild northern sky. He stands in place a few seconds to give himself a cut point, then says 'OK, scene' as though he's actually talking to someone. Trudy reels herself back to the charging station, where she wiggles her rear into place and powers down. Jon does a level check then trudges over to pick up the heavy charging block, all four drones attached, and lug it through the rusty door into relative warmth. Christ, how he yearns for a best boy to carry the kit around.

Just eighteen months back, his Channel 4 show, *Mr Mangan's Mythmakers,* was doing thirteen eps a year. In it, he exposed the artists, tricksters, moguls and fools behind a string of modern myths. He had a team of researchers. The crew totalled sixty at peak. Now, with advertisers fleeing to experiential platforms, nobody much has an actual TV show. Jon sure as shit doesn't. Today anyone can make and transmit content. What it means in reality – even for a high-end B-lister like Jon – is that the only person involved in making his show is him. He's putting out the same show format – though now it's called *MYTHIC* – but on 1/60th of the manpower. Plus he has to do it in VR; or whatever the cool kids call it these days. Long time since Jon was one of them.

He hurries down slimy spiral stairs to the main platform level. This is where the nerds of the Cockaigne free-data collective have their mess room; where they've agreed to let him do his vox-pops.

Cockaigne. Through the eight months Jon's spent hunting this invisible crew of anti-state hackers, they've developed a kind of cult status, as has their leader, the infamous Hairy Jacko. Now at last Jon's wangled an invitation, he's struggling not to be disappointed by the dingy reality of their rusting hulk of a North Sea base. And the hackers themselves have turned out to be just the kind of pedantic, self-important – not to say malodorous – counter-culture fellow-travellers you find at any art happening in the Mission District. After twenty-four hours he's yet to get anything solid from the tight-lipped techies – at least nothing on the central subject of his film, the mysterious tech rebel known as Hairy Jacko. Without Jacko, there's nothing here but a bunch of sullen punks and limited shower facilities. It took four months to negotiate this visit and he didn't come here expecting these guys to spill the beans on their super-secret capo; but he'd hoped he could at least rile someone sufficiently to drop a provocative hint or two about Jacko. Maybe even something punchy enough to use as blinkbait. He needs to pull at least another 100,000 views, or he risks losing his sponsor. Though who knows, with all these new Strangers suddenly in LOVE with him? Maybe now his next audience will be in the millions. He wishes he could believe those stats but they just seem hokey.

Either way, he needs to get his final interviews in the can asap. The four hours of grimy twilight they call 'day' out here are almost over. At four on the dot the hire chopper that's eaten most of this month's budget will arrive to carry him back to Felixstowe.

At the bottom of the spiral stairs, Jon feels his way along the damp corridor with a hand on the studded iron plate of the wall. As he pushes into the mess room, light streams over him. The steamy murk turns the lenses of his specs solid white. He removes his glasses, puts the charging rack down on a blurry metal cabinet just inside the door, and wipes his glasses on his T-shirt. He's too short-sighted to see the faces of the hackers but the ripple of giggles is surely directed his way. Given that he's the artist celeb, and the rabble in here nerds, it's ironic he should feel like the class dweeb walking into prom.

This is where the hackers gather to eat. It's also the 24/7 hub for an overlapping racket of coding projects. The sweaty air and rusty ill-finished room feel super-familiar to Jon. Twenty or more young men and women in the uniforms of a hodgepodge of counter-culture tribes, plus at least as many computing devices, piled across tatty sofas and folding chairs. Three or four of them are wearing the full-head pig masks that are the network's brand marque. Jon smiles to see tacked to the wall a shitty repro of his own posterised Elyse Martingale print from 1998. *Or we shall route around it.* The hackers crawl over each other, completing and collaborating, passionate to create things as good as they possibly can be. This is all too familiar. These kids don't look like outlaws. They look like artists.

A husky thirty-something guy in a Tintin T-shirt looks up from his crablet and notices Jon at the doorway. He hops up nimbly as he can and shakes Jon energetically by the hand.

'I'm Colin,' he says, as though Jon's meant to know who that is. 'So,' he goes on, conspiratorial, 'I heard why you're with us. You may be interested to know Jacko is here. Now.'

Jon's heart begins a frantic BPM. Holy fuck, he's about to get the scoop of a lifetime. Down by his side, the fingers of his left hand twitch to start his mesh recording. The quality's never as good as from camera drones, but for something like this, who gives a shit?

'Here?' he says. 'On Seatopia? When did he land?'

This Colin person frowns and looks slowly around the mess room. Attention is moving away from screens and onto him.

'He's been here a while in fact,' says Colin carefully.

He closes in on Jon and whispers in his ear in a wave of coffee breath.

'In fact, he's in this room. Right now. As we speak.'

Colin steps back grinning, patently delighted at Jon's astonished staring round the room.

Seatopia's origin story was written early in the new millennium by a clique of anarchist-crypto nerds, though the structure dates back to the Second World War. It stands on two massive concrete legs in a section of deep ocean eleven kilometres from the East Anglian coast; one of a series of free-standing fortress platforms put up by the British to defend against attack from the North Sea. The military abandoned it in the fifties, after which it was occupied by a sporadic succession of smugglers, pirate radio stations and survivalists – all taking advantage of its position just outside British territorial waters. The first cypherpunks moved in around 2006, by which point the base had been standing empty for nearly a decade. Right away they began to restore the rotting hulk to a habitable base with reliable power generation. Each of them must have had their reasons for wanting to live outside the reach of the

UK authorities, but they shared a single purpose in building Seatopia. Their ambition was equal parts idealistic and commercial: they were setting up a data haven.

The platform stands above the sea on two fat tubular legs, each twenty metres in diameter. The right leg contains the Cockaigne crew's sleeping quarters. The left is packed with five storeys of server racks, linked by a living system of Ethernet cables and flashing router boxes. A system of generators and backup generators and backup-backup generators powers the data centre round the clock. A system of pipes keeps seawater running through the heat transmission panels surrounding the machines, sucking out their infernal heat and spewing it into the sea where it can warm the fish. A massive snake of fibre-optics runs out of the leg below sea level, across the ocean bed, from where it comes ashore at Harwich. Another cable heads the opposite way, towards other hubs on the continent of Europe. The machines chatter constantly in their cells, receiving and transmitting gigabit flows of data more tightly encrypted than the Pentagon. The Seatopians have no idea what the data is, or whose it is, or whether any of it's remotely legal. That's the whole point. Information should be free, whatever the cost – whoever gains, be it anarchist hackers, rogue nations, drug lords, child pornographers or assassination networks. Thanks to Cockaigne, which took over Seatopia when it was founded some time in the mid-2010s, anyone in the world can now enjoy total freedom from surveillance, for a modest payment in any of fifteen encrypted digital currencies.

Everyone in the mess room is by now laughing openly at Jon. Including, he's sorry to see, Suze – the cute girl with the piercings and old-style ink tattoos who he had a roll with last night. Her lean, grubby body and her greasy ginger hair put him in mind of a vixen, as did the heady musk she'd acquired over three months' voluntary exile on this station. Now her face is curled in an ugly cackle.

Colin puts his arm around Jon's shoulder and nods at the table by the serving hatch, where cereals, tea and coffee are kept. A muscular lad with a nose-ring and a leather waistcoat hops off the table and gestures with a ringmaster's sweep of the arm. There are suppressed snorts of laughter. Suze has her head cocked back and is rolling her tongue behind her lower lip, staring at Jon in amused defiance. He looks at the breakfast serving table. It's exactly as you'd expect: a chaos of spilled sugar and caked Shreddies stuck to ancient Formica. Strung all over the wall above the table are strands of bunting made from banknotes, each cut diagonally in half in zig-zag lines. Banknotes of all countries – presumably those of Seatopia's resident hackers. Slices of cut-up credit card.

'This is the altar,' says Colin from behind Jon's shoulder, 'where we each make our sacrifice when we arrive. We cut the cord that shackles us to the enemy.'

He goes over to the table and picks up a giant pair of pinking scissors on a length of chain. The other end of the chain is attached to the neck of a life-size mannequin of a man, dressed in a black business suit, white shirt and black tie. The mannequin's wearing the pig mask. On top of the mask is an unkempt brown wig. Around its bottom is an ill-matched black fake beard. Pinned to its chest is a handwritten label: JACKO. Jon's cheeks are hot – and not because of the steamy air of the room.

'Yes, great,' he says. 'Mock the ageing non-techie.'

Colin's grin is replaced by bewilderment.

'No mockery intended,' he says, letting the shears dangle. 'I happen to be very interested in your work. I was hoping you might admire this little bit of fakery. You came here to learn about Jacko? Well.' Colin waves his hand at the cash bunting. 'Here's what he taught us. *Money is control. Freedom is its absence. Cut the cord.*'

The whole room's watching Jon with earnest intent. He's no idea whether this is wind-up or sincerity but it's not a great set-up for vox-pops. As he opens his mouth to speak, the door bursts open behind him.

'He's coming!' screams the gothy girl at the door.

Her boots clatter away and up the stairs to the helipad. After a beat, the whole room's on its feet and bundling out into the corridor. Jon's carried along by the sweaty jostle. He looks back along the hallway, which is crammed with overexcited hackers heading up. His camera drones are back in the mess room. He summons Esther, the smallest and nimblest. She catches up as he's manhandled up the spiral stairs.

On the helipad, the afternoon wind is up. It bites through the technical fibre of Jon's jacket and pushes through his teeth, leaving a tang of salt. He joins the milling cluster of Cockaigne members at what he estimates to be the south-west corner of the helipad. Easily forty of them – perhaps the whole crew. He follows their gaze through the clouds and spray towards a grey-pink glow on the horizon.

Something is approaching. Something large and indistinct against the North Sea skyscape.

After the wind-up downstairs, Jon's trying hard not to be excited. When he was young, he called himself an artist. He believed the way to make art real was to make things happen in the physical world. After a while, it stopped being art and became something different. But being here in this moment? Having the nous to track down Jacko? That's what art is, now.

The grey shape approaches. It's maybe a kilometre off. Jon screws up his eyes. Even through the whipping spray penetrating his mesh, this doesn't look like any kind of aircraft. He glances to his right to check that Esther's recording. She is. He pulls up a video window on his mesh to monitor her feed. It's blank. Black. He looks up to Esther. Her LEDs show *ON* and *RECORD* – but the feed is dead.

He spots Colin a couple of bodies away and shoulders over to tap him on the shoulder. Colin turns wild eyes on him.

'I've got no picture,' says Jon, raising his voice against the wind. 'My drone – she's getting nothing.'

He immediately regrets using the female pronoun. Colin looks blankly at him a moment, then turns back to gaze up at the milling cloud. It's two hundred metres away now.

'That's because,' he says, 'her camera's pointed at Hairy Jacko.'

SWING A CAT

'I'm sorry,' says the skinny Asian lad. 'I don't know why I did it.'

He blurts this out within three seconds of opening the door. He barely has time to clock Alex standing in the porch and he's apologising. For what?

This scruffy-haired teenager in a metal-band shirt looks out of place on the threshold of the stuffy Edwardian terrace. Its hallway's tiled in busy black-and-white chequers, walls blank white, hall table straight from Handy Frank's. It has the air of a private clinic.

The boy squints at the air around Alex's head. She turns to see what he's looking at but there's nothing.

'O–kay,' she says. 'Apology accepted, I guess?'

The boy blinks at her, then at her chest, then his eyes plummet to her shoes. There's a dapple of bum fluff on his upper lip. He's a scrawny seventeen at most. She floats the contact card into her field of vision.

'I'm looking for an Abul Ala Ayyash?' she says.

The boy says nothing. A woman's voice comes from the rear of the house, riding on cooking smells, speaking maybe Arabic. The first word is *Abul*. The kid gives Alex a sheepish look and turns to shout back in the same language. Then he steps out into the porch with her, setting the door to. The shrubby front garden is shaded from street light by walls of privet.

'Are we live?' says the kid, still looking around.

Alex twigs. He thinks she's filming this. He must know her vlog. But why would he think she's door-stepping *him*?

'You're Abul,' she says.

'What are you using?' he whispers. 'Mesh? Implants?'

'Not recording,' says Alex, though of course she is. Everything's recorded in the Strange. 'You gave Mickey Gallant two emails. Now he's dead.'

The kid's eyes all but pop out of his skull.

'Not here,' he says.

The robot cat furls between Alex's calves. It's black and lean, its movements fluid. It gazes up at her with blank silver eyes then skulks into the humming darkness beneath the desk.

'She's called Elyse,' says Abul.

'I've never seen one move so smoothly,' says Alex.

'Late model Samsung. I got her in exchange for – some work. Then modified her some.'

Alex surveys the multiple screens and keyboards on Abul's desktop, the stacks of hardware on the shelves above. Everything arranged by size and tagged with colour-coded strips of tape. Alex's mesh ticks off brands and prices where it can. Even this comes to over fifty grand.

'Looks like you earn quite a bit from your – work?' she says.

Abul sits at the desk. Alex jumps as something chitinous scuttles out from under the desk and clatters up his leg. It's a crablet, though not one of the smooth consumer models. It looks like something from an HR Giger nightmare.

'Freelance mostly,' he mutters. 'I'm going to disable location on your mesh.'

'Oh, sure. OK. I suppose.'

Abul grunts in acknowledgement and fiddles with a homespun device, using his long legs to swivel his chair from side to side. Back downstairs when Alex mentioned Mickey, he clicked into a focused, somehow adult mode. He smuggled her past the voices of his mum and dad with the polite insistence of a close protection officer, up to his little bedroom. Like the hallway downstairs, this room is fitted out like some halfway house, in cheap self-assemblers. Now he's up here, Abul's reverted to 110 per cent teenager. He hasn't looked once at Alex. She sits on the neatly made brown covers of the bed. Abul's looking the other way but the muscles in the back of his neck tighten.

After a moment, he hops up and crab-walks to her. Without meeting her eye he lowers a lanyard round her neck. Dangling from it is a credit-card sized circuit with two red wires attached. Each wire ends in a plasticky sausage with a clawed opening like the mouth of a hookworm. With a slight cough Abul reaches in to fix these tiny black mouths to points on her collarbone. He's careful not to touch her skin. The second red worm goes onto the head of her dragon. He steps back.

'That's your geolocation fascia,' he says, still not looking at her. 'The blanker cheats it. It puts you at randomly different coordinates. Everything else will work as normal.'

'OK. Thank you.'

'But if you come near a Stranger they'll still ID you by proximity.'

'Got it, chief,' says Alex.

She pats the bed beside her. Abul scuttles back to the safety of his desk and wakes his screen.

'When you answered the door,' she says to his back, 'you apologised. But not because of what happened to Mickey. You were surprised when I mentioned him.'

Abul types. Alex detects a flowery scent. Violets? This has to be the least smelly teenage boy's bedroom on the planet. Not that Alex has much experience of teenage boys' bedrooms – not since a few early disasters.

'And,' she says, 'when I told you Mickey was dead, you knew I didn't mean natural causes.'

Abul stops typing. He turns slowly and looks directly into Alex's eyes for the first time since he hustled her up here. His eyes are wide and pecan-brown. He has a sweet, anxious face.

'I'm really very excited to meet you,' he says. 'You're one of my top twelve anti-corporate journalists.'

He speaks in a stop-start rush, like a barrel striking an occasional rock as it rolls down a hill.

'I am?' says Alex. 'Top twelve? Well, thank you. I guess.'

'Actually, specifically you're my number seven, but you need to understand how weird this is. No disrespect but you're not gifted and there's no way you could trace those mails to me. So somebody must be naming *names*. And that's—'

He comes to a stop, breathing hard. Alex studies his face.

'It's a betrayal of your privacy,' she says.

Silence back. He won't look at her.

'OK,' says Alex. 'OK, yes, somebody gave me your name. He called himself Jacko.'

'Bullshit,' says Abul. 'Jacko's not real.'

Alex blinks at him. Even she's questioning whether that crackpot half hour was real, when Jacko materialised in her life. Certainly Harmony thinks she's making the whole thing up. Half an hour back, when Alex was following the shifting path to Abul's house, Harm rang.

'I just got home,' she said. 'From the *hospital*, remember? And what do I find? Someone's smashed my favourite Indian light. With a *rounders bat*? And I mean – where even are you?'

In a flurry, Alex described the giant vintage computer screen, the blue man, Mickey's ghostly farewell. She tried to get across the urgency of seeing Abul. The nearness of danger.

'Jesus,' said Harm, 'you have stopped taking the meds.'

'This wasn't a hallucination. It was so unreal I can't describe.'

'How else,' said Harmony, 'would you describe a hallucination?'

'These are the emails.'

Alex sits up. With lightning keystrokes Abul tosses windows onto his big flat megalith of a screen. She gets up and leans over his shoulder. The blocker device swings on its lanyard. Each window contains an email. Alex hunts for the ones to Susan Hardiman's office but all she can see are jargon-heavy messages about encryption, data.

'The Hardiman emails,' says Abul, 'were part of a cache we pulled from a man who worked for a security business called Occidental Data Partnerships.'

Alex notes the 'we' but doesn't pick him up on it. She pulls up a plastic stool to sit beside him.

'You're sure this is OK?' she says.

Abul's fingers assume a holding pattern over the keyboard. He turns to her in surprise.

'Of course. I can trust you. You're Alex Kubelick.'

Alex struggles to know what to say to that.

'Yes,' she manages at last. 'I am.'

Abul goes back to punching up windows.

'There wasn't much useful information in these emails,' he says in his lurching monotone, 'though they helped us break into Occidental yesterday.'

'The demo in Swindon,' says Alex. 'That was on our news bulletin. Didn't someone die?'

Abul pauses a moment, then his lean fingers return the keyboard. A cluster of emails hops forward. Alex slides her stool in, making Abul stiffen. All the mails are from Sam Corrigan. Alex sees the one she read out on-air and lets out a breath.

'It's true,' she says. 'You're the source.'

'Most of the mails were quite boring. But the ones from Mrs Hardiman's constituency office were interesting because they sounded like they might be to do with official corruption. That's one of the things we look for.'

Again, 'we'.

'I thought they would be interesting for you which is why I gave them to Mr Gallant. I knew he feeds you stories.'

Alex sits back and studies Abul's profile. He works his screen, eyes darting between emails.

'How would you know that?' she says.

'I've just now done a search of yesterday's haul of emails and found more mails from Occidental that mention Ms Hardiman.

I'm afraid I haven't spent much time on these recent emails. I'm mostly looking for something else. Something – older.'

Is he trying to distract her?

'Seriously,' she says. 'How would you know Mickey and I work together?'

'I wanted you to do well in your new job. I like to see you do well.'

Something lands on the desk. Alex jumps to her feet but it's just the cat.

'*Someone at the door*,' says the cat in a posh female voice. '*Two men. Mesh.*'

The cat has no mouth but its head ducks and bobs as it speaks, as though forming words. From below, the doorbell chimes. Abul's mother shouts something from the kitchen. There's a banging of interior doors.

'Wait wait wait,' says Alex. 'This is—'

The cat sits by the screen and makes as though to wash itself.

'I can help you,' says Abul. 'With your compliance enquiry. My routing data prove those mails were sent from Corrigan to Hardiman's office. I can fake up datestamps when I send them to you so that it looks as though you had all this information before you went on air. When you show that to your colleagues you'll be in the clear.'

He's so pleased with himself. Alex rubs her temples.

'What? No, I don't care about the compliance thing. I need to know why Mickey was killed. Why Corrigan was bribing Hardiman. The answer has to be in these emails.'

Abul nods enthusiastically. He goes back to making windows dance upon the screen.

'I can help you, Alex. Yes, I can help you.'

Downstairs, the front door clicks open. There's a murmur of male voices.

'No, hold on,' says Alex. 'There you go again. How do you know about the compliance—?'

Her eyes have been distracted by the emails riding around Abul's screen. Now they land on the little terminal window sitting static at the bottom right. This is where Abul's been typing commands at super-speed. At the bottom of this window a command prompt awaits his next entry:

```
$thimblerig > _
```

The cat stands and arches its back.

'*Gun*,' it says evenly.

There's a shout from downstairs. Abul leaps to his feet, sending his chair wheeling back across the lino.

'Wait, stop!' says Alex. 'Thimblerig? Your user name is *Thimblerig*?'

'Something's happening,' says Abul.

A man cries out downstairs.

'Oh, shit,' says Alex. 'Thimblerig. That's the Handyman's name. You're the—'

'*Shots fired*,' intones the cat, at the exact moment a double blast sounds from downstairs.

There's a scream – a man's scream, from the gut – then another hammering shot. Abul tears open the door and runs onto the landing.

'*Abul*!' hisses Alex, scrambling to follow.

Out on the turn of the first-floor landing she grabs his arm. He glares at her in confusion. The front door's directly below their feet, hidden from view by the landing floor. Alex holds her mesh against her chin and tilts her head. She sees the ghost-forms of two men standing directly below. The cat was right: they're Strangers, or she wouldn't be seeing them through the floor. The men step further into the hall. Alex kneels, pulling Abul down by the arm. They peer through the banisters into the ground floor hallway. The top half of a man's body is splayed out there, arms forming a 'V' over the chequered tiles. His face is cherry-red pulp. Beyond him, a headscarfed woman appears in the doorway to the back of the house. She sees the man's body and stops short, then her eyes lift towards the front door and her hands go to her mouth.

Before she can complete a gasp, red powder explodes from her face and a boom sounds. She falls back limp, face a bloody wreck.

Abul half stands, starting to cry out. Alex clamps her hand over his mouth and puts all her weight into dragging him backwards in a crouching walk. As she wrestles him to the bedroom, her mesh shows one of the figures below walking forward towards the woman's body. His head comes into view through the banisters. It's double human size, smooth and bubble-white. As the full figure emerges she sees who it is.

Casper the Friendly Ghost.

Alex pushes Abul back through the bedroom door and toes it shut as silently as she can. She guides Abul to the bed where he sits obediently, then she hurries to the room's one window. Peering out through the plastic venetian blind she sees a little roof sloping below over the front porch. Could they climb onto it? Even if they did, there's a car parked directly outside the gate. At its wheel, someone in a helmet. Ant-Man?

'*They're on the stairs,*' says the cat, standing to alert on the desk.

Alex turns, and through the walls sees the traces of the men, making their way upstairs. She looks around, glowheart pumping, seeking an out. Could they hide in the little wardrobe? What use would that be? These aren't casual burglars.

'The hatch,' whispers Abul, using the stool to climb onto his desk.

He reaches up to open a loft hatch in the ceiling.

'No,' hisses Alex, 'we need to get *out*.'

'Precisely.'

He reaches a hand down. Alex, who's shit out of other options, takes the hand and lets him manhandle her onto the desk. She grabs the edge of the hatch and heaves herself up. Out on the landing a door opens. Alex turns to look. The men are searching rooms, starting with the bathroom at the rear.

'You're sure this works?' she whispers, indicating the blocker round her neck.

'Yes, yes,' says Abul, grappling her up.

This messy manoeuvre ends with his hands planted against her buttocks.

'Sorry,' he whispers, though he doesn't move his hands.

Alex scrambles onto the dusty plywood of the attic floor. It's pitch dark but there's a weird sense of space – wider than she'd expect. She swivels round to reach for Abul, who passes her the cat.

'Oh, for fuck's –' she whispers, tossing the cat into the dark of the attic.

She hears its feet scrabble for purchase. She reaches down again for Abul, who's squatting at the keyboard.

'Come *on*!' she says.

On the giant screen Abul hits the return key on a command:

```
$thimblerig > kill
```

it says.

'Kill who?' she says as she heaves him up.

Abul struggles up through the hatch. As soon as he's through, they slide it back into place.

'Oh,' he says. 'No, not kill *someone*. Kill the *data*.'

In the darkness, Alex's mesh kicks in, outlining the low attic space as it stretches out to her right. Her mesh must be getting this wrong. It's showing a room several times longer than Abul's house is wide.

'Come on,' he whispers, standing and brushing himself down.

By light from the cat's eyes he tiptoes along the impossibly extended attic. Since he hasn't yet walked into any walls, Alex follows, placing her feet with care. Looking down through the floor she sees the forms of the two men entering Abul's room and making a beeline for the desk. The computers. Casper's in the lead. The other one has a cape. Alex, Abul and the cat have left the bedroom well behind them. They must be over the next-door house.

Abul leans in to whisper to her.

'My group lives in a row of five houses,' he says. 'The attics were knocked together years back. There used to be a lot of illegals staying here on and off, when things got bad – the boats, the fences?'

'Sure, of course.'

She hadn't figured this out, but it makes sense. Abul is of Syrian origin. And his parents—

Again, she sees the woman's face replaced with an exploding ring of red. Not a replay from the Strange: her own brain screaming the memory.

'God, Abul, I'm so sorry. Your mum and dad.'

'What? No. That was Waleed and Manal. They were residents. Organisers.'

They've reached the end of the long empty space. Alex turns back to check on the men. They're still in Abul's room, poring over the computer.

'But they were good people,' says Abul.

She turns to see his frown picked out by light from the cat. That seriousness. That focus.

'Someone just walked into that house,' he says, 'and killed them.'

'It has to be the people who killed Mickey. They're looking for me.'

'No. For me. Or why come here?'

He squats down and puts his hand on another hatch. What he's saying makes sense. Those men made a beeline for his computer. Maybe this isn't to do with Mickey.

'Can you see any more of them?' he asks, pointing at the hatch. 'Inside this house?'

Alex looks down and scans.

'No Strangers, no,' she says.

Abul slides the hatch away. He pokes his head through, then turns to slide down his legs and lowers himself into the room. He's surprisingly nimble. The cat takes a sideways glance at Alex then jumps down into his arms. Alex lowers herself down after. Abul reaches up to help her. Which again seems to involve his hands all over her arse.

The empty room is a mirror of Abul's bedroom. The floral paper's been sliced from the walls, leaving jagged teeth along the skirting boards.

'Perhaps it's because of Mr Gallant,' says Abul. 'Perhaps because of Occidental Data Partnerships. Either way the information we need is in those emails.'

'But you just wiped your data,' she says.

'The data's in here,' he says, reaching down to pick up the cat, which furls in his arms.

'In your head?'

'No,' says Abul, holding out the cat. Its legs droop from either side of his hands. 'In here.'

The cat turns to look at Alex with aluminium eyes.

'*Time to go*,' it says.

CASH-FLOW CRISIS

Mr Ox grabs the chair one-handed. With a roar he hurls it at the face of his Vice President of Finance. It strikes the wall, exploding a framed photograph of the martyr Trump, then lands in a mess of glass, one leg bent sideways. Had Ms Okapi been present in reality, this would have harmed her severely.

Already that section of wall is decorated with seven or eight dents where items of office furniture were hurled at people's ghosts. It was only two months ago this office was redecorated. It is for the best Mr Ox conducts so few meetings with actual people present.

Ms Okapi's ghost hasn't moved from her power stance, hands on hips. She didn't flinch when the chair flew at her face. He admires this, but it is also evidence of her constant jostling after power.

'This report is unacceptable,' he says.

'The report,' says Ms Okapi, 'is the truth. In the current trading period, we have lost over fifty per cent of darknet trading – our highest-margin business stream. If you care to review my analysis you will see: the great majority of these losses are due to the actions of the Cockaigne group.'

Mr Ox picks up his 3D printer and smashes it onto its stand. Smashes it again. Again. The casing buckles. He smashes it down again. Metal and plastic gubbins tumble from a breach in its rear. He tosses it aside. It catches on its own cables and drops to the ground.

'Cockaigne!' he shouts. 'Cockaigne! If tell me, it is Googple who are eating your lunch – or even that pomeshany, Musk – I would fathom this. But a rag-tag army of schoolboys? This is who has killed our cash-cows?'

'As an operational matter, you should take that up with Mr Lemur.'

Mr Ox kicks the rubble of his printer into the corner of the room.

'I have done so,' he says. 'Believe me.'

Which reminds him: he must be sure to compensate Lemur's family for their loss. A new condominium in the Lebyazhy district should suffice.

He breathes hard, like his animal namesake. With the incompetent Lemur out of the way, the operation to squash the Cockaigne insects is under way. Mr Ox cannot understand how this has not already happened, when the client has given them a way to raise an army from air. Yet over and over, Mr Lemur failed to staunch the activities of that claque of online guerillas. Now, though, just today, the client has provided data on the locations and identities of several of Cockaigne's key personnel. To be fair to Mr Honey Badger, he has done an excellent job acting on this information, with very little time to prepare. Though it seems the Ayyash boy – Thimblerig – has evaded him.

Ms Okapi's voice draws him back to the room.

'Our Emoticoin reserves are holding out,' she says. 'It's the short-term revenue hole I wish to draw your attention to. For now, this is a cash-flow issue but the hole must be plugged before our capital reserves are depleted.'

'Depleted?'

Mr Ox moves over to the quarterly dashboard the woman has thrown onto his dark windows. He studies the projected revenues, profit and—

Bozhe moi.

'How long?' he says.

'Three weeks. Four. Revenue flows are volatile.'

Mr Ox screws his eyes tight and peruses the rows and columns. He is a fool for numbers, but any way he looks at it, Okapi is correct. If things continue as they are, the greatest partneka network in history will fall off a cliff within a month. How can this be, when he has followed every dictum of the great business gurus?

'When do you report to shareholders?' he says in a near mutter.

'Friday next week.'

'Very well,' he says, still not looking her way. 'And for now these data stay with us, yes?'

'Need-to-know, sir.'

'Very good.'

'Will that be all?'

He turns to the woman. Behind her power-dressing and over-elevated shoes, there is a sense of duty. She is the best of his C-suite team. He has long thought of her in terms of succession, in spite of her gender.

He nods. Her image starts to disperse.

'And Ms Okapi?' he says hurriedly.

The woman reappears, snippety-snap.

'Sir?'

'I apologise for my earlier breach of our Core Behaviours. As a senior leader I should set a better example. Kindly award yourself a compensatory settlement for my gross example of workplace bullying. What can I offer?'

'Now you mention it, sir, I have had my eye on the new Mondan Electron Mesh. The Platinum Prestige Edition.'

'Have Ms Pangolin order the top-end configuration. Express drone delivery.'

'Thank you, sir.'

Her image disperses fully. Mr Ox turns back to the window. The figures and charts have vanished with their creator, so he stares instead at the volatile graph formed by the ever-adapting skyline of Minsk. His plummeting numbers remain as an after-image. He may have dealt with the bulk of the threat presented by

Cockaigne, but too late. He no longer has time to rebuild his darknet revenues. The situation requires a vast injection of cash in a matter of days – at the latest– before the shareholder meeting next Friday. When it comes to their investments, Mr Ox's non-executives have less patience even than he.

Everything now depends on their completing Project Domino to the client's satisfaction. With that done, Occidental will receive a healthy capital inflow before next week is over. A 4 per cent commission on a billion dollars? That, as Mr Ox's father would say, is larger than the erection of a field mouse.

Here is Mr Ox's only remaining avenue. As Professor Margary Kramer says in her seminal *No is Not the Answer: Now What's the Question?* – 'No two ways around it, buster!'

The die is cast. The client shall win his – or her – billion-dollar bet next Monday. Mr Ox will receive his commission; and Mr Honey Badger his true deserts.

All shall be well.

LEAVE TO REMAIN

Everyone's dark. Every Cockaigne chatroom has gone post-apoc-
alypse. Thimblerig roots out the news. Police raid. Tip-offs. A
warning at the top of every thread:

DO NOT POST: COMPROMISED.

He doesn't know what to do. The others have vanished with
not even an encoded message to signal their path.

He's been in difficult situations before. In the past two days he's
seen three people die. He's been chased and shut up in a cupboard
and surrounded by corporate monsters. All though these trials
he's thought and acted clearly. This must have been something to
do with the release of adrenalin – the way it stimulates blood
glucose in the brain. Now though everything's different. What
he's feeling is actual panic – though nobody would know this to
look at him. He's retained his calm mask ever since he and Alex
Kubelick snuck out of the back of number 27 late last night and
made their way through back gardens and under a flyover and
over a stretch of floodlit shopping centre car park to the Holiday
Inn Express by the station.

The first thing Thimblerig did when they got to this hotel room
was have a pee. The second was to sit at the desk and plug his
crablet into the cat. He switched to headsup mode and set the
crablet over his face and hunted the boards for some trace of his
Cockaigne cohorts. The cat curled on his lap as he worked. Its

batteries warmed his legs. Alex Kubelick was clearly exasperated by his withdrawn silence but doesn't want to explain anything. He just wants to work out why he's been uprooted yet again from the life he's known.

Giving up on the Cockaigne boards he returns to the store of emails he hacked from Occidental Data Partnerships. He wishes he could return to the older emails and dig out connections between the corporate bully Doug Raynor and the chat persona *drainer.* The one who sold out his father. But that will have to wait. Last night he saw Waleed's dead body on the hall floor and Manal shot in the face. That was real. He knows what's real. Unlike Alex Kubelick he chooses not to coat his world in a comfort blanket of corporate content.

The experience keeps returning to him as he types. Each time the scene replays he sees some new detail he didn't notice at the time. The white bowl of the shooter's head-mask. The crown of blood drops that scattered around the doorframe as Manal was thrown back by the bullet. The more this happens the less these memories translate into recognisable symptoms of emotion. After a while none of it seems real. The death of those caring and attentive people apparently means less to Thimblerig than the fake scenarios of the Strange do to people like Alex. How can this be? Perhaps he's cold. Perhaps he's in what the self-help vlogs call shock. Never mind. Sitting mining data in this bland hotel room he's entered the clearest-headed analytic state of mind he's experienced in a long time. Never mind the neurological basis of this. It's useful.

On the inset video feed of his headsup he sees Alex sitting very still on the corner of the bed. She's thinking hard. He's glad she's there. There's something about the way she speaks to him compared to most adults or non-technical people in general. She uses a direct form of language he finds helpful. She doesn't address him as though being a hacker makes him somehow subnormal.

He made a stupid mistake when he let her see his Cockaigne handle on the screen. Thimblerig. It was a schoolboy error to use

it as an account name on his home network. Imagine if the police
or some corporate thug ever saw that. He wonders if that's going
through her mind as she sits in silence on the bed. Or is it her dead
friend Mickey Gallant?

She stands without looking at Thimblerig and vanishes into the
bathroom. The taps go on and Thimblerig hears her splashing
water. Then she starts making unpleasant choking noises. Only
when these ugly noises stop and the shower turns on does
Thimblerig activate the microcamera he earlier suctioned to the
light fitting at the top of the vanity mirror. He fills his field of
vision with the blueish image. Alex has her back to the camera as
she undoes the impractical number of buttons on her old-fashioned blouse. Impatient for the scene to fast forward Thimblerig
loosens the cord of his tracksuit bottoms.

This footage won't need much post-production. The hard light
of the bathroom works in his favour. Alex pulls off her light silk
top. Thimblerig feels in his backpack for tissues. As she steps out
of her narrow skirt and stockings and her loose silk knickers he
gets to work on himself. Her bottom is muscular and so so smooth
and pale. She leans over the bathtub to fiddle with the shower
settings. He wishes he'd placed the camera a little lower to get a
view between the tight curves of her thighs.

She steps into the shower and pulls the frosted glass screen across
the bath. Thimblerig pauses the recording. His thing goes soft.

After a few minutes the shower judders to a stop. Thimblerig
starts up the recording as Alex steps out. While she grabs for the
towel he has a perfect view of her lean wet body. Her freckled skin
sparkles like gold in the artificial light. She throws the towel over
her head and bends forward to dry her mat of red hair. The towel
obscures her body. All this shifting about is frustrating. Then she
moves the towel to savage her face dry. Her small breasts shaking
at the camera are enough to send him to a finish. Some kind of
relief surges through him but it's tinged with weirdness. He's not
so cold he doesn't realise Alex is in an unhappy state. He feels bad
for watching. Perhaps. Or bad because it should be him who's

sad. Again it claws at him: why does he feel nothing for Waleed and Manal?

He'd known them for years. They managed the row of houses for a wealthy and public-spirited importer named Mr Wassouf. They'd been doing this ever since he bought the properties in the late 2010s. That was when the situation turned severe for settled families. The two of them kept on looking after the houses as the people who lived there were gradually settled or returned. All except Thimblerig. He still has nowhere to be.

While Alex finishes drying Thimblerig cleans up with more tissues and a Wet Wipe. The cat watches unmoving as he wads the gunky tissues into a ball. He zips up and looks around for a bin where he can put the tissues. There isn't one. He unlatches the crablet from his face and lets it dangle from his neck. He looks around with increasing anxiety for somewhere to hide the soggy mess. His fingers are getting wet.

He reaches his free hand into his backpack. If he only had a plastic bag. His hand lands on rubber and he pulls out his scrunched-up pig mask. He looks between mask and tissues. The lock on the bathroom door clicks open. He shoves the tissues into the mask then pushes the mask into his backpack. As the bathroom door opens he throws the backpack onto the bed and sits back down at the desk. By the time Alex walks out of the bathroom with the towel wrapped round her he's latched the crablet over his face. He wipes his sticky hand on his jeans and watches Alex stride around the double bed to collect her hat and mesh from the side table. As she puts on the hat she glances at him. She can't tell whether he can see her through the crablet. He moves his fingers over the keyboard to make it look as though he's still at work.

Dressed only in hat and mesh and towel Alex moves to sit on the bed. Making space for herself she picks up the backpack and places it at the end of the bed where it teeters then falls. Thimblerig leaps up from his chair in a vain attempt to catch it. As it lands the pig mask flops out onto the floor. Alex leans over to scoop up the mask with a sharp look at Thimblerig. He sits back down. His

heart is thumping. She looks curiously at the pig mask then back
to him.

– OK, she says, so I guess you can see me?

She sits back on the bed and starts tossing and catching the
deflated pig-head. The towel rides up revealing bare thighs but
Thimblerig can only watch the mask as it rises and falls.

– Getting a good eyeful? she says.

She throws the mask higher. Thimblerig whimpers involuntarily but the tissues stay lodged inside as Alex catches it. She leans
forward to him.

– Right, she says. What I thought.

Thimblerig keeps up his silent fake-typing. Alex holds out the
crumpled mask.

— So you're one of them? she says.

When he fails to respond she takes hold of the mask's neck-
hole and makes as if to put it on.

– So, she says, if I wear this do I get to be a hacktivist too?

– Stop! shouts Thimblerig, ripping off his crablet.

Alex pauses in the act of lifting the mask to her head.

– Oh, she says, so it's OK for you guys to go masked but not us
mere mortals?

Thimblerig stares back. She shrugs and holds the mask out to
him by both ears. The wad of tissues drops onto the carpet with
a splat.

– Oh, sorry, she says, what's this?

She reaches to pick it up

– No! shouts Thimblerig.

She grabs the tissues.

– Ew, she says, this is all . . .

There's a pause. Abul's heart races. Alex drops the tissues.

– I'm getting dressed, she says wiping her hands.

Without looking at Thimblerig she vanishes into the bathroom.
He hears the splashing of water then silence. He doesn't use the
camera. From the floor the pig mask stares at him with a serene
grin. He kicks it into the corner. A creeping thought comes over

him – of unseen eyes spying on his every move. The sensation of is unfamiliar and unwelcome. He hasn't felt it since his last brush with the UK's Border Force. He's always thought he's smart enough to evade any surveillance. This new sensation is making him uneasy.

He returns to his emails. This isn't just to distract him from the creepy feeling he's getting from the pig mask. He needs to find something he can offer Alex – as apology but also to distract her.

Alex returns fully dressed. She sits on the bed and watches Abul stare into the crablet wrapped around his eyes. She clears her throat.

— OK, listen, she says. Jacko sent me to you because he said you had information that'd help me understand why Mickey Gallant died. But things are . . .

She stops. Stares at the hands she's winding in her lap.

– Look, she says, I'm not sure I want to be anywhere near you at this point. Sorry.

She looks at him. Looks away. He removes the crablet and lets it hang around his neck.

— I'll be fine, he says.

She gives him a sharp frown.

— You can't go back to that house, she says.

He shakes his head in agreement.

— The police will be there, he says. My equipment is incriminating. Even wiped. I need to stay out of sight.

— So where?

— All the data are inside the cat. I'm not going anywhere until I've solved this.

Alex gives him a long and level look. He wraps the crablet back around his face and watches her in a corner of the display. She watches him silently for a very long time. Then she takes a deep breath and speaks.

— You do know I have a bone to pick with you? she says.

Thimblerig frowns behind his crablet. Why can't she go? She said she would go. There's no conversation he wants to have with her.

— At some point, she says, we need to talk about the way you've treated me and my wife.

He keeps typing and staring into the display. On the feed Alex folds her arms. The way she calls that lady her 'wife' makes him uncomfortable. It's not that he doesn't like women. Or lesbians. He isn't a sexist. He dislikes the manosphere bullies as much as he does the feminazis. Anyone who thinks their type of person is better than another type. *All should be shared equally regardless of moiety* (© Elyse Martingale 1958).

Alex clears her throat.

— At some point, she says, I want to explain to you how it's made me feel.

Thimblerig swallows. There's nothing he can say at this moment. Nowhere he would less rather be than in the chair in front of Alex Kubelick. They both know what she's talking about. She's his biggest and most rewarding project. Her home address and email came from domain name records for her vlog. With these he hacked her social media. Her credit-card records he social engineered from an online retailer. Once he owned her he began his work. At first it was only jibes but when she stopped reacting even to rape threats he escalated. He created the Happy Handyman persona in October. That was just after her confrontation with the man who runs Handy Frank's. Quite soon after she had her breakdown or whatever you want to call it and shut down her vlog. Then things went quiet. At least until Thimblerig heard she'd got a job on the radio. Then he started to make things happen to her in the real world. At no point did he ever expect the actual Alex Kubelick to show up on his doorstep. Or rescue him from gunmen. Or undress in front of his camera.

Now she's here it's clear she's not going to let him get away with silence. She's still Alex Kubelick. He unpeels the crablet from his face.

— I really liked the way you attacked the corporations, he says.

— O-kay . . . ?

— But then I started to notice how you always told people what to do.

— And I'm not allowed to do that because . . .?

— I'm your biggest fan. Honest.

Alex does this half-laughing, half-snorting noise and pinches the top of her nose with her thumb and finger.

— Seriously, she said, you lads have the weirdest way of showing you like a girl.

— What are you saying?

But he knows what she means. *You lads*. You nerds. You young men who don't know how to interact with people. Who never leave your bedrooms.

Of course it's true that Thimblerig does spend a lot of time in his bedroom. Or he did until last night.

— I'm not saying anything, says Alex. I thought you might have something to say to me.

He doesn't. He's sick of explaining.

— I had this image in my head, she says, of some forty-seven-year-old, eighteen-stone guy. But you're just this kid. You seem relatively well adjusted. So honestly, I'd like to understand why you'd say those hateful things. *Do* those things.

She looks like she's about to cry. Thimblerig wants to cover his face with the crablet but his arms are glued to his sides.

She has a right to ask. She's only seeking information. But why do people always assume there's some grand reason for everything? Maybe she wants him to spin her some sob-tale. Something that will give him a *psychology*. Then she'll *understand* him. As though people are anything but random balls of meat and hormone.

She's exactly like his case officer. The way she always needed to write down some *diagnosis*. Abul Ala lost his father in Aleppo and his mother on a Zodiac off the coast of Kos. Poor Abul Ala. He made his own way north. When he set out from Turkey his Adidas trainers were proudly white. When he reached Calais they were held together by a crackled icing of gaffer tape. Such a heroic child. Only natural he'd vanish into himself. Be rude to ladies on the Internet.

wise nod

stroke chin

A tragic consequence of shameful times.

Fine. Whatever. Just don't make Thimblerig watch while you exercise your northern European guilt on him.

Alex is giving him a look that could griddle a fish. He fiddles with his crablet and avoids her gaze. She gets up and yanks it off him – scraping his neck. The cat arches its back and lets out a static hiss. Alex towers over him. He thinks she might hit him or break the crablet.

— I have more emails! he says in a rush. On . . . there?

Tentatively he points at the crablet in her hand. She looks at it then shoves it into his hands with a shrug. He slips it onto his arm as the cat furls back into his lap. He selects a cluster of mails and throws them onto her mesh. She gives him another sharp look – meaning *this isn't over* – then flicks her fingers in the air. These mails were sent by Doug Raynor to a public relations man called Sam Corrigan. Instructing him to use 'any methods you deem appropriate' to stop the bail-out of Handy Frank's.

— Jesus, she says, reading. I was right. The bribe was so Hardiman would *kill* the bail-out, not secure it. Your guy Raynor is trying to take down Handy Frank's.

He hopes she won't notice how selective he's still being with the emails.

— I need to take this to them, she says. To the Gunnells.

She bustles around the room grabbing stuff and pulling on her jacket.

— This is what I should have done in the first place, she says. The bail-out announcement is Monday. Less than two days. I need to go. Now.

She stops and turns to Thimblerig.

— I should only be a few hours, she says. You're staying here?

He nods his head about a nanometre but she seems to accept that as an answer.

— Because we're not done yet, she says. OK? Somehow I'm going to end this thing and then I'm coming back and we're going to talk. With no staring at your feet or distracting me with emails.

— Just don't go within ten metres of a Stranger or they'll detect you. Blanker or no blanker.

— Yes, all right! You told me once.

— You're the one who chose to use that dumb corporate platform.

— Don't lecture me, Abul. I happen to find the mesh helpful.

— Because it plasters the world with lies?

— Can we just focus on the people trying to kill us?

But Thimblerig can't let things hang. He never can.

— I thought you believed in finding out the truth? he says.

Alex puts on her super-reasonable voice. Her super-patronising one.

— And the Strange helps me *do* that. It makes the world smarter.

— Why would you want intelligence in the world? Intelligence belongs in your head.

She gives him a look like she's trying to work out whether that was the smartest thing ever or utterly stupid. But it's true. Most people are bad users of the world. Good users hack it to make it work better. Bad users take whatever corporate illusion someone chooses to impose on them. The lack of choice makes them happy.

— I don't actually have to justify myself to you, she says. This has been a very tough year. *You've* made it tough. You. I don't need you judging me. All right?

He nods then shakes his head. His father always told him to beware of people who gave themselves up to false gods. He meant the regime. Capitalism. Radical Islam. But in the world today no god is falser than the Strange.

— To be accepted in the Strange, he says, you have to wear a mask.

— This from the kid who hides behind a pig mask?

— I thought you were part of the fightback but you're just another drone.

— Oh for— Sorry, she says, making to go, it's clearly not worth having this conversation. There's some actual important stuff I have to deal with.

— I like your vlog very much. You used to *fight* the corporations. What happened?

She turns at the door. A bright flush is climbing over the collar of her thin white shirt.

— What, she says in a horrible cracked voice, because you were a subscriber you think you can tell me how to live my life? And fucking troll me?

— Subscriber? Huh.

There's a pause then she gets the message.

— You little shit, she says, storming over to him. You pirated me, too?

— Copyright's a prison.

— Oh for fuck's! Copyright's my livelihood, you smug-ass troll!

— It's in the nature of information to make itself free.

— No, sorry. Forget it.

She turns her back on him and makes elegant mimetic gestures with her slender fingers.

— My car'll be here in five, she says quietly.

She still isn't looking at him. He stares at the stupid brown mass-produced carpet and waits for her to go.

— How do I contact you? she says. I'm guessing not through the Strange.

He reaches for his crablet and sends a link to her mesh.

— You can chat me here.

— Right, she says, checking it. 'Thimblerig', of course.

There's another awkward silence. She turns back to him. He can't stand looking at her bruised and angry face. He used to think she was pretty.

— I could call the police, she says, to come and pick you up.

— No police, he says.

— We can't know you're safe here.

— No police.

She gives him a long look.

— You're illegal.

He flinches. That word. Like his whole person is against the law.

Her eyes defocus.

— OK, my ride's here, she says. You're sure?

He nods. Still she hesitates at the door as though trying to find something to say that means a thing. He coils up into himself. Why can't she just go?

Eventually she does.

As soon as she slams the door shut Thimblerig hurries to the bathroom and rips the camera off the light fitting. He places it on the porcelain edge of the bath and smashes it with the butt of his multi-tool until fragments litter the tiled floor.

He stands there until his breathing returns to normal. Then he walks back to the desk where he dons his crablet and messages Lucky Ghost.

SOME RANDOM

He's on the point of uninstalling the new Encounter. It's called *Agents Down*, which sounded excellent in the store, but after a few hours' play it's turned out to be one of those art-house indies where nothing actually happens and you're meant to find that deep. He's all for trying something new – that's why he has his mesh set to Random Encounter of the Day – but he's no truck with artsy crap. There's enough boredom in the real world. Isn't that why people play in the Strange, to rise above their drab old day-to-days?

He crosses the waste ground behind Mesh Warehouse, watching yet more empty status messages. He's on the point of burning the Encounter and replacing it with a favourite Martingale ep when he sees the woman climbing into a driverless car, a hundred metres ahead on Sedgeborne Drive. His display goes nuts with making her affordant. His mesh is a little slow so for a second he sees her street self – flowing red hair, neat tweed suit – before she's rendered as a muscular slav in a zip-up silver one-piece, her shaved hair revealing a fat scar down the back of her head.

<Katya Smolensk>

say the green console characters above her head.

<Enemy agent detected>

The words swoop round the vehicle as it hums to speed and glides away. He hurries to the roadside and jogs along the pavement after the car, calling up a driverless.

<Bogey sighted>

he says.

<Message acknowledged>

<Tac team deployed>

comes the rapid reply.

A block and a half ahead the car glides to a stop, at a red light on the junction to Amberley Road. Once it gets onto the main road he'll never catch it. A lime-green driverless swoops up from behind and pops the door to its two-seater cabin. He hops in. The car ahead pulls left onto Amberley Road, heading out of town.

'Follow that car!' he says. 'Top legal speed.'

The driverless lurches forward, makes it through the light, and corners left at speed.

<in pursuit>

he tells base.

The graphics on this Encounter are exceptional. This is no back-bedroom job. The driverless veers left and right as it overtakes a slow-moving van, keeping pace with the car. His heart races at the pursuit. He's completely sold on the Encounter. He has to admit, the hours of nothing were a brilliant touch. What a great way to lull the player into a false sense of calm, make the action all the more engaging when it comes.

Boredom as an ingredient of gameplay: he can see that catching on.

Katya Smolensk's car leaves the main road at the start of the 50 MPH zone approaching the M25. His car follows. An ad scoots in, promoting a paid upgrade. Normally he'd dismiss it, but he's keen to know what the Encounter's offering. He flicks his head to read the blurb. It sounds pretty cool. They actually issue you with physical repro weapons to use in the Encounter. The problem with most stories is, the objects never seem totally real when you handle them. He orders up a Glock and a couple of grenades for a total of 320 ECSTASY. The order agent gives him the spinning wheel for a couple of seconds then lets him know the delivery drone will rendezvous with his driverless in fifteen minutes. As long as the target car keeps moving till then, he'll be playing fully armed when he engages.

This is going to be awesome.

TRIGGER ISSUE

'*Nobody home. Piss off.*'

The gate's voice shouts inside Alex's mesh. She swirls a finger round her ear to tone it down. She caught maybe forty-five minutes' kip on the road. It might have been better not to sleep at all, the way her head is pounding now. Her skin's taut and in spite of the shower she took at the hotel, it's already raw and sweaty. Behind her, the driverless minicab completes a three-point turn. Wheels crunch gravel as it accelerates up the long straight drive between the rows of plane trees.

'Special delivery,' says Alex to the gate, holding up an empty Jiffy bag she found in her satchel. 'For a Mr Francis Gunnell.'

The gate's a two-metre plane of battleship grey, set into a red brick wall.

'Thumbprint required,' she adds hopefully.

All she gets in reply is a dull click. She waits. She must be insane to come here. The maniacs who live beyond this gate could well be responsible for Mickey's death, but they're her only lead.

When she came here last autumn with a killer exposé on the Gunnell family, she was riding high, her vlog numbers at a peak. She scammed her way through the gate with exactly this courier ploy, then marched up to the door of the mansion, cam drones in formation around her. Did the thought enter her mind that she was alone with a man she'd reason to believe was a borderline gangster, on the secure grounds of his country mansion? If so, it was elbowed aside by the three minutes of tape she thought she was about to capture.

Because thanks to Mickey, Alex had a source who could testify to the illegal sweeteners the Gunnells had paid three months before to the chair of the West Midlands planning committee. In exchange, they'd secured a superstore plot at a peppercorn payment. Mickey's source had carried in his own hands the envelope of readies and the shrink-wrapped package of blow.

In the face of her accusations, Gunnell was warm and condescending – like some delightful but sexist uncle. Alex couldn't understand his easy confidence, when her drones were tracking his every move, until a stony *crack* sounded from behind her. She spun around to see one drone lying inertly on the drive. A second later the other three followed suit, dropping from the air and smashing to the ground. Then a battering ram drove into her chest, sending her spinning backwards onto gravel.

She looked up at the thickset man standing over her in green overcoat and fedora. His face was blanked by darkened mesh, his neck coated with cobweb tattoos. Connor Gunnell, the son.

The interview ended with Alex dumped outside this very gate in muddy tears, Connor's boot prints in her ribs. The physical onslaught was swiftly followed by a legal one. Unable to afford a lawyer, Alex had to face alone the slick team of City partners assigned to represent Gunnell. Over six gruelling weeks, they twisted the facts into blunt-edged weapons and used them to pummel her into submission. She'd trespassed, they asserted in firm but reasonable voices, and threatened a defenceless old businessman. Thank goodness his son had arrived in time to quite rightly defend his ailing father and their property. Those weeks of legal convolution, far more than Connor's size twelve boot, were the weight under which Alex eventually buckled. They ended when she signed whatever papers those smooth-suited men laid in front of her, just to make them let her go. Then she retreated home into the most savage attack the black dog ever visited on her. She'd be under it still, if it weren't for the comforts of the Strange.

One thing she'd never understood about the aftermath of her visit: according to Mickey, nobody ever laid a hand on his source, the man who delivered the money and coke. Which made no sense. Before Connor laid into Alex, Francis out-and-out told her he knew where she got her information. He said he was going inside to make a call that would 'cut it short, right here, right now'. Alex realised with horror she must have given away some hint that let Francis figure out which of his men had blabbed. As soon as she stumbled away from the mansion she got on the line to Mickey to tell him to warn his source. But Mickey assured her all was well. Last time Alex asked him, the source was still working for the Gunnells. So who did Francis call that day? What source did he 'cut short'? Where could he have thought Alex could have got her information, if not from his own bag-carrier?

Alex blows into her hands and stamps the gravel. Whatever happened that last time round, she's back again, on the slender hope that Abul the Handyman's email evidence is enough to turn two proud and furious semi-gangsters to her favour.

Thinking of Abul makes her shiver. She sincerely hopes that bundle of tissues wasn't soaked with what she thought it was soaked with.

Something flutters past her head. She turns to see a drone dart off into the trees.

'Where did you come from, little 'un?' she calls after it, but it's vanished.

There's the hum of a speaker powering up. A green LED illuminates on the camera panel.

'You have got to be fucking kidding me,' says a flinty male voice in her head.

'Hello, Francis,' says Alex. 'Long time no beat me up.'

There's a pause, then a long sigh.

'If you'd asked me to tell you the very last interfering skank I'd expect to ring my doorbell—'

Alex leans forward against the gatepost, placing a hand either side of the camera and staring out the lens.

'If you think about it, Francis, I was hardly going to come here by choice.'

'Thought we'd shut down your pissant web page.'

'Nobody says web page any more, Francis. And no, it was me who shut it down, though you and your lawyers were a big help.'

'So what does that leave you? Horny dyke sub who can't resist another taste of our Connor's steel caps?'

From behind Alex comes a crunching sound. She looks back up the gravel avenue but it's empty. The flanking rows of plane trees rustle in the breeze. The fields to either side are bare scrub, blanched by February sun. Farm machinery fires up somewhere out of sight, then rattles to a stop. Alex shrugs and turns back to the camera.

'It's a delightful offer,' she says, 'but how would I tell you about the secret plot to sabotage your government bail-out?'

The best thing about landing your killer question is the pause that follows. Alex always counts the pause.

– three, four, five –

Her record is sixteen.

– seven, eight –

'You'd better come in,' says Gunnell.

Huh. Decisive.

There's a buzz like a thirty-ton hornet, followed by a repetitious klaxon. A police light spins and flashes red at the top of the gatepost. Alex steps back, grinning at the drama as the gate separates along its centreline and parts towards her. From behind her a loud *crack!* echoes across the fields. Something punches her in the shoulder, throwing her forward against the sharp rim of the gate. Her jaw cracks on metal and she falls. A shot of pain spikes out from her shoulder blade.

Something makes her roll away the second she hits the ground. A second shot punches gravel up from the spot where she was lying. She keeps rolling and scrambling over the gravel, shoulder screaming. A third and fourth shot ricochet off the wall with a *SPANG! SPANG!* She reaches the grassy verge and the ditch that fringes the drive. She uses her good arm to drag herself head first into it and lands in mud.

She pulls her face out of the cold sludge. Like her sensei told her: *reflexes excellent; aim terrible*. Her ears ring and all of her aches. Running feet approach across the gravel – no. They're running past. She tries to push herself up but her right arm's defunct. She rolls onto her left side, muttering '*ow ow ow*' then lifts herself gingerly with her good arm and raises her head over the rim of the ditch.

'*Get down*!' shouts Gunnell, still inside her ears.

She lands face-first in mud. Fire bursts across the top of the ditch, roasting her back. There's a cosmic *BOOM* then a stinging rain of gravel. She lies still as dust falls on her, breathing as best she can through the muck piled over her head.

Male voices, shouting. Short bursts of automatic weapon fire repeat across the fields like whip cracks. Booted feet land in the muck near Alex's head. She levers herself up, shaking off dirt. Francis Gunnell blocks the sky in a stained Barbour coat and flat tweed cap. He reaches a hand down. Painfully, she raises her good arm. He grasps her forearm, helping her up with a care backed by burly force. She stands panting in the ditch, clutching her useless arm.

'Connor droned that fucker,' he says without looking at her.

His face is cracked and worn like unmaintained cement. He nods towards the drive, where a figure in a green overcoat stoops over a prone superhero. Déjà vu from the outside.

'So,' he says. 'Now I have *two* unexpected guests who have explaining to do.'

Alex finally notices the large black revolver in his hand, which is pointed at her stomach.

'AND,' he bawls towards the prone man in the cape, '*WHICH ONE OF YOU FUCKERS IS GOING TO MEND MY FUCKING GATE?*'

Alex turns to look at the buckled remains of the plate-metal gate. Even this small movement rattles her brain inside her skull. A wave of nausea rises up her throat. She collapses forwards over Gunnell's arm and lays a streak of vomit onto the green slew of mud at their feet.

Then she's gone.

HOT TAKES

Almost all of Abul Ala's memories before the age of seven take place in the workshop – the one in the basement of his family's apartment building in the Sayf al-Dawla district of Aleppo. The apartment itself was on the seventh floor. Abul Ala can't remember its layout. He does recall the sense of light and air so high above the hot and dusty streets. From there you could almost pretend the crumps of mortars and the cracks of tank shells were just the normal sounds of a busy market district. He knows he spent long afternoons playing on the green tile floor of the balcony. He remembers how the wrought-iron grille threw patterned shadows over his Lego. But those memories are faint and smudged as old tattoos. The only room he remembers clearly is the basement workshop – that dim space with its whiff of burning oil. It was there he learned his electronics skills. And it was there where he hid while his father was gunned down before him on the concrete floor.

His mother he remembers less and less. He can't even reconstruct the boat journey that the two of them took from the Turkish coast. He remembers his mother putting her phone in a ziplock bag before she boarded. He remembers the fat yellow suitcase that he helped her drag onto the dinghy. He remembers the plasticky waterproofs of the sailor who pulled him from the water. Nothing in between. Somewhere between the scuppering of the dinghy and his rescue by an Italian launch he lost hold of his mother's hand but he doesn't remember when or how this happened.

Why is that moment of separation lost to him when he can remember far more prosaic times from years before? What does it mean that he can't even call up his mother's face but that dim-lit basement is vividly present? He pushes his head back into the hotel pillow and closes his eyes. The scrappy chaos of the workbench is laid out in front of him. He smells the bitter spice of solder and sweat as his father reaches from behind to guide his son's hands in their work – not once correcting his student's clumsy fumbles. Not even when the circuit collapses for the dozenth time. Abul Ala's father gives his son the space he needs to keep on trying until the connection's finally made. The lesson: keep on failing until you succeed.

The image of the breadboard circuit is so vivid Abul Ala might as well be watching an instructional video. Yet he can't see his father. Within the memory he tries to turn and see that frowning stubbled face. He can't. The image that presents itself is not from the basement at all. Not even from life. It's dragged up from a vintage news report that Abul Ala found years later on YouTube. Most of that juddering sequence focused on a white reporter who spoke with earnest intent into the camera – but for a few seconds in the second minute it cut to Abul Ala's father as he strode past smashed-up vehicles overshadowed by wrecked apartment blocks. Over his black T-shirt he wore a khaki cotton jacket. An earpiece dangled by his neck. He trained his pistol at the ground as he shouted directions at a group of running men. Then the image returned to the self-important reporter.

That memory is second-hand. But Abul Ala knows he can also recover a living image of his father if he dares. The moment when the men came. The moment when his father appeared breathless at the basement door and – without a word – grabbed Abul Ala and shut him in the tool closet under the stairs.

Thimblerig hugs his arms around himself as he lies on the hotel bed. He sees what the boy Abul Ala saw that day as he peered out through a ventilation hole drilled low in the door. He watches his father kneel and place his hands behind his head. He

sees a man with a black mask step forward and hold the muzzle
of an AK-47 to his father's head. He thought he understood what
he was seeing through that tiny peephole. He thought the masked
man was preparing to kill his father. In retrospect he knows the
terrified young man in the mask was only standing guard. He
was probably no older than Thimblerig is now. This was not an
assassination but a kidnap – and the young man wasn't alone.
His brothers had sent him down to check the basement while
they headed up seven storeys to the empty apartment. Empty
because Abul Ala's father was down here and his mother at the
market.

Thimblerig wills his younger self to understand this. Wills the
boy to act with common sense. But the scene plays out as it always
does. By the tiny slice of light inside the closet young Abul Ala
extracts his grandfather's Webley Mk VI revolver from the dusty
tea tin on the shelf. Gedo had proudly served in the Republican
Guard when that was still a thing a man could do with honour.
This pistol was the single trophy he left behind. Now it's the
grandson's turn to handle the weapon. Working quietly as he can
Abul Ala flips opens the firing cylinder. With jelly fingers he takes
the three remaining .455 cartridges from their carton and loads
them in the cylinder. Before he knows what he's doing he's sliding
the barrel of the loaded gun out through the ventilation hole and
lining the front sight at the masked man. His father's eyes widen
at the sight but his slender face stays calm. The masked man is
screaming something Abul Ala can't make out through the rush-
ing of blood in his ears. Before he can draw breath his finger
squeezes the trigger. It doesn't pull. It squeezes – just as father
taught him. 'No!' cries a voice from far away.

Then it's dark. Thimblerig's lying on a bed in a hotel. At the
exact same time he's lying on dusty concrete in a basement in
Aleppo. His head pounds. He tastes sick in his mouth. The gun
lies by his right hand. He makes to lift it but the pain in his wrist
prevents him. The cupboard door flies open. Light pours in
around Abul Ala's father as he kneels and takes up the pistol.

Here's the image Thimblerig retains like a smartphone picture. The compassion and rage in his father's eyes as he glares down at the fool his son's revealed himself to be. A child sprawled on his back in a bright blue Adidas tracksuit. His father kneels and holds the boy for a bare three seconds. Then he covers Abul Ala with a heap of ancient oilcloths from the corner of the closet. The door closes and the memory breaks apart. There are two gunshots. Then shouting. Then another gunshot. Then nothing.

Abul Ala stayed immobile under those rancid cloths. After a time he wet himself. As the pee warmed his legs he began to weep. After some more time he stopped. Maybe the dehydration staunched his tears or maybe this was the point when his insides began to harden like cement. He didn't cry again. Not when two of his cousins thought to look in the basement and found his father's body. Not through his flight nor at any time during the hardships that followed.

How angry he was to be left with mother and not with father. With the one who was weak enough to slip from that boat in the arms of some wave.

He opens his eyes and gazes at the halogen downlighters in the ceiling. Now he can see back with a measure of logic he knows his father would have died whether or not young Abul Ala had shot the jihadi. The two older men would have soon come down from the seventh floor. Instead of shooting Thimblerig's father there and then – as they did in reality – they'd have taken him away for good. He'd have died after days of agony as did the other eight militiamen that Raynor betrayed that day. By squeezing that trigger Abul Ala spared his father torture but he sentenced him to death. In return his father faced down the two men with the two remaining bullets. Made it seem as if it was he who shot their brother. They took him out in a single shot while Abul Ala lay hunkered in the cupboard. In some sense he's been hiding inside that cupboard ever since.

His father taught him two things. How to engineer electronic systems. How to resist. Enough for him to become a man. But a man is small and has no hope.

— God gave all creatures fear, said his father, for a single reason. So that they can rise up in the face of danger. Fear is a fuel. Do not waste it in cowering and hiding.

And where is Thimblerig now? Holed up in a bare hotel room under the constant thrum of air conditioning. He flattens his back onto the bed – just as he lay on that concrete floor. Still only watching. Watching Alex on the camera even after she tried to help him. Watching all the other women he's creeped on. Never before has he had to look one in the eye.

He was rude to Alex. But only after she'd sneered and mocked him. Maybe he shouldn't have given her those emails. He knew they'd make her leave. He was only giving her what she wanted – evidence about Handy Franks – but he didn't tell her a fraction of the truth. She's walking into danger. What right did he have to choose what he did and didn't tell her? Information should be free.

He checks the time on the crablet clamped to his forearm. Half an hour since he last looked at it. He was too overwhelmed by the news of death and disaster from everywhere outside. And what does he feel as he lies here immobile? Nothing. The parts of him that should be capable of emotion are gnarled and twisted as desiccated figs.

— *The enemies of progress dealt us a savage blow last night,* says a perfect but flat reproduction of Elyse Martingale's voice.

Thimblerig lifts his head and turns to the voice. The cat is sitting on the desk with paws furled under its chest. Its eyes are dimly lit. Lucky Ghost has returned.

— How many? he asks after a long pause.

As if it matters any more.

The cat stands and articulates its alloy spine. It leaps onto the bed and saunters up Thimblerig's prone body then plants itself by his arm. It glances down at the crablet's screen. For some reason he twists his arm to shield the display. The cat's blank eyespots scrutinise him.

— That I know of? It is hard to be precise. I have seen reports of seven fatal shootings and twelve arrests for hacking-related offences, just in this country. Impossible to know the total number.

Thimblerig swallows.

— Seven people killed?

— Plus of course your two housemates.

Steadily the cat returns his gaze. He doesn't say anything to that. He's alone with only a robot for company. There's no reason he can't react. But the eyes of Elyse are on him from inside the cat. He needs to think. The logic is wrong. But why? How can he read data when it's just a random scatter?

— Why kill some of us but arrest others? he says. Why not kill us all?

There's a time delay before Ghost replies.

— If I were to hazard a guess, I'd say expediency. Some of you their roughnecks could reach right away. For others, they had to rely on the authorities to do their dirty work. Evidently speed is of the essence.

While Thimblerig chews this over he unhooks the crablet from his arm and lets it scuttle around his tummy looking for a place to clamp its legs. Usually the tickling sensation calms him.

— This must be Occidental, he says. You've seen the emails. But none of it fits a pattern.

He's grepped and diffed the data left and right and thrown up lots of fascinating data points but he can't align them into a meaningful structure. Business emails are unbelievably boring – even when death and deception lie under their surface. Ninety-seven per cent are HR announcements and passive-aggressive office politics.

What he has established is that a lot of criminal acts are happening very soon. This is not a sophisticated interpretation but it's as good as he can get to. Example one: something will happen to the entrepreneur Sean Perce's RedShot One Mars probe. The first-stage rocket will launch next week. The algorithm turned up a cluster of negative words connected with RedShot – including *detonation*. Then something bad but unstated will happen to the artist-slash-vlog host Jon Mangan. Then there's Handy Frank's. The fact that they won't get their bail-out makes Thimblerig sad. It'll make a lot of people sad. Everybody loves Handy Frank's.

A raft of events and attacks unconnected by anything other than their badness. And by the PR man Sam Corrigan. For months he's been amping up the profiles of all these celebrities and companies and rockets. Winning them LOVE from millions of Strangers without any of them knowing why.

There's another common theme. Everyone doing Occidental's dirty work is being paid in Emoticoin. Thimblerig's putting together a transaction graph of all the payments. All the Emoticoin came from a single account. A massive stockpile of game currency it's mathematically impossible for him to locate. It contains far more than even a syndicate of human players could ever assemble. So whose account is it?

— A day ago, says Thimblerig, I understood at least one thing. I knew that Occidental was going to use the banking hack. Kaa. But now that's the only thing we know for sure *won't* happen.

— *After you destroyed the final copy.*

— Now all I have is this noisy mess of criminal stuff. I told Alex Kubelick about the attack on Handy Frank's. But there are dozens of bad things I didn't even mention.

—*Wise lad. Keep your cards hidden from mirrors and new friends.*

— There has to be a pattern. So many Cockaigne killed or silenced all at once. Why?

Before he's finished speaking a great big stupid light bulb goes off over his head. Ghost says something in reply but he's shut down inputs. This is one of those moments when the data align and logic flows cleanly through. Of course there's a link. Ghost already said it but he didn't hear her. He clamps the crablet back on his arm and composes a search. The script returns the outcome.

— I was looking so hard at the individual data, he says, I missed the obvious.

There's another of those Ghost-pauses.

— *What do you mean, dear?* she says at last.

— Monday, he says.

He's pleased to have condensed the pattern among this noise into a single word.

— *What do you mean, dear?* she says again.

She's stuck on a loop. Like maybe she's a bot after all? Thimblerig strokes the cat's smooth skull. It rubs its sharp ear against his hand.

— You said yourself, he says, the attack on Cockaigne is messy because it's being done *quickly*. And I realised. The crimes in these emails are separate – but they're all timed to happen early next week. 87.3 per cent of them will happen on Monday.

It's 10.00 Saturday morning. Whatever's coming starts in two days.

The cat places a paw on Thimblerig's chest. He freezes. Something about that gesture invades his space in a way a robot shouldn't do.

— *Whatever the reason,* it says, *you're not safe, Abul Ala. Our first priority must be to keep you invisible.*

He pushes the paw away and gets up from the bed.

— You used my name, he says.

Short pause.

— *Are you with friends? At a hotel?*

— You know my name.

— *Certainly I do. Did you think I'd not have found out every-thing about you before we started down this road? I don't put my trust in just anyone.*

Trust. Exactly. Nothing works if people have reason to suspect each other.

The cat makes to jump up into Thimblerig's arms but he pulls away. It reels as it regains its balance then sits back on the thin brown duvet. It cocks its head.

— *Your safety, Abul. Don't be distracted. If you're with friends you need to leave now. For their sake. If you're in a hotel, do you have an anonymous way to pay? Think, lad.*

Alex and he never spoke about money. Maybe he could hack the payment system. But he'll need money at some point: that's how the world is. But can he take it from Ghost? If Thimblerig had to choose to trust one single user in the world he'd choose her. Over Eponymous even.

— *Don't tell me where you are. Don't tell anyone. But if you need a way to pay let me send you a fold of Emoticoin. Get yourself a room somewhere and pay anonymously. With Coin.*

He thinks of the day he met Ghost. When she outed Eponymous to demonstrate her skills. She could have shopped him to the authorities a hundred times. She never did.

Thimblerig wakes the crablet on his arm.

— Thank you, he says. Yes. Send me Coin.

MOTHERSHIP

The world is purple. Every shade of purple. Think Paisley Park, but more violet.

Waves of mauve sand coat the landscape. Intermittent clumps of plum rock form shade from the lavender sun. Hairy Jacko never knew there were so many shades of purple. Manifesting in his blue ghost-form, he's the one note of contrast in this steaming desert. He crouches behind a low rock, watching a convoy of three giant raisin-coloured wildebeest march past him, thirty paces from his hiding place. Each of the massive creatures bears on its back a wooden cabin large enough for three or four passengers. The portholes of these cabins are curtained with patterned cloth.

Purple patterns.

From behind another cluster of rocks, just beyond where the three enormous beasts of burden are passing, Jacko spies movement. A lithe form leaps into the air and performs a spectacular and pointless spin, landing just in front of the leading wildebeest. The convoy stumbles to a halt.

Jacko smiles. Dani's chosen to manifest here as a slim but busty half-leopard half-human creature with purple fur. Her lance has a giant amethyst embedded in its blade. Her skimpy hooded muslin shift is tied with a belt that's laden with yet more no doubt hard-won purple weaponry – hand axes, laser guns.

There's a shout from inside the cabin sitting atop the first beast. The leopard lady raises her lance and fires off three rapid bolts of purple fire. Her fire's returned. The leopard leaps into the air, still shooting.

Jacko doesn't want to get caught up in this dreary gameplay. From his vantage point he watches the cat-woman leap again, even higher, flipping right over the first beast. With doubtful physics, she pauses in mid-air to rain fire onto the makeshift wooden cabin. Then she spins to the ground and lands in a crouch, punching the ground. Fire's returned from the cabin on the second beast. The flame-bolts strike the ground where the leopard-woman was standing but she's in the air, incinerating the second cabin and its screaming occupants with pulses of purple light. She lands briefly on the ground then is aloft again. She lands on the back of the third beast, where she wrenches off the cabin door and steps inside. Magenta light pulses from the portholes, accompanied by screams that sound remarkably like the last lot; then at last there's silence.

The leopard creature steps wearily from the cabin. Jacko ducks out of sight as she scans the horizon and leaps down in a reverse pike. She lands on her hind legs a few metres from Jacko's rock. She's lean and lovely, if you go for furries. The Rey-style strips of mulberry cloth that dangle below her weapon belt reveal slim human legs, their purple fur uncovered. Distractingly sexy, depending on your taste. From the ground, she surveys the saddle-bags of the nearest beast. The game's about to move onto some tedious business with booty and haggling in some purple souk. Jacko loses patience.

'You still play this Guild Wars BS?' he shouts from his hiding place.

The creature drops to a defensive crouch. Jacko steps out.

'I thought the whole point of these mesh-head games,' he says, 'was to interact with other people? Not mass-produced sprites.'

Seeing Jacko's blue shape emerge, the creature relaxes. Jacko seats himself on the rock.

'They're called Encounters,' she says, 'you hairy tool. Not games. And by the way, what the fuck are you doing in my universe?'

'Hello to you, too, Dan. I thought you gave up swearing for Christmas?'

'I make an exception for you, pissflaps.'

Jacko grins from behind his incorporeal beard. The creature makes an inhuman gesture with the claws of a forepaw. The desert scene wipes away, replaced by bare brick walls. As the transition passes over the purple war leopard, she transforms into Dani Farr. Dani's standing in an area of bare-boarded floor that she's cleared for gaming. She's dressed in black T, black jeans and scuffed black boots. Her hair, which was purple last time Jacko saw her, is black as well – as is the strip of gossamer mesh that hovers around her eyes and ears. The only note of purple is the livid wine-splash of birthmark on her jaw.

In spite of himself, sentiment washes over Jacko at finding his remote self back in this room after so many years.

'Don't I get a welcome back kiss?' he says.

'From my fat arse.'

'Sounds all right.'

'To a perv. I hope your hard-on's well-hidden behind that filthy caff table.'

Hard to know what she's thinking behind the blacked-out mesh. She uses banter as a shield.

'I'm not at the caff. Not in the UK, strictly speaking.'

'Oh, you're on the platform?'

'London's too hot. The whole grid's hot. Anywhere your poison can reach is no place for me.'

She marches up to his ghost and points at him with a hand that's coated in haptic flower tattoos.

'OK, cockpanda. I know where this is heading. Why don't I hang the fuck up now and save us the bother?'

'I'm not here to trash your service.'

'That would be a first.'

She storms off to the fridge. Jacko follows.

'There's bad voodoo being done,' he says. 'Right now. Dead people bad. The Strange is the channel.'

Dani freezes in the act of extracting a beer. Turns to him.

'Dead people?'

'It's escalating. I can't track down the source.'

'Wait. Stop. Why are you here and what are you doing with my service?'

'*I'm* not doing. *People* are doing. Bad people I can't trace. They're using the Strange to fuck with the actual world.'

'Bullshit. What happens in the Strange stays in the Strange. That's the whole point, you bag of dicks.'

She flips open the bottle and passes it to Jacko, then remembers herself. They both laugh. This little moment cuts the hostile vibe. Dani swigs the beer and waves the bottle in a *go on if you must* gesture that he's seen a million times. He follows her to a tattered and familiar sofa. She pats the empty spot and he pretends to sit. They sit in silence as he works out how to frame the thing in a way that won't piss her off. She chugs her beer.

'There are millions of Emoticoin moving around in the Strange just now,' he says. 'Why?'

'Because it's where people prefer to be.'

'Millions of pounds on magic purple lances?'

She's about to snap back but stops herself. She fiddles for a while with the paper round the wet neck of her Grolsch.

'You know *The Electronic Radical*?' she says.

'I gave you your first copy.'

'Then you've got a short memory. Right there in chapter one, Elyse says freeing our information will mean we won't need companies any more.'

'*Why interact,*' quotes Jacko, '*through the medium of a banking house or Limited Company? When we hold our own means of information, we shall negotiate terms of life directly with one another, as individuals. We shall execute our own liberty, free from the bitter regimen of Capital.*'

'Are you reading that or do you remember it?'

Jacko taps his forehead.

'Robot Boy,' she says.

He smiles. She makes a big sweeping pass with her bottle.

'We're building a society,' she says, 'a nation, almost. It's not Britain, it's not anywhere.'

'You're serious?'

'Everything known. Invisible from the state. I learned that lesson the other time.'

Jacko nods. He knows exactly what she means by *the other time*.

'And in this picture,' he says, '*we* is you and your Jorah Mormont lookey-likey sugar daddy?'

'*GAH!*'

She lashes out with the beer bottle, letting it fly at where his chest would be if he was actually there. It hits the back of the sofa and lands in a puddle under his crotch. They both look down at where he's apparently wet himself.

'You were perfectly happy,' she says quietly, 'to take Sean's pay cheque for a while.'

'Until he fired me.'

'For cracking your own employer and stealing his data, Gray.'

'Jesus! Name!'

Dani puts her hand over her mouth.

'Sorry,' she says, 'sorry. I mean "*Jacko*". Apparently.'

Jacko stands and walks away from her. Paces about the space, being careful not to hit the concrete walls of the little storage room where he actually is.

'Oh, c'mon,' says Dani from the sofa. 'Jacko. I said I'm sorry. Jesus.'

'You of all people know conversations on here are keyword-searched.'

'It's hardly an uncommon word. I might have been talking about paint.'

'In a colour that isn't purple or black?'

'Huh. Point.'

Jacko walks back to crouch in front of where Dani's sitting. This was always the best way not to aggravate her: get his head below the level of hers.

'Think of social engineering. Systems are hard to hack but people are easy, if you know the levers. Phone calls from "the IT department". Phishing scams.'

'That's always been true.'

'But imagine there was a system that knew what everyone felt and believed, every second of the day. Imagine it was set up to tell them what's real.'

Dani wrinkles her nose in that way where she looks like an angry eight-year-old but is actually thinking hard.

'So,' she says. 'I guess your standard mode of discourse is still the mansplain?'

OK, no. He tries again.

'We're programmatic animals. We have two ways of thinking – fast and slow. Screenlife's too quick for us to engage the rational system. We're that vital bit more stupid when we're in the screen-world. We live for the stimulus/response of small rewards. Upvotes. Cites.'

'You know how much you sound like the *Daily Mail* right now?'

'Your Strangers are being played. Made to think stuff, feel stuff. It's coming to a head any day now.'

'Listen, says Dani. 'Shit. Can we be totally cards on the table?'

'I thought we are being.'

'Ever since you vanished into your *War Games* fantasy—'

'*I'm* in a fantasy world?'

'You keep coming up with these wilder and wilder stories. It's like the Bilderberg Group was set up specifically to get at you.'

'You know nothing about what I've been doing. On behalf of you. On behalf of everyone.'

Dani leans forward, punches her heart with her fist.

'My. Fucking. Hero.'

The middle finger of the fist pops up. Jacko looks at it a moment then peels off his headset and chucks it at the actual sofa that he's kneeling in front of in a concrete chamber hundreds of kilometres from Dani's studio. He stands and draws in a breath. Now he's out of the Strange he can smell the sea air and rising mould that permeates everything on Seatopia.

He steps to the slit window in the curved wall. Through the grey sheen of the scratchy Perspex and the salt coating its exterior, he watches the North Sea churn and splinter. There's a gale blowing up. It'll be deafening by nightfall. This might be the loneliest place in the word, if it didn't have the best connectivity. The main fibre-optic pipe to the European mainland passes directly under Jacko's feet. Hence why the refresh rate of his conversation with Dani is so lifelike.

It was a mistake to go to Dani. There's too much shit they've been through, never dealt with, since their years as on-again-off-again partners – whether professional, romantic, sexual, or a bit of everything. Impossible to just have a conversation. Yet this is too urgent, too essential, to let their mutual bullshit get in the way. He needs to go back in and reason with her.

He walks back to the sofa and picks up the headset. Takes a breath and puts it on.

'What?' says Dani.

She's pulling another beer from the fridge. She shuts it. There's a dent in its frosted metal frontage.

'Did you just make that?' says Jacko, walking over to inspect the damage.

'I guess I must love you after all.'

He laughs. She swigs at the beer, then waves the bottle in a strange loop, clearing her blackened mesh. Her eyes are heavy with eyeliner. Crow's feet cluster round their corners. Jacko draws his real and mirror selves upright and begins.

'OK, so I'm going to say something and all I ask is that you listen.'

Nothing back. Her black eyes stay level on him.

'You can call me a paranoid as much as you like,' he says, 'but I'm telling you something's happening. You know me. I follow patterns in the data. Was I wrong when things got bad for you that one time?'

'Gah!'

Dani slams the beer down on the counter and walks straight through him. Back in his physical body, Jacko shivers at the intrusion. He turns. She's heading for the stairwell door.

'What did I say?' he shouts. 'Genuinely?'

As soon as he opens his mouth he hears that old whine in his voice. What a charmer. Dani stops in her tracks and turns. Oh: she has tears in her eyes.

'Fuck but that was *different*,' she says. 'I could *see* those cocksuckers trolling the living shit out of me. I didn't need telling.'

'Well, now you do,' he replies carefully. 'The Strangers are being used, even if you can't see it. Dani, seriously, what did I say?'

'Look, you're just *wrong*, OK? Accept it for once. We're not *doing* anything.'

'I'm not saying *you* are. *Someone* is.'

'Oh, oh what, your *bad men*? That doesn't sound remotely paranoid.'

'Oh for—!'

He gets a grip on himself. That took, what, ninety seconds? And they're both miserable. How were they ever a thing?

'There are Strangers with guns,' he says. 'Bombs. Someone is sending them real-life weapons on drones and giving them missions to hurt people. And this is just the latest in a series of – I can't describe them – *anomalies*, OK? Things being nudged out of place.'

Dani reaches under her mesh with a balled-up fist and shoves tears away. She's listening, though.

'Public figures,' he says. 'Brands. Someone's selected them and is priming your Strangers to love them. They're painting public sentiment by numbers, setting them up for – for *something*. Over the past couple of days, it's accelerated. People have started dying. Something's coming, Dan. A finger is coming to knock down the first domino and then – I don't know what.'

Dani's expression hasn't changed but he can see the glint in her eye. She has something to say.

'You know what?' she says. 'You're right. A finger is coming. Oh. Here it is.'

She flips him the bird. She must see the hurt in his eyes because she comes back kinder.

'Look,' she says. 'I get that you're serious but you must see how you sound.'

'Bonkers?'

She gives him a wide-eyed look that says, *D'uh, right*?

'What would even be the point,' she says, 'of making people feel good or bad about stuff? They already have the feels. Major major feels. Feels is what we trade in. A few more won't make a dent.'

'Not arguing. But it's still true.'

'So, OK. All I'm saying is, if you have evidence, show me. Or if you're so sure – fuck! *Do* something about it.'

'I don't have the evidence. This script kiddie does.'

'Then ask *him*. Or her.'

'Trying. But he's in the thick of it. He needs help.'

'Oh, Jesus. Then like I said, *do* something.'

'I am. That's why I'm here. To ask you to shut it down.'

'To what? Shut the *what*?'

He gives her the Serious Look.

'Oh, what – the Strange?' she says. 'You, my friend, are having a genuine laugh.'

'No, but think about it. It's the only way to stop this. This manipulation is happening through the Strange.'

Dani stares at him a little more, then something coughs up out of her. A laugh like a dybbuk set free.

'Oh fuck!' she shouts. 'Oh FUUUUUCK! Oh Jesus Christ how am I so cocking STUPID?'

'What are you—?'

Dani strides towards him. Magics her hands. His view is hurled backwards from his body and up into a high camera angle. His hazy-blue avatar stands below him, frozen. Dani rolls back for a roundhouse punch and smashes it in the face. His head snaps back and lolls appallingly from his neck.

'*Fuck! You*!' she screams.

She punches a chunk from his left shoulder. Then lands another blow in the centre of his chest. His head cracks off and falls to the ground. How the hell did she take control of the hack that cut him into her space? She looks up towards his viewpoint, balling fists by her sides.

'You are never coming in here again. I'm closing your pathetic back door that you seem to think I haven't known about for ever.'

He tries to speak but that isn't an option. She's silenced him, exactly as he did to Alex Kubelick yesterday.

'Of all the times,' says Dani in a vicious spit, 'you've tried to own me in some stupid shit of yours, this is—'

She turns away, gets back control, then turns towards his viewpoint.

'Close down the Strange?' she says. 'Fuck you up the actual arse. Time's up. You're gone.'

More prestidigitation with her fingers. Jacko goes spinning backwards and lands in the concrete room on Seatopia, actually staggering. He pulls off the useless headset. All its LEDs are dark. It's bricked. He chucks it onto the sofa again and sighs.

Plan B it is then. He hurries off to find the others. Outside, the shushing of the gale is mounting like the breath of an angry sea god.

SQUAD GOALS

This Batman has a gun.

Thimblerig has the hotel CCTV up in the corner of his crablet's display. So he sees the Batman round the corner in the hallway. His first thought is that Batman carrying a firearm is completely non-canon. Then something about the man's movements tells him this is not a game. By the time the door to the room bursts in Thimblerig's already inside the built-in wardrobe opposite the bathroom door. He crouches down to peer through the ventilation grille built into the wardrobe door. Second time in two days he's been holed up inside furniture.

The first thing to enter his field of vision is an AR16 fully automatic assault rifle. It works its way into the room at shoulder height. Thimblerig saw the gun on the CCTV but that shaky image didn't reveal that the gun is covered in bright pink enamel – like a ladies' crablet. Guess fashion marketing's reached the arms trade.

The Batman edges into view behind the gun. Through the slats of the vent Thimblerig has a close-up view of the man in the costume. Judging by the visible bottom half of his face he's in his twenties. Black. He's holding his caped shoulder high behind the butt and his cowled head is bunched behind the sights. It's like the stance of a trained serviceman but even ignoring the costume there's something off about it. Like a child playing bang you're dead. Thimblerig was barely eight when he left Aleppo but you don't forget the sight of a trained man holding a gun.

The Batman works his way along the narrow space between bathroom and wardrobe. He stops directly in front of Thimblerig and stares at the ground. Peering sideways through the vent Thimblerig makes out the cat sitting in the Batman's path. It's looking up at him with its grey impassive face.

— هاجمي shouts Thimblerig through the grille.

The Batman starts and looks his way. In speeded-up time, the cat coils into a shape that's more armadillo than cat – then rockets like a piston at the Batman's face. Its front paws close like a calliper on his cheeks. The Batman drops the gun. It swings on its strap. He swats at the cat but it clings on. He grabs its torso and tugs. Blood pools under its paws but it holds fast. Those claws are centimetres long – one of several modifications Thimblerig made to the factory build. Hard to pull her off anything she's locked herself onto.

The Batman lets go of the cat and grabs for the bright pink gun slung under his arm.

— Jesus shit! he shouts. Turn down haptics!

The cat swings from his cheeks as he waves the rifle about. Her paw falls away from his near cheek with a hunk of flesh attached. The Batman shouts out and squeezes the trigger. Fire bursts from the muzzle. With a boom that shakes the flimsy wardrobe door, a wild strafe chews across the room. It bursts the bedclothes into a white cloud then smashes through the computer gear on the desk. Chips of wood and metal burst up like geysers.

— Turn down haptics! shouts the Batman.

The cat flails at him with the claws of its free paw. It's hanging with a single paw from the flesh of his cheek. He swats at it with the rattling muzzle. Bullets dig a trench in the ceiling. He grapples with the juddering gun. The strap's tangled in his cape. The cat takes a swing directly at his masked eyes. He staggers back and smashes against the door to the hallway. The gun swings towards Thimblerig. He drops to the floor of the wardrobe as firecracker impacts pulverise the wood.

The gunfire stops. From outside the wardrobe the Batman speaks quietly.

— Huh wait what? he says in that eloquent way mesh-heads have.

Thimblerig stands and peers through the random lattice the gun's made of the wardrobe door. The Batman lies prone on the carpet outside. His head's uncovered – making him look younger and more scared. He's looking around like a creature waking from hibernation. The pink firearm lies tangled in his cape. The cat is sitting to attention by his Batman panties. Snared on its right paw is a tangle of cloth. The man's mask – which contains his mesh. This Batman is suddenly seeing the real world.

Thimblerig pushes open the remnants of the wardrobe door. It bumps into the Batman then drops sideways and hangs skew on its remaining hinge. The Batman's eyes catch his. From outside in the hallway comes a shout and a door slam. Footsteps run off.

— This is real? says the Batman.

He touches the mess of his left cheek and stares at the blood on his fingers. He tries to get up. The cat hisses and furls into attack configuration.

— وقفي says Thimblerig.

It unfolds into a sit.

The Batman leans his back against the bathroom door. He untangles the strap of the gun and places it gingerly on the ground. Pushes it away with his foot. How did he know to come here? Thimblerig knows how to stay invisible. He steps over the Batman's legs to extract the cowl from the cat's claws. Holds it up for the Batman to see.

— What were you playing? he asks.

The Batman might as well have Tweety-Birds circling his head.

— When you called out to turn off haptics, says Thimblerig, you thought the pain you were feeling was inside the game. You were surprised to see real blood. You thought you were playing an Encounter. Chasing a ghost. But it was me. What was the Encounter called?

The Batman stares. If he's a serious player he probably hasn't left the Strange in months except to sleep and shower. A sudden removal of mesh can be disorienting.

— It's called *Agents Down*, he says at last.

Thimblerig tuts. He goes to fetch his crablet from the bed but it's distributed in a thousand shards across the shredded bedding. So he gets his backpack from under the mangled desk. He has to shake off a bunch of crud that's fallen onto it but it's undamaged. He digs out his spare crablet then pulls on the Batman's cowl and lines up the eyepieces. The mesh gives the room a gauzy look.

— You can't play with that, says the Batman. It's tuned to me.

Thimblerig tuts again then spoofs the mesh by telling it his crablet is the hotel's local network. Beneath the showy genius of the algaerhythm mesh are pretty stupid at the I/O level. It's not hard to trick them with a false flag. Once inside he restarts the game.

A thumping soundtrack kicks off round his ears. The words AGENT DOWN crash into the room in shouty 3D. The title wipes away. Animated laser sights and busy readouts of non-data weave across his field of vision. The game is screaming kill alerts. Pinging them directly at Thimblerig's torso. Instructing him to shoot himself.

He roots out system level. Beneath the playscreen the gameplay engine is deeply confused. Thimblerig's status shimmers between player and target. On the one hand the game thinks he's W@yn3 M@n510n23 – the man sitting stunned on the carpet. On the other it sees him as someone called Mustafa Kalim who's from a sleeper suicide cell. Hence why it's trying to get him to assassinate himself.

He sits on the one intact corner of the bed and hooks the crablet over his thigh. He decouples Kalim – the target jihadi – and sets his location to {null}. Now other players won't have a location for him. Though they'll know the location of this room. The game will probably latch on to Thimblerig again as soon as another player gets him into their line of sight. Conclusion: he needs to send Mustafa Kalim somewhere other than where Thimblerig actually is. Draw any other players away from the room.

He selects GHOST from the main nav and chooses a suitably racist jihadi character from a game design library. He starts modding it into the game.

— You'd better go, he says as he works.

The unmasked Batman looks down at the gun then up at Thimblerig.

— But my cowl? he says.

— You really want to put it on again after where it led you?

The man looks at the devastation of the room. Then he scrambles to his feet and runs off down the hall. Thimblerig walks to the gun and squats by it. After a pause he picks it up and slings it over his shoulder.

— *IT'S REAL!* comes the man's voice from the hall.

— *DROP YOUR WEAPON!* comes another voice.

Which is interesting given that Thimblerig has the Batman's weapon.

— *YOUR GUN'S REAL!* the Batman shouts.

There's a rattle of gunfire. Thimblerig jumps to the door and pushes it shut as best he can on its kicked-in hinges. No way of knowing how many more players have been brought here. It might be just this one. It might be a hundred. He has maybe thirty seconds before this new arrival gets to the room. He steps away from the door and instructs Mustafa Kalim – his ghost terrorist – to move. Kalim steps out of Thimblerig's body like a soul exiting a corpse. He opens a fake door and walks through the real one. Briefly his arm appears through the real door and shuts the ghost one.

Melded reality is confusing.

Gunfire rattles from the hall. Good. That should draw away any players heading for the room. But the game's still looking for Thimblerig's face. He has to leave the room fast but as soon as he does he'll be spotted by a camera or Stranger or some other form of surveillance. He needs to create enough audio-visual white noise to confuse the algaerhythm. As the gunfire continues in the hallway and the shouts mount up he has a quick chat with the hotel's security system and persuades it there's a fire in the lobby. The ceiling gives out a glooping sound like Willy Wonka's chocolate chutes then a hiss starts from the spigot above Thimblerig's head. Blue fire retardant liquid gushes out. A siren starts yammering.

With the sticky liquid starting to coat him Thimblerig holds open his backpack for the cat. It jumps inside and goes to sleep. He shoulders the bag and steps to the door. He straightens his mask and raises the gun to his shoulder then eases the door open with his foot.

In imitation of how W@yn3M@n510n23 entered the room Thimblerig leaves it.

SLEEP WITH THE FISHES

'No we are not bastard well letting him go!'

Francis Gunnell's voice echoes around the bare brick cell. To emphasise his point, he punches a stack of Black & Decker cartons, leaving the middle box jenga-ed out of kilter. Then he lights his roll-up cigarette.

'But,' says Alex, 'if he says he was in a game—'

Gunnell's finger is in her face.

'That grenade nearly blew my gate off its hinges,' he says. 'What kind of bollocking game is that?'

'He doesn't exactly look like a terrorist, though?'

They're standing at the arched entrance to a cellar vault. While Alex was out cold, the Gunnells dragged the shooter in here and tied him to a chair. He's unconscious now, but he was evidently awake long enough for Francis to extract information from him. She doesn't care to think about how. The man's right ear and the side of his freckled face are clodded with red, his spike of ginger hair matted with sweat. From the neck down he's dressed in a superhero costume Alex doesn't recognise – red with a dark blue strip across the shoulders. Yellow starburst on the chest. A mask hangs around his neck.

'He looks,' says Francis, peeling a fleck of tobacco from his lip, 'like an utter prick.'

A wave of nausea envelops Alex. Sparkles dance at the edge of her vision. She looks around for somewhere to sit, locates the orange plastic school chair she was sitting in when she first came round. She winces as she sits, at the pain in her shoulder. When she woke she assumed she was a prisoner. Perhaps she is. But with the shooter here she seems to have become the lesser of two evils. The Gunnells have even cleaned up and bandaged her bullet wound.

Gunnell glares down at her, strip light slicing his craggy face in half. She swallows back sick. So here she is again with the human template for the grinning Happy Handyman logo that graces the signboard of every high-street store and out-of-town warehouse. Even twenty years ago that cheeky homunculus must have been a rosified version of this bludgeon of a businessman. Impossible to imagine him ever making a thumbs-up. Though he does have that trickster gleam in his eye.

He grinds his roll-up into the brick of the archway and walks to the unconscious Stranger in the chair. He places his hands on the man's shoulders.

'If you like Captain Dickhead so much,' he says, 'maybe I should hand him back his gun, see what he does with it this time?'

Alex shifts in the chair, wincing at the pain from her shoulder. Gunnell has a point. Her shoulder is proof this is not a game. The bullet that struck her scapula was very concrete indeed. The Gunnells have patched her up pretty neatly, but it's like she's been kicked by a mule. To keep from blacking out, she leans her head back against a shelving unit packed with cartons of light bulbs.

Gunnell strolls to the filthy workbench running down the opposite side of the vault. He picks up a roll of silver gaffer tape.

'Or,' he says, 'maybe I should be tying *you* up, too? What d'you reckon?'

He tosses the tape roll in his hand. Alex's heart begins to thud. This cave-world is too raw and too loud. This is no Encounter. There's no way to take the measure of this situation. Last time she came to this house she was assaulted. Just because the Gunnells have taken her in and patched her up, doesn't mean they don't mean her harm.

'People will be here, Francis,' she says in the calmest voice she can muster. 'They were following my mesh before you shut it off.'

'Yeah? Interesting.'

He picks something off the workbench: Alex's shoulder bag. From it he pulls out a little metal box, holds it up for her to see. Shit. Abul's blanker.

'Give me back my bag,' Alex says.

But Gunnell's registered her shock at seeing the device.

'Connor tells me,' he says, 'this little hoosits was masking your location. More fool you, girly.'

He tucks the blanker back in the bag with a smirk.

'*I* came *here*,' she spits. 'Think about that, you hard-boiled brontosaurus. Your bully-boy son kicked seven shades of hell out of me that last time, but I came back. Why?'

'What do I care?' says Francis, slamming her bag onto the worktop. 'You fucked my business. You fucked *me*.'

'OK,' she says, 'you need to listen to me, Francis.'

'Need? *Need*?'

Gunnell wields the roll of tape. She shields her head with her arms but he spins and hurls the roll point-blank into the Stranger's face. The man's head bounces as though his neck is rubber. Alex clamps a hand over her mouth.

'Every fucker these days,' says Gunnell, pacing about the space like a caged lion, 'telling me what I *need* to do. You want this bail-out, Mr Gunnell? You *need* to rationalise your business. You *need* to shut stores. You *need* to use more bastard robots. You *need* to assume the position so we can fuck you up the jacksie till your nose bleeds – then you *need* to tell us afterwards how much you loved it.'

'Jesus Christ,' says Alex.

'Seems to me there's a few things *you* need to do for *me*. Like tell me how come you're still shitting on my business six months after we made you stop?'

As Alex's eyes follow Gunnell around the room, they catch something, then lose it. No: there it is. A vast spray bottle of Cillit

Bang cleaner, standing on the workbench. She makes an involuntary croaking noise, like she's got a wishbone in her throat.

'Oh, God,' she says. 'It *was* you. This is where Mickey died.'

'Mickey who?'

'Mickey Gallant!' she says. 'Christ, why would you do that? Don't you *want* to stop Occidental?'

'You keep using these names like I'm meant to know them from a steaming turd.'

'*Fuck you*!' she shouts, trying to stand and failing. 'Dickless fucking bully!'

'*Shut* it!'

'You deserve to be ruined! I hope you lose every fucking penny!'

'Christ on a bike! I do not know any Mickey Grant, OK?'

'*Gallant*!'

'I don't. Care. I don't *know* him, OK? Fucking hell.'

Alex's brain catches up with her mouth. No. It doesn't make sense for the Gunnells to kill Mickey. She might have believed that yesterday, back when she thought Corrigan was bribing Susan Hardiman on *behalf* of the Gunnells, to get her to support the bail-out of Handy Frank's. In that version of reality, Francis had a reason for stopping Mickey.

Now Alex knows different. The emails Abul showed her at the hotel prove she had it exactly the wrong way round. The bribe was paid to get Susan to *reject* the bail-out. By turning up evidence of the bribe, Mickey was doing Francis a favour. No reason to kill him.

Plus, there's no way the Gunnells are responsible for this Stranger attacking her at the gate. Francis is genuinely baffled by what the guy was up to, and now she comes to think of it, Captain Whoever isn't the first Stranger to attack her in the past two days. She'd forgotten that weird incident outside Corrigan's office, when Tony the Tiger knocked her off her bike. Someone way more tech-enabled than Francis Gunnell is pressing the buttons on this.

So, OK. Francis didn't kill Mickey. Even so he's holding a man hostage and assaulting him. People are still shooting real guns at Alex.

She hauls herself to her feet. When blackness sweeps into her vision, she sits back down again.

'I'm calling the police,' she says weakly.

'Oh no. That is something you are not doing.'

'So what am I, a prisoner?'

'Look around you, darling.'

It's true. The long vaulted cellar outside the arch does resemble a medieval dungeon. It must run the whole length of the manor house. It's lined with shelves, all packed to the gills with cardboard boxes.

'Where the hell is this anyway?' she says. 'Your sex dungeon?'

Gunnell comes and stands beside her. He lights up again, takes a few contemplative puffs. He's calm again.

'It was the wine cellar when I bought this pile,' he says. 'Now it's overflow storage for the Thanet branch. I hated to see a big old space go to waste.'

There's something weighty and dispiriting about all this well-stacked *stuff*. Alex tries to calculate how many boxes there are down here; and fails.

'Like *Raiders of the Lost Ark*,' she says, half to herself.

'What are you bitching about now?' says Francis.

Alex leans her head back against the shelves and looks him in the eye. Get him talking. About anything. Keep him calm.

'You never hear of mass-dormant consumer goods?' she says.

His expression of contempt returns.

'Mass whatty?'

He draws on his cigarette, then uses it to point at her.

'You know what you sound like?' he says. 'You sound like those fucking civil servants they've had here crawling over my business, playing jargon bingo.'

'Excuse me for having an economics degree. Mass-dormant goods means things that a lot of people own but which stay unused most of the time. Things people don't get value from owning. Like my pasta machine.'

As soon as Alex says this she feels a stupid pang. Harmony bought her that doohickey, which has taken up cupboard space ever since the one time she made linguine with it.

'*Pasta machine?*'

'Posh house like this, Francis, I'm sure you've got one. But how many times did you actually use it?'

He's giving her a very, very level gaze.

'My Jules did,' he says at length. 'All the time. Might be around here still, somewhere.'

He takes another long pull on his roll-up, then raises his eyebrows, waiting for the penny to drop. And it does. Alex had forgotten what happened to his wife, Julia. The attack took place in this very house. A break-in, while Francis was off conquering yet more turf. Julia lasted four hours, according to reports. Alex studies his red, exhausted eyes. Is there an explanation there for his brutality, or a consequence?

'Sorry,' she says, not quite sure why she'd apologise to this man; except that he's turned remarkably human in the last few minutes. Human, and exhausted.

He shrugs and turns to look along the endless tiers of boxes.

'So your point?' he says.

'My point is, *tools* are mass-dormant. Unless you're some DIY nut, you buy the particular screwdriver you need to put up that one wardrobe or whatever. You use it once then it goes in a drawer. First this stuff sits down here unused for months and months. Then somebody buys it. Then it sits unused somewhere else. Tonnes and tonnes of dormant stuff, all up and down the country.'

Gunnell is staring now in open fury. He jabs the lit end of his cigarette towards her, sending daggers of hot ash through the dark air.

'Fuck you,' he says. 'Fuck everything about you.'

He hurls the cigarette towards the unconscious Stranger then advances on him.

'OK, hold on,' says Alex. 'I didn't mean to—'

But she did. She wasn't trying to calm him. She was deliberately winding him up. Idly Gunnell takes hold of the Stranger's chin. Gives it a hopeful shake.

'Good thing for you,' he says, 'there's someone else in here for me to hurt.'

He balls his other hand into a fist and raises his eyebrows questioningly.

'Oh Jesus, don't,' says Alex.

She wants to leap up and stop him; but she's more likely to pass out right there in the chair. Francis rolls back his meaty fist as if to land a blow on the Stranger's face. She turns her head away, sick of swagger. Sick of this dank sub-world she's landed herself in. Sick of people dying and being hurt. Everything pounds like an overbaked soundtrack.

'Suit yourself,' says Gunnell, dropping the man's head and raising his hands in mock surrender.

Alex launches herself up and stumbles off along the main cellar, thinking she might vomit any second onto the dusty stone floor. With its dank vaulted ceiling, ill-lit side-chapels and row after row of consumer durables, it's like some wrecked cathedral has been taken over by market traders. She stops by a cluster of shrink-wrapped plastic lawn chairs. Her shoulder is pumping pain signals into her brain. She puts a hand on it, then quickly removes it when the jolt of pain hits. She sits on one of the chairs, the wrapping cracking under her, and holds her throbbing head between her hands. Her powered-down mesh presses into her cheeks. She'd forgotten she was wearing it. Dumbass: she can use it to call the police.

She finds the toggle at its corner; boots it up. The domino-mask logo of the Strange fills her vision then fades. The room warms. Her glowheart lands beside her, shuddering with competing colours. Forest floor, ambient thrum. Gentle birch twines around her, shielding her from Gunnell. She waits for the comfort to hit but it doesn't flow. This is all too dislocated for the Strange to muzzle.

An echo of footsteps hurries down a distant staircase. Something red swoops in on Alex. She jumps up but is instantly faint, so she drops back into the lawn chair. The red thing is a pair of words, hovering in the air.

‹kiss him›

Forest and basement whip away, replaced by a monochrome fifties’ café. Hoots and shunts sound from the platform, along with the chatter of long-dead people with a train to catch. Leather soles slap flagstones. The door of the tea shop opens and there stands the square-jawed version of Connor Gunnell, dressed in his finest overcoat. It’s Charles – the character – not Connor who hurries to her.

‘You must know I never wished for this to happen,’ he whispers in perfect Received Pronunciation.

He leans in to her and they peck cheeks politely, coolly. He places his folded *Times* on the café table. Alex doesn’t know if what he just said is part of the Encounter, or if it’s real. She draws a breath. The oily flavour of the cellar air jars with the tea-room fug.

‘May I?’ says Charles, nodding at the opposite chair.

‘I don’t—’ she begins

Is she herself or her character? Charles sits, placing his hat on the folded paper.

‘Thank you,’ he says, ‘for meeting me here.’

It comes out ‘*Thenk* you’. He watches two ladies pass the table. The same two women from the train compartment – the ones who disapproved of Mickey. Poor Mickey.

‘I must explain what you saw that day,’ he says. ‘With Roger.’

OK, who is Roger now? Has Alex missed an instalment?

‘Listen,’ she says, ‘I’m not – this isn’t the time for—’

‘It was not I who did those things. That is to say, of course it was – but the man I was then – he disgusts me.’

A flicker of agony passes over his face. Alex’s next line is

‹I think perhaps I have always known›

‹about these predilections›

Predilections?

‹but I would not let myself believe›

She claws the line away.

'Connor?' she says. 'Why are you doing this? We're in the middle of—'

'If you never wish to see me again, I shall understand.'

Alex stands. Hard-core Strangers play their Encounters no matter what's happening in the real. *Commit to the game*, the motto has it. But this is insane.

'Please,' she says, 'stop. Your dad's about to do I don't know what to the guy in the cape.'

'I have not always been kind, I realise. But there is more at stake now than our marriage.'

'No.'

'Whatever spark of duty remains, Elyse, I must ask—'

'No. I'm not playing.'

Alex rips off her mesh. Back in the dark cellar, Connor is sitting in shirtsleeves on a shrink-wrapped plastic chair. He's pudgier, grimmer than his Encounter self. The spider's-web tattoos extend from his neck down to his forearms.

'It's true though,' he says, standing. 'We're connected.'

His true voice is a softer version of his father's. He moves in on Alex.

'Mate,' she says, taking a step back, 'there's nothing connecting us except physical assault. Back up a little.'

Connor's on her, too close. It's the moment before an attack. Sexual? Physical? Both? Yet it isn't that. This man needs something from Alex, but it isn't that.

'You know how it works,' he says, in the whisper of a doomed conspirator. 'The Strange doesn't put two people together unless there's something – *shared*.'

He hits the last word like a punching bag. Lets it dangle. It takes Alex several seconds to catch on, then an insane bark of a laugh bursts from her.

The Encounter was telling the truth. Or a version of it. The 1950s' husband whose *predilections* dare not speak their name.

'You're queer,' she says.

Panic soaks into Connor's eyes like tears. He throws a look over Alex's shoulder. She turns to see Francis approaching, wiping his hands on an oily rag. Connor grabs her arm but she yanks it away.

'It was you, wasn't it?' she whispers. 'You hurt Harm.'

'I did what?' says Connor.

'My. Fucking. Wife.'

'I – didn't mean for that to – I thought the flat was empty. She surprised me.'

'Right. So inconsiderate of her, showing up in her own home.'

'I never wanted to hurt you either, Alex. I know you're—'

Francis arrives, dangling Alex's bag from his paw. Alex looks from father to son to father. She has a lever now. She came here powerless but now she *has* something on that vicious fuck-up, Connor Gunnell. One word to his dad. One word – she'll get her own back.

'Noisy cunt doesn't have a clue why he's here,' says Francis. 'I had to muzzle him.'

A wave of anger rises in Alex, an urge to blurt out what she knows. She throws a furious look at Connor. Sees his terror. Damn damn damn. Whatever he's done to her, to Harm, she's not the one to out a guy to his gangster dad.

Francis reaches into Alex's bag and extracts the plastic Happy Handyman figure. He holds it up to her with an amused smile.

'That's not mine,' she says.

Francis shrugs and flips back the mannequin's head. He takes a cigarette from behind his ear, pops it in his mouth, then flicks the neck-stump of the miniature him. On the third try a flame emerges. Francis cups the flame and lights up, then flips the head back into place.

'Didn't have you pegged as a tobacco girl,' he says, returning the Handyman to the bag. 'Would have had you down for vape.' He drops the bag onto a plastic-wrapped chair, smokes for a few seconds, then says, 'Occidental.'

Alex wrinkles her brow.

'In what way?' she says.

'You mentioned that name when you were flipping out back there.'

He rolls his weight towards her, cocksure. Alex takes two small steps back, catches herself, stands firm.

'Did I?' she says.

He's right on her.

'What,' he says, jabbing his lit cigarette towards her face, 'do you know about them?'

Alex slaps the hand away. Francis balls his fist, cigarette poking from the fingers.

'Whoa, whoa, whoa!' says Connor, putting a hand on his father's forearm.

The men lock eyes. The fist stays primed. Alex steps out of range of those grisly knuckles.

'Piss off out of the way, son. She's got something.'

'So ask her.'

'Oh, what, you're on her side now?' says Francis.

Alex shivers. She remembers this feeling from the last time she was here, of stumbling into a hard-boiled geezer movie.

'We talked about this yesterday,' says Connor. 'Remember?'

'You're saying just let her go?' Francis yanks his hand free, faces off against his son. 'She reckons we should let the prick in the bodystocking go and all. You agree with that?'

Or maybe this whole thing is just another Encounter. One that started Thursday morning, with the slap on the pavement.

'Maybe she has a point,' says Connor. 'I mean, what the hell *do* we do with him?'

Thoughts of Thursday remind Alex she's supposed to report back to her compliance hearing on Monday. Day after tomorrow, fat chance. All of that's a whole turn of the world away.

'I've a few ideas,' says Francis darkly.

'I'm getting,' says Alex, 'a fascinating insight into the gangster thought process.'

Francis points at her with two fingers, cigarette burning between them.

'Still not too late to dump the pair of you under concrete,' he says.

'Fucksake,' says Connor.

Everything's spiralling into nonsense. People are chasing Alex with guns. Mickey's dead. She goes on the run with a teenaged boy who's been harassing her online for a year, then drops in on the men who physically assaulted her. But these two meatheads are somehow at the centre of this. She has to get them to stop playing *Lock, Stock* and focus.

'There are more of them,' she says. 'Maybe a lot more.'

Francis folds his arms. Frowns.

'I'm listening,' he says.

'This one isn't even the first. Last night two more came after me and—'

She breaks off. Let's keep Abul out of this.

'—and they killed two bystanders. Day before, someone else killed a contact of mine – the one who gave me the Hardiman email. Then, seconds after I get here, this guy turns up. He followed me, but he doesn't know why. How does that make sense?'

'There are more?' says Connor.

'Is your gate still sound?' she says.

'Depends how many more grenades they decide to chuck at it,' says Francis.

He stands with arms folded a few more seconds, then comes to some kind of conclusion. He heads for a videophone mounted by a metal-reinforced door, picks up the handset and presses a key. The screen lights up.

'Well, fuck me,' he says, then turns and raises his eyebrows at Alex. 'Company.'

Alex walks over. On the screen, a Sylvester the Cat and a Tweetie Bird are advancing along the drive towards the camera. Sylvester has a long tube balanced on his shoulder.

'Is that – a bazooka?' she says.

'We're moving out,' says Francis, chucking something to his son.

Connor catches the keys his father's thrown. He goes to a shelving rack, reaches up and pulls down two full duffels.

'Some kind of RPG,' says Francis, still studying the video screen. 'Not that I'm an expert.'

He turns off the screen. Connor hands him a duffel.

'Let's move,' he says. 'Gate won't last more than one or two of those.'

Connor heads out of the door. They've prepared for this, like survivalists digging an apocalypse bunker under their Kansas farm.

Francis shoulders his duffel and picks up Alex's bag, which he holds out to her.

'You're coming with us,' he says. 'I still have questions.'

'What about the guy?' she says, nodding towards the chamber where the superhero's tied up. 'You can't just leave him.'

'He stays there,' says Gunnell, 'and he thanks his stars I don't gut him.'

He waves the bag again. Alex snatches it and follows him through the door to a dark stairwell. Connor's already vanished upstairs.

'And why,' she says, 'would I want to go with two men who attacked me?'

'Because, snowflake, the alternative is getting shot.'

'And that's my choice? A bullet or an abusive man? Where did you get the idea you can tell me what to do?'

Gunnell rounds on her. She winces as he presses his bulk against her shot-up shoulder.

'Are you the one,' he says, 'with the whole fucking establishment trying to crush you? No! Don't tell me who's the fucking oppressor, all right?'

'Let me go. Right now.'

He grabs her chin. She tries to shrug him off but he uses his mass to back her into a corner of the stairwell.

'This is *on you*,' he says. '*You* brought this here. I should take this,' he places his free hand on a red extinguisher clamped to the wall, 'and cave your pretty head in.'

The back of Alex's head is pressed into raw brick. The smell of cigarettes coming off Gunnell makes her gag.

'Only reason I haven't,' he says, 'is because you mentioned Occidental Data Whatnots. If you get me to those cunts—'

Alex wriggles her good arm free and shoves him in the chest. He barely budges.

'*Awroight you slaaaag*!' she shouts in his face.

He starts back, baffled.

'You what?'

'*I know it wuz you, Fredo*!' she screams, changing accent.

Gunnell looks disgusted.

'What the fuck are—?'

'More of them!' shouts Connor down the stairs. 'Seven or eight. They're getting in position.'

'Shit!' says Gunnell.

He glares at Alex then charges up to join his son. When he gets to the turn in the stairs he stops and leans over the handrail.

'You coming, twinkletoes?'

Alex stares up at him. More attackers. The first guy followed her; these others followed him. That's why they're arriving in dribs. So the first guy must have spotted her back in Crawley, when she got into the driverless.

She swallows. Oh shit: Abul. Whoever's after her knows where she started her trip – a car park's width from the rear entrance to the hotel where Abul's hiding out. Now she definitely has to call the police. Except she promised Abul she wouldn't.

Abul the Happy Handyman. So she made a promise to a guy who's done nothing but harass and ruin her. So what? She should—

She should what? Leave a teenager for Strangers to kill? Call the police and let the Home Office deport him to the boiling catastrophe of post-Assad Syria?

'Jesus fucking *Christ*!' she shouts at nobody.

Francis blinks down at her from the top of the stairs

'You coming,' he says, 'or do you want a rocket-propelled grenade up your cunt?'

PRAWN COCKTAIL OFFENSIVE

All's quiet when Thimblerig edges out of the hotel bedroom – apart from the shush of fire retardant squirting over him. As the blue-dyed liquid soaks his clothes he sets the pink butt of the assault rifle to his shoulder and jogs along the soggy carpet past blank numbered doors. The hotel must have evacuated its inhabitants. Any Strangers who came here playing *Agents Down* have left in pursuit of the fake sprite Mustafa Kalim.

Turning the corner Thimblerig nearly stumbles on a body. The game identifies it as a fellow agent downed by the terrorist. Thimblerig pulls up his mask. Lying there is the bare-headed Batman. The front of his suit is wet with blood. Thimblerig pulls the mask back on and keeps walking.

His view of the beige corridor's cartoonified by the primary-coloured renderings of the Strange. To the right the mesh keeps relaying snatches of events from W@yn3M@n510n23's life. One young woman keeps returning. She must have meant a lot to the man. Thimblerig shivers as she croons hotly in his ear. He doesn't like whispering. Ads keep passing for condoms. Pornography. Hook-up services. Thimblerig doesn't know how Strangers can live this way.

He trots down the four flights to the lobby. There's nobody about here either. Through the blue-spattered glass Thimblerig sees four or five cars parked out front but not a human in sight. He doesn't want to exit that way – the police can't be far off. Instead he heads for the restaurant at the rear of the hotel.

Presidents and pop stars leave through the kitchen. Why not Thimblerig?

The restaurant entrance is behind a frosted glass screen with a sundial etched on it. As he approaches it a fat green arrow appears and rattles from side to side with jaunty physics. It takes a few seconds of goggling at the arrow before Thimblerig understands what it's trying to tell him. He turns and sees a Shrek climbing in through a window.

The Shrek has forced open the casement and is climbing through it but his fatsuit's got stuck in the narrow space. Head and shoulders are through but below his little brown waistcoat his belly is wedged. He grunts and wiggles with his beady mesh eyes fixed on Thimblerig. The barrel of a green assault rifle is wedged beside him.

Thimblerig backs towards the restaurant. The Shrek starts to work his arm around the squashed-in stomach of his suit. He's going for the gun. Thimblerig raises the shaking barrel of his own weapon and frames the Shrek in the sights. The Shrek stops wriggling and stares at the gun from behind fake eyes. The tip of Thimblerig's finger touches the trigger. Unsteadily he trains the gun on the Shrek – who again starts struggling through the window. Directly over Thimblerig's head the sprinkler continues to coat him in watery chemicals. From somewhere comes a siren. His finger twitches on the trigger.

Thimblerig was seven years four months and six days old when he had to choose between killing a man or losing his father. Ten years later he has the choice to kill or be killed. The Shrek would gladly shoot him but he's being duped by a dumb game. Does anyone deserve to die for being stupid?

The Shrek's belly pops out of the window and he tumbles forward. His gun clatters onto the smooth wet tiles. Thimblerig runs for the restaurant. His Nikes skid in pooled water but he rights himself and makes it round the screen. He tears past unlaid tables towards the kitchen door at the far end of the restaurant. Before he's halfway there a chatter of gunfire bursts from behind him. He changes course and dives for cover. He skids over puddled tiles and lands with a painful splash by the salad buffet then keeps on skidding until he hits the breakfast counter by the wall. The gunfire's stopped. He scrambles behind the salad bar and pushes his back against it. He's panting hard.

He slips off his backpack and drops the Batman mask onto the wet floor. He pulls out the pig mask and puts this on instead. The mask smells even nastier than usual. After a second he remembers why. But he can't take it off now. No telling where they have cameras.

The salad bar he's huddled behind is a cuboid two metres long with chilled aluminium tubs on top. The tubs are filled with salads. Unhelpful. He can't fight off the Shrek by throwing roasted pumpkin seeds. In front of him the breakfast bar is built against the restaurant's wall. No doors there. The only exits are the entrance where he just came in and the kitchen door at the far end. No way of reaching either without being gunned down.

In a glass splashback behind the breakfast bar Thimblerig watches the Shrek's reflection enter the restaurant and crouch by the maître-d's station. He scans the room with weapon to shoulder like a pro gamer. For a moment his reflection seems to look directly at Thimblerig. Then it turns away. Then he raises his weapon and steps out. Thimblerig hunkers against the cabinet as above his head bullets punch vegetable fragments into the air. A shower of lettuce and couscous falls over him. A dressed prawn lands in his lap. The gunfire stops. A persistent thrum remains.

No – that's not right. The thrumming isn't the aftermath of the shooting. It isn't coming from inside Thimblerig's ears but rather from behind the warm wood panel his back is pressed against.

What now? His right hand's on the handguard of the rifle. He has cover. He could shoot back. And either kill or be killed. Not a choice he wants to make. But what other options does he have? No point in shouting out the truth: that this is real and not a game. The fate of the Batman proves that the game's insured against this. It must be muting anyone who speaks the truth. What option does he have but gunfire?

Without warning the sprinkler system cuts out and the alarm stops sounding. A flurry of drops splashes onto the floor. In the quiet that follows Thimblerig hears the Shrek's feet slap slowly towards him across the wet floor.

He picks up the sticky prawn from his lap. It's chilly to the touch.

Aha.

A WALL OF UNHAPPY MONEY

Alex has barely made it to the top of the cellar stairs when the first explosion rocks the house. She half-ducks, half-falls forwards out of the cellar door. Another explosion sounds – this time close enough to rattle the shuttered windows of the service corridor.

Her bandaged shoulder twinges as she raises herself from the chilly flagstones. She scans the corridor in both directions. Where the hell has Gunnell gone? She was only a few seconds behind him. In spite of everything, that rough and pitted man is her way out of here, and her only lead.

This must have been the servants' section of the house – all white-wash and bare stone. At each end of the corridor is a white panelled door. She flips a mental coin and heads left. She's barely made it halfway down the corridor when the shutters of the nearest window blow inwards, followed by a cloud of flame and noise that smashes Alex backwards and sears her face. She lands hard, jarring her bad shoulder on the wall. She starts to cry out in fury – then stops when a hairy grey face appears at the window. It leers at her from behind enormous pink sunglasses. On its head is a tiny fireman's helmet. It heaves itself up onto the window ledge where it teeters for a second. The elephant costume hangs to its feet like a shaggy dress.

Snorky, Alex realises. This is Snorky, from *The Banana Splits* – the weird-ass twentieth-century kids' show that Harm teaches in the first module of her cultural-studies course: *They were different times: the norming of sexual abuse through light-entertainment tropes: 1968–1983.*

Framed in the high window, the giant plush toy turns and reaches behind itself. A lime-green machine pistol borne by a hovering drone descends from the air and lands in its hand. The drone dips and shoots out of view as the Snorky turns to Alex. Through its shades, it takes careful aim at her.

'Hey – no!' she says, scrabbling to her feet.

A shot booms out. Alex flinches – but it's the Snorky who buckles forwards. A second shot, and his chubby shoulder is flung back in a spout of blood and acrylic fur. He falls back from the window ledge. Staggering to her feet Alex turns to the source of the shots. Francis Gunnell is standing in the doorway at the end of the corridor. His left arm is crooked, creating a rest for the barrel of his shotgun. His long waxed coat gives him an *Easy Riders* dash.

Alex looks back out through the wall. The Snorky is raising himself to his hands and knees. He's alive. She's got to stop the killing, but first she needs to stop Strangers finding her.

'Come on if you're coming,' says Francis.

'Just a second.'

She reaches into her shoulder bag and pulls out the blanker by a dangling cable. With trembling fingers she attaches its suckers to her tattoos. Just like Abul showed her.

'OK,' she says. 'I'm ready.'

Alex follows Francis at a run down a white-painted corridor. As they turn a corner, Gunnell pauses to shove a fresh shell into his shotgun. Alex stops to lean on an upright chair, struggling for breath. Her shoulder's throbbing dangerously. Through her mesh, she sees a fat figure barrelling towards them, just around the bend.

'There!' she shouts, pointing just as the grinning man-dog appears.

Gunnell clacks his gun shut. The dog skids to a stop and raises its own puce shotgun. Gunnell spins towards it as Alex flings the chair at the dog. The gun discharges. The chair takes the bullet, then jars against the dog's gun-arm. Gunnell's shotgun booms. The dog's chest explodes below its red bow tie. Its floppy cloth tongue flails as it falls.

'No!' shouts Alex, turning away from the sight.

Gunnell strides past the dog, reloading, and knocks on the door at the corner of the hall. Alex steps carefully past the wreck of the coslife dog, averting her eyes. The door opens a crack, then fully. Connor's on the other side.

Alex follows Francis into a triple garage. He hands his duffel bag to Connor, who locks the door behind them, giving Alex a careful frown. There's a Bentley and a spiffy Land Rover, but Francis and Connor walk past these and vanish behind a white van at the far end. As Alex rounds the back end of the van, Francis looms out and grabs her arm. Pain strikes her bandaged shoulder as he shoves her against the rear doors.

'Hey!' she says.

'Take that off,' he said, pointing at her mesh. 'I'll get you out of here, because I'm not a total cunt. But you are not recording me.'

Alex's heart punches her chest in an angry volley. Ever since she put the mesh back on, her glowheart has thrummed with purple electricity. Down in the cellar she thought the insanity of the past few days might wash her away. Her mesh is keeping her alive.

'I need it,' she says.

Gunnell grabs the mesh and yanks it off her face. She cries out as though he's hurt her, then realises he hasn't. Mesh clips are designed to give way.

'You fucking don't,' says Gunnell.

In the real, Francis is no longer a demon walking the earth; just an ageing tough guy, furious at how the world has turned. He slides open the side door of the van.

'You're getting in back with me,' he says.

Without the Strange to soften them the concrete walls are closing in on Alex. She climbs obediently into the van. Francis slides the door shut, shutting out most of the light. He points at the bench seat running along the side of the fibreglass cabin. Alex sits and fumbles for a seat belt; straps herself in. Francis sits on the opposite bench. Up front, Connor fires the engine. There's a metal grille between him and the rear of the van. Through the windscreen, Alex sees the garage door crank open, letting daylight in. She braces herself for shooting, but none comes. Connor revs up and the van leaps forward, rattling Alex and Francis like dice in a cup.

'Ease up!' shouts Francis.

They crunch forward onto gravel. Through the windscreen, Alex glimpses a red-brick wall, a tree. Without her mesh, she's no idea what's going on outside, how many Strangers Connor's passing as he corners violently, then accelerates onto bumpy terrain. At one point there are three rapid pops and the van swerves mightily to the right. Alex is thrown forward against her seat belt. Then Francis lurches forward as the van swings the other way. A cattle grid rattles under the wheels and high gateposts whoosh past the windscreen.

'We're out,' says Francis. 'Back gate.'

The van accelerates onto smoother ground. The only sound is the rush of tyres on tarmac. Are they out of danger? In the absence of anything else to look at, Alex and Francis stare at one another. The van corners. Still no shooting. Connor calls out over his shoulder.

'I think we're clear.'

The first thing Alex does when they park up in the lay-by is message Abul on his 'Thimblerig' address. Francis won't let her have her mesh so she has to borrow his antique smartphone. While she waits for Abul to respond she calls Harmony. She tries to summarise what's going on but totally fails.

'You're high on this, aren't you?' says Harm's crackled voice. 'You know who'll have to mop up when you come down?'

The noise of the traffic drowns her out. In this off-road parking spot Alex and the Gunnells are hidden from the view of any Strangers driving by, but the scrawny trees can't cut out the road noise. Alex cups her hand around the phone.

'Are you hearing me?' she says. 'There are people after me with guns. Dogs and superheroes and I don't know – elephants!'

'OK, Ally, breathe. You're wearing your mesh?'

'No no no, this is not an Encounter.'

'Because elephants carry guns.'

Gunnell is watching Alex from beside the van. She walks away from him, towards a wire fence marking off a scrubby field.

'I'm not saying they're real elephants.'

'So you *are* playing a game.'

'Oh for—. Stop it. This is not an Encounter.'

All that's going on, Alex could persuade herself this *is* some crazy-ass Encounter – except that Gunnell has stripped away her mesh. This world has no overlay. The sun's white light irradiates the field, undoctored. Washes everything clear.

'I need you,' she says quietly.

'What was that?' said Harm.

Alex's words are lost to traffic noise. Harm says something else but it breaks and crackles. The call cuts out. No signal. Alex waits for it to return but it doesn't. She walks back to where the Gunnells are blowing into their hands and slaps the phone into Francis's paw. Connor doesn't look her way.

'So,' she says, 'where now?'

Having a destination means having a clue what's going on. For now, it makes sense to be in the middle of nowhere. At least that reduces the chances of armed Strangers stumbling onto them.

'Nowhere,' says Francis, nodding towards the van. 'You and me are going to have that chat about Occidental Data Partnerships.'

In the petrol-scented calm of the van's interior, Alex explains as clearly as she can about the emails and Susan Hardiman. She leaves Abul out. She can't work out whether she's feeling protective of, or repulsed by, the little shit. Somewhere during the escape from the mansion she's made a decision to run with the Gunnells, but they're nowhere near her friends. She's not yet angry enough to put Abul into any more danger.

Gunnell nods through her narration, beating time on his thigh. 'I knew it,' he says, 'but I never made the connection.'

He bangs on the wall of the van.

'Oi, son!' he shouts.

After a second, Connor's head appears.

'Those Occidental cunts we brought in last year,' says Francis. 'Didn't I say they were up to something?'

'You said you'd get them checked out,' says Connor.

'Way they claimed to know all about that virus.'

'I told you, it wasn't a virus. It was an object injection attack.'

'God,' said Alex. 'I'd hate to have to eat dinner with you two.'

'Not much chance of that,' said Connor, giving her a look laden with meaning.

She avoids his eye. He hops down out of the van and slides the door shut. His father turns to Alex, 100 per cent business.

'So there was this bunch of spotty hackers,' he says.

'*Crackers*,' says Connor, climbing back into the driver's seat and slamming the door. 'Hackers is generic. Crackers break things.'

Francis looks like he's about to punch him.

'Go on,' says Alex.

'So they locked down our computers, and that, with this – this—'

'Ransomware,' says Connor, starting up the van.

Francis turns him a sharp look.

'Where we going?' he says.

'Anywhere but here. All it takes is one Stranger to make us. We're too exposed.'

He pulls the van into the stream of traffic.

'Are you sure?' says Alex. 'At least we're sheltered here.'

He takes no notice. Alex buckles up. Francis doesn't.

'So,' he says, turning back to Alex, 'these hackers send us this ransom demand. And three hours later, who do you think shows up at my front door?'

Alex leans closer in to Francis.

'Me?'

'Spouting this dead-on shit nobody else had got close to. Stuff you couldn't have known—'

'—unless I was working with these hackers.'

'*Crackers!*' shouts Connor from up front.

'You thought I was with them.'

Connor steers sharply. Francis grips his seat and glares at his son until the van steers straight.

'So by now,' he says, 'I'm wanting to cut this thing off before anything gets out. And lo and behold, that very afternoon I get a call from this Occidental Data shower, offering me all this techie protection.'

'Network security,' says Connor.

'*Oh*, I says to myself, *it's my lucky day*. So I tell them all about the ransom-whatnot.'

'–ware,' says Connor.

'And, *oh*, they says, *we have just the thing. All you need is give us a wodge of monkey money and let us walk all over your network. We'll make you secure as a bank*. Fucking idiot, am I?'

Six months back, the day Alex door-stepped Francis, he told her he was going to *cut off her source*. She thought she'd somehow given away Mickey's contact – the bag-carrier who leaked the dirt on Francis. The idea she'd put that man in harm's way was one of the mess of things that pushed her into depression, but it turned out that the Gunnells never laid a finger on him. She never understood why. Now she does. It was because Francis thought her information came from these hackers.

Or crackers.

Which means Alex never gave anyone away. She punished herself in vain, for that at least.

Gunnell watches her chew this over.

'They've got something on you,' she says. 'Occidental. They're going to use it to scupper your bail-out.'

Occidental staged this hack on Francis, stole a bunch of data from him, as much as six months ago. That means they've been preparing this current whatever-it-is for a long time. Now, according to Corrigan's emails, they've used the hacked information to prepare a dossier. They're going to release this on Monday, giving the government air cover when they back-peddle on all the bigging up they've been giving Handy Frank's. Calling it *A national treasure* and *The friendly face on every high street*.

'And for some reason,' she says, 'this information is hot enough to justify—'

She points behind them: meaning the guns, the costumes. Gunnell nods, keeping Alex pinned in his stare.

'So why,' he says, 'do *you* give a shit all of a sudden?'

Alex returns the gaze unblinking. Her eyes and head are on fire.

'They killed my friend,' she says, though Mickey was never that.

Gunnell studies her a little longer then shrugs.

'All right. So what's our play?'

Everything has been about getting to this moment – persuading Gunnell to talk to her. She's no idea what happens next.

'Ah,' says Gunnell, turning to look forward through the windscreen. 'Right. Well, so much for you.'

Except.

'Hold it,' she says. 'What did you mean by "monkey money"?'

Gunnell doesn't look at her. It's like she's been dismissed. But he answers.

'The hackers wanted their ransom in toy money. The stuff from your game.'

'Emoticoin?'

Gunnell looks at her.

'So?

All these dark acts, fuelled by pseudo-money. And the people shooting at them are Strangers. The Strange is the thing that binds this whole affair together. Suppose for a moment it's not that someone's *using* the Strange. Suppose the people behind this are the people who *run* the Strange?

'I need to call someone,' she says.

Francis pulls out his phone. He makes to hand it to her, then reconsiders and extracts a wire from another pocket, winnows it into the bottom of the phone. Then he plants the business end in his ear. An ancient hands-free. He heaves himself over to sit by Alex and hands her the phone.

Alex dials from memory. The phone rings once, then a clipped male voice says, 'Yes, hello?'

'Hello, Lukaš.'

'Alex? I can barely hear you.'

His distant voice is a still point in all the fury.

'I'm in the back of a van,' says Alex.

She glances over at Francis, who gives her a thumbs-up. He can hear OK.

'Where are you headed,' said Lukaš, 'that you need to ride there in such style?'

Where indeed?

'From what I am seeing,' says Lukaš, 'you are moving rapidly over the Alaskan tundra. Is there some fault with your mesh?'

'I'm not on my mesh.'

'But listen, Alex, I'm glad you've called. I'm embarrassed to ask when you have your compliance investigation to deal with, but I was hoping there might be an opportunity to speak on your programme next week.'

Alex's stomach knots up. Here she is, on the run from gun-toting cartoon characters, and Lukaš is using her for PR.

'However,' he says, 'I haven't heard from – ah—?'

'Siobhán. I'm sure they'll have you up. I'll give her a call, OK?' The show – the compliance enquiry – they're a lifetime past.

'I appreciate that, Alex.'

'But there's also something you can do for me.'

'Of course.'

Boredom is creeping into his voice.

'You had that consulting contract with Mondan?' she says. 'Helping Sean Perce and Dani Farr develop Emoticoin?'

'Alex, I can't speak about confidential—'

'Meaning you did.'

A brief pause.

'I suppose it's no secret.'

'Yesterday you told me Perce controls the supply of Emoticoin.'

Another long pause.

'There are confidentiality clauses—'

'Meanwhile he's buying up companies left and right. Marching into new markets, replacing traditional suppliers.'

'I really wouldn't be able to—'

'So let's say he wanted to move into DIY.'

Beside Alex, Gunnell sits intently, shoulders rising and falling with his breathing.

'Hardly a natural step for a tech firm,' says Lukaš after a pause.

'Let's say he did. Could he use his shadow currency to take down a rival? Pay bribes? Does that kind of thing go on in these cases? In your opinion?'

The phone crackles. Alex had forgotten how hot your ear gets using a mobile phone.

'We are not speaking over the Strange?' says Lukaš.

'Plain old telephone service,' says Alex.

'Very well then. Since you press me.'

Actually, all she's done is ask, but she knows when not to interrupt.

'You must understand,' he says, 'I am not pleased with myself at not having acted on the following information.'

Beside Alex, Gunnell tenses up.

'Two months ago,' says Lukaš, 'I ran a strategy session for Perce's executive team. We were scenario-planning new ventures. At one point, I led a mind-mapping exercise on mass-dormant consumer goods. You know what I mean by this.'

Alex and Gunnell catch each other's eye. *Pasta machine*, he mouths at her. She nods with a grin. This weird intimacy in the droning closeness of the van.

'Sure,' she says.

'To Perce, such underutilised goods represent areas of significant opportunity. If he can get his users to share their underutilised possessions through the Strange, they will use his service more.'

'And,' says Alex, 'undermine traditional suppliers.'

'During the exercise, Perce's strategy director, a Mr Pemberton, commented that tools are an ideal, untapped category for such sharing.'

Gunnell lurches forward, as though looking for someone to hit. Alex holds up a hand.

'Drills, hammers, screwdrivers,' says Lukaš, 'what have you. These valuable items, lying as they do, unused, in attics and sheds. Ripe for lending. Then Pemberton said, *Of course, there's nothing to stop Handy Frank's stepping in and doing this if they had the will to innovate.*'

Gunnell mutters something dark.

'Excuse me?' says Lukaš.

'Nothing,' says Alex, placing a hand on Gunnell's waxed sleeve. 'Go on.'

'There was,' says Lukaš, 'some laughter at this juncture. One could attribute this to the usual – I believe the term is – "bro attitude".'

Alex smirks. He does have a way of talking like her nan.

'But then,' says Lukaš, 'Perce said something I found distinctly odd. *No need to worry about those dinosaurs once the dossier lands in Whitehall.* After which, everybody laughed harder. Excluding me.'

The van rumbles over an uneven surface. Alex is knocked sideways into Gunnell. She shifts away. This makes complete sense, and also no sense at all. When did people start killing each other over DIY equipment?

'When you came to me yesterday,' says Lukaš, 'asking about Susan Hardiman and Handy Frank's, I should have mentioned this, but it stretched credibility to believe these things were connected.'

'They're connected, all right,' says Francis Gunnell. 'Connected as my fist is going to be with Perce's pretty face.'

Alex sucks in air. There's a pause.

'You might have let me know we had company?' says Lukaš.

'Lukaš Caron, meet Francis Gunnell. Francis – et cetera.'

Lukaš makes a noise Alex can only presume is laughter.

'Well, well,' he says, 'what interesting company my former students keep. Good day, Mr Handy Frank!'

'Is it?' says Gunnell, whipping out the earpiece and standing.

Alex ducks back as he clambers past, steadying himself with a hand on either wall of the van. Up front, he and Connor start an animated conversation.

'Listen, Lukaš,' says Alex, 'I don't mean to be rude – you've been really helpful, but I need to be getting on.'

The van is making a series of sharp left turns, jolting in and out of motion.

'Not at all,' says Lukaš. 'I can only hope I've been of assistance.'

'You have,' says Alex. 'Thank you.'

She ends the call with a soft *boop*. She tries to stand, remembers the seat belt and unclasps it. She gets up and joins the huddle at the front. Francis has his finger on a page of an *A–Z*.

'Apparently,' Francis shouts through the grille, 'he pretty much lives there, up on the thirty-fourth floor.'

Connor nods.

'We're going to Perce?' says Alex. 'Now?'

Francis cracks a warm and genuine smile. Alex smiles back, then remembers what he's capable of.

'What are you planning?' she says.

'Nothing stupid,' says Gunnell. 'There are cameras all over that building. We need to call him out. Record it. That's not me and Connor's forte.'

He grins again and she understands. He wants her to confront Perce in his lair. She nods, though the prospect terrifies her.

She and Francis grip the grille as the van leaves a roundabout onto a main road.

'So,' he says, in an unnervingly casual voice. 'If it wasn't those hackers, how *did* you find out about my little Brummie deal?'

Alex stares at the road ahead. Shit. Has she walked into this, after everything? Now he knows she had another source. Without knowing what she's about to say, she opens her mouth; but before she can get out the first word there's a loud *CRACK*! from the side of the van. Everything lurches to the left.

'Shit!' shouts Connor, wrestling with the wheel.

There's another crash against the side of the van. Alex grabs at Francis for support as the van mounts the verge. A scream of brakes throws them hard against the grille.

'I can't—!' shouts Connor.

The van rears forward and up, then lands with a *CRUMP*. Alex is airborne for a second then the back of her head smashes into the grille. Then nothing.

GIVE ME FREON OR GIVE ME DEATH

The wet footfalls of the Shrek are bearing down on the salad bar where Thimblerig is hiding. He needs one more minute to do his work. He doesn't have a minute.

He twists around and slides open the metal panel on the side of the salad bar. He clambers into the humming warmth of the void inside. It's dry. The whole snug space has been isolated from the spray from the sprinklers. Between him and the Shrek is a solid metal panel. It's dented by bullets but unpunctured. To his left the refrigeration unit thrums.

He manhandles the pink assault rifle past his body and places the muzzle up against a metal ventilation grille that's facing towards the Shrek. No chance of aiming. But he isn't intending to hit anything. He wedges the butt against his feet and finds the trigger guard with his fingers. He takes a breath and squeezes the trigger.

The gun kicks like a stallion. The world inside the salad bar explodes in light and sound. He holds the gun as level as he can while it thunders. Then he lets the trigger go.

He ears scream a sharp and constant note. He twists his neck to see the damage. Through sparkles he sees that the vent has popped out – leaving an opening the size of a mail slot. He peers through. Nobody in sight. Best of all: no corpse.

Leaving the gun in place he wriggles back round and opens his backpack. The contents – including the hibernating cat – are dry. He extracts a long flathead screwdriver from his cache of Handy Frank's acquisitions and pokes his head and arms out of the same opening he crawled in through. Keeping his body inside the cabinet to avoid touching the wet floor he reaches out and unscrews the access panel to the refrigeration unit. Behind this is a dusty array of fins where the coolant runs. Behind this will be the compressor that pumps freon through the system. All of which is important for just one reason: the piston inside the compressor is powered by mains voltage.

Another rattle of bullets hammers the unit. Each shot echoes like a kettle drum. Without bothering to aim Thimblerig twists around to give the trigger another squeeze. The gun gives his shoulder a painful jolt but he holds on a few seconds longer through the horrendous din. Then he lets the trigger go.

Silence. If he was the Shrek he'd back off now. Try another tack. Maybe double round to approach through the kitchen instead. At least that's what Thimblerig would do if a) he was playing this game and b) it actually was a game.

He stretches his head out of the cabinet and peers past the dusty heat exchange to locate the long black tube of the capacitor. He nudges this aside with the screwdriver. Behind is the mains relay. When he touches the screwdriver against the first screw the LED at the tip of its handle lights up red. Mains electricity.

It takes another twenty seconds to get the wires in place. Then Thimblerig spins around again to look out through the vent. The Shrek is approaching from the kitchen. He's surprisingly quiet for such a big ogre. Seeing him tippy-toe through the dining tables in a near-horizontal crouch would be funny if he wasn't holding an assault weapon.

The Shrek takes cover behind the nearest table. He has barely five metres to cross to get to the salad bar. The green hillock of his back rises and falls behind the table. Thimblerig tightens his fingers around the stock of the gun and thinks of the rewards the game must be piling onto this man.

Thimblerig no longer has the gun trained on the Shrek. He's using it for a much more basic function. As a pole. The barrel is pointing out behind him with the mains flex draped over it. At the end of the flex the exposed wires are dangling five centimetres from the sodden floor.

There's a crash somewhere nearby. Perhaps a fire crew or police bursting into reception. This is enough to jolt the Shrek into action. He straightens up and charges towards the salad bar. Thimblerig holds out for one second – two. Then he yanks the gun back into the salad bar. The mains flex falls to the floor.

There's a *ZATZ*! and a burst of gunfire. The room's lights flicker and die. Thimblerig's finger finds the trigger. There's a chance the Shrek is still on his feet. Maybe his booties' rubber soles kept him safe. Though that's unlikely with his whole costume drenched in sprinkler water. At this range the full 240V would have made a circuit up one leg and down the other.

After what feels like ten minutes of silence – but is probably thirty seconds – Thimblerig lowers the gun and peeks out. Around the end of the salad bar the lovable ogre Shrek is snoozing peacefully. His bright green assault rifle lies beside him.

Thimblerig steps out of the cabinet. The exposed ends of the mains flex are still lying on the soaking floor but with the fuse blown they're no danger. He kneels by the Shrek and tugs on the mask until it pops off. A wiry baffle of hair springs out into a sphere. The Shrek turns out to be an older white woman. She must be thirty-five or something. Thimblerig lays the mask on the floor and uses the heel of his sneakers to grind the circles of mesh in the eyeholes. Then he kneels in the wet and manoeuvres his ear to the woman's mouth. Would he be able to tell if she's alive? Before he can come to any conclusion there's a shout from the reception area. The police have heard the shot. Thimblerig grabs his gun and rucksack and runs-slash-skids into the kitchen.

As he tears past the massive stainless steel units he tries to grab a knife from a magnetic rack. His hand lands instead on a ladle. Not wanting to stop and correct the mistake he grips the ladle tight and shoves out through the fire-escape door.

At the rear of the building is a yard surrounded by a high brick wall. Thimblerig's standing on the platform of a loading bay. The fire door slams shut behind him with a crash the police will surely hear. He vaults off the platform, half-twisting an ankle on the rough concrete, then runs to the gate at the back of the yard. On the other side of the gate's fat metal bars the side road's empty. Beyond this is a patch of tarmacked ground where a couple of dozen cars are parked. The afternoon light is fading. Here and there lights are flickering on.

He struggles with the gate's lock mechanism but all he manages to do is scrape his fingers on the catch. He pushes and pulls at the gate but it doesn't budge.

A big black Mercedes glides up the driveway on the other side of the gate and comes to a halt directly in front of Thimblerig. He steps back from the gate. The car's registration plate reads HNY 8@D63R. The windscreen is deeply tinted. This is not the police.

The front passenger door opens. From it climbs Doug Raynor of Occidental Data Partnerships. He raises a handgun at Thimblerig. The gamer in Thimblerig says its a .45 Glock 37.

Raynor strolls up to the gate with the gun trained on Thimblerig's stomach. The driver's door opens and another man slides out. Thick-set. Shaved around the sides of his head. Aviator shades like a nineties' footballer. An automatic machine gun slung over his shoulder. He rests the gun against his hip and points it at Thimblerig. He grins with teeth that are 60 per cent black amalgam filling.

Raynor holds out his free hand and makes a beckoning motion.

— The bag, he says. Hand her over, Mr Piggy.

Thimblerig grabs hold of two bars of the gate. Makes as if to shake them.

— Oh sorry, Mr Raynor, sir. I don't think I can fit it through these heavy heavy bars.

He has no idea what he's saying or doing. The locked gate. The guns trained on him. The armed police who are probably about to burst from the fire door any moment. All of this has somehow squeezed him out of reality. Whatever the reason, this burst of sarcastic courage certainly aggravates Raynor. He steps forward to reach the gun through the bars. He places its cold muzzle on Thimblerig's forehead.

— Then, *kid,* he says, you can take out your backup disk and pass it through. *Or* I can shoot you in the head and reach through to take it myself.

Thimblerig feels the weight of the backpack on his shoulders. Raynor seems to know exactly what he's after. Though at least he doesn't know the incriminating data's actually inside a cat.

— Shoot me in the head, says Thimblerig, and I'll fall backwards. The bag'll be out of your reach.

— Try me.

— No, if it's OK with you I'll just stand here.

— Thirty seconds, kid. Then boom.

Thimblerig could unsling the rifle from his shoulder but these men would mow him down before he even got a hand to it.

Wait: there's something in his hand. The ladle. He holds it up to Raynor who looks at it baffled. Somehow this lunatic moment gives him strength.

— One false move, he says, and I will take you both out with this.

Raynor gives back a vile grin with zero emotion behind it. It's the face of a badly rendered game villain.

— Look, he says, I'll tell you what. Hand over the bag this second and I'll only shoot you in the kneecaps instead of the balls. Before I kill you.

Sirens. Distant but getting closer. Raynor's eyes flick towards the sound then meet Thimblerig's. His gun's drifted down a little. He levels it back up.

— Mr Honey Badger? says the driver. We have company.

Raynor swallows and nudges the gun at Thimblerig's face. He makes to speak. Then the sky goes black above them. Raynor looks up and when his eyes widen Thimblerig follows his gaze. A cloud is descending on them at speed – a dark grey cloud ten metres across that churns and shoots out grey jets like the base of a waterfall. Raynor and the driver start to back away. Then vanish as the cloud envelops them.

As it swirls around Thimbelrig it gives off a staticky hum. A boiling vertical tunnel has formed around him – just wide enough for him to reach out both arms if he wasn't frozen to the spot. Six or seven posts of the gate fall inside the tunnel along with him. Everything else has vanished.

He takes a few steps backwards. The grey cyclone follows – keeping him at its centre. As it moves with him it envelops the gate-posts. He's alone in the belly of the storm.

Thimblerig ducks as a shot rings out. Then a burst of machine-gun fire. Then a pause during which all he can hear is the rattling of the cloud. Its surface is moving too fast to pick out details but it looks like liquid metal broiling over rapids. Raynor's Glock is ejected from the cloud and lands at Thimblerig's feet. The driver's machine gun follows shortly after.

A smaller cloud separates from the whirling surface and hovers in front of him. The churning movement stills and resolves into several dozen tiny drones all hovering in formation. They're about the size and shape of badminton shuttles. Moulded from carbon fibre polymer. Tiny fin-like propellers rotate at super-speed to hold them up.

The drones advance in formation and land on Thimblerig's chest where they attach themselves to his T-shirt. Another deputation moves forward and does the same. This is the cue for a frenzy of mini-swarms to land on different patches of his body. Pretty soon he's covered in humming clusters. His clothes start tugging upwards. After a beat his feet leave the ground. In another twenty seconds he emerges from the top of the tunnel-cloud. Still no sign of Raynor or the car.

As Thimblerig rises into the air, the whole swarm follows below him. Once they're level with the flat roof of the hotel the direction of travel changes to horizontal. They pick up pace. Their bearing is roughly east and a little north.

He's become somebody's special delivery. The question is, whose?

DRONE SHOT

Someone's shouting but Alex can't hear over the sound of the fireworks display. By focusing all her attention into her eyelids, she forces them open and strains to see against the sunlight blaring through the rear windows of the van. The floor's tilted at a dangerous angle. The fireworks display is going on just metres away: mighty explosions accompanied by cymbal crashes.

Alex is piled in a heap on the plywood floor, up against the rear of the driver's seat. There's a boot in her face. She moves it away. It belongs to Francis. She crawls up his leg and body; touches his rocky face. A face bruised by age. He's breathing, at least, but he's out. He wasn't the one shouting just now, so who?

The van's interior is a thundering echo chamber. Somewhere beneath the explosive noise, the voice is still shouting. *Popcorn!* it cries. *Popcorn!*

The noise isn't fireworks, Alex realises, it's hammer blows on the van's exterior.

'*Popcorn!*' shouts the voice. '*The fucking popcorn!*'

It's Connor, up front. That's who's shouting. Alex lifts her head to see but her shoulder starts to spasm. So she rolls onto her back. There's nobody in the driver's seat. All she can see through the smashed-up windscreen is a thicket of trees.

The hammering peters out. Only now does it occur to Alex that it was gunfire, not hammer blows. Someone was strafing the van.

Now it comes back to her. Before she blacked out, another vehicle rammed them, drove them off the road. Strangers. The Strangers have found them.

'Shotgun!' cries Connor's voice from the driver's footwell. 'The *shotgun*!'

Shotgun. That's what he was shouting. Not *popcorn*. Alex rolls over and forces herself to her knees. Her world heaves as she half-stands under the low roof and takes a wary step towards Connor.

'Where?' she says.

The gunfire starts up again. A volley smashes through the rear-door windows behind her. She cries out and stumbles forward. Her wounded shoulder lands on something solid. Diamonds of glass litter the floor, cutting her palm. The sound she thought was cymbals? That was the windows smashing in.

'The gun!' shouts Connor.

Alex is lying across the duffel bags that Connor loaded into the van, back at the mansion. Her cheek's pressed against something long, thin and solid. She reaches into the duffel and pulls out a pump-action shotgun by its butt. She holds the chilly rod across her palms and stares at it.

'*Up here*!' shouts Connor.

Alex scrambles up and searches the metal cage separating the driver's cabin from the rear of the van but finds no hatch or gap.

'I can't get it through,' she says.

'Then *use it*!'

'What? But I—'

'Just cover me long enough so I can get back to the wheel. Or we're *dead*.'

Alex looks towards the shot-up windows at the rear. The doors, and the van's right wing, are pitted with dents like acne scars. Bullets hammer metal in a fury. She hopes to Christ they don't make it through to the canister of spare fuel that's latched to the side wall of the van. Every few seconds another shot ricochets through one of the windows. If she goes anywhere near the doors, she's bound to get hit.

Unless.

Stumbling at the slope of the floor, she scrambles over to Francis's prone body and searches the pockets of his waxed coat. Her mesh is in his inside chest pocket. Attached to the mesh is Abul's blanker. She puts on the mesh and pockets the blanker, then scans through the side of the van.

There are two Strangers, standing at a rise above the tilted van. By the roadside, Alex guesses. With the blanker on, she can see them but they won't see her unless they get line-of-sight.

'Abul,' she whispers, 'you're a misogynist pig but I've got to say: cheers.'

'Safety's on the top,' shouts Connor. 'Above the trigger. Flip it to red.'

She finds it, and does. The Strangers are making no effort to come down from the road. They're just emptying rapid-fire weapons into the side of the van, not caring if anyone sees them. Like they're playing a game.

Which is, of course, exactly what they're doing.

'Chamber a round,' shouts Connor. 'Pump once to rack it.'

Alex grasps the ribbed brown slider running along the bottom of the barrel. With a wave of nausea, she gives it a single rapid pump. The gun latches like in a first-person shooter. It's primed. She can kill somebody. She has to find a way not to do that.

She crouches and moves to the rear doors, holding the gun high to shield her face from the occasional splinter pinging off the shattered windows. For a microsecond, she wonders why she isn't freezing in terror. In the story she tells about herself, she'd have crumbled by now, retreated to the corner of the cabin to weep. What she's actually doing is coolly scanning the positions of the Strangers through the side panel of the van. The one on the left's still firing, while the other fiddles with his gun: reloading.

She gets into position at the rear. After a few seconds the pounding of the bullets stops. The left-hand Stranger has turned his weapon towards the ground to reload. His mate's still fiddling with his.

Here goes nothing. Alex breathes fast, three times, then moves to the window, puts the stock against her right shoulder, and aims through it.

At the top of the verge, by a vintage Nissan Micra, stand two Imperial Stormtroopers. Their neon pink weapons are trained on the tarmac. No. They're Wehrmacht soldiers, in crisp blue uniforms. Alex's hands tremor on the gun. The man on the right flickers white as he raises his weapon. He's back to being a stormtrooper. Alex pulls the trigger as he fires. Recoil kicks her right shoulder and she staggers back, pumping another shell into the chamber. The van's rear doors dissolve, revealing a low wooden platform. Beyond the ornate iron banister at the back of the plat- form, railway lines snake off towards the hissing train from whose caboose two Wehrmacht guards are taking aim with their Mauser rifles. The van lurches forward. Alex lets off a wild shot towards the soldiers, then falls backwards onto the plywood floor.

'That did it!' shouts Connor.

The van racks and bumps over rough terrain. From under the axles comes a cacophony of scraping. Already bruised and battered, Alex is being shaken about like a die in a cup.

'Easy!' she shouts.

The rear doors of the van have reappeared. Alex uses the bench seat to pull herself up and staggers to them. They're crashing along a stony track through a wood of spindly trees. The railway lines have gone. Instead, a thick layer of dry branches carpets the track. A few hundred metres behind, through trees, Alex glimpses the blue Micra pelting after them. Then it's the rear end of a vintage train, careening backwards along the tracks. They hit a straight patch. Track and Micra reassert themselves.

'Are you getting the trains again?' she shouts to Connor but he doesn't reply.

'Not helpful,' she mutters, to nobody in particular. This is not the time for Connor's Encounter to nose back into their story. And where the hell did the Second World War soldiers come from? The story's getting tangled.

Peering out of the grimy window, Alex can just make out a blanch-white figure sitting in each of the car's front seats. Both Stormtroopers are back. At least she didn't kill either of them.

'They're still on us!' she shouts to Connor.

'So shoot them!' he calls back.

The car's closing in along the winding path. The train thunders ever closer along the tracks. The car takes brief flight as its wheel strikes a rock. Even if Alex wanted to shoot the stormtroopers, which she doesn't, the Strange knows now where she and the Gunnells are. More Strangers are bound to follow. What she needs to do is make the way impassable. Scanning the cabin for inspiration, her eyes land on the fuel can. She kneels to loosen its cap. A waft of honeysuckle rises from its sloshing interior. It's full. All she needs is a source of flame.

She trips and stumbles back to Francis, who's now dressed in the black wool uniform of a mid-twentieth-century railway guard, complete with peaked cap. She searches his pockets a second time. The cabin stutters violently between the van's rear, and the dim-lit interior of a train's mail carriage, post sacks heaped to either side. Alex locates a box of Swan Vestas in the breast pocket of the jacket. Empty. She searches the other pockets. Nothing.

She crawls to where two Royal Mail sacks are lying on the floor. As she lifts the sacks to tip them out, each morph into one of the Gunnells' duffel bags. A clanking mess of weapon-ready tools tumbles out. Nothing that could start a fire.

Shit. Alex drops the empty duffel onto the pile of tools. No point asking Connor for a light. He doesn't smoke tobacco. How in hell does Alex make flame in the back of a moving van that's trying to become a steam train? She lets out a mighty sob of frustration. Then she remembers the Happy Handyman.

She fumbles for her shoulder bag and extracts the mannequin, plants a kiss on top of its winking head. Now all she needs is a cloth. Her eyes land on Francis's feet, which are once again clad in twenty-first-century work boots. With fumbling fingers, she unlaces his left boot and tugs it off. He doesn't stir. She peels off his ribbed black sock. Its smell is musty, like a favourite armchair.

Staying on all fours, she scrambles to the rear of the van and unlatches the fuel can. Against the lurching of the van, she tries to tip a little petrol onto the sock. She ends up with petrol over her hands and knees. Fumes rise, leaving her dizzy. She shakes her head to clear it, then stuffs the sodden sock into the neck of the can.

Three rapid cracks sound from behind the van. Shots – wide of the mark. Through the metal of the doors, Alex watches the Stranger in the passenger seat leaning his gun out of the car window. They're close. A hundred metres, tops. Another volley of shots pings off the back of the van.

Alex grips the handle of the petrol can in her left hand. The van doors have gone again. The Nazi train is steaming towards them. With her right, Alex cracks back the head of the Happy Handyman and flicks the lighter wheel. Her hand's engulfed in a halo of flame.

'Shit!' she cries, dropping the lighter.

'What?' calls Connor.

The trains and track drop away, replaced by the dented rear doors of the van. Alex shakes her hand but the sticky flame keeps eating into the flesh of her hand. It leaps to the dangling sock, which goes up in a stinking ball of orange flame.

'*Shit! Shit!*' she shouts.

With a single motion, she reaches to the can behind her, then launches it through the smashed-in window. A sonic boom sounds, followed by a tremendous *WHOOMPH* as two whole carriages of the pursuing train whip-crack into the air, in the slow-mo of a fever dream. Alex drops and rolls onto her flaming hands, smelling spit-roast.

'*Jesus Christ*!' says Connor. 'What did you do?'

Alex rolls onto her back and stares at the reddened mess of her right hand. Idly she thinks of a poster she had on her wall as a child, of the surface of Mars. Smoke tails up from the carbonised front of her tweed skirt.

'That wasn't real,' she says. 'The train. That was the Encounter.' She turns to shout to Connor. 'Can you see in the mirrors? Are they OK?'

'They went off the road. Hard to tell, past the fucking fireball.'

Hugging her right hand under her left armpit, Alex kneels up and grabs hold of the back door. The conflagration reaches ten or twenty metres into the air.

'Oh, shit,' she says. 'Holy fuck.'

'Wood's pretty dry,' says Connor. 'We're outpacing it.'

Alex watches the smoke recede through the rear windows. Could anyone survive that? Did she just kill two people, for the sake of her own skin? She slumps onto the bench seat and puts her head back against the jostling side panel. After a minute or so she realises that the weird sound droning in her ears is her own weeping, rattled by the motion of the van.

'You OK back there?' says Connor.

Things have gone from insane to bat-shit. How can a battle for the market in hammers and nails lead to a daylight attack on the open road? There has to be more. This thing has got to be bigger, but for the life of her Alex can't see beyond her own little corner of the picture.

The van slows and tilts upwards. Alex dries her eyes with an undamaged patch of sleeve, and uses her left hand to guide her up to the grille. The van bumps up a grassy verge and onto the road.

'We'll need new wheels,' says Connor as he manoeuvres onto the hard shoulder. 'They've had eyes on the van. And it's shot to shit.'

'I thought,' says a gravelly voice from somewhere, 'I couldn't hate these fucking hipsters any more.'

Alex turns back to see Francis rising from the floor like a hard-boiled Lazarus. The van starts moving on the level. The quiet of tarmac under rubber is a crazy relief.

Francis is staring at his feet in bemusement.

'Where,' he says, 'is my fucking sock?'

SHORT

The cloud of drones makes dull but effective company.

After they lifted Thimblerig from the hotel delivery bay his altitude rose fast and he began to get chilly in his sodden clothes. His rescuer had thought of that. Before too long a deputation of delivery drones appeared with a one-piece quilted bodysuit. The drones got in sync with the flight path of Thimblerig's cloud. In mid-air they removed his backpack and manoeuvred the suit onto his legs and arms. Then the suit zipped itself up and a hood popped over his pig-masked head. Now he's super-snug as he cruises over the grey map of London.

His backpack is floating in front of him. He reaches into it and wheedles out his crablet. The cat's head appears from the bag.

— *You, my lad, are full of surprises*, says Lucky Ghost.

— Not me, says Thimblerig against the hard brush of wind.

The cat regards him evenly as he attaches the crablet to his puffed-out sleeve and fires it up. First thing he does is pull up a map and confirm that the soft green checkerboard moving below him is Suffolk. He zooms out the map. Sure enough he's heading for the North Sea coast.

He's pretty sure this is a rescue rather than a kidnap. Just as well. If he's to get to Doug Raynor he needs an ally. He had one of course. Alex Kubelick. She threw everything into helping Thimblerig and what did he do in return? A creepshot video. A few distracting morsels of information. Surly silence.

Thimblerig shivers inside his quilted suit. He's only just realised. The Strangers found him at the hotel. Alex Kubelick must have been spotted.

He mutters a short prayer. On an impulse he can't quite track he fires Alex a warning.

Thimblerig: It's not just Handy Frank's
   See other emails
   Note all timed for Monday
   Note all paid in Emoticoin
   Something's about to be tripped off

He thinks for a moment then types some more.

Thimblerig: Like dominoes
   Handy Frank's will get pushed first

He attaches a new package of emails, including the ones about Sean Perce's Mars rocket and the celebrity Jon Mangan.

— *Well, now*, says Ghost. *Where on earth are your little helpers conveying us?*

The cat's peering down over the flap of the backpack. Thimblerig follows its gaze. Through the patchy spaces in his retinue of drones he sees the dishwater surface of the ocean churning fifty metres below his trainers.

— No idea, he says to the cat.

Why is he being so reticent to Ghost? It seems he's more inclined to spill secrets to Alex Kubelick. The cat's looking at him again. A layer of condensation has formed on its head.

— Here, says Thimblerig, pushing its head down into the backpack. We don't want you to rust.

The cat says nothing as he zips her inside. They fly on through the wet slap of ocean sky. As Thimblerig tracks their progress on the wet screen of his crablet one of the drones attached to his sleeve fritzes out and tumbles towards the sea. Another swoops in from the wider cloud to take its place. This is happening so often he's stopped noticing. These tiny drones have way too little power to carry Thimblerig this far without recharging their torsion batteries. So a constant cycle of replacement drones has been nudging in to replace the ones that die.

He checks the screen again. He doesn't know exactly where the platform is but it's eleven kilometres from the shore. Which means it should be coming up round about – now. He looks forwards. Directly ahead a grey-black oblong protrudes from the wavering surface of the North Sea. A sharp-edged intrusion in the soft texture of the sea.

The tabletop form of Seatopia becomes clearer as they descend. Thimblerig's stomach lurches and his ears pop as they move towards it on a tight diagonal. The wind is salty, brisk and wet. In less than a minute the drones have set him gently on the helipad. They place his backpack beside him and disperse so quickly into the wind and spray it's like they were never there.

He stands a while alone enjoying the sensations of the open sea. This is the highest point of the wartime platform. From here he can take in miles of interference patterns rolling and intersecting over the grey-green plane of the North Sea. It's quite beautiful. Mathematically speaking.

His peace is shattered by the clank and thud of a fire door. Wrapped in an ancient parka at the stairwell entrance stands the hairiest man Thimblerig has ever seen. He's looking punchably pleased with his own brilliance.

— *WELCOME*, he shouts over the wind, *To SEATOPIA!*

He makes a gesture like the cheap conjurer he is. Thimblerig has never wished so strongly for a witty rejoinder but that's never been his style. Instead he says what's on his mind.

— I need to pee.

Hairy Jacko and Thimblerig stand a careful distance apart in the deepest chamber of Seatopia's server farm. In the near-dark they're watching LEDs run a lightshow across an array of servers that's wrapped around the long curved outer wall. The router lights flicker like a stop-motion cityscape at night. This semi-circular catacomb is halfway down Seatopia's eastern leg. A good ten metres above sea level – though in this bluey light it could be deep beneath the ocean. Only the highest-grade sysops and router engineers are normally allowed this low.

— We're pretty certain these belong to Occidental, says Jacko.

It's hard to hear him over the staticky hum of the server rack and the gurgle of coolant seawater being pumped through pipes around the room. Thimblerig moves a notch closer.

— They're officially run by twelve different clients, says Jacko, but my ears pricked up when we started getting requests to hook ever more kit into the same deep layer. With identical non-functional requirements. So I had a good look at these servers . . .

He breaks off. It's as though he's inviting the obvious question. Thimblerig can't not ask it.

— You're – breaking your own crypto?

Jacko shakes his head. His beard rasps against his parka.

— Just traffic analysis. Packet headers. Nothing the authorities couldn't do if they had the nous. You guys did a good job doxxing Occidental last week . . .

This is the first time Jacko's acknowledged that Thimblerig's anything more than a non-swimmer. He wishes he was recording this conversation. But nobody can record Hairy Jacko unless he wants them to.

— . . . all we've done is connect the operations your cell's been uncovering to the network locations of these machines.

— Still though, says Thimblerig, you're breaking anonymity.

Jacko gives him a dark look from under his thick brows.

— Nobody believes in free data more than me. But there are limits, you know? Our people—

He breaks off and walks over to check a router array. Thimblerig thinks about his friends who've vanished and died. He guesses Jacko's thinking of the self-same thing.

Thimblerig knows he should keep his mouth shut but again –
that isn't his nature.

— But up to now, he says, you've been totally happy to take
Occidental's money?

Jacko spins round.

— Only to fund operations. You try running this level of solution without paying customers. All we've ever done is hold their
data.

— As well as pimping connectivity to Sean Perce?

— We're keeping access open.

— So Perce can sell more of his snake oil?

He thinks for a second Jacko might clout him but instead he
breaks away again and sits at the sysadmin terminal beside the
door. He drums his fingers on the desk and pretends to read a
status screen.

Seatopia's not just a free-data hub. It's one of a surprisingly
small number of places where the physical Internet enters the UK.
These islands are only tenuously connected to the continent – digi-
tally as much as politically. There are only a few points where
anyone's been able to make the vast investment needed to run
undersea fibre-optic to Europe or the US or West Africa. Sean Perce
controls not only these cables but also most of the inland hubs. He
pays Jacko's crew to maintain this crucial line from the Netherlands.

Jacko stops drumming the desktop. He's watching Thimblerig.

— You need to give me your data on Occidental, he says.

Thimblerig's hand goes to the backpack where the cat is sleeping. He shakes his head but he doesn't mean 'no'. At least he
doesn't think he does.

— I've turned up – a short, says Jacko.

Thimblerig frowns.

— A short-circuit? Don't you have engineers for that?

— A short on the *market*, says Jacko. A billion-dollar bet that
the UK's about to go to shit. You need to help me stop it.

SANCTUM SANCTORUM

'I'm here for Dani Farr.'

The receptionist's a beehived woman with improbable cheek-bones and pursed vermilion lips. She clearly doesn't know whether to gape or laugh in response to Alex's request. After a few seconds of cognitive dissonance she recovers.

'I'm *terribly* sorry but Ms Farr is indis*posed*,' she says in a front-desk sing-song. 'You do realise it's eleven at night?'

She blinks through her sheeny mesh and waits for Alex to crumble. Alex blinks back at her. Presumably nobody ever asks for Dani, at any time of day, and most definitely not some wild-eyed woman who seems to have set fire to her own clothes. But Alex needs to see Dani. So: what are the magic words to get her past the goblin at the gate?

Alex tucks her burned and crackled right hand under her jacket. It's decided to start reminding her again how much pain it's in. She looks around the reception area. It's weird to visit the Strange in an actual physical building, after it's enfolded Alex so completely for so long. This place is reassuringly solid: white-washed brick and dark hardwood, decked out by Alex's mesh with the foliage of her default wallpaper. From memory, this cavernous room was converted from a derelict synagogue that had been hidden undiscovered for years on this Brick Lane side street. First time Alex visited, this was the office of an upstart social media shop called Parlay. Now it's the HQ of Parlay's more successful offspring, the Strange.

'Look,' she says to the receptionist, 'I get it. I just marched in off the street like a madwoman in a charcoal suit.'

The woman's eyes are travelling sceptically up and down the wreck of Alex's clothes.

'But,' says Alex, 'she'll want to see me.'

A drawn-on eyebrow goes high.

'You just need,' says Alex, 'to say to her—'

Her throat locks up. What exactly *does* this woman need to say to Dani? Everything's churning too fast. Alex has been thrown sideways, as in a tightly banking aircraft, barely clinging on. Now that momentum's landed her here. Bombing up here alongside the Gunnells she somehow persuaded herself that Dani's the one and only ally she needs in the forthcoming confrontation with assailants unknown. Maybe it's because she met Dani once, years back, and thought she seemed like a human being. Maybe it's because a few hours with the Gunnells was enough to turn her off testosterone for life. Either way, the Strange is the source of all this crazy, and Dani Farr's her best route in.

It was touch and go getting here. Connor kept thundering along unreliable B-roads in his wreck of a van, wind whipping through the spaces where the windows were, until they found an out-of-town industrial park in the lee of the M25. They parked up in a row of rusty manual-drive vans that looked as though they hadn't seen service in a decade. Connor extracted from a duffel bag the bits and pieces he needed to steal one. The third he tried – a sky-blue number with the words *FRESH2U CATERING SUPPLIES* fading on its side – actually started. They piled in and made it to London in half an hour, keeping to side roads to avoid CCTV. No telling when the theft might be detected. Alex checked for messages en route. One from Abul at last. Apparently he was alive enough to send her another stash of emails from Occidental. She read through them slowly, jaw setting harder with every swipe.

The truck dropped her at the kerb outside Dani's office. She hesitated when she saw so many Strangers passing by on the Shoreditch pavement, but none of them paid her any mind. As she hopped down from the van, Francis gave her the Happy Handyman thumbs-up, which she returned. Jesus, she thought, as she slammed the door – look at me, old mates with the psycho thug. But they'd been through a lot, the three of them, in the past few hours. Francis whistled her back, proudly brandishing a device he called 'the front-door key' – a home-made ratchet with two long handles and, at its business end, a large flat hook moulded from sheet metal. This, he explained, would get him through any push-bar fire door from the outside. It was going to be his entrée into Perce's notoriously Fort-Knoxed HQ building, round the corner on City Road.

Alex has a strong sense the Knuckle Brothers won't make it within a kilometre of Perce before his private security catches up with them. Even if they do, the man can handle himself. Let the alpha males battle it out. Alex's hunch is there's someone here more biddable than that human eel, Perce. Also with fewer Y chromosomes. Dani's the key. Even though she created the Strange, it can't be her who's using its currency and players to cause this mayhem. The woman has always bared her soul for every Stranger to see. It's impossible to imagine her faking anything. Let alone something this big.

The receptionist blinks and cocks her head. Alex's mind is running on bullet time. She needs to find a code phrase that will gain her entry before this woman calls security.

The mails sent by Abul were the things that finally revealed the scale of the thing. Up till then, the story was all and only about the bribe paid to Susan Hardiman. From Alex's compliance charge through to Mickey's death to the mad pursuit by costumed Strangers, everything seemed rooted in a simple battle over the Handy Frank's bail-out. The first batch of emails Abul gave her, back at the hotel, seemed to confirm this. The fake security business, Occidental, was behind the bribe, was using the Strange to bring the Gunnells down.

Yet even as Alex struggled to nail down the truth, some part of her knew this didn't stack up. Sure, there were tens of millions of pounds at stake in this corporate chicanery. Sure, the Gunnells were borderline crims. But the sheer scale of the madness, the deaths, spoke of something more. As she read the new stash of mails from Abul, her mind crash-zoomed to a much wider perspective. As Abul said, Handy Frank's is just one of a row of dominoes. Only the first to fall.

Alex is a storyteller. She scrapes together fragments from the mess of reality and shuffles them about until they form a concrete narrative. This is what's happening now, inside her head, even as she stands at the reception desk of the Strange. She can make out the shape – but not the through-line.

On Monday, Frank's will collapse, unrescued by government. Britain will draw in a breath, astonished to see this monolith of the high street crumble. Shortly after, Sean Perce's RedShot mission to Mars will crash and burn on its launch platform, incinerating the aspirations of everyone who believes that Britain might for the first time take a lead in the race to escape the bounds of gravity. Then – it would have seemed crazy to think of this a couple of days ago – the late-morning bulletins will announce the tragic death of much-loved vlogger and artist Jon Mangan. And so on, in a three-day parade of awful. A chain of events, all horrendous to the people of Britain, though barely anyone will raise a shrug beyond its borders. An insulated cataclysm of strictly local heroes. In a matter of days, a population who believed they were riding high on the new emotional economy will plunge into despair – and the Strange will be the gateway through which disaster is loosed.

Alex doesn't understand why anyone would want to do this. It seems like Abul doesn't either, though he's gone dark again so who knows. But this catastrophic fall? This overnight swing from triumph to despair? Surely this is something grand enough – insane enough – to justify murder and mayhem – though to who? A foreign power? Some supervillain in a mountain lair?

Either way, this tinfoil-hat conspiracy is the thing that Alex needs to persuade Dani Farr is happening, is real, and she has to convey this information through the very narrow channel offered by one frosty receptionist.

Well, again: her job is telling stories.

'Was there a message at all?' says the receptionist, in words that can pierce Kevlar. 'Because—'

'Tell Dani,' says Alex, 'the Strange is about to flood. Tell her the first drop lands on Monday at eight a.m. Then it'll be a torrent.'

The woman gapes at Alex as though she just threw off her clothes and started twerking around the atrium. This isn't going to work.

There's a microsecond burst of white, like a flash bulb.

'I know you,' says the woman in black.

The woman is standing behind the receptionist, exactly where there was nobody a second ago. She's ruffled and confused, as though she's just woken. She's less brightly lit than everything real around her. A head shorter than Alex, she's leaner than in the publicity stills, though the birthmark on her jaw's there. She studies Alex in silence. This is rather like being checked out by a mountain lion. Then she speaks again, in a scratchy estuary accent.

'You were at the hotel,' she says. 'That time with the minister. How many years back? I lose time.'

So, yup: this is Dani Farr.

Alex was indeed present nine years ago when everything went to shit for Dani and the government minister. Alex was meant to host that ill-fated press conference, on the day TakeBack was born – the fake hacker movement that morphed into the genuine collective called Cockaigne.

Which makes her think again of Abul and everything he's done to her. But Abul must wait.

'Your hair was blue,' says Dani, 'not red. You were waiting in the wings with Sean before he—'

'Before he pegged it to his car?'

Dani giggles, which is kind of girlish, and ducks her head in a nod.

'Heh. Yep,' she says. 'Pretty much.'

Her gaze goes in and out of focus.

'So you're – Alex?'

Alex nods. She's what: star-struck? Things are moving too quickly.

'There's something going on,' she says, 'in the Strange. The first domino is about to fall. Monday morning.'

Dani's turn to nod.

'The black algae. Yeah, I've been watching it. You'd better come up.'

She does stuff with her hands. Compared to most people's mimetics, Dani's are artful, like a Hindu dancer. She vanishes. The receptionist cocks her head, reading her mesh. A bright smile washes across her face.

'You can go right up,' she says to Alex. 'Fifth floor.'

'C'mon in,' says Dani, holding open the door.

The room takes up the whole length of a converted factory attached to the rear of the synagogue. Victorian wood floor, airbrushed brick walls, original ironwork. Big skylights covered by taut blinds. At the centre, a huge desk of plain design with a neatly ordered array of tech. At the far end, a ratty sofa. Alex tries to control her urge to dance across the parquet. She's heard about this room from a number of young male employees she inter-viewed for her vlog piece on Dani. Each of them found their way up here and one way or another ended up on that very sofa with Dani. Yet none of them saw the room. The sex was always on some distant planet, some sword-and-sorcery realm. Guess Dani doesn't like having sex in the real, or doing much of anything there. In this bright open space, she lives unencumbered. Nice game if you can get it – but then, she did create the Strange.

The two women walk to the desk and sit on the smooth ergo-nomic chairs. This close up, Dani smells faintly musky. Not bad, just lived-in. It's actually quite sexy. On the desk, the three screens are live with organic flows of colour, populated by shifting info-graphics and flurries of numerals. In the centre of the middle screen is a black patch, tendrils cloying outwards into colour. Numbers rattle at its borders like bottled wasps.

'The black algae,' says Dani, placing a finger on it. 'Far as I can make out, it started growing a couple of months back, but in the past few weeks it's ballooning.'

Seems like they're buddies now, or something – or Alex happened to arrive at the precise moment when Dani wanted someone to talk at about her 'black algae'. Maybe when you spend your whole time in the Strange you come to expect that a random stranger will turn up on your doorstep with a vital piece of information, just when you need it. Life exhibiting game logic.

Alex squints at the living data

'What is—?' she says, 'I mean, *where* is this?'

'In the algaerhythm. This is a map of what everyone in the Strange is feeling, right now – as read by the algaerhythm. The sum of seven million glowhearts. I'm zoomed in but what you're looking at is roughly thirty per cent of all human experience in the country right now.'

Alex watches the colours do amoeba moves around each other, the black dominating by slow degrees. It makes her queasy.

'So – I'm in there somewhere?' she says. 'What I'm feeling right now watching this is already part of it?

Dani nods.

'A tiny drop in an ocean of feels, but yeah – it's a hall of mirrors.'

Alex is having trouble zooming her brain to the right scale of perception. For as long as she's been in the Strange, it's seemed personal. Her glowheart was her constant companion, a regulator for her wayward emotions. Now she has a God's-eye view, she doesn't much like seeing her highs and lows translated to tiny inflections in a national trend-line.

'The black, here,' she says, 'that's negative emotions?'

Dani glares. OK, whoa – maybe they're not quite friends just yet.

'There are no negative emotions,' says Dani. 'Just strong ones and weak ones. Anger's a weapon. Despair's when you see the heart of things. Better either than sickly joy or love. The black algae's not an emotion, it's an invasion.'

For Alex, another fragment slides into place.

'It's making the Strangers crazy.'

'People have always wanted to play stories with each other,' says Dani. 'Since we were just apes. We still let children make-believe but then we drum it out of them when they reach their teens. Grown-ups've outsourced their fantasies to actors and writers. TV. The algaerhythm changes that.'

'It permits us to play,' says Alex quietly and mostly to herself.

'It tracks what you're feeling and finds a story better than your reality. The black algae's different. It only lies.'

'How did it get there?'

'I was hoping you could tell me that.'

Alex tears her eyes away from the roiling screens. Dani's looking directly at her. Into her.

'I mean,' she says, 'you *are* with Jacko, aren't you?'

'So, all right,' says Jacko, 'Since you've decided to listen to me.'

It's still weird having the mesh back on, though it was only yesterday Gunnell forced Alex to take it off. She thought she couldn't live with the world as it was. Then everything exploded. After that crazy dose of real, the shapes and shades of the Strange are tinny and intrusive. But she needs to keep it on to bring Hairy Jacko into the room.

It's Sunday morning now, eight a.m. and Alex has finally had some shut-eye. Dani's swivelling in her chair. Alex has her butt planted on the edge of the desk. They sip from the foamy bowls of coffee Dani whipped up in her kitchen area. They managed to catch about four hours – Alex on the sofa, Dani in her chair – before Jacko returned the whisper that Dani sent him on some redundant channel. When she patched him in, one red-brick corner of the room transmogrified into the concrete bunker where Jacko's sitting at one end of a mouldy orange sofa, murky in grey-green light. At the other end of the sofa, Alex is confused to see, sits Abul, cat curled on his lap. The top of the cat's head has been flipped back to allow a chunky cable to be plugged into it. It doesn't seem to mind.

The two men look like they're in the room but, according to Dani, they are in fact off on some North Sea oil rig. Or something. Alex is confused on this point. She's also unclear how the hell Abul has transported himself there overnight. Seems he's had adventures of his own.

Seeing Abul is making her mind do several colliding somersaults at once. Fear and disgust at his months of trolling, at the way he was creeping on her back at the hotel room. At whatever the hell was in those tissues. Guilt at having left him to a peril he seems to have evaded. A strange affection for his dogged, literal-minded urge to do good. Then looping back to fury at all the wrong and horrible shit he's done. For a teen, he's a bundle of contradictions, and her feelings about him won't resolve. She's choosing not to use her glowheart to break this down. She has it suppressed, for now. She wants to face this head on, unaided. She'll decide for herself what to say to him next. For now, the two of them are pretty much ignoring one another.

Jacko taps the cat's rear end.

'So moggie here has been storing a batch of email data Abul lifted from Occidental. Here—'

He waves into being a new wall, off to Alex's left. It's a patchwork of glowing grey-white rectangles. Alex picks up her coffee and walks to it. A motherlode of mails. Way more than Abul chose to share with her, before she headed off to possibly die.

'The missing pieces,' says Jacko, 'of a jigsaw I've been putting together for a while. They show that – how to explain this quickly, Abul?'

Abul starts at being brought into the conversation. He's been silent, apart from one embarrassed 'hello' to Dani when she patched him in. Since then he's sat and stroked his cat and fiddled occasionally with the baseball cap and mesh that Jacko's forced onto his head. Now Jacko's question unlocks him. He blinks at

Dani for a second then starts speaking in that uninflected tone he uses to relay information.

'Occidental Data Partnerships is not a security firm. It's a protection racket. Though that's a misnomer also because they're really not protecting anybody. They're currently preparing for their largest ever operation. An attack on a number of well-known institutions and individuals using an algorithm inserted into the Strange. The algorithm shows people a skewed version of reality. It alters the way they think and feel. It makes them do things. They've been building up these people and institutions and making people feel unnaturally excited and optimistic about them.'

He pauses for breath.

'The black algae,' says Dani.

'Ooh,' says Jacko. 'Is that your new horror fanfic?'

Dani glares.

'I know about this,' says Alex. 'A whole bunch of terrible is landing Monday morning. Anyone who tries to stop it gets attacked by killer Strangers.'

Abul flinches.

'You've seen them?' Dani asks him.

He flicks a glance her way and nods quickly. Then he does something strange. He leans forward to whisper to the cat. Then he sits back, casting a millisecond glance at Alex.

'These emails,' says Jacko, 'paint in a picture by numbers. It'll be one gut-blow after another. Public figures will die. National institutions fail. One event on its own would be shitty but this will be a domino effect. It'll be like, Christ, what's happened to this country of a sudden? These people are hacking the public mood.'

There's a still silence. Dani leans forward over her desk, fists balled together in front of her.

'You weren't kidding,' she says. 'There actually is some giant conspiracy?'

Jacko shakes his head.

'Not a conspiracy. A company. An incredibly effective one, headquartered in Belarus. A client of mine, as it happens.'

Over by the wall of emails Alex puts up her hand.

'Can I just—?'

Everyone turns to her – human and ghost – but she's not 100 per cent sure of what she's about to say.

'We do all realise,' she says, 'that this is insane?'

'It's real,' says Jacko.

'No, no, I know you're right. I just mean . . .' She gestures at the mails. '*Why*? This is so *cruel*. Why go to such unimaginable trouble, just to harsh everybody's mellow? You don't do murder to make people feel bad. Unless – is this like some foreign power, attacking us by destroying the national mood? Although, why would that – oh. Hang on.'

'Fabulous,' says Jacko. 'This is like, *please show your workings*.'

Dani gives him the finger. He grins.

'No, no,' says Alex, 'I get it now. It's *money*. Mood equals money. This is designed to tip the financial markets.'

Mood equals money. She's heard that aphorism recently.

'Bingo,' says Jacko. 'Top marks to the lady hack. A national mood-swing that'll crash on the markets like a tsunami. Which is presumably why someone's taken a billion-dollar short on the British economy.'

Nobody speaks or moves. There's only the low buzz of Dani's electronics. Jacko beams. Jesus – how that man loves to generate drama.

'Can someone do that?' says Alex.

A short: a bet that something will fall in value. Like, I think Googple's share price will go down next week because I have inside knowledge that some government's about to make them pay their taxes for once. So I get a bank to sell me an option that GPL will drop five points. A betting slip, essentially. This is normal stuff. As a student, Alex wrote an essay on the role that shorting played in all three of the big financial crises of the new millennium, but she's never heard of someone betting on the fall of a national economy.

'My other bit of detective work,' says Jacko, waving into place another false wall, at a right angle to the first. 'Which I didn't connect to all this other stuff until today. I keep tabs on weird activity from the big banks. Tiny things that can act as canaries for bad shit that's about to go down. Past month, I've come across over three hundred market instruments, purchased from a range of counter-parties – bets on indices, commodities, individual stocks. On their own they're business as usual. But put them together and they equate to . . .'

He pauses for effect.

'Go on, you beardy twat,' says Dani.

Jacko grins and puts a Doctor Evil pinkie to his mouth.

'– *one billion dollars*! If and only if the value of the London markets drops twenty per cent next week.'

Alex walks to the new wall. This is her territory: money trails. Here at last is the real story. A blanket of illusion just got lifted. She should have been chasing *this*, instead of racing after penny-ante scandals. She forgot that human emotions and cold hard readies are just two different manifestations of the same set of forces. Two sides to the same Emoticoin. She works her way across the electronic chits on Jacko's wall, piecing the short together. You'd never know these were part of a single operation. The deals are registered to a plethora of investment trusts, shell companies. Offshore shenanigans. It must have taken someone months to piece these all together. Jacko has to be some kind of genius for jigsaws.

'Shit me,' says Dani. 'These Occidental dudes are hard core.'

'Except it's not them,' says Jacko.

'Excuse me?' says Dani. 'You just told us—'

'Yes, sure, Occidental's making the bribes, running the Strangers. Doing the bads. But they're strictly implementation, not strategy. An outsource provider. They never do anything off their own bat. They're extortionists, not investment wizards. I'd bet a billion of my own cash they didn't make a single one of these deals. They're working for someone.'

'I know who,' says Abul, in a voice as deep and quiet as a tube train passing in the earth.

It's like they all forgot he has the power of speech. Even his robot cat seems to gape up at him. He doesn't move; just speaks in that level voice.

'Controlling how people feel. Brazen raids on other companies. Only one person round here does that kind of thing.'

'Hold it,' says Dani. 'Let's not bring that tired bullshit into the room.'

'Offering people freedom,' says Abul, still staring at the floor. 'But controlling them day and night.' Now his furious eyes bore into Dani. 'That is who Perce is. Your boss.'

The cat shifts in his lap. He whispers to it. What is it with that cat? Dani stands, her presence electric. Maybe this is some enhancement she's applied to herself in the Strange, but Alex is forced to break her survey of the trades, just to take it in.

'I seriously don't need to hear this shit,' says Dani, 'from some bargain basement Anonymous.'

'Now, Dan—' says Jacko.

'No! Do you never stop to think how Sean pays for his extremely expensive hair products? For all this cool tech shit? Do you? No? *Advertising*, for fuck's sake. We're an ad business. This kind of economic collapse would bring Sean down. Cradle. Baby. All.'

Jacko stands and walks out of his zone of virtual concrete. Breaking the fourth wall.

'No, no,' he says, 'but think. This is the *Strange* attacking us. Bribing people in Coin.'

'Fucksake,' says Dani. 'You think I wouldn't know if Sean was doing with *my* platform? I'm telling you, this is the black algae.'

'So racist,' says Jacko.

'*FUCK OFF!*'

'Coin, though,' says Jacko. 'Hundreds of millions of Emoticoin. Seriously, who has those kinds of resources?'

'Exactly!' says Dani, her voice cracking with the force of the word. 'Exactly. Sean is a Coin *billion*aire. You think he *wants* it to crash?'

That stops Jacko in his tracks.

'Crash *Emoticoin*?'

'Come on, Brainiac. Do the maths. You think Coin'd survive this – this domino hack? The value of Coin is pegged to human emotions. It'll be the first thing to fall. Sean'll be fucked.'

'And,' says Jacko quietly, 'now I come to think of it, they *are* planning to blow up his rocket tomorrow, too.'

'Oh, what the fuck?' says Dani. 'RedShot?'

Alex has been working her way down the wall of market trades. At its end, she freezes. Reads again to make sure she didn't invent it.

'Worm in the guidance system,' says Jacko idly.

'Can I say something?' says Alex.

Dani nods distractedly. Jacko doesn't seem to hear.

'But maybe this is an inside job?' he says. 'A mole here?'

'Can I—?' says Alex.

'There can't be many people with this kind of access,' says Jacko.

Alex has been scanning the companies responsible for the trades. Most are random, single-purpose, the addresses offshore: Cayman, Monaco, obscure crown Pacific territories. But one, on a contract tucked down to the bottom right of Jacko's wall, is listed to an address on Kingsway, central London. It's called Vaclav Holdings. And who does Alex know with a pale white office at that address?

'I know who did this,' she says. 'And I know how to stop the killing.'

Well: that got everyone's attention.

'The algaerhythm is a community,' says Dani, 'not an entity. To wipe the black algae, we need to turn it off completely. But there's no kill switch.'

The in-fighting's over; the council of war has begun.

'I've pushed it out of every device and server within a three-kilometre radius of this building—'

'Guess that explains why nobody shot at me when I got here,' says Alex.

'—but it'll take days – weeks – to erase it completely. I'm pissing in the ocean.'

Alex has always divided people into two camps: those who *talk* about getting things done, and those who *get* things done. Earlier this morning, as the group broke into bickering, she was afraid they were the former. Seeing the speed with which they've flipped to problem-solving, she realises she was wrong.

Problem 1 is how to stop the black algae fucking everything up tomorrow morning. After which, problem 2 is how to stop a vast criminal empire killing them all. And problem 3: how to get to the man behind this whole psychotic caper.

And Alex, who's hanging back to let the techies work things through, has a problem 4: when to call Harm, and what to say to her when she does.

'We could pull the plug on Occidental's servers,' says Jacko. 'They must be running a lot of this operation from there. They'd know we were on to them as soon as we did it, but we can make it happen like—'

He snaps his fingers. Dani shakes her head.

'This is already out there,' she says. 'In the Strange and in the real world. The domino hack –' everyone's silently adopted that term '– is the sum of ten thousand little pieces. We need to stop the whole thing – or at least say eighty per cent of it. Or everyone with Internet access is going to see the bad stuff happen. How can you stop ten thousand different things at once?'

In the silence that follows, Abul lifts the sleeping cat off his lap and places it on the sofa cushion. He stands and steps out of the concrete corner that's been borrowed from Seatopia. He walks to where Dani and Jacko are huddled together.

'Have you tried,' he says quietly, 'turning it off and on again?'

It takes a second for them to register, then they all turn to see who's spoken. Dani frowns at him.

'Turn off the Strange?' she says. 'I already said that's not enough. And it'd take too long.'

'Not the Strange,' says Abul. 'The Internet. Why don't we turn off the Internet?'

'Ah,' says Dani, giving Abul a smoky look that clearly alarms him. 'Now this one, I like.'

PART THREE:

ECSTASY

'Some people, like myself, just aren't satisfied with being law-abiding, calm people.'

— Dread Pirate Roberts 2, interviewed on *Motherboard*

THE EMPTY CAN

Mr Ox rides the early morning streets in a silent black Mercedes. Two hours have passed since he landed at the private airfield. It has been many years since he intervened directly in an operation but he is weary of Mr Honey Badger's prevarications.

Mr Honey Badger is full of talk. He uses the same potent words as Mr Ox's business gurus, but with him it is nothing more than chatter, designed to conceal his weakness and venality. He should never have been allowed free rein over Occidental's UK entity. The whole endeavour has come to the edge of failure. In the future, Mr Ox will not listen to a man's chatter: he'll look into his heart. He recalls his mother's expression: *It's the empty can that makes the most noise.* If only he had heeded those words!

The driver eases the Mercedes to a stop, two blocks from Perce's ludicrous glass tower. Mr Ox steps wearily out of the car and watches the screens at the building's pinnacle spew consumcrist hubbub over the dark city. It is just before midnight. Mr Ayyash and Ms Farr will be setting about their plans before too long. As he walks, Mr Ox turns up the volume on his earpiece, tuning back into these young people's conversation. It is interesting to hear such enterprising folk plan their counter-measures.

Mr Ayyash is speaking. This young man, only seventeen, has run rings around Mr Honey Badger. Ayyash's gambit might even have succeeded, had the client not granted Mr Ox audio access to so many of his conversations. Ayyash has identified a vulnerability Mr Ox himself did not spot, in spite of extensive scenario-planning workshops. For a moment, Mr Ox considers offering the lad a job when the dust of conflict settles. But no. He knows this type, has been disappointed in them too often. The boy is as principled as he is gifted. A shame, but he must suffer the same disciplinary procedure as his cohorts.

Mr Ox pauses to compose a message on his satellite communicator. This vintage platform is far more secure than mobile email services. He copies in the full list of subcontractors, on- and offshore, types in the code words required to activate them. The list includes Mr Honey Badger. The man may not have leadership qualities but he's effective on the ground. Also in the air. This will be his final test before he undergoes his performance-review meeting with Mr Ox.

As Ox presses 'Send', another of his mother's dictums comes to mind. *When a job is to be done well, it should be you who does it.* This they say in the UK also. He checks his firearm, reseats it in his shoulder holster, then resumes his steady walk towards 404 City Road, London EC.

A block away from the building he takes a sharp right down Kingsmere Alley, past a row of darkened industrial units. He stops by a patch of waste ground. He pulls a Gagarin keyring from his pocket and locates a shiny Yale key. He turns this in the oiled lock of the aluminium gate, which snaps open with a *SPANG!* Closing the gate behind him, he heads for a low brick structure by the wall of the next-door warehouse. His leather soles crunch glass as he crosses the weedy ground. Stopping at the hut, he locates the padlock key. Whistling, he pulls back the hasp and opens the door. Inside, a series of iron rungs descends into blackness. He takes hold of the mossy top rung and places a foot on the ladder.

Mr Ox descends into the dark.

POINTS OF FAILURE

'You haven't told him?' says Alex's transmitted voice.

Dani looks up from her screens. Alex is sitting across the desk from Dani, her ghost bumping up and down, revealing the fact that she's really in the back of a moving van. We could code out that bouncing, thinks Dani. Stabilise the image. Make it more real.

'No way would Sean let me kill the net on the day of his launch,' she says. 'Can't see us persuading him it's cripple the business this way, or let it die completely.'

'Or that the only way of stopping his spaceship from blowing up is stop it launching.'

Dani nods as she hammers out code.

'He's going to look a total prick,' she says. 'Which is so very not his favourite thing. Seriously, he's best out of this.'

Alex's ghost turns to have a muttered conversation with someone just out of shot. One of the Gunnells. Weird to be hooking up with that pair of dinosaurs. Desperate times.

'You getting close?' says Dani. 'I can't track you with Abul's doohickey on your tattoos.'

'Hopefully neither can those pricks at Occidental. We're in Clerkenwell. Connor's looking for a car park where we can hole up until it's time to make our move.'

Dani nods again, leans back to stretch her aching shoulders. She looks around the frosted glass equipment cabinets lining the walls to her left and right. The three young engineers working on the equipment are moving with the controlled urgency of the best systems people. They're setting up for everything to fail in a few hours' time.

This room's in Mondan's deep basement. It's a side chamber of an ancient stretch of decommissioned sewer that links the lower levels of Dani's building with the headquarters building at 404 City Road. It's where they run their cable. A good 30 per cent of the nation's Internet passes through these routers every millisecond. A host of other businesses rent access and rack space here. None of them has clearance to enter this room.

'Do you honestly think we can make it?' says Alex. 'It's nearly four already.'

Dani checks the status updates rolling up her left-hand screen.

'My guys have the other big inland hubs locked down,' she says. 'Manchester, Edinburgh. Then there's the points of entry to the country – looks like Porthcurno's pretty much sewn up. That's like seventy-five per cent of international traffic. East coast, let's see? No. Nothing reported yet.'

'Seatopia'll come through?'

'Jacko's a whining cunt but he couldn't bear for us to see him fail. Plus, his crew are hardarse. They'll be OK.'

She's trying to persuade herself more than Alex.

'From seven a.m.,' says Dani, 'if someone wants to connect to the Internet, the best they'll have is a satellite station. And as soon as we take the cable down, those stations'll be flooded out with traffic. We take out our twelve pinch-points: poof. No Internet.'

'Plus London?' says Alex.

'Plus here. We take out our *thirteen* pinch-points and it's bye-bye twenty-first century.'

'Pre-Martingale.'

'Right.'

Most people see the Internet as ubiquitous, invisible – inevitable. But it's only bundles of wires running through repurposed conduits beneath the pavement. Plus a few very very busy switching points. The backbone comes down to an insanely small

number of physical cables. Which is why, come six a.m., all Dani's
team will need to do is take out thirteen pinch-points mapped out
across the nation – and in its coastal waters. The good news is
that because of Sean Perce's acquisitive efforts over the past two
decades, every single one of these locations is now owned by
Mondan, and so accessible to Dani. With the exception of
Seatopia, which nobody owns. Take out these thirteen spots and,
if Dani's right, no Internet. If she's wrong – well, she's not wrong.
At seven o'clock the Goliath of the wires will be felled by thirteen
simultaneous sling-shots.

London's the key. It's where everything comes through. If
London stays up, even without the international links or the
regional hubs, there will still be a functional Internet over large
swathes of the UK. And 'London', in this context, means this
cavernous room, three storeys below ground.

There was a joke once, on some old-timey TV show whose
name Dani can't remember, where an incompetent IT manager is
duped into thinking the Internet's housed in a single black box
she can hold in her hand. Funny, yes: but this room beneath the
London pavement is to all intents and purposes the Internet. For
the UK, at least.

'And you're OK with the infinite me's?' says Alex.

'I'm ninety per cent there. They'll be ready.'

'OK, listen, we're parking. I should get going.'

'When you get to the studios, the zombies'll be there.'

'I appreciate it. Really.'

Poof: no Alex.

Dani continues coding up the zombies. Five thumps sound
from the corridor. All three engineers look up.

'Did you hear that?' says Dani.

They all nod in unison and continue looking at her. Guess it's
her job to check. She hops up and sticks her head out of the door
into the tunnel. All still. The ancient brick walls are lit with halogen arc lights, giving the tunnel a Harry Lime vibe. Maybe the
noise was a security guard slamming doors? Dani's tasked them

with keeping the tunnel sealed off. She's stripped out permissions on the access doors to herself and a few trusted others.

Catching movement from the periphery of her vision, she turns to look. Where the tunnel bends up ahead she thought she caught a shadow moving across the brick wall. A shadow like the moon obliterating the sun.

'Hi?' she calls. 'Hello?'

The shadow's gone, if it was ever there. Dani shrugs and returns to her keyboard.

'Just nothing,' she says to the engineers as she types. 'Stop shirking, fuckers.'

They grin and return to work. Dani being an arse is reassuringly normal.

DEAD CAT BOUNCE

'Your lads'll go for the package now?' says Myles. 'It's candy-coated.'

Susan Hardiman, MP, neither confirms nor denies. Myles Hendrix is a decent type, but at this moment he also happens to be the lead partner from the Handy Frank's legal team; and Susan's not about to give away the game over a sneaky fag.

'Bearing in mind,' he says, gazing out over the dark concrete alley of London Wall, 'you don't have long to get the signatures. If you want to announce at nine.'

Susan smiles but says nothing. The two of them are leaning on the bannister of a raised walkway outside the entrance to Myles' firm, Eaves and Perivale. The occasional driverless vehicle passes unwanted beneath them. Otherwise there's nothing to hear but the grinding of the City's lungs. So many windows already lit up in the high blocks around them. Traders hitting the Far East markets. Or maybe it's just that when you make that much money you don't give a shit about leaving the lights on over the weekend?

'Now, Myles,' she says, giving the man her coyest power-flirt, 'I thought we were on our break?'

He flicks her an appraising look, then draws on his cigarette with a post-coital smirk. Jesus Christ, the man actually thinks he's pulled his opponent in the middle of a negotiation. There is no accounting for the stupidity of a preening male in a three-piece.

'Can't blame a man for trying,' he says.

He's right, though. There's a timetable. Susan and her legal team are here for one reason only: to string the Frank's legal team along until eight thirty. Then, just when they think their bail-out's sewn up tight, the City will belch, and the sour cloud will fan across the country, tickling the storefronts of every high street in every town. By lunchtime, Handy Frank's will be the bellwether for all that's failed.

There's a buzzing from Susan's bag.

'Excuse me,' she says.

Myles nods, still drunk on inhaling his own sex appeal. Susan walks further along the concrete balcony, extracting her phone. It's Sam Corrigan.

'Does nobody on this project understand the need for discretion?' she says.

'Hello to you, too, Susan.'

Corrigan's voice is dressed up in a velvety filter.

'They've already hacked your emails, Sam.'

'And yours.'

Over by the railing Myles is pretending not to pay attention. Susan turns her back on him and whispers into the phone.

'Why *exactly* are you calling me?'

'My client's been on. We need to move the announcement forward.'

'Don't be absurd. It's five in the morning and I still have legals to complete. I won't be in a position to brief my comms team for at least two hours.'

'Well, that's OK because I'm taking over comms on this.'

'Sam. I have an entire press office to deal with media announcements. I do not need the help of some slick-suited lobbyist.'

'Susan. Your press office is a bunch of lifer public employees who wouldn't know how to put spin onto a tennis ball, let alone a story of this magnitude. We need to double down on the negatives. Use key trigger words. We don't want the public missing the severity of the decision you're about to make. Luckily I've got your statement right here in front of me.'

Susan glares out over the City skyline.

'Am I permitted to see this statement?' she says.

'Not over email. Obviously. You'll see it when you get to the press conference at seven forty-five.'

'And if I don't like what's in it?'

'Then you'll smile and read it the fuck out to the cameras.'

'You seem to be forgetting, Sam, which of us is the minister of state. I will make the announcement I approve. At a time of my liking.'

'Yeah, well. Remember when we met that one time? At Sheeky's?'

'An excellent lunch I'm hardly likely to forget.'

She lards her words with enough irony to penetrate even Corrigan's Teflon manner; but he takes not a bit of notice.

'Maybe you missed the fact,' he says, 'that I was wearing mesh?'

Susan's stomach knots. After leaving a sufficient pause for his message to sink in, Corrigan continues.

'If you found a bunch of emails hard to rebut this week, let's see you deny a wraparound video. You bought the ticket, Susan. Whatever gave you the idea it had a return portion?'

'Fuck you.'

'Yeah, I thought you'd end up seeing things from my point of view. Seven forty-five, Susan.'

The call ends. Myles is looking her way with undisguised suspicion.

'Shall we?' says Susan, stubbing her untouched cigarette on the pristine concrete. 'I think our comfort break is over.'

INSIDE LEG

They can hear the helicopters but they still can't make them out through the North Sea moonlight. The sky's too full of Jacko's drones. Maybe it's one helicopter. Maybe three.

Thimblerig stands on the icy helipad with Jacko and seven other members of Cockaigne. Hard to believe Doug Raynor – the man who betrayed his father – is heading directly to him on an attack bearing.

It was late into the night before one of Jacko's team spotted the name *Raynor* on an air traffic clearance at the heliport. Thimblerig's heart leapt. All along he's worried that by helping Lucky Ghost he's lost sight of his true target. Now Raynor – the very man he's sought so long – is heading for Seatopia. He can strike two birds with one stone.

He turns to the man standing by him in the orange all-weather jacket. They nod invisibly at each other. This man was introduced to him as Colin but he instantly recognised him from the photo Lucky Ghost once shared. Colin is Eponymous. They've been giving each other insiderish nods of recognition ever since but haven't mentioned a thing out loud. Need to know.

The dull chug of the helicopters is louder. Jacko steps away from the pack.

— Showtime! he shouts.

Everyone snaps into motion. Colin departs with another nod. Jon Mangan – the artist – heads downstairs with his group. Everyone so matter-of-fact. As though they're heading off to perform routine maintenance. The people flying towards them at 150kph are coming to kill them. If they fail in their tasks every person in the country will suffer.

Thimblerig saw as a child what comes of a country when the institutions holding badness in check give way. Since he arrived in the UK things have been on a downward path. The agents of reaction and violence keep gaining sway. Today's attack would tip things. With all at stake they've no choice but to act. And Thimblerig will make Raynor suffer at last.

Jacko grasps his elbow. A thicket of beard-hair is spilling over the collar of his parka. In the wild sea light he looks like some crazy ancient mariner.

— It's time, he says.

Four a.m. They make for the stairs. The rest of the crew will hold off Raynor's men while Thimblerig and Jacko complete the work. Or they won't. At times like this Thimblerig isn't a seventeen-year old. He's the wizened veteran of an electronic army. He follows Jacko down the stairs into the warmth of the hallway. When they reach its end Jacko bends to heave on the iron trap-door with a great amount of puffing. Its rusty hinges groan but don't budge.

—Do you want help? asks Thimblerig.

Jacko ignores him so he looks out through a west-facing port-hole. It's too misted up to see. He rubs the glass but the seascape is getting less and less distinct. It isn't salt or condensation obscuring his view. The hazy cloud of drones is thickening by the second.

— The first wave is programmed to get into the fan vents of the choppers, says Jacko.

He's right behind Thimblerig. For all his ungainly posture he moves like a ghost.

— Think Luke Skywalker and the ventilation shaft, he says.

Thimblerig steps aside to give Jacko a better view.

— The second wave will go for the rotor engines, says Jacko. If we're lucky none of them will make it to the station.

He means 'hopefully we'll kill them all remotely'.

— Ready? he says.

Thimblerig nods and follows Jacko down the metal rungs into the left leg of Seatopia. He pulls the trapdoor shut behind him then spins the rusted but well-oiled wheel to lock it. He puts all his weight into pulling it tight. Now it's just Jacko and Thimblerig inside the leg. Plus the entire UK–Europe traffic of the Internet. They head down rung-by-rung into the dark and damp. Something stirs by Thimblerig's right ear.

— *He's coming to you?* whispers the cat.

Lucky Ghost is with him. In his backpack from where she can gently counsel him. Only she knows why he's seeking Raynor.

— I'm going to look him in the eye, he whispers. Make him tell me why he'd sell himself to the insurgents. Betray my father's unit.

— *And then?*

Thimblerig reaches an iron platform near the base of the west leg. He steps off the ladder. Ghost is right to ask. He needs revenge but is he prepared to carry it to its conclusion? As he once did to the extremist in the basement workshop?

— I think, he says to the cat, that—

A bulky arm reaches past his face and rips the cat away. It gives out a static hiss as Jacko holds it at arm's length.

— Hey! shouts Thimblerig.

The cat's claws snick out. Thimblerig opens his mouth to command it to stop. The cat rears back its top half to strike at Jacko's face. As its claws whip forward Jacko pushes a small black rod against the side of its head. It slumps in a dead collapse. Jacko tosses it into the corner of the platform where it clatters like a tin can in a dustbin.

— That's my cat! shouts Thimblerig.

— Is it though? says Jacko, breathing hard.

Thimblerig runs over to pick up the limp cat. He turns it over and holds down the power switch in its belly.

— I can't even hard reboot, he says. What did you do to it?

Jacko holds up the black rod.

— EMP, he says.

Thimblerig uses the back of his hand to shove away the useless tears clogging his eyes.

— Why would you do that? he says. She's protecting me. I'll need her when . . . when he . . .

— What were you telling it?

Thimblerig cradles the cat.

— Listen, you amateur, says Jacko. This place may look like a shitheap but information-wise it's pure. Hermetic. Nothing travels in or out without my control.

— I was talking to a friend.

— Whose name is?

More glaring. Jacko comes over and kneels down.

— You weren't born yesterday, he says more kindly. We're talking information security. One pinprick opening and the dam's breached. You know this.

— Lucky Ghost is one of us.

— A Cockaigne? Bullshit.

— She's my source. I tell her everything and she shows me truth.

— Your spirit guide, huh? And you're speaking to her through that thing's mic?

Nodding at the cat.

— I suppose.

— At what times has the mic been on?

— It's been . . .

Something shifts inside Thimblerig. A realignment. All the times he's followed Ghost's counsel it's seemed to lead to victory. *Seemed* to.

— You've had it on full-time?

Thimblerig just looks at him. Jacko lets out a breath and sits back against the corroded plate-metal wall.

— Shit. Well that explains the stream of encrypted data that's been following you around like a series of farts. So tell me. How do you think Occidental knew to send these men?

Thimblerig starts.

— The helicopters! We need to—

Jacko waves him off.

— There's time. We've broken Occidental's messaging. The instruction to attack Seatopia only came through yesterday – *after* we planned the Internet blackout. *After* we let the others know Jon Mangan's here. Then all of a sudden, Raynor gets a message mentioning 'fresh intelligence'.

— What's that to do with me?

— Why I chose to let some random script kiddie into my—

— It isn't me! I'm not— I hate Raynor. He – I have reasons.

Jacko's nodding slowly. His mournful face looks sadder than ever.

— Seriously, I believe you, Abul. I don't think you even know you've been betraying us.

— But I haven't!

Abul realises he's on the point of tears. Like some girl.

— It must be Alex Kubelick they're following, he says. In the Strange. We should never have let her trust a corporate platform. She doesn't know how much she's been giving away.

Jacko's shaking his head.

— And when you were at that hotel? Was Alex with you when they found you and attacked you?

Thimblerig stares at the prone body of his pet. His companion.

— Because, says Jacko, do you know how I miraculously got those drones to you and pulled you out? Again, intercepted chatter. They knew where you were, Abul. They knew, because they're inside your lame toy cat. Your Lucky Ghost has turned you traitor without you even knowing.

— No, says Thimblerig. That's not true. Ghost helps me. I – I can prove it. Earlier this week she helped me steal a hack off Raynor. It hurt him. He was so *angry*.

— So they're not friends. Doesn't mean they're not working together.

Thimblerig's about to protest when he remembers the phone conversation he overheard while hiding in the cupboard at the data storage site. A conversation between Raynor and an unknown man. A man whose authority Raynor challenged. Now he understands the argument he overheard. Kaa was meant to be part of the domino hack but Raynor scuppered that. Straight afterwards Ghost told Thimblerig to destroy the hack.

Do as you must, the voice said to Raynor then. *This is but a single domino.*

Thimblerig thought he'd come up with the phrase 'domino hack' on his own. But the word was already embedded in his subconscious.

And later. At the hotel when Ghost gave him a fold of Emoticoin. She passed him a secure network address where he could retrieve a cache of Coin. He didn't even question whether the address was safe. Why would Lucky Ghost send him into a hacker's honey-trap?

But she did. That's how the Strangers found him at the hotel. Lucky Ghost hacked his location and his data. She's been with him the whole time. He thought she was helping him fight Occidental and get to Raynor but he's been working for them all along. Their hacker for hire. And now he's brought Raynor to Seatopia with guns and helicopters.

— We need to tell Alex Kubelick, he says.

EMERGENCY LANDING

'*JUST FUCKING LAND IT!*' screams Doug Raynor.

The pilot can't hear over the hailstorm of drones smashing onto the chopper. Raynor leans across the mercenary to his right and peers out of the window. The Seatopia platform is just ahead but all he can see is seething metal. They're going to have to trust in gravity.

He's strapped into the middle seat in a row of three, facing forward at the back of the chopper, a hired goon to either side. Three more grunts facing opposite. Pilot up front. All staring around in horror and doing fuck-all. This is what you get when you hire in a hurry: greenhorns with no service record.

Raynor unlatches his seat belt and makes to get up. The chopper lurches and Raynor's thrown into the man facing him. They bump helmets and their bodies crunch together. The engine overhead chokes and grinds. The chopper bucks like an electric bull. Raynor is thrown at the roof of the cabin then slammed down into the footwell. The chopper smashes into something with the sound of a demon screaming. Raynor rattles around the footwell, the boots of his men flailing into his sides. The chopper grinds across some surface. Raynor's stomach lurches as they spin with an almighty scream of metal. Then a deafening *CRUMP!* and he's thrown against first one row of legs, then the other. They've stopped.

Something lands with a juicy plop on Raynor's face. Hot sauce and a stench of molten iron. He lifts it. A stump of gore protruding from an ostrich egg. No: a severed head in a flight helmet. He throws it away. It lolls where it falls, astonished face staring up.

Raynor wriggles onto his back, body crying out in pain. His head's lower than his feet. The chopper's at a tilt. He looks over the seated knees to either side. Fragments of searchlight break through the window of the upward-facing door. The roof of the chopper has crumpled inwards like wet cardboard, crushing the heads of the pilot and the men with their backs to the front of the chopper. With one exception. The head of the man in the centre has been replaced by a spear of metal that's sheared in from the front of the chopper, through the man's neck and into the cabin. A rotor blade. Raynor can't imagine what could have made it bend into the chopper at such an angle. Blood drips from its underside.

At the rear of the cabin, the two remaining men are strapped into their seats. The far one shakes his head as though to ward off a fly. Then he sniffs the air and stares down at Raynor, who follows suit. Gasoline. Specifically, the thick, sweet smell of aviation fuel. Also burning rubber.

The two men wrestle with their seat belts as Raynor raises himself into a crouch. A great vice crushes his ribcage from either side. He struggles for breath.

'Need – get out,' he manages to say, then coughs up half his lungs.

Ignoring the muss of blood, he twists around to face the near-side door – the one closest to the ground. Outside its fractured glass is a grey mass of tiny drones, in their thousands.

'Mask up!' he shouts at the men, pulling up his own.

The seal of the gas mask burns his skin. Something bad has happened to the side of his jaw. He activates the mesh in the eyepieces of his mask and turns to check the men have done the same. They each give a thumbs-up. Their names and stats scroll round them.

Raynor pulls back both legs and kicks at the door, which smashes outwards. Another twist of the vice staunches his lungs.

He chokes a spatter of his own meat onto the inside of the mask, which is starting to smell like a butcher's shop.

The drones surge in and coat him. Second time in two days he's been caught in a swarm of these fuckers. Sign they've come to the right place. He slides out blind under his own gravity. As he lands he rolls aside to give the men room. The drones whip sharply at his mask and combat suit.

Willing the pain to fuck off out of his life, Raynor flips to schematic. The greenline trace of a helipad clicks into place. The data was gathered by the Occidental team who came out here years back, when they started renting server space from Cockaigne. In the process, they managed to walk around every square metre of the platform, embeds logging everything for future reference. Raynor scans the greenline terrain and locates the door to the stairwell on the far side of the mangled chopper. Then he looks down. Directly below him, twenty-six bogies are clustered. From their huddled posture, they're working crablets and desktops. Running the drone attack. Also with them, one of Raynor's targets: the Internet star Jon Mangan. Not the Ayyash kid, however. Raynor keeps scanning.

Beyond, and further down, two more figures. One is Ayyash. Judging by their location near sea level, they're in the data link room. Which makes them Raynor's other targets. More than that: his ticket to prove himself. There's no margin for fucking this up. Ox was super-clear. Raynor's on the platform with two objectives: a) stop Cockaigne cutting the cable and b) kill Jon Mangan. Twenty-one heavily armed men against a rag-tag crew of stoners and nerds, plus one ageing artist. It should've been fish in a barrel. Now Raynor's down to these two guys.

He chambers a round in his automatic. Still liking those odds.

'Heads low and follow!' he says into his helmet mic.

He links hands with the green ghosts of his two surviving men, like a junior high outing. They work their way through the vicious cloud. The ground is slippy. Even through Raynor's mask, the smell of fuel is overwhelming. As they work their way round the mangled chopper, Raynor's mask pieces together the scene. It wasn't only *his* chopper that crashed here. The lead chopper crash-landed first. Its side is flattened against the stairwell cabin. Next, his own chopper hit the deck and slid smack into the first. Now he understands how a rotor blade managed to decapitate one of his mercs. It belonged to the first bird. Pierced the windshield and popped off that guy's head like a Pez dispenser. Kudos to both pilots, who found their targets blind. Though they weren't the neatest landings.

Scanning vitals, Raynor sees what was obvious: everyone in both wrecks is dead. He also sees the heat signals of flames lapping round the pilot's console.

'Move!' he says.

The human chain works its way round the wreckage to the stairwell cabin – and stops dead. The first chopper's flattened against the door, blocking it.

'Come around!' he calls, leading the procession around the cabin.

He puts out an arm to stop the men falling off the edge of the helipad. The cloud of drones is too thick to see through but the display is telling him that, below the rim, there's a four-metre drop to the main deck of the platform. On this side of the helipad the deck protrudes a fair way beyond the edge. If the schematics are accurate he can simply drop off the edge and land on the main deck. Of course, the other two sides of the helipad – to the north and south – protrude out over open sea. So if his display is wrong, he'll plunge a hundred metres into frozen ocean.

Well – you got to trust the data, right?

'If you hear a thud, follow,' he says. 'If it's a splash, try back a ways.'

He sits on the edge of the platform and before he has time to reconsider, slides feet-first into the mist of drones.

When he hits hard deck he rolls, ignoring the fissure of pain that opens up down his right leg. He keeps rolling, making room for his comrades to land. Stops when he collides with something hard and oily: a barrel.

The next man lands and rolls off in a different direction. Then the cloud of drones lights up orange as flame fills the air, silhouetting the rim of the helipad. A second later comes the boom of an explosion, followed by a groan of metal. Then a second blast. Flaming crap showers the deck. The air's aflame with belches of burning fuel. Hundreds of red-hot drones drop like sparks from a Catherine wheel, lighting fires across the deck. The surviving swarm lifts up and peels away. The stench of burning plastic invades Raynor's mask. He chokes. Pain jolts through his chest. He'll be lucky if he makes it long enough for Ox to murder.

No, he's made it this far. This is his opportunity. He clambers to his feet with the aid of the oily barrel. The deck's lit up by a pile of flaming wreckage. No – not wreckage. A man. His second guy was about to jump from the helipad when the chopper exploded. The force must've tossed him off the edge. The flames dancing round his corpse are showing no sign of going out. Thing about air fuel: it's sticky as fuck.

So much for that guy. The other man, though, Raynor heard land. He scans the deck on his heads-up, sees the survivor climbing painfully to his feet. They give each other rickety thumbs-ups and pick their way towards the structure under the helipad. There's a godawful scream. They freeze, then realise that was the sound of two dozen nerds whooping from inside. Dumb shits think they took out the whole crew. The two men resume their approach. It's dark under the helipad but there's a strip of light at ground level, exactly where the schematic shows a door. They flatten themselves against the wall to either side and Raynor scans the interior. All the nerds are clustered round their machines, save one who's lurking just inside the door, on the stairs to the helipad. Raynor unclips a concussion grenade from his belt and signals to his man, who shoulders his machine gun. Raynor puts his free hand on the door handle and pushes the door inwards a crack.

Unlocked? Seriously? Dumb shits.

Raynor opens the door wide enough to throw in the unpinned grenade then pulls the door shut. He counts three. The shockwave hits.

'Go!' he shouts, throwing the door open.

His man leads in, strafing in measured bursts. They move together along the over-lit corridor down the centre of the structure. To their right, the stairs to the helipad, where the prone form of a kid is lying. Shaved head, leather waistcoat. A whole lot of ink. The man's head jumps as Raynor puts two rounds in it.

Shoulder to shoulder they proceed to the open door halfway down the corridor: the entrance to the mess room. On his mask, Raynor sees a nerd approach from inside the room. A long black shotgun barrel edges out the door. Raynor signals to his man, who strafes it for ten seconds, sending ricochets from the iron walls. The shotgun vanishes.

Up ahead, at the end of the corridor, Raynor spies the trapdoor. His two targets are directly below it. He signals at the mess room door.

'Take them,' he says. 'Confirm the kill on the artist.'

The man opens fire. Under his cover Raynor runs to the trapdoor. As he passes the mess room, he catches a glimpse of the occupants juddering under the impact of the gunfire. He skids to a stop and tries the trapdoor. It's locked from below. Behind him, gunfire comes in controlled snatches. He turns to look through the wall. The ghost of his man is just inside the mess room, kneeling to fire from behind some kind of cover. The rest of the room's littered with corpses but his man's taking fire from two hostiles at the side of the room. They're standing with their backs to the room, taking turns to spin and fire pump-action rounds.

Raynor dodges his head from side to side to understand the parallax of what he's seeing. No, they're not in the mess room. They're in the kitchen next door, firing through a hatch. Raynor steps to the kitchen door, unpins a concussion grenade, counts to two, opens the door, rolls in the grenade and slams the door on the astonished faces of the two hackers standing in the dilapidated kitchen with shotguns raised. He slams the door. The blast shakes it. The ghosts of the men are thrown back; then they crumple. Raynor opens the door and puts two slugs into each head. His pistol jams on the final shot. He checks the magazine: three rounds left. Piece of shit knock-off automatic. He chucks it away. And steps back to scan the mess room through the wall. All vitals down. Everyone dead, including his guy. He strolls round to see.

The mess room is a charnel house. The bodies of the Cockaigne crew litter sofas and floor. Their equipment is scrap metal. Right in front of Raynor, on his back, lies a handsome middle-aged dead guy. The mask throws up the ID. *Jon Mangan.* Mission 50 per cent accomplished. The original plan was for Mangan to be stabbed by a stalker in a London street. Then, for some reason, he took it upon himself to hole up on this platform. Now the story is, he's fallen victim to a gang war while making a documentary. Just as big a downer for his recently pumped-up fan base.

Down to the left side of the door, behind a wheeled metal cabinet, lies Raynor's final squad member, one eye of his mask blown out and bloodied.

'Good work,' says Raynor, unhooking the Heckler & Koch machine gun from the man's shoulder.

He retrieves two spare clips from the merc's belt then, for good measure, lets off three single rounds into Mangan's body. Then he shoulders the strap and heads back to the trapdoor where he fixes two charges onto the metal plate over the lock. He sets a timer to thirty seconds and saunters back into the kitchen, shuts the door behind him. A boxed-in wave of sound and fury ripples across the plate-iron wall, leaving a humming aftershock.

Raynor tries to open the kitchen door but it's jammed. He braces his feet and gives it a heave. It flies open. He rights himself before he falls, straightens his combat jacket and heads out into the hallway.

The fluorescents have blown out but light still spills from the kitchen and mess room. The metal walls are scarred but intact.

Everything else – the little mailbox fixed to the wall; the hung-up waterproofs and life vests – is ripped apart and scattered. A fire extinguisher's busted open, leaving an impact crater and a splurge of foam all over the wreckage. The little porthole at the end of the hall has popped out, bringing in salty spray.

The end of the trapdoor has buckled up. The lock's gone, leaving a gap in the twisted iron. Raynor heaves on the handle. The trapdoor flies open, throwing him back on his butt. He crawls to the edge of the aperture, peering through the floor to get a bead. His hostiles are five storeys down, moving together, manipulating controls. As predicted, they're in the link room, getting ready to disable the undersea flow of data. When Raynor single-handedly stops them, no way Ox will ditch him.

He peers down the rectangular shaft. Looped iron rungs are bolted all the way down the concave wall of the left leg of the platform. On the way down, the ladder passes four or five levels. The bottom of the shaft is dark.

Raynor lowers his legs onto the ladder. Working his way down with his left hand, he uses his right to train the machine gun into the darkness below.

ZOMBIE APOCALYPSE

The street is filled with Alex. Dozens of her.

With *Alexes*, perhaps?

With *Alices*?

Either way, two hundred slender women are crammed around the van, all dressed in identical natty tweeds and bottle-red waves of hair. They mill about, casual, cramming the West End street. Each is Alex, down to minute detail.

The van pulls up. From the driver's seat comes a tut.

'Look at these pricks,' says Francis Gunnell from behind the wheel.

'Must look bonkers without a mesh?' says Connor from the passenger seat.

Gunnell Senior nods. At the rear of the van, Alex looks out through the tinted glass. To her, the street's an inverted *Where's Wally* – a crowd where every single person is the one you're looking for. Most of the Alexes milling about around the Corporation's forecourt are ghosts, placed there by Dani as chaff. A handful are real Strangers, modded against their will into yet more Alexes.

This early in the day there'd normally be no one here; but this morning the black algae's brought a crowd of gaming Strangers, all of them deep into *Agent Down*, to stake out the place. In the real they must all be gawping around in confusion. How to find their target when everyone, including themselves, has *become* that target?

The game doesn't know Alex is here. Abul's blanker's hiding her location. The black algae needs a Stranger to land eyeballs on her.

She grips the handle of the rear doors. In spite of her attempts to resist the lure, she checks her glowheart. It's firing stripes of FEAR and DISGUST but the overwhelming shade is the deep crimson of RAGE, driving hard through all other emotions. She turns to Francis.

'You know what happens next?'

He keeps his eyes fixed forward.

'I know for some reason I've been cast as the fucking chauffeur.'

Alex grins.

'Just don't kill any of these guys, OK? They know not what they do.'

'Yeah, yeah,' says Francis, waving her away.

'You look after your old da, yeah?' she says to Connor as she swings the rear door open.

He nods without turning. Alex jumps onto tarmac and into a sea of herself.

The van pulls away to circle the block. She takes a few tentative steps. At first, she tries dodging the other hers, but it soon becomes clear she doesn't need to. Dani's set the ghosts to avoid each other. Casually but confidently they walk their own trajectories, passing a whisker from one another but never colliding. They acknowledge each another with the slightest nod, eyes turned down, half-smile on their rosebud lips. Weird. Alex knows that expression, but from inside.

She does her best to emulate their behaviour – the easy stride, the nods, the smiles – as she makes her way to the revolving doors of the Corporation. A distance of forty metres. Dotted about the crowd are twenty-three would-be assassins – or that was the number Dani gave her. Maybe more now.

Once through the doors she needs to reach the turnstiles. Assuming her security pass hasn't been deactivated, she'll be able to swipe her way through. From then on, any Stranger who follows will find their mesh deactivated. No Strange inside the Corporation. For the first time ever, Alex is grateful for that ban. The spell of the black algae only works while a Stranger's mesh is active. After the gates she'll have a free run to the studio.

Hopefully.

She's barely halfway across the forecourt when an Alex Kubelick walking past blinks out of existence. Dani blinks into place in its place. Her black eyes are wild, her cheeks flushed and her birthmark livid red.

'I'm sorry,' she says, 'I can't keep them—'

She blinks out of sight. One by one, silently, the Alexes start to vanish. Slowly at first they flick away, like someone's hitting CTRL-X over and over.

CTRL-X CTRL-X

The vanishings get faster and faster. The street clears of tweed-suited bodies, revealing stray individuals. Mostly men. A few women. Some in civvies, many in full-body coslife. All armed with primary-coloured weapons. All looking urgently from Alex to Alex to Alex.

CTRL-X CTRL-X CTRL-X

The few dozen remaining Alexes are still walking easily around. Alex forces herself to take a few more steps at the same pace but there are fewer and fewer of her to camouflage her shaky, all-too-human self.

CTRL-X CTRL-X CTRL-X CTRL-X

She wills herself not to look around. She's less than ten metres from the doors. Only three Alexes left between her and the building. One blinks out, replaced by a young man in a red-and-black costume. A Deadpool. He's standing in front of the central revolving door, head cocked sideways, studying Alex. The real Alex.

CTRL-X CTRL-X

The other two Alexes fritz out of existence. The real one falters to a stop. She rips off her mesh and stuffs it in the breast pocket of her jacket. Nothing changes. Reality and the Strange have collapsed into each other. In both worlds, the Deadpool stands at the top of the steps, looking down at her. Under his full-face mask, his jaw twists into a grin.

'Mom!' he says, raising two bright yellow pistols.

CAVEMAN DAYS

'I'm sorry,' says Dani, 'I can't keep them—'

The great hand smothers her face.

She presses her back against the server cabinet. The hand closes on her head like it's picking up a tennis ball. There's a static fizzle round her face then the hand withdraws, balls up her crushed mesh and tosses it away.

The huge man with the jet-black pudding-bowl hair steps back and studies her with button eyes set deep in a pocked face.

'Now it is just us,' he says in a voice like a robot Benedict Cumberbatch.

The lilac refinement of Dani's mesh-world is stripped away. The basement burns with unfiltered glare. Two of the engineers have fled. The other, Davin, is frozen by the router racks, staring at the big man, Ox. She tips her head at the door – *g'wan, go!* but he shakes his head. Ox turns a blank look on Davin. Jesus, guy: run! Honestly. You give a guy one tumble – OK, in fairness two or three – and he thinks he's got to be your hero.

Ox grunts and turns to Dani. Are they speaking in grunts now? Here outside the Strange it's caveman days. Dani glances at the wad of sparks her mesh has been reduced to. Ox follows her gaze then looks back at her. Sympathy riddles his scaly face.

'It is perfectly feasible for you to leave this room unharmed, Ms Farr,' he says. 'However, I regret to say I cannot allow you to protect Ms Kubelick.'

Oh, shit, Alex. She'll be a sitting duck. Without her mesh, Dani can't turn the Alexes back on.

'Nor,' says Ox, strolling over to the racks, 'can I allow you to deactivate this equipment.'

The big man pats a flickering router cabinet. Davin scuttles along the racks, making distance. That cabinet's one of over a hundred, but somehow this man knows the exact one they're planning to trip off first. Ox shrugs. A thought crosses his face like a storm front

'Or, of course,' he says with a friendly chuckle, 'I could kill you! That would be simpler, no?'

'Oh wait, wait,' she says, finding speech at last. 'I understand. You get your rocks off scaring women. That's fine. Would you like to spank me, too?'

She gives him her shit-eatingest grin. A dark blankness crosses his face. His jaw tightens. With unfeasible speed he pulls a pistol from his jacket and, without taking aim, shoots Davin in the groin.

GOING ON AIR

The van mounts the pavement and tears across the forecourt. It passes in front of the revolving doors a metre from Alex. The Deadpool is flung up and sideways, both guns firing wide. Alex is thrown back by the van's wake and lands hard on her right arm. Pain erupts from her burned palm and her shot-up shoulder. The Deadpool skids across the flagstones like a cast-off action figure. The van does a screeching 180, its rear end piling into three Darth Vaders standing with orange rifles trained.

The van comes to a stop. Alex touches her shoulder. Her hand comes away bloody. One of the Vaders is moving painfully. Are the others alive? Is the Deadpool? Dear Jesus, she hopes so. From the passenger window of the van Connor screams, 'GO!'

Alex goes, ignoring the pain in her shoulder. She launches herself up the stairs towards the revolving doors. Gunfire cracks the tarmac around her. She ducks as she runs. Behind her, the van surges forward. She hits the centre door, bullets landing on the glass, and throws her weight into the revolving door. Reluctantly, it starts to turn. It's only moved a few centimetres when someone throws themselves into the opposite compartment. A Catwoman. The two women stare at each other through the glass partitions as the door revolves with them both inside. The Catwoman tries to level her red rifle at Alex. Its barrel taps glass. There's no room to get a bead in that tight space. The door completes its half-turn. The Catwoman steps back out of it and levels her gun on Alex, who stumbles backwards into the lobby. The Catwoman's body buckles. Her gun flies up, firing wild, muffled by thick glass. Behind her, the van screams to a stop. The passenger door's open. Connor's inside, shotgun on hip.

The Catwoman struggles up. Behind her mask, her eyes are desperate.

Alex holds up a hand to tell Connor, *enough, stop* – that poor woman has to know she's been shot for real – then she turns and runs at the security barriers, yanking her pass from around her neck. To her right, a Human Torch and a Thing are reading magazines in the waiting area. They scramble to their feet when they spot Alex, readying weapons. The female security guard steps out towards Alex, raising a hand. She hasn't seen the armed Strangers.

'Hey!' she shouts as Alex makes the barriers.

There's no time to swipe. Letting her momentum carry her, Alex scrambles up onto the turnstile and over the barrier. She lands hard on marble as gunfire breaks out behind her. The stair doors are to her right. She half-staggers, half-runs across the remaining ground, catching a glimpse of the Human Torch raising his gun at the guard.

'Hey!' she shouts, finding her footing and waving at the Torch. 'Over here!'

The Fantastic Two turn their weapons on her as she smashes through the stairwell door. They fire too late. Alex barrels upstairs. She's banking on the Strangers vaulting the barriers after her, in which case they'll immediately lose the Strange and see what's really going on. She's pretty sure they won't kill the guard. But what can she do except carry on? She keeps running up the stairs, spinning round each bend with a hand on the rail. She makes level 5 and bursts out into the open-plan bullpen, where she brakes hard.

Here's the weirdest thing yet: the normality of this scene. It's exactly as it was on Thursday morning when this all kicked off. The show's already on air. Across the banks of desks the studio's lit up and humming. That's where she's headed, but first she runs to the balcony and looks down into the lobby. The Fantastic Two have made it to this side of the security gates, where they're engaged in a raging argument. The Thing's taken off his head and is staring in confusion at his gun. The security guard's shouting from the far side of the barriers. Good. Alex turns and fast-walks towards the studio. As she passes each tier of desks, the astonished head of her colleagues bob up like meerkats.

'Oh. Alex,' says an assistant producer whose name escapes her.

The AP tries to manoeuvre herself between Alex and the studio. Alex stops her advance and stares the girl down. She takes a half-step back.

'I'm – um,' she says, 'I mean you're a bit early for your – you know – meeting?'

She means the compliance hearing. How pointless and tiny that affair seems now.

'Alex!'

A small voice. Somewhere near at hand.

'Alex Kubelick!'

The voice is coming from her left breast. She touches it, baffled.

'Hello?' she says to her chest.

'Um, Alex?' says the AP. 'Are you OK?'

Alex pulls her scrunched-up mesh from her pocket and holds it in front of her mouth. It shouldn't work in here.

'Hello?' she says again.

'Oh Alex!' says her mesh in a tinny voice. Its nano-size speakers aren't designed to be heard from so far away.

'Abul?' she whispers. 'How am I hearing you past the blocker?'

She holds the balled mesh to her ear.

'That's just a software restriction,' says Abul's voice. 'Not physical. I need to tell you something.'

'There's no time. I'm at the studio. He'll be here any moment.'

'And we're under fire. But you need to know. My cat. My cat overheard everything.'

Alex lowers the mesh and stares at it, then returns it to her ear.

'Abul, this isn't the time for—'

'Not the cat. A voice speaking through it. A user called Lucky Ghost. She's been speaking to me in the voice of Elyse Martingale. Guiding me. But now Jacko—'

A tremor passes down Alex's spine. The primal sense of being watched, from somewhere off the side of the forest path.

'Someone's been in your cat?'

'Lucky Ghost.'

'And you *let* her?'

'Jacko says it must be someone at Occidental. They've known our plans at every stage. They're here on the platform, right now. It's my fault.'

Alex curses silently.

'They know about the Internet outage?'

By way of reply, Abul's voice produces a tiny inarticulate wail.

'You little—' says Alex. 'I thought you were the kid genius?'

'I'm so sorry.'

The tiny speakers in her mesh start emitting some kind of static. Is Abul crying? Alex holds the ball of gauze away from her face in disgust. Yesterday, when she found out Abul was being chased by the killer Strangers, she couldn't help feeling a morsel of sympathy. When she saw him work with Dani and Jacko on the outage, she felt a prickle of something like admiration. The kid's been through so much, achieved so much, but she'll never forget his secret identity. Thimblerig, the Happy Handyman. The man-boy who viciously harassed her online for a whole year. Nobody in this picture is who they say they are. Now the arrogant dork's fucked the whole thing up for everyone.

Except what if he hasn't? What if she can *use* this information?

She puts the mesh back on. Nothing changes visibly – Abul's only using audio.

'Abul?' she says.

'Yes? Hello? They're almost on us, Alex.'

'OK, OK, but listen. When we planned this next part – the studio. Did you have the cat with you?'

'I don't know. I—'

'Think! Dani patched you in. You were standing in some kind of kitchen?'

'I don't – no, wait. The cat was in the mess room. In my bag. I was making tea.'

'And did you give her the details, after?'

'I didn't have time. This was just before we found out Raynor was—'

'OK then. OK. We can make this work.'

'Alex, I'm . . . I'm so—'

'Yeah, well look: add that to your list of things to be sorry about, OK? And give hell to those vicious shits.'

There's a sound like paper being screwed up. Abul's cut the line. Alex scans the faces of the production team. They've broken off their busy-making and are openly staring.

'You want the news?' she says to them. 'There.' She points down towards the street. 'The news is out there. Go and see. Fucking hell.'

She turns and storms past the AP, the dead mesh flapping round her face, towards the sound-baffled studio door.

FULL-STACK

Thimblerig cuts the call and listens for movement from the shaft outside the door.

The link room's a semicircular bunker five levels down the left leg of Seatopia. It might as well be a museum of Second World War sea defences. Ranged around the arc of its outer wall are large iron lockers. Their dark green paint and serial numbers are corroded by time and ocean. Remnants of wartime notices are fixed with rusty tacks to the cork-board over the desk where Thimblerig sits. This was the station's armoury – though it's empty of weapons now.

The atmosphere's clear of the salty mould that permeates the rest of Seatopia. The room is crisp and fresh as any modern office. Cockaigne sealed and air conditioned it when they converted the left leg into a server farm for their data haven. This chamber holds the vital switching gear – black stacks of routers housed in four locked cages at the centre of the room. Cable spills from the top of the cages like blue and yellow hair. Knots of it vanish into the ceiling. In the low light of the room the equipment's LEDs throw a busy sheen over the small grey shapes dotted all around the knots of cables.

Thimblerig sits at the desk and uses his crablet to watch Doug Raynor descend the ladder. A pink dot on Raynor's sprite tells Thimblerig he's carrying the machine gun collected from his dead colleague. When Raynor reaches the third level Thimblerig gets up and clamps the crablet to his forearm. He moves across the room to the central locker whose well-oiled door stands open for him. This position opposite the door has a clear view between the router cages. From it Thimblerig will see Raynor enter the room. He already has one foot inside the locker when the question stops him. The same question that's been shredding his resolve all night. If he stays in the locker how is he going to confront Raynor? When does he look that man in the eye and ask him why he betrayed his father?

He turns to look at the door. Then back to the locker.

This moment's as well rehearsed as the rest of the operation. Ever since the explosion up above he's been tracking Doug Raynor's diminishing squad. Now the man himself is clambering down the shaft. He's heading here. To the link room. How does Thimblerig know this? Because Raynor's mask is currently showing him that the only two surviving human beings on this station are working together in this very room. Though Thimblerig's the only one here.

From outside the door comes the clang and slap of rubber soles stepping off the metal ladder. As the door nudges inwards Thimblerig decides: no more hiding in furniture. Besides, he'll be able to run things better if he's moving about. He quietly shuts the locker and pads to the equipment cages. Through the metal grille he watches the door swing open. A figure in black combat gear eases into the room with a machine gun at his hip.

Raynor scans the room. He's relying on the tech in his mask to find his targets. Not his eyes. The mask says Thimblerig and Jacko are in the cage nearest the door. He can see them now – hard at work on some complex task. He thinks it's because he's so stealthy that the two of them have failed to look up from their work.

Playing on what your target believes to be his strengths – that's the best kind of social engineering.

Raynor pads around to get a bead on the non-existent Thimblerig and Jacko. This easy stealth is a contrast to those lumbering gamer Batmans and Shreks. As he circles the cages

Thimblerig mirrors his movements to keep out of line of sight. Just in case Raynor decides to use his eyes.

The crablet vibrates minutely on Thimblerig's arm. That's the signal that Hairy Jacko – who's in the cable room one level below – has pulled the plug on the North Sea cable. The Internet is down. Or at least the bit of it that connects the British Isles with the European continent. Thimblerig chances a glance at the time on his screen. It's seven a.m. Bang on schedule. And Raynor hasn't even noticed because he's in the wrong room. One of many things he's failed to notice as he plays out his Gerard Butler fantasy is that this equipment has nothing to do with undersea cables. It's just the gigabit routers that run the internal network of Seatopia.

Raynor's reached the door of the equipment cage. His mask is telling him he's standing two metres behind Jacko and Thimblerig as they work at the racks. He braces the stock of the machine gun on his hip. The real Thimblerig pads towards the cage. He's out in the open. If Raynor bothered to lift his mask he'd see him straight away.

Thimblerig draws his breath in sharply. He's just noticed that Raynor's machine gun is not only pointed at the ghosts of him and Jacko. He's just walked directly into its line of fire.

That's when Raynor pulls the trigger.

THE FINGER

Dani fights down bile. Four years she's spent in the Strange. Four years her world's been whatever world she chose. Her battles and strife curated for her. Now her mesh is torn away, she's no choice but to look at the sorry wound that Ox's bullet has made of Davin's upper thigh. The wound that's opened in her world.

Davin has stopped screaming. He's gaping at the sodden mess and panting like he's just run a marathon. He has the presence of mind to press down on the wound, but how long before he bleeds out?

Some animal sensation rises in Dani. It comes out as a low groan. This is how feelings are, let free. This is everything she'd cut away. It's raw and brutal and it hurts her all the way from throat to groin. She stares at Ox with eyes she knows are brimming with tears.

Some years back, her life was dropped in a blender and pulverised. All the fantasies she'd acted out online were laid bare on national media. She fought back, as she's always fought back, and she kind of won. But the experience altered her. She no longer recognises the ballsy tiger she was in her twenties. She no longer wants to face off against the world. She stepped out of her timeline and into a self-coded world, like a serpent swallowing its tail. Is she even capable of fighting any more?

Ox returns the gun to his jacket and folds his bear paws in front of his crotch. His wine-barrel chest rises and falls with the heavy breath of a fat man, but he's no ordinary fat man. He's the ogre from the margins of the story. The monster under the bed.

Dani flattens herself against the wall, weeping openly, waiting to be blasted away, certain she will be.

'I see,' says Ox, 'we have reached a point of understanding.'

He checks his watch.

'My, my. Seven oh four a.m.'

He looks at Dani, gauging her response. Seeing something there through the blurry mess of tears and snot.

'Yes indeed,' he says in his flat narrator's voice. 'Somehow I know this detail. Seven a.m. What else, you may wonder, do I know?'

He's right. Dani's brain has latched onto this detail. He knows they're trying to shut off the net. Maybe he could have figured out for himself that it's their only remaining play. But the exact timing? They only agreed to that a few hours ago, and only Dani, Alex, Jacko and Abul ever discussed it. Nobody else knows – not poor Davin, not Cockaigne. Ox's eyes wrinkle with kindly pleasure at seeing her shock.

'Yes, yes,' he says. 'A traitor.'

Dani wipes her fist across wet eyes, feeling the physical surprise of no mesh. Her heart thuds as she raises her right hand and gives Ox the finger. His eyes widen with fury but – thank Christ – he doesn't take out his gun.

'Bull,' she says, 'you planted a mic. Hacked our gear.'

'Disappointing,' he says. 'Believe me, I understand your frustration. But please—' he starts to amble around the room, keeping himself between Dani and the exit '—I'd ask you to consider. I know what you know. *You* know I know this. Your deadline is passed. Even if your colleagues succeed in knocking out one or two of your twelve – how did you describe them – *pinch points*? – you and I both know London is key. So . . .'

He shrugs. The movement of those shoulders under the double-breasted jacket is like whales turning under the surface of the ocean.

'. . . we both know I have won,' he says. 'And really, Ms Farr. Is it not better for things to be out in the open?'

Dani's nodding. Ox smiles to see this, though the trace of a thought is troubling his forehead.

'You're right,' she says.

He keeps nodding and smiling but his face creases into a frown.

'You're right,' she says. 'We both know I can't get to those racks to switch off the routers. Except – oh, what if I can do that remotely?'

Ox doesn't move but all at once he's locked in position – ready to strike. Careful, now.

'Except, no,' says Dani. 'Because in order to activate that remote command I'd need access to some form of device, wouldn't I? And you very wisely ripped off my mesh and shot my engineer.'

Minutely, Ox relaxes.

'Except,' says Dani, 'the thing is that a mesh is only one half of the input/output that hooks you into the Strange. It's for viewing, not doing. Think about it. How do people control the Strange?'

He's openly baffled. His hand twitches towards his shoulder holster.

'We use movements,' says Dani hurriedly. 'All parts of our bodies but mainly hands. Our tattoo embeds read them. And, sure, it's harder to use mimetic controls when you can't see the feedback on your mesh, but sometimes I set up a very simple gesture so I can be sure I'll get it right. One I could do with my eyes closed. Or with my mesh ripped off.'

'A simple gesture . . .' Ox says quietly.

Dani nods.

'You got it, Ox. Like giving you the finger. And you might be able to shoot me before I managed to do even that, except – oh, I already did it, you brutal piece of shit.'

He turns to the racks and at last he sees that they're powered down. They have been ever since Dani flipped him the bird. He turns on her, panting with fury. She forces herself to keep it up. Not long now. He takes a step towards her.

'And,' she says quickly, 'there's a counter-command. I can turn the Internet back on. Except, oh – if you kill me I won't be able to tell you the command.'

The trammelled flesh of Ox's face is livid red. His black eyes shoot death-rays. But he stays where he is.

'So,' says Dani breezily, though her breath is giving out, 'it turns out I *do* know something you don't.'

Her eyes dart to the chrome box on the desk, a metre from her right hand: the perforated white panel behind which sits its speaker. The old-style backlit display. This isn't finished until she turns that thing on.

'Perhaps it's true,' Ox says, 'that I can't kill you. But this one?' He moves with that uncanny speed to Davin's rumpled body, heaves him up by the scruff of his hoodie. 'This one I think I can kill.'

Dani looks around for some out but the reality crashes in. Davin's livid face as Ox calmly places the muzzle of his pistol against his temple.

'So,' says Ox. 'Would you kindly turn your machines back on, you whore?'

BLUE SCREEN OF DEATH

The Internet's a tenacious creature. It was built that way. Give it an instruction, it'll keep on trying to execute it, even when its first, second, third and one hundred-thousandth attempts have failed. So it takes a while for everyone to register the loss. For a time, Britain's in a state of buffering. Users of mesh and screens across the land continue to gaze at the ever-rotating wheel of doom. They drag their fingers down through the air to refresh; but nothing happens. So they wait.

Sanjeev Kapur is running late; or not strictly speaking *late*. The Metals desk doesn't open until 11.00 and his specialities, zinc and copper, don't have their sessions until afternoon. But commodities are global, and constant; and Sanjeev makes a point of being in by 7.30 every morning. He has ambitions, and in his line of work, progression means presence, at any hour when the high-ups might be there. Any hour when opportunity might present itself.

Yet here it is, already 7.13 and he's only just leaving London Bridge Station. His train arrived bang on 7.01 but there was a malfunction with the automatic platform gates, which stopped letting anyone through. A deep throng of commuters had formed at them before the dimwits at the station thought to turn the gates off manually. It took fully six minutes to clear the crowd.

Today of all days: such a crucial time in the commodity markets. The new, super-light zinc alloys that have just been announced are kicking off a revolution in drone manufacture. That's important, of course, but what's much more important is the impact this is having on the market price of zinc. For a smart guy like Sanjeev, who did his research and saw this coming, it's a time to clean up, but only if he's at his screens, owning the trades as they come about. The present time is a time of wonders. Every week, new opportunities arise for arbitrage. But you need to be present when the opportunities arise.

Knowing he's late, Sanjeev's on his mesh before he's finished jogging down the ramp from the station. At once there's something fishy. The mesh is rendering the usual constructs and infographics – his price tracker widgets are lined up in his field of vision – but they're flatlined. They keep refreshing but to no avail. Sanjeev restarts his mesh and picks up pace as he heads for the bridge. At a jog, he can make his desk in fifteen minutes.

He's halfway across, his mesh still trying to restart, when he sees the rain. It's all across the City, though there's not a cloud in the hazy February sky. Something's wrong about the rain. Sanjeev slows to a stop. All across the bridge, others are starting to do the same. There is in fact a cloud, though it's a funny kind of dark, low cloud, lower than the tops of the City towers. The rain falling from it is thick and grey. Some kind of solid material; not water. Sanjeev squints. It's as though an army of furious gods is hurling metal balls down onto the City.

As he stares into the rain, a hard-edged thing strikes the side of his head. He cries out, half-falling under the impact. The thing bounces onto the pavement. He touches the skull beneath his hair. The fingers come back bloody. He squats and picks up the projectile. It's a small drone, cracked and powered down, its blades crumpled. He turns it in his hand, then looks at the thick grey rain ahead. Now he understands. Every single drone in London is simultaneously falling dead.

He stands. A million drones, bricked and smashed at once. What a demand this will create for the new models. What an opportunity. Imagine how the price will have moved by the time the markets open. He drops the drone and sprints for dear life towards the north end of the bridge, into the wounding metal rain.

Encounter artist Debbie Salvas wakes with a certainty: today's creation will be the one that changes lives.

Her dream lingers. In it, the elements of a story that, if she moulds it right – draws out its meaning before it can fade – will speak to every living being, about some truth. In the dark of the bedroom, she feels on the nightstand for her mesh. Carefully, so as not to disturb the sleeping form of Anatole, she turns onto her back and drapes her mesh over her face. It launches the familiar surge of colour and meaning, then stalls. This is frustrating, though not unusual, but Debbie needs to get it started before she loses the thread of the story. She restarts the mesh.

What *are* the threads of this story? If she can repeat it to herself during this frustrating wait-time, she'll maybe hold on to it until she can set it down.

It's the story of a parallel now, where everybody lives in their own self-created world, just like the Strange, but without the need for mesh or embeds. The ability to mould reality exists in all of us. This is a peaceful world. It contains no wars, no countries, as each individual has the means to create whatever they desire. But this young girl – Eliza. She's a little like the young Debbie. Spunky, pragmatic. In the dream, she journeys to the elders of this world, to ask a question. It's a long journey, with many tribulations – Debbie will fill these in later – but at length she reaches the plain white zone where the elders live. In their state of elevation, they've no need to mould their world into any one reality. They exist in the pure geometry of thought.

The mesh has returned to that weird state of light-blue haze. Debbie sighs and with a dismissive flick of her fingers, restarts it again.

In spite of Eliza's young age – she's twelve? Thirteen? Something like that. In spite of this youth, she strides boldly into the white chamber of the elders to await her turn. At last she reaches the front of the line. The speaker for the elders says, you may ask one question only. And she asks them—

Dammit, what is with this mesh today? Debbie tries every mimetic she can think of.

Eliza asks, in a world where I can get anything I desire, what is any of it really worth?

And the elders say—

Now this is weird. Her mesh has thrown up a message.

⟨sorry guys normal service will be resumed etc⟩

⟨might be a while tho⟩

⟨laters⟩

Now it's not responding to any commands.

Debbie gives out a huff of frustration and tosses her mesh onto the bedside table. Anatole grunts and turns onto his back. Uh oh. And yes, sure enough, within three seconds he's snoring. Debbie elbows him in the ribs until he turns onto his side. The snoring tails away.

Now: what was she thinking about?

Crispin Hart's internal biology is malfunctioning.

Here he is, sitting in the early morning on his smart-loo, trying not to consider the mess his rear end is extruding. It disgusts him that his body's mechanisms should keep on failing in this noxious fashion; that they should produce these streams of ill-formed, stinking *stuff*. Crispin's mission is to control and manage every aspect of his life through technology. His house is timed and managed to perfection. Temperature, humidity and light rise and fall on calibrated curves throughout the day, and in response to his progress through the property. His own self, too, he's upgraded component by component, as bionics have evolved and his budget permitted. His circulatory, respiratory, limbic and pulmonary systems are as regulated as his juicer or his garage door. His diet has migrated 100 per cent to Soma, the innovative Total Food System created by a sparky Californian start-up. This system was developed by technologists who were as frustrated as Crispin by the inefficient rottenness of human biology. Using the latest nutritional science, they've crafted a powder that, when dissolved in tepid water and consumed every eight hours, can deal with a human's nutritional needs without the need for festering, stinking *food*.

And yet, and yet: ever since Crispin migrated to Soma his stomach has been converted to a factory for diarrhoea. He's sent an accelerating series of queries to Soma Customer Services, but has as yet had no response. He's found nothing in the FAQs. It horrifies him to think that this reaction might be unique to his own body; that the titans of technology who live on Soma are more regular than his deficient physicality.

He leans forward, propping elbows on knees, and strains a final time. Is he done? He prays he might be – last Thursday it took him two hours to leave the house.

'Two sheets,' he says to the toilet paper dispenser.

Nothing happens. Well, that's his fault. He keeps not enunciating clearly enough.

'Two-oo sh-eet-ss,' he intones at the sleek box.

Still nothing. And nothing in response to his next two tries.

He tuts and reaches under the box, fiddles for the end of the roll, and tugs. Tiny servos whine in complaint as he extracts a few shreds of paper. Eventually he has a handful. Gamely, he sets about himself and does the best job he can in these disgusting circumstances. He can feel what a horrible mess is back there still.

'Flush,' he says to the toilet.

It does not flush. He tuts again. He'll deal with that situation later. First he needs to clean himself. With his pyjama bottoms round his ankles, he shuffles onto the bidet.

'Warm jet,' he says to it.

Nothing happens. He repeats the command, then sighs and presses the chrome controls at random. He's not sure how manual operation works – he's never had cause to use it. Eventually the bidet produces a trickle of cold water; but he can't make the plug go down. He splashes a paltry amount of biting water up himself then ruins a towel wiping hands and backside clean.

'Open,' he says to the laundry bin, without expectation.

Predictably, the bin stays closed. He pulls at the lid but can't get it open. He balls up the soiled towel and drops it on the terrazzo floor, then toes it gingerly behind the bin.

Shaking at these unsanitary goings-on, he does up his pyjamas and heads to the door. Perhaps the guest bathroom will cooperate more reliably. If not he'll have to restart the house again.

'Open,' he says to the door.

The door stands smooth, inert and shut.

'Open,' he says again, panic rising in his chest.

The door stays shut. He fingers at it. There's no handle, so he unhooks his towelling dressing gown and tugs on the hook. The door does not budge.

Nothing for it but to do a full restart. Except his mesh is on the dressing table in the bedroom and his crablet is on his office desk. He looks around the windowless room. It contains no devices except the suite of immaculate but unresponsive porcelain appliances. He turns back to the door.

'Open,' he says again. '*Open!*'

He grapples with fingernails at the door's seal but gets no purchase. Even if he did, how could he possibly overcome the MagnaSafe system that secures each interior door in his home?

He turns his back against the sealed door and slides to the floor. After a few minutes, he begins to weep. Each time he breathes in, his nose fills up with the putrid stench of innards rising from the SmartPotty.

The countdown screens suspended from the ceiling are all frozen with *01:45* to go. The giant wall display – which should be showing the feed from the RedShot launch platform in the Irish Sea, plus a schematic of the ship's flight path to the orbital rebuild zone – is showing the cyan logo of its manufacturer, rotating on black. The array of indicators on the console banks are also dark. Sean's mesh, like that of his team, is blue-screened.

Sean slams his fist onto the console. The rows of engineers to either side jump in their chairs, in unison. He gets up and paces around. How to fix a system crash with two minutes to go, when everything's suddenly bricked? His people have been warning him for days about weird anomalies creeping into the navigation code. System behaviours that simply weren't there in any of the test launches. He's been ignoring them. Guess they were right.

Deepak, the project manager, is hovering by Sean's shoulder. Traditionally, he's the only one allowed to talk to Sean during a rage.

'So-o-o –?' he says in that drawn out way he has.

Sean turns full hairdryer on him.

'I get it! All right? But you do not have permission to give me "I told you so"s. We need to *fix* this.'

Deepak blinks at him in confusion.

'This isn't – a system problem here,' he says, as though talking to a moron.

Sean makes to speak, then looks around at the dead screens, dead terminals, his own dead mesh.

'Our Internet's down?' he says.

A laugh punches up from inside his throat. He pats Deepak's shoulder. So he *was* right. There *was* no problem with the launch software. He was right. His guys were wrong.

'Well, OK then,' he says. 'Let's get it back up. We can restart the countdown at T minus five.'

Nobody moves.

'Come on, Jesus!' Sean paces around the seated engineers, clapping hands in their faces. 'It's not like we don't have network techs here.'

'But Sean,' says Deepak, trailing behind him. 'It's not just *our* Internet.'

Sean brakes. Turns to Deepak. For the first time in living memory, uncertainty's creeping up the back of his neck. He'd forgotten what that felt like.

'Wh—?' he says. 'Wh—?'

He slaps his own face. Deepak looks horrified. Goddammit, this is not the time for his voice to conk out.

'We're not sure there *is* an Internet,' says Deepak.

Throughout the country, this chilly February morning, a lottery begins: which technology will work as normal, and which will fail? It quickly becomes clear that nobody knew what would happen when the Internet went away. Nobody predicted which big things or small things would work or fail. Some of the most basic appliances – coffee makers, crossing lights, vending machines – stop responding to any prompt, while some of the most complex – CAT scanners, heart monitors, air traffic systems – continue to work, or revert to some unconnected backup system that doesn't rely upon the wider world of data. Nobody knows for how long these depreciated platforms will go on providing life-sustaining services. Nobody wants to be the one who trusted lives to the redundant and unknown. So, one-by-one, flights are grounded and diverted; all but the most urgent operations cancelled; transports and logistic networks shut down. Degree by degree, Britain grinds to a halt.

In their homes, people wake to a new – or very ancient – reality. When their newest, closest devices fail, they fish in drawers for old smartphones; then for these old smartphones' chargers. Yet even when recharged, they're useless. Mobile networks and landlines are all down.

People hunt for some other way to fill their information voids. They recall the vintage radios sitting under a skein of dust in their kitchen cupboards. They haven't turned them on for months or years but for one reason or another they haven't thrown them away. Without much expectation, they turn them on. At first the displays say, scanning, and stick there, but when the people tire of this terse message, they toggle their radios from DAB to FM. It takes a few seconds for the radios to recall what FM is, but once they get the hang of it, their speakers pop with a fresh signal, and a reassuring voice emerges. A voice from an age when information took time to percolate and, because of this, had greater weight. A time when this self-same voice, measured and assured, delivered the news through our morning radios.

'—happy to report that our FM and AM services do seem to be working nationally,' says Thomas Causey. 'Listeners may rest assured we'll continue to broadcast on these channels and will report on the situation at it unfolds. Now, over to Lucy Nevins with the news.'

'Oh – Alex?' says Lukaš. 'How—?'

Lukaš Caron's ghost-white features just turned three shades paler.

'How nice to see me?' says Alex. 'Bless you for that.'

The acoustic seal on the door farts shut. The look of shock on Lukaš' face is very good news. He wasn't expecting Alex. No way he'd have shown up for the interview if he was. He's already seated at one of the guest mics on the central console. Arranged in front of him are his notes, a glass of water, a little rectangular device the size of a smartphone. Tom Causey and Sally Robsart are sitting directly across from him. All of them are looking at Alex, who's barged in while Tom's pre-recorded intro is playing. It's just a few minutes before the interview begins. The studio's in that state of silence it takes on while a piece of tape is playing in the background. Tom, Sally and Lukaš will be about to hear the intro on their cans but the room's on mute.

'So,' says Alex. 'I'm here for my close-up.'

Tom places his headphones silently on the desk and stands.

'Well now,' he says. 'I look forward to hearing some of this new journalism I've heard so much about.'

Sally hasn't moved. Her eyes track from Alex to the control room. Siobhán's there, shouting something towards the studio as she marches around to the door. Alex isn't great at lip-reading, but the word 'fuck' definitely crops up.

Tom taps Sally on the shoulder. She flinches, looks up at him. He points at the door. Sally nods and pulls off her cans. She's halfway out of her swivel chair when Siobhán storms in.

'We have literally seventy seconds of tape left,' she hisses. 'And in case anyone needs reminding we are at this point the only news source standing in a national crisis.'

'Hi, Siobhán,' says Alex.

'Yeah, fuck off, Alex,' says Siobhán.

Tom glides over.

'A word,' he says to Siobhán in the Voice of The Nation.

Sally sits, befuddled, at the exact same moment Lukaš stands.

'I should really—' he begins.

Siobhán points a scarlet fingernail his way.

'You should really *sit the fuck down,* Prof. Only reason you're on my show is you seem to be an expert on Sean Perce and the Strange – and this morning Perce has turned off the Internet. You come on my show? You stay on my show.'

Lukaš sits.

'Siobhán?' says Tom in his Jedi voice. 'Alex knows what she's doing. And you can hardly call this a normal morning.'

Siobhán's aware as anyone that there's zero time. She allows herself three seconds of glaring before letting Tom lead her into the corridor. Sally hops up and follows. Lukaš twists round to look through the glass at the studio director, hoping for some cue. The director shrugs and points at his ears. Lukaš dutifully puts on the cans. Just before the door shuts, Siobhán pokes her head in and points the fingernail at Alex.

'Literally do not fuck this up,' she says, and heaves the door until the acoustic seal engages.

Alex bends down and inserts under the door the metal wedge provided to her by Francis Gunnell. This is going to get messy. Can't have Siobhán interfering. She walks to Tom's chair, tracked by Lukaš. The chair still holds Tom's warmth; and his voice still emerges from the headphones when she puts them on. As she leans in to the mic the intro package ends.

'This is Alex Kubelick picking up for Tom,' she says, radio voice kicking in. 'Professor Lukaš Caron, thank you for joining us.'

Opposite her, Lukaš sits bolt upright, black cans perched atop his preened white coiff.

'Good – morning,' he says, as though discovering for the first time the concept of morning.

'Professor Caron, in Tom's piece we heard him trying and failing to get Mondan to account for their bizarre actions this morning. The country is hurting. The authorities seem unable to force Mr Perce to turn this vital service back on. You know the man, you've worked with him. Why has he taken away our Internet?'

Lukaš licks his lips. Whatever confrontation he was expecting, this ingénue approach has disarmed him. Alex studies the man – her teacher, her counsel. Something in the same genus as a friend, though never quite that.

'Sean is—' Lukaš begins, then stops to sip his water.

Alex waits, eyes trained on his. He clears his throat.

'Sean is an often inscrutable man,' he says, 'but he is a principled one. If he's taken this step, I must assume he believes – falsely – that some threat is present on the Internet.'

'A threat?' Alex blinks in fake confusion. 'What kind of threat could there be that would require such drastic measures?'

'As I say, Sean is clearly mistaken.'

Alex nods. Hunched forward over the mic, her eyes haven't left his. He'll keep playing this game – keep claiming everything's green in the garden – until his lackeys can get the net back online. Then he'll act as shocked as anyone else at the terrors that are then unleashed. What he doesn't know is that in the next five minutes, he's going to call off Mr Ox and stand down the domino hack. He won't even know he's done it until it's too late. Provided Alex doesn't fuck this utterly up.

She swallows. She's let dead air run too long.

'Interesting,' she says. 'I thought the reason for the outage was to stop you having anyone else killed?'

Lukaš is utterly still, drained of colour. His grey eyes scissor the air. She tries to overlay onto him the things she knows he is: the client of the criminal network, Occidental Data Partnership; the man who's gathered the means to buy a one-billion-dollar bet that the UK economy will fall into ruin. The man who talks the talk about the abstract nature of money, yet who seems to want a whole lot of it for himself, and doesn't care who dies along the way. She can't square it all. It's only because of a single slip, one trade among hundreds registered to his true location, that she even knows it's true.

'Let's start, shall we,' she says, 'with the government bail-out of the Handy Frank's DIY group? And the officials who've been bribed to pull the plug?'

To add to this, she's pretty sure that Lukaš is also the anonymous voice called Lucky Ghost. The one who's been guiding Abul as a fifth columnist in his hacker circle. Abul hadn't worked this out, though he knows his ghost companion is the traitor in their ranks. Lukaš must have charmed Abul utterly. Spoke to him in the voice of Elyse Martingale. There's something so ingenious and awful about that choice – speaking to an orphaned immigrant as an older woman; to a rebel hacker as the poster-girl of the digital anti-state. That's how Alex knows, without a shadow of doubt, that Lucky Ghost is Lukaš, and not some Occidental minion. Only he would choose to personify Elyse in wooing Abul. He's a master at recruiting wide-eyed acolytes. Alex was one, too, twenty-four hours ago.

Now she knows the truth behind Lucky Ghost, Alex also knows Lukaš has been present all along. He's overheard how she and the others are moving against him, but he hasn't heard it all. He doesn't know what's about to happen.

'I don't know anything about a bribe,' says Lukaš now, in the flat voice of an electronic reading device.

Things are moving. The net is down. Dani, Abul and Jacko have done their jobs. It's Alex's turn to finish this.

'This?' she says. 'Really, still? All right then. Let me tell you what you've done.'

NOT GOING TO LIE TO YOU

Say this for Cockaigne – they have excellent toy guns.

Raynor sprays Thimblerig's and Jacko's ghosts with bullets. The Koch rattles at his hip with hyper-realistic recoil. The mesh in his eyepieces renders the gunfire – and his earpieces the deafening rattle of bullets. Maybe a combat veteran should notice that the way the corpses are bucking about under his rain of bullets is kind of overdone. The Cockaigne team only had four hours to modify these animations from generic shoot-'em-up game-build components and the result's more Tarantino than Scorcese. But Raynor's so high on adrenalin and fury he doesn't seem to have noticed. If he didn't have a mask on he might notice the lack of cordite smell – but he does have a mask on.

The gun stops jolting. Raynor's emptied the fake clip. It's time for Thimblerig to step into the action. He types a couple of lines of code into his crablet. Raynor ejects the clip. A formation of grey blobs drops from the cables that tangle above his head. Some engulf his helmet. Others limpet onto his midriff and form a lumpy waistband.

— Oh, what the fuck? he shouts as his helmet's lifted into the air.

He grabs at the helmet and pulls it back towards his head.

– Ow! Shit! he cries, letting go of the helmet so he can swat the seething mass of drones that are butting at his stomach.

The helmet zooms up to the ceiling. It's now completely encrusted with drones. Then his webbing belt is whipped off – with his ammo and pistol dangling from it. He grabs at its severed end as the drones sweep it off towards the open door. Helmet and belt swoop in formation out through the door. Raynor runs after but the door slams in his face. A lock rattles from outside.

Up to now this is all according to plan. What Thimblerig does next is unplanned. He takes a breath and steps out from behind the cage.

Give Raynor this. He only gawps for a couple of seconds before snapping into a braced stance and letting rip with his gun. It rattles. Nothing else happens. Raynor lowers the gun and stares at it.

— Can't shoot a ghost, says Thimblerig.

— The fuck? says Raynor, glancing back at the cage – seeing no corpses there.

Raynor and his men had mesh in their masks – and Cockaigne cracked mesh technology years ago. Not to the same extent as Lukaš Caron but enough to paint false pictures and sounds. That's what's been happening to Raynor ever since the drones brought down the choppers. Most of the Cockaigne crew are sealed up in the sleeping quarters in the right leg of the sea plat-form. From there they've been spinning Raynor and his men a melded reality tale of heroic conquest. Of mowing down a room-ful of enemies who were never actually there. Of his last surviving man being shot down by armed enemies – while in reality a drone buzzed up behind the man and dosed him in the neck with a tran-quilliser pen. Of his pistol seeming to jam. Of taking the weapon of his fallen comrade – which was really a toy gun the drones had slung over the shoulder of the showroom dummy that lives in the mess room.

We all crave stories. We all want to be their heroes. That's how social engineering works. People hear the narrative they need to hear. Even if it's thinly stitched together from jailbroken video games.

Thimblerig takes a step forward. Raynor snaps his gun back into position. His shaved head is sweaty and flushed red. His right eye's puffed up in a pool of purple. A gash runs down his left cheek. He breathes hard, staring at Thimblerig like a man who's seen his own ghost.

— Go ahead, says Thimblerig, taking another step towards him. Shoot me.

Raynor jerks the gun. Thimblerig takes another step. The barrel's only a metre from his stomach. Raynor pulls the trigger and the weapon rattles. Thimblerig smiles. Raynor's eyes flicker as he figures it out. He glances down at the gun then throws it at Thimblerig's face and dives for him.

Thimblerig's head cracks against concrete as they land. Raynor pins an arm across his throat and extracts from his jacket a serrated knife as long and shiny as a sea bass. He grins.

— Guess those buzzing little shits forgot something, he whispers.

How did the scanners not pick up the knife? Raynor holds it horizontal over Thimblerig's face. It isn't made of metal. Some kind of ceramic?

— Gonna gut you, kid, says Raynor.

But all he does is pant. His eyes keep darting back to the cages where the corpses of his victims ought to be.

— Why the hell were you just standing there, you little prick?

— I was meant to hide, says Thimblerig in his most monotone voice.

— Then fuckit, why?

— I needed to look you in the eye.

But the man isn't listening. He's staring towards the door where his mask and weapons vanished.

— How the hell did you—? he says. And what about—?

He looks up at the ceiling. Towards the site of his supposed victory. His face is a mask of horror. He's broken. Not physically. This type of man will keep on crawling until you chop his limbs off. What's shattering him is working out how much he's been duped. Learning he was the clown all along. Not knowing how much of what he's just experienced is real. How much fake.

Here's the moment.

All Thimblerig's life he's been the child in the under-stairs cupboard. Looking out as his father faces off the young man with the AK-47. Not this day. This day he returns the stare of the enemy with a calmness that takes his whole will. Keeping his voice steady he speaks the words he's waited half a lifetime to say.

— Why did you betray my father, Mr Raynor?

Raynor leans back.

— Huh? The beardy dude? He was never even there, you cocksucker. Nor were you.

His legs are on either side of Thimblerig's torso. Pinning him to the floor.

— Ma'moun Ayyash, says Thimblerig. Captain in the Aleppo First Division. Whose group you betrayed in August 2015 to Jabhat al-Nusra. Ten men taken and killed! Ten! What did they pay you? No client so evil that a 'security contractor' will turn him down when dollars are waved before him?

Raynor listens to this with mild amusement fluttering over his bruised face.

— Kid, he says. Seriously. I don't know what movie you think you're in but I have priorities here. So let me tell you what you're going to do.

— You think I don't know? I have your chat files!

— What's going to happen now is, I'm going to walk you to that door and you're going to tell your friend outside . . .

— Don't even try to deny you were operating in Syria ten years ago.

— So I was in fucking Syria! What the hell am I supposed to have to do with a bunch of jihadi cocksuckers like Jabhat al-Nusra?

— I have a record of your communications. Giving them the locations of ten senior officers in the First Division militia.

— No you fucking don't.

— Using the name *drainer*.

— Not me.

— I know it's you! How can you—

— You have no fucking idea what—

— Betraying your own country—!

— Crazy-ass paranoid horseshit—!

They're shouting over each other.

— Whoa, whoa! shouts Raynor. Hold it – *djh, djh, djh*!

Thimblerig stops shouting.

— Think about it, says Raynor. Why would I use a handle so close to my real name?

Thimblerig stares back.

— Jesus! says Raynor. What would even make you think that was me?

Thimblerig draws in a breath. Oxygen hits his brain. For the first time he thinks clearly. Why has he believed so long that Raynor is guilty? In spite of all his detective work, the only evidence he ever really had was that Lucky Ghost gave him data. But now he knows that Lucky Ghost's a liar. He lets Raynor's weight push his body into the concrete floor. He never did have a lead on his father's death. He never will. To think he could simply hack his way through the lies and counter-lies of a dozen warring factions in the midst of an ancient disaster.

He'll never know why his father died. Or rather he's always known. It was because the world's unjust and humanity vile.

Raynor's eyeing him carefully.

— So, he says. Now we cleared that up?

He flips the knife round in his hand so the serrated edge points upwards. Places it under Thimblerig's ear.

— You have ten seconds, he says, to instruct your friends to turn the cable back on or—

A vast boom rips the silence. Raynor cries out as he flies sideways off Thimblerig. The knife clatters over the floor. At the door, Jacko shoves a shell into his smoking shotgun.

— I thought you were going to stay inside the locker? he says. You muppet.

Thimblerig gets to his knees and brushes himself off – though the floor is spotless.

— Sick of cupboards, he mutters.

Jacko's hangdog face goes even more crumpled as he frowns at that. Then he steps forward and trains his gun at Thimblerig.

— Seriously, he says. Don't.

No – the gun's not pointing at Thimblerig. It's pointing *past* him. He turns to see a fat streak of blood that's worked its way across the floor. At its far end Raynor is frozen in the act of dragging himself towards the knife.

— Fuck you, hippie, he says into the floor. I'm a dead man anyway. But with your scalp? And his? Who knows?

— Yeah, says Jacko, resting the gun on his arm. Except your mission's over. You just don't know it yet. Thimblerig?

— Pleasure, says Thimblerig.

He's glowing inside that Jacko used his handle. Kicking himself for caring.

He raises his right arm – where the crablet still clings – and calls up the Sonos control panel. Presses *FM RADIO*. This was the second job he was meant to do from inside the locker. Two seconds later Alex's voice springs forth from half a dozen speakers.

— . . . *prove beyond doubt,* she's saying, *that Occidental Data Partnerships are guilty of this bribe. Of harassment. Even murder.*

The audio is warm and hyper-real. Say this for Cockaigne: they have the best sound system.

— This is live, BTW, says Jacko.

— The fuck? says the bloodied Raynor from the floor.

— *Listen*! say Jacko and Thimblerig in unison.

TUNNEL VISION

Ox is on a roll.

'Not bad,' he says to Dani. 'This fellow is quite the tough guy. Many would be unconscious by now. But you know what? I am holding back. What will happen, do you think, if I apply something closer to full strength?'

Dani has slid down against a router cabinet. She weeps on the ground, refusing to look at the thing that Ox is doing to her friend. She can't stop herself hearing, though. The next sound she hears is a mallet striking a melon.. Then the low hard grunt a tennis player makes when serving. She balls her eyes tighter, keeps her head down.

'But you're right,' says Ox. 'This is dull. Anyone can be meat to a tenderiser. I feel the need for something more . . . specific.'

Dani looks up. Ox is standing where he was before. Cradled in his left hand is Davin's head. But Davin has gone. Or his face has. In its place is a side of tenderised meat. His body hangs limply, held up by that great paw on his head. She screws up her eyes. Sobs rack her. Then she forces them open again and stares knives at Ox. He turns a quizzical expression on her.

'I wonder, for instance,' he says, 'could I crush his skull with my hand? Is this something I could do? Do you know, in all my years I've never tried this?'

Davin spits out blood and fragments of tooth.

'*Bugv*,' he says.

That was meant to be, *fuck off*, but his voice is as pummelled as his face. Ox gives him a smile. He looks like the father of an exhausted but victorious athlete. Dani shifts herself, sitting upright against the wall.

'Fuck you,' she says on Davin's behalf, though without much conviction.

'Disappointing,' says Ox. 'You have thirty seconds before I break this man. I will not demean myself by counting out loud.'

He stands perfectly still, watching Dani. Involuntarily, she glances up at the clock on the opposite wall. Seven thirty-seven. Then she looks back at Ox.

Then she remembers: It's time.

She reaches up onto the desk to her right. Ox watches her fumble about but seems to decide this isn't a threat.

'Fifteen seconds,' he says.

Dani's fingers find the old-model Pure DAB radio. She pulls it off the desk and lets it fall into her lap. Its white plastic finish has aged to a pale olive green. Ox looks down at it blankly, then at Dani.

'The signal down here's not great,' says Dani, 'but it works.'

Ox is no longer able to hide his confusion. You can tell how much he hates being left out of the loop.

'Believe me,' says Dani kindly. 'You're going to want to hear this.'

She presses the On switch and holds up the radio, its speaker facing Ox.

SPEAK TRUTH UNTO NATION

Alex stops talking. The studio falls silent, save for the low hum of the room's systems. It's as though she can hear the attention of the nation, vibrating back across the airwaves. What's their listenership, right now? How many tens of millions? She hopes it includes the two men who are her real and only target audience.

Lukaš takes another sip of water. His hand is steady as he raises the glass, but it's already empty. He replaces it on the felt surface of the desk, picks up instead his little rectangular device and spins it around obsessively as he speaks.

'Your story fails to hold water,' he says. 'I hesitate to expose a former student's solecisms in such a public forum but I have been somewhat hijacked this morning, and I feel I must.'

'I'm all ears.'

'If I may characterise your story: some dramatically named criminal conspiracy has arranged for a series of bitter shocks to strike our nation this morning.' He clears his throat. 'Via the Internet and the Strange?'

'Good so far.'

Behind the glass of the control booth, faces are lined up in the light from the screens. The studio producer and engineer. Siobhán, Tom and Sally. All rapt.

'Handy Frank's being,' says Lukaš, 'but the first target. The purpose of this is to wipe value off the UK economy; an economy that has been falsely boosted by the calculated manipulation of many people's psychological states?'

'Specifically, emotions.'

'As you say. These shocks will earn some mastermind figure – a figure you for some as yet unexplained reason imply is me – a billion dollars?'

'Thereabouts.'

'And the reason you and your colleagues have committed the wanton act of disabling the network access of an entire nation? You are, in this hysterical story, some kind of hero?'

'I'd say antihero at best – but go on.'

Lukaš leans back with an almost sensual smile. The utter certainty of his success.

'Yet,' he says. 'Even if one accepted the scale of this conspiracy, this series of planned shocks, who would gain? There is no billion-dollar derivative pegged to the failure of the UK economy. As you well know, the futures market is highly regulated. Such a thing would have been detected.'

Alex snorts. Not an attractive noise.

'Not one contact. Hundreds. I've seen every one of them.'

'Ah. Now. You admit to seeing documents that could only have been obtained illegally.'

'It defies belief that so many separate organisations would independently take out shorts with the exact same term.'

'Yet you have no proof.'

'And while most of the shell companies are registered to who knows where, this one—'

She throws the first paper across the table. Exhibit A. Lukaš makes a point of extracting his half-moon specs and balancing them on his slender nose.

'*Vaclav Holdings*,' he says. He looks over the top of his glasses. 'I trust you are not going to make the somewhat racist claim that a company named after a Czech national hero must be registered to me, a Czech national?'

'At your address.'

'At the address of the London School of Economics. Not so hard to fathom that someone at that address might purchase an over-the-counter financial instrument.'

He still doesn't get it. He still thinks all he needs to do is beat her in an argument. Because that's all he's ever known how to do. He doesn't understand the real stakes. Alex leans forward into the mic, glares at him between the line of monitors at the centre of the console.

'A few days back,' she says, 'when I told you Mickey Gallant had been killed, you didn't bat an eye. But when two minutes later I told you about a bribe paid in Emoticoin you jumped a mile.'

'Claims worthy of a conspiracy theory vlog.'

'I thought it was odd. But I didn't have time to think it through. But really: who's a world expert on money and Emoticoin? An expert in the role of sentiment in the national economy? Who has access to big investors with the kind of capital to fund a massive buy-up of short contracts? Who's been adviser to Sean Perce ever since the Strange was a thing?'

Lukaš removes his glasses with weary sorrow.

'I hesitate to say this,' he says, 'but if you go on I fear the listening public – not to say your employers here – will need to hear something of your psychological history.'

Alex glances into the control room. Everyone's staring ashen-faced. They're wondering whether to stop this. Except this is fucking good radio. And the only media channel in the country right now.

'So,' says Lukaš, 'are you done?'

A note of anger has entered his voice. Alex's little denouement has served its purpose.

'For now,' she says.

'Then let me spell out the main flaw in your logic. Let me explain to your listeners why it is self-evidently *you* that is the criminal party here. Not. I.'

'Oh, now this should be good.'

She wishes she had the confidence she's claiming. There's still too much at stake; too many moving parts.

'Let us suppose for a moment,' says Lukaš, 'everything you say is true.'

'Suppose away.'

'You and your friends commit this act of – if I may say – information terrorism, by taking down the public Internet. You claim to have done this to prevent a catastrophe on the UK markets. Yet your actions will bring about precisely this catastrophic effect. Are having it as we speak. *You* are the cause of the catastrophe, Alex.'

'Nuh-uh. We're stopping the worst of it. Right now, nobody else is being killed by unwitting Strangers. The evidence we've put in front of Serious Crimes will stop a dozen other acts of sabotage. Handy Frank's is going to get its bail-out, Lukaš. No government could turn its back after a minister took a bribe.'

'Yet the Internet down? Do you even understand the impact of this?'

'Do you?'

'I know it's enough to bring about a fall in the markets. Enough, I warrant, to trigger these mythical short contracts you claim to have illegally seen. So – suppose I was the villainous mastermind of this scheme. With the Internet turned on, my scheme goes ahead and I get my billion dollars. With the Internet turned off, the same result. I win either way.'

Triumphantly he plants both palms on the console.

'This,' he says, 'is the flaw. Your act of terrorism *could not* prevent such a scheme. Which proves you are doing this for some other, malicious end – and attempting to pass the blame onto me. How.' His palms beat the console in time with his words. 'Dare. You?'

'Easy on the table-thumping. Tends to get a bit boomy.'

Lukaš sits back in his chair, a blond Cheshire Cat, and folds his arms. The ghostly row of spectators behind the glass is captivated. Alex leaves it a single beat then leans into the mic.

'Here's the thing about your big short, Lukaš. I've read those deal contracts. And there's no recourse for you if the markets are closed during the days covered by your short. You only get your money if the index value of the markets falls. But a market doesn't rise or fall when it's closed. If the Internet doesn't come back on in the next –' she checks the studio clock '– thirty hours, your short is null and void. You don't get a penny.'

Lukaš hasn't moved but the muscles holding his smile in place have shifted almost imperceptibly into a grimace. Very suddenly he lurches forward, almost leaving his chair. On reflex, Alex pulls back. Then he gets hold of himself and eases back down, wheels the chair forward to the console where he sits bolt upright and addresses the mic, gazing into the middle distance.

'It seems to me that the British people will be appalled at your suggestion of keeping the Internet down for a whole two days on some fairy-tale premise. This can only confirm that you are the villains of this piece, not I.'

'The evidence is all being made public.'

Lukaš snorts.

'Not if there is no Internet! Can you imagine that businesses – government – will allow you to keep so many points of presence down, for so long?'

Here it is, now. Make it clear.

'You said it yourself,' she says. 'Whatever happens this morning, the markets are going to tumble. But your plan was to wipe them out entirely, for a generation. And which asset would fall the fastest and furthest in this scenario?'

'In such a state of chaos as you've created it is hard to predict.'

'No, it's easy. In order to crash the markets, Lukaš, you were planning to kill Emoticoin. That's how this domino hack was going to work so fast and so effectively. For months – maybe years – you've been manipulating millions of Strangers. Making them work for you, telling them what to feel, building the value of a digital currency that's pegged to emotions instead of the real world. When people feel good, it booms – it's been doing that for months. When overnight they suddenly feel bad – it crashes. And that's what was going to set off the domino fall that would trigger your short. So clever.' She gives him a little round of applause, which gratifyingly irks him even more. 'Seriously, genius. But you know the really, really stupid thing you got wrong?'

Silence now. A silence burning with hatred. Ah, Lukaš, you never were the careful, caring mentor, were you? This is who you always were.

'Do you know,' she says, 'who currently has the largest holding in Emoticoin? I'm talking globally.'

'If I was that man you claim I am, I would presumably know the answer to your question. But I am not.'

'Then let me tell you. It's a Belarusian conglomerate called Occidental Data Partnerships. My friends have been watching their transactions for some time. And it turns out they have a *lot* of Emoticoin. About a tenth of the global supply. They like paying bribes in it. Receiving ransoms with it.'

'No.'

'O-o-oh, yes. Funny, really. The people who are going to suffer worst from your masterplan are the people you've hired to carry it out. Guess you never explained the mechanics to them. Guess you like keeping information to yourself.'

'Now of all times it is deeply irresponsible to spout unevidenced conspiracies.'

Alex can tell his heart isn't in it any more. He knows she has him. She leans into the mic, maximising the resonance of her voice.

'How do you think Mr Ox will react when he hears that, in taking this contract from you, he's been ruined? From recent experience, I'd have to say: people don't like it when you try to destroy the company they've built from nothing.'

Silence. Lukaš has hold of the edge of the console. He looks like he's about to break off a chunk.

'Well,' Alex says. 'We won't have long to wait. You see, Mr Ox is listening to this now. That's right. Wave to the mic and say, "*Hello, Mr Ox*."'

Lukaš leans forward, frantic calculations ticking behind his grey eyes, and picks up his little device.

'So I guess the tables have turned,' she says, as he taps at the face of his little black metal slab. 'Now that you're—'

Her body freezes and her throat locks up. Her arms and shoulders spasm, sending rockets of pain down her back. Her head drops forward towards the desk. Gagging for air, she forces it up so she can look at Lukaš: what's he done to her?

— *My dear girl*, says a soothing, antiquated voice. *One must admire the fight in you.*

Sitting across the desk from her, where Lukaš was a moment ago, is a long-faced woman in a green wool twinset, a tidy string of pearls resting over her full chest.

— *And yet*, says the woman in her spectral voice, *it can only be in vain.*

Alex still has her mesh on from when she was talking to Abul. Now Lukaš is in it, and in her embeds. His little device—

She forces her left hand up towards her mesh. Beneath the skin of her forearm, the metal of her tattoos heaves back against her bones and muscle. When the pain becomes too great, she lets her arm slap back onto the console and glares at Lukaš. But it's Elyse Martingale who returns her stare, with compassionate concern. Around her the studio blurs into a psychedelic world of colour.

— *And do think, my dear*, says that doyenne of the past century. *Why would you resist my wholly rational endeavour?*

Something invisible lands against Alex, shoving her back onto the floor. The chair falls back under her. Her head smacks into the floor. The sea of colours soars down on her, accompanied by a shrill whistle and a furious drumbeat. An invisible foot lands on her midriff, forcing air from her lungs. Hands grab her lapels and haul her into a sitting position. Through the keening baffle of her mesh she hears someone pummel on the glass of the studio door, but Francis's wedge, it seems, is working all too well.

— *Why*, says Elyse's voice, close up to her ears, *must it always be the brutes and Philistines who inherit power?*

Alex's head smashes back against the carpeted floor. Starbursts and a hot ringing fill her eyes and ears. The unseen Lukaš hauls her up and smashes her down again. A crimson chord thrums in her ears, lovely as the Strange. Her head strikes the floor a third time. The singing of her blood fills her skull like a water bomb.

— *It is long past time,* says Elyse, *that those with intellect seize hold of the means of production of information. Of capital.*

Through the riot of colours a five-pointed spaceship hovers above her head. The heavy base of a swivel chair. Light explodes at the back of her eyeballs.

— *Those who stand in the way of the inevitable tide,* says Elyse, *shall be swept away.*

Never mind who outwits whom. All the smarts and the bluff, it comes down to this. A forty-something man's weight and muscle overwhelms a thirty-something woman.

The chair's base lands on Alex's face.

THIS

Ox pockets the satellite phone.

'I have no signal,' he says.

'Yeah, line of sight, you idiot!' shouts Dani.

She's kneeling by Davin's unconscious body, feeling for heartbeats, breath. There's maybe a flutter on the side of his neck. Or maybe it's her own pulse pumping in her fingertip. The radio show has flipped to a recorded message. Something just happened in the studio.

Ox surveys the room and nods.

'This operation is over. There are calls I must make if I am to avoid further outlay.'

He reaches a club of a fist down to Dani. She shies away. He wiggles the fist, encouraging her to take the little white rectangle protruding between his thumb and forefinger. She takes the business card. The hump-backed silhouette of an ox in livid orange. She turns it over. *Occidental Data Partnerships*, it says in sleek designer writing. Underneath, an IP network address. Nothing more.

'We have had rebranding,' says Ox. 'Reflecting our values of dynamism and efficiency, but also touch of humour. This humanises us, the branding agency believes.'

She stares at him. He looks slightly apologetic.

'It is always somewhat awkward,' he says, 'to have been on opposing sides of a deal. However, should you ever require our services – well. You have my IP.'

He's about to go. She needs to make something happen. Some trap, some unexpected twist nobody saw coming. She can't let him just walk out of the room.

Ox walks out of the room. Dani slumps back against the wall with Davin's head still in her lap. She'd like to cry again, or scream, or thump something. Separated from her glowheart she barely know what she feels any more.

Davin's head shifts. A tremor passes down his right arm. Dani sits forward to see if his eyes are moving. They aren't. She puts her head back against the cool glass of the router cabinet.

'I really hate that guy,' she says to nobody.

PART FOUR:

' "Free" inevitably means that someone else will be deciding how you live.'

— Jaron Lanier, *Who Owns The Future?*

UP NEXT

On a clear afternoon, this early in the year, Parliament Hill is London's version of God Mode. As Alex listens to Connor chatter on her flip-phone, she gazes down a full green slope and out across the bottle-city of London. Children's kites wheel through the mad blue shout of the sky.

'OK, wish me luck though,' says Connor at the other end of the line.

'Luck,' she says idly, leaning into her stick to take the pressure off her sore right leg.

'And you? Is your date there yet?'

'She will be,' says Alex. 'I'm meeting someone else first. This guy.'

'Ooh, a tall dark handsome stranger?'

'He's half those things at best.'

'Do tell.'

'I will. *After* you give me the post-mortem on tonight.'

'Will do, babes,' says Connor.

'Excuse me, *babes*?' says Alex, but Connor's already cut the line.

She closes the phone and leans into her stick to limp up to her favourite bench. She sits with care and watches the kites circle overhead.

Connor's the least convincing gay man since Matthew Broderick in *Torch Song Trilogy*. Strictly speaking he belongs in jail, not on Grindr. Still, Alex has taken him on as a kind of project. This is after all the age of reconstruction.

She watches the elemental pull of the wind on the sinews of the flyers' arms; their feet making anchors on the true earth. She looks down at her own skinny forearms: the rivulets of scar tissue where her tattoos were excised.

Connor's not only rebuilding his personal life, but also Handy Frank's. The firm's become a touchstone for how the country evaded the worst of Lukaš' domino hack, a year back. Within hours of Alex's broadcast, Susan Hardiman was sacked as Minister for Competitiveness. The first thing her replacement did was announce that the government would indeed bail out Handy Frank's, as soon as Francis stepped down to face justice. Connor got off with a hefty fine, in exchange for cooperation with the police. He stepped straight into his father's shoes, causing not a little protest. Everyone – especially Harm – assumed that Alex would speak out against the man who beat on her and on her wife, but she didn't. Among so many vicious men who'd lined up to assault Alex over the course of that terrible year, it was Connor who turned out to have at least a strain of the good guy.

Plus everything's different now. So many accounts have been wiped clean. The Internet blackout lasted just a few days but it was a junction point. As was Alex's own blackout, which lasted a little longer. Life hinges on moments when you almost die, as Alex would almost certainly have died on Bluescreen Monday, if it wasn't for Connor.

The plan was that the Gunnells would wait outside in their van while Alex confronted Lukaš in the studio, but Connor was restless after cat-and-mousing with so many Strangers. He took advantage of the mayhem to vault the security gates. He located the studio by following the trail of staffers on their way to witness the news event of the decade, and reached the control room in time to see Lukaš mount the console and assault the frozen Alex, and the vain attempts of the security guards to enter the studio. Seeing Lukaš wield the business end of a swivel chair over Alex's face, Connor flipped up the pump-action shotgun from beneath his long green coat and put a shell into the reinforced glass. He clubbed his way through with the butt of his rifle, leapt through the fissure and piled onto Lukaš.

The phones being down, the Gunnells ferried the bloodied Lukaš to Paddington Green police station while Siobhán drove Alex to hospital. The doctors reckoned another blow or two would have crushed her skull. They patched her up well, though she's lost movement in her face and right leg and the left side of her head's complaining in this morning's cold.

Lukaš lost far more than the few million dollars he'd sunk into defunct futures contracts. He was behind bars only a few weeks. On the first morning of his trial, he was on his way from the cells to the prisoner transport vehicle when he took two rapid rounds of sniper fire to the side of the head. He died in mid-fall. Shooter and weapon were never found. One year on, he's like a false memory.

A magnificent red box kite figure-eights perilously near the ground. Alex draws in her breath but the teenage girl at the strings wrestles it back into an updraft.

As well as being a year since Bluescreen Monday, it's just four days to Alex and Harm's second wedding anniversary. This being a Sunday they're celebrating today, with a visit to the heath. They never had the chance to celebrate their first anniversary, what with Alex being spark out in a private room at University College Hospital, hooked up to a suite of vintage medical gear that didn't need the Internet to function. Harm sat by her bed for the full twelve days it took her to come round, and was beside her for the whole six months of physio. She'll be here soon – though hopefully not so soon she'll bump into Alex's other visitor. Hard to know how she'd react to seeing him.

Hard to know how Alex herself will react.

A ragged cough makes her spin round. A lanky kid in a parka is hovering awkwardly on the path. Alex's shoulder twinges at the sudden movement.

'You surprised me,' she says to Abul. Thimblerig. The Happy Handyman.

He looks down at her with his usual gangling lack of grace.

'You're not wearing mesh,' he says.

'I don't any more.'

She shifts painfully, pats the space beside her. Abul stays standing, fingers tapping the slats of the bench's back.

'It's the same for ninety-seven point three per cent of the population,' he says. 'Before Bluescreen Monday mesh use was in the high sixty per cents.'

'Seriously,' says Alex. 'Sit. It – it hurts to twist round like this.'

Abul coughs again and darts round to sit the maximum distance away from Alex. They watch the kites for a time. Well. This is awkward.

'You work for Perce now,' she says. 'With Dani.'

'I'm the youngest Chief Data Scientist ever at a FTSE 100 or Fortune 100 firm.'

Alex smirks to herself.

'You do know it's kind of dickish to talk about your achievements?'

'For you it is.'

Alex shakes dizziness from her head. She can still get so whacked out, after even a gentle walk uphill.

'I watch the metrics every day,' says Abul. 'One hundred and sixteen new reconstruction projects launched in the UK just this morning. And this is a Sunday.' He rolls up his parka sleeve to reveal the crab-like computer still clamped to his arm, reads from it. 'Here. Silver Solder, a drop-in engineering class run by retired IT professionals in Cardiff. Carecoin, a digital currency to reward people who care for relatives.' He gestures at the screen. 'My team would never have come up with these.'

He's listing projects from the Great Reconstruction. Projects Mondan provides with tech and connectivity, and with inward flows of Emoticoin.

' "*Your team*",' she says. 'There's a weird thought.'

'One hundred and twenty-eight people.'

The four unconnected days that followed Bluescreen Monday crippled the nation, forced it to rediscover itself. With no private worlds to shelter in, people stepped out onto the streets and started mucking in. Volunteers donned fluorescent tabards to patrol their neighbourhoods. Kids in pig masks set up drop-in centres where people could inoculate their tech against the black algae. It was like they'd woken from a sleeping spell. Mondan's leading the charge to muster these efforts, helping communities build micro-economies, now the macro one has withered away.

Dani's vision of the Strange was never wrong. It was a place where people could share and exchange beyond the control of banks or governments – just as Elyse foresaw. The better parts of the Strange remain, even after the black algae manipulated and destroyed the heart of it. Emoticoin is still a thing. With the economy in shreds, with banks so unwilling to lend actual pounds sterling, people use Coin to restart and run their local economies. Mondan injects the funds they need. Abul and his fellow hackers have turned gamekeeper to keep the system running.

'You talk like everything's fine,' she says. 'Like we didn't fuck the economy that week.'

'We stopped something far worse.'

Dani kept the Internet down for ninety-six hours. Longer than it took to render Lucky Ghost's billion-dollar short null and void. The evidence of the domino hack was enough to persuade the government to slap on a state of emergency until Lukaš Caron's dark magic could be undone. Until Dani could unravel his black algae strand by strand. Which in the end meant disabling the Strange for ever, leaving every Stranger alone, their memories and the ghosts of their loved ones eaten away for ever by black algae.

'Do you think,' says Alex, 'I don't spin myself that same ends-justify-the-means horse-crap, every time the pain keeps me awake at night? It's still crap, though.'

'You checksum the good and the bad and you evaluate what remains. We left a net positive.'

The twinges in Alex's skull are back with a vengeance. She stops talking and waits for them to subside. She can take another painkiller in half an hour.

'You know Doug Raynor became a police informer?' says Abul. 'When he heard your interview, he knew he'd nowhere to run. Based on his information, Interpol's taken apart most of Occidental's operations. Because of you.'

'I didn't know that, no. Thanks, I suppose?'

During each of the five times Alex has been in the same room as Abul, he's always managed to come out with this kind of transparent, positive declaration, while not looking anyone in the eye. It's impossible not to warm to him a little when he does this, yet that doesn't mean he isn't the monster who tormented her for months. The contradiction hurts. This is the first time she's been alone with him since that hotel room, during the disaster. She's been so afraid his stillness and his buried anger would be triggers for her panic and horror to rise again. For now, though, there's nothing but a tremor in her throat. For the umpteenth time, she glances down at a glowheart that isn't there. She's having to get used to reading these more ancient signals of her own emotions.

'I guess, though,' she says, then coughs when the words come out choked. 'I guess Ox is still out there?'

Abul puts his hands together prayer-style and clamps them between his thighs. Down the slope, the girl with the big red kite has fallen under its force. A younger girl is helping her up. Perhaps a sister. Still Abul says nothing.

'Do you ever think about the dead?' says Alex.

He seems not to hear. She's never been able to tell whether he's completely cold, or he just withdraws in face of questions he finds difficult.

'The police told me the numbers,' she says, 'while they were working out whether to prosecute me. There's Mickey, of course.'

While Alex waits for the rising tears to retreat, she watches the older girl unravel the strings while her sister holds steady the kite.

'Waleed and Manal, too,' she says. 'The man Francis shot at his mansion, the one who bled out. One of the Vaders Connor ran down. All the wounded.'

Abul continues to inspect the dusty path.

'Those guys I firebombed in the woods survived, thank God,' says Alex. 'Though the one trapped in the car had second-degree burns all down his body. And then,' she chances a look at Abul's profile, 'then there's the guy you shot at the hotel.'

'I didn't shoot him.'

'Oh! He responds.'

The kid's blank face cracks. He screws it up as though struck by a sudden pain in his gut.

'Why are you being so cruel?' he says. 'I thought you asked me here to talk.'

Alex can't keep the anger pent up any longer. She stands without the help of her stick, raising her height unsteadily over Abul. He hunches down further.

'Why so cruel?' she says. 'Oh, well, let's see, shall we?' She slaps him across the shoulder. 'Shall we start with the six months of vile harassment?' She thumps him again, between the shoulder blades. 'Or with you trying to get me fired?'

She raises her hand to hit him again but suddenly he's up, furious face directly in front of Alex's. She stumbles back from the apparition he's become.

'You want to talk about the dead?' he says through clenched teeth. 'Say boo-hoo for this person or that person? Does that make you feel better? You don't know what you're talking about. I thought you meant something but you're just another rotten smart-Alec!'

'Wow. Sorry to be such a disappointment.'

He jabs at his own chest, fingers clustered into an arrow-head.

'Do you have any idea,' he says, 'how many people I saw die while I was still a child?'

Alex's mocking grin falls away.

'All my cousins,' he says. 'All! My mother. That night on the dinghy it was so dark I couldn't tell where she even was. Then she was nowhere. My father, *in front of me! BECAUSE of me!* You don't know *ANYTHING!*'

He stops abruptly, horrified at the words that have just cascaded out of him. He shoves his whole right wrist into his mouth, bites down on it and turns around. He takes a few steps away along the path then stops. Alex pushes her hands deep into the pockets of her raincoat and watches him. The tails of his parka flap around his legs.

'How old were you when you left?' she says to his back.

'Eight.' She can barely hear him. 'I was eight.'

Probably the same age as the younger of the kite-flying girls down on the muddy slope. The one who's leaping with joy to see the bright red plaything soar again. Alex picks up her stick and walks towards Abul. His whole lean frame is shaking under his coat. She opens her mouth to speak then closes it. Does any of this give him the right to avoid her questions?

No. It really doesn't.

'You were wrong before,' she says, in a gentler voice than she was expecting. 'I don't want to punish you. Well, I kind of do, but that's not why we're here.'

'Then what.'

Good question.

'I want you to tell me why you did it.'

Still he doesn't move – though the shuddering's stopped. She walks around to face him front-on. He keeps on glaring down at the path. She grabs his chin and forces his head up. Wild-eyed, he yanks it away. But he's looking at her now.

'Why?' she says. 'Come on. I'm standing right here. There's nobody else. Tell me why you would say and do such vile things?'

'I've stopped, haven't I? I haven't done a thing to you since we met. To any woman.'

'That is so far from making it OK.'

'It was meant to be a joke.'

A single dull laugh bursts out of Alex.

'A *joke*? Fucking hell.'

'To get a response! When you always ignored every single sensible message I sent you, why not?'

'Sorry, what, you used to message me? Before?'

'Men throw insults at each other all the time. Banter. Exactly like the things I said to you. Why do you – why do women have to make such a thing of it?'

'No. Sorry, no. Men don't. Not like you did to me.'

'It's only in fun. Like – like every time a newbie girl comes onto the groups we ask her to—'

He stops dead. Guilty fear bleeds into his eyes.

'What do you ask her, Abul?'

Alex's voice has a knife-sharp edge that's unfamiliar, even to her.

'To . . .' he gestures circles in front of his chest. 'To show us . . .'

'Oh, you mean her *tits*?' Alex gets her face close to his, to read what's in his eyes. 'Jesus, you do. That's the price of admission, is it?'

He turns his head away.

'They're fine with it,' he says. 'Not all girls are like you.'

'What, because I'm not a *sport*? Well, OK then. Should I show you them now?' She steps back and starts unbuttoning her raincoat. 'Will you let me in your gang then?'

As she starts unbuttoning her shirt, Abul turns away.

'Don't be horrible,' he says.

'This is horrible? This is?' she buttons herself up again. 'Fucking Christ, do you have any idea how it feels to see an image of yourself having—'

The composite of her being raped by that demonic Happy Handyman flares up in her mind. It's never far away, that image. Tears are welling up. She musters fury to repel them.

'I didn't know!' he shouts. 'How was I supposed to know you'd get so upset?'

'That *rape threats* would upset me? How little imagination does that take?'

He strides up the grassy slope. She rushes around to get in front of him. He brakes and turns. Again, she moves into his path. Her hip screams complaints.

'You told me you were my biggest fan,' she says. 'When we met, you actually told me that. How could that possibly be true and yet you kept on attacking me, even after I'd just – just – melted down? I was *broken*! But you kept at it.'

'I don't *know* why! It was something to do.'

'It made you feel good. It must have done. It made you feel powerful.'

'They were just words.'

'Bullshit. You hate women. You must. Why do you hate women, Abul?'

He's staring at her with open fury. If she wasn't riding her own wave of anger, maybe she'd have the headspace to be afraid of him.

'Because I'm a Muslim you think I hate women?' he says. 'Because I'm brown?'

'Oh no. No, no. We're not playing that game. *Because you're a troll* I think it. I *know* it.'

'I've always respected women.'

'Oh, Christ! Name a single woman you've treated with respect. And do not tell me your sainted mother.'

'Elyse Martingale.'

Alex reels back and lets out an ugly crowing laugh. She walks back down to the path, leaning hard into her stick, then turns to shout up at the rumpled, glaring boy.

'That's it?' she says. 'The only example you can give me has been dead for fifty years?'

'Dani Farr. Half my team at Mondan.'

His voice is very small on the darkening hill. Alex turns her back on him and eases herself back down onto the bench.

'So,' she says, 'you've actually met some living women. Congratulations. That must be terrifying for you.'

Abul stumbles down to the path and stands at the end of the

bench, hands towards Alex in a kind of supplication. His fury has morphed into misery.

'You,' he says. 'I respect you. When I met you it was different. You were brave and strong and you beat Professor Caron. I was so wrong. I kept those emails to myself because I was sure I could solve the problem on my own if I dug deep enough. But I didn't. *You* did and he almost killed you.'

She gives him a long look, studying his face against the glare of the sinking sun.

'OK, well, thank you for that,' she says. 'I guess. Though actually I couldn't have done that without your help.'

'I don't do those things any more,' he says. 'I promise. I will never do them again.'

He moves around to sit beside her. She can't stop herself from rearing away but he's babbling so fast now he doesn't seem to notice.

'I don't want to hurt people,' he says. 'I never meant to do that. I'm – I am really very sorry.'

Alex nods but says nothing. Wasn't this exactly what she was after? An apology? Truth and reconciliation? Was she expecting that to make her feel better? Did she think she could fix every single man, just by confronting a single screwed-up teen?

She takes a deep breath.

'OK, let me just try this out,' she says. 'Tell me if this is anywhere near correct. Then maybe we can leave this for now.'

The two girls are still down there, even after all their fellow kite-flyers have packed up and left, eking out the last of the failing afternoon light. The older girl takes the full force of the kite as it rises.

'Before,' says Alex, watching it surge upwards, 'you lost at everything. Your father, your mother. You couldn't save them. Trolling me, the others, was a new kind of game you stumbled on. You happened to be very good at it, and the points you scored made you feel good. Powerful. They were your Emoticoin. Ten thousand RAGE, each time you made a woman cower from her screen.'

She glances over at Abul's expressionless face. Seeing nothing there she turns back to the kite and continues.

'But on Bluescreen Monday you won. *We* won. Everything changed for you then. You have a job title now, and a corner office. And what I think is, *that's* the reason you don't troll any more. It's not that I taught you anything. It's just that you no longer need to. Does that make sense?'

Abul shrugs and bites his lower lip. It doesn't look like he buys a single word of this, but he's back to his old inarticulate self so it's hard to know. Alex leans back painfully and both of them watch the single remaining, bright red kite. Sitting in silence like this, looking out over London, you might think the two of them were friends. If you didn't know anything about anything.

Time stretches out like a frayed rubber band, ready to snap. Alex is the one who breaks it.

'So if you're such a big Martingale nerd,' says Alex, 'I guess you've seen this new Lucky Ghost? She's got like twenty million followers. I've been following her. She says incredible things.'

'Oh, well, that's me.'

Alex swivels her whole upper body round to look at him: not without some pain.

'Sorry?'

'I'm Lucky Ghost now.'

He blinks at her in confusion, as if what he just said was the most obvious thing in the world.

'You're – excuse me?'

'Professor Caron didn't need the name any more. I thought it would be a way to help people fix the damage. Speak without them knowing it was me. I mine our data and extrapolate ways we can connect groups in need with groups who have what's needed. I share these ideas through Lucky Ghost. I can't speak in Elyse's voice like Professor Caron but people seem to find it useful.'

OK, if this is true, score a positive point for Abul. The new Lucky Ghost he says is him – that online voice has been central to the Reconstruction. Helping people and communities raise themselves back up by their bootstraps.

'What is it about a long-dead academic,' she says, 'that's made one person after another assume her mantle?'

'I don't know why anyone else does.'

In spite of all the bad done in her name, Elyse's clarion call for transparency and sharing has shaped this time. She staked out combat lines between authority and liberation. It doesn't matter who inhabits her ghost. If Abul can redeem himself by being the latest Elyse, all power to him.

'Fair enough,' she says. 'I don't really know why any of us does anything, either.'

There's a force that draws us to the voice that happens to speak for our age. The voice that reveals the things we need to change. Some epochs never find their voice, or follow a false one. This time cannot be one of them; there's too much left to fix. Maybe some other voice will speak out soon, and be found and heard. Until it does, let Abul go on channelling the late, great Elyse Martingale.

The sun is low in the sky. Alex shakes back the sleeve of her mac to check her five-year-old smartwatch.

'Oh, hell,' she says, 'the time. I keep losing track without my mesh. Harmony – my wife. She'll be here in about minus three minutes.'

Abul's immediately on his feet, agitating to go.

'I am sorry,' he says. 'Really. Please. Tell me if there's anything I can do – anything *we* can do. Medical? Tech? Coin?'

When Alex smiles it's only a little forced. She doesn't think she wants to see Abul again. She doesn't think she needs to.

'I'm good,' she says. 'I have everything.'

With a quick nod and a furtive look around, Abul scurries off along the path, towards the east. Alex watches him until he sinks behind the brow. Then she looks around for a sign of Harm approaching from the west.

A year back, when she came back into consciousness, she'd lost everything – everything but Harm. The headaches were overwhelming. She couldn't walk until slivers of metal were grafted onto to her skeleton. It took months of physio to get her teetering along a rail. She still needs her stick to walk to the corner shop.

But she also lost a ton of shit she never knew she was carrying. The constant anxiety over status, well-being, viewer counts. The drumbeat she imagined was the necessary part of her. When the security blanket of the Strange was ripped away; when she rode the explosion that Lukaš set off; defeated him, then fell to him: it switched her off and on again. She's cleaner now, she thinks. Free of the knots that were clogging her emotional muscles.

Down below, on the slope by the kite-flying girls, a woman in a yellow duffle coat is standing with her back to Alex, watching the box-kite slice triumphantly through the vacant blue. The woman wasn't there the last time Alex looked. Now she turns to smile at Alex. It's Harm, of course, nodding at the kite with a lovely smile. Then she turns back again and watches the girl bring it neatly if effortlessly to the ground. Then she turns to Alex again and smiles. Then she turns away. For a second she's trapped in the video loop that Alex used to hold her in, within the Strange. Then, as the girls run to retrieve the grounded kite, Harm turns wholeheart-edly back to Alex. She smiles and lowers her head to trudge up the hill towards her. The spell's broken. She's her real self.

Alex settles her plated, patched-up body into the bench and gazes up into the fading light. Let this unfeigned moment stick around a little longer, and we're good.

ACKNOWLEDGEMENTS

Profound thanks are due as ever to my agent, Cathryn Summerhayes, and to my editors at Hodder, Anne Perry, Oliver Johnson and Sam Bradbury, for giving this book life – as well as to the whole Hodderscape crew, including Sharan Matharu, Kerry Hood, Rosie Stephen and Fleur Clarke, for helping me share it with the world. Thanks also to those early readers, wise counsellors and drinking buddies who helped me wrestle the book into shape, including fellow Faber Academy alumni Molly Flatt, Laura Powell, Julia Wheeler, Georgina Aargyrou, Judith Wilson and Wendy Mantle; Liz Barnsley; and all my brilliant fellow Prime Writers.

Lucky Ghost was written between January 2016 and February 2017, and that volatile period has had a profound impact on the finished book. Though I'm in no way qualified to comment in depth on the Syrian Civil War, behind Abul Ala's backstory lies a wealth of material I read and watched in an effort to better understand that escalating disaster, but which never made it into the final manuscript. If you're interested in learning some of the human stories behind the footage from Greek beaches, I'd encourage you to look at the output of Rami Jarrah and his ANA New-Media Association. I'd also like to thank Ronak Housaine for helping me correct my Arabic and some other details.

The way the Strange codifies human emotions is, sad to say, no fiction. As our data shadows grow longer and deeper, they're increasingly being read for their emotional, as well as their literal, content. To marketers, this emotional content is a seam of gold, but there's also a wealth of fascinating psychological theory behind this commercial exploitation. The system of emotional metrics behind Emoticoin is very loosely adapted from the theoretical work of Robert Plutchik and others. Plutchik's 'The Nature of Emotions' (*American Scientist* 89, 2001) is a good place to start.

Lucky Ghost is also a story about money: what it is, whether we can live without it; and how it can be manipulated by those who understand its weird dynamics. I'm very grateful to Duncan McCann at the New Economics Foundation for his lucid explanations of currency and capital. If the ideas in this book have captured your interest I'd recommend Felix Martin's clear and challenging book *Money*, which first exploded my naive preconceptions on this subject.

I'd also like to thank Victoria Wakely and the staff of the Today programme for the opportunity to watch good old-fashioned news radio being made.

Finally, thanks as always to Alice, for helping me take the life-changing plunge that meant I could write this book.

WANT MORE?

If you enjoyed this and would like to find out about similar books we publish, we'd love you to join our online SF, Fantasy and Horror community, Hodderscape.

Visit our blog site
www.hodderscape.co.uk

Follow us on Twitter
🐦 **@hodderscape**

Like our Facebook page
f **Hodderscape**

You'll find exclusive content from our authors, news, competitions and general musings, so feel free to comment, contribute or just keep an eye on what we are up to. See you there!

In the best books, the ending often comes as a shock.
Not just because of that one last twist in the tale,
but because you have been so absorbed in their world,
that coming back to the harsh light of reality is a jolt.

If that describes you now, then perhaps you should track down
some new leads, and find new suspense in other worlds.

Join us at www.hodder.co.uk, or follow us on
Twitter @hodderbooks, and you can tap in to a
community of fellow thrill-seekers.

Whether you want to find out more about this book,
or a particular author, watch trailers and interviews, have
the chance to win early limited editions, or simply browse
our expert readers' selection of the very best books,
we think you'll find what you're looking for.

And if you don't, that's the place to tell us what's missing.

We love what we do, and we'd love you to be part of it.

www.hodder.co.uk

@hodderbooks

HodderBooks

HodderBooks